Alisha Franklin

The Mourning Dove

TRAFFORD

Note for Librarians: a cataloguing record for this book that includes Dewey Decimal Classification and US Library of Congress numbers is available from the Library and Archives of Canada. The complete cataloguing record can be obtained from their online database at:
www.collectionscanada.ca/amicus/index-e.html
ISBN 1-4120-5958-5
Printed in Victoria, BC, Canada

Printed on paper with minimum 30% recycled fibre.
Trafford's print shop runs on "green energy" from solar, wind and other environmentally-friendly power sources.

TRAFFORD

Offices in Canada, USA, Ireland and UK
This book was published *on-demand* in cooperation with Trafford Publishing. On-demand publishing is a unique process and service of making a book available for retail sale to the public taking advantage of on-demand manufacturing and Internet marketing. On-demand publishing includes promotions, retail sales, manufacturing, order fulfilment, accounting and collecting royalties on behalf of the author.

Book sales for North America and international:
Trafford Publishing, 6E–2333 Government St.,
Victoria, BC v8t 4p4 CANADA
phone 250 383 6864 (toll-free 1 888 232 4444)
fax 250 383 6804; email to orders@trafford.com
Book sales in Europe:
Trafford Publishing (uk) Limited, 9 Park End Street, 2nd Floor
Oxford, UK ox1 1hh UNITED KINGDOM
phone 44 (0)1865 722 113 (local rate 0845 230 9601)
facsimile 44 (0)1865 722 868; info.uk@trafford.com
Order online at:
trafford.com/05-0859

10 9 8 7

Glory to God for this novel
and the gift of writing.

I dedicate this book to my sister.

For the cover, my sincere thanks go to
my friend and artist,
Elaine Classen.

To Adam and Joey, my grandsons,
my thanks for the graphics, and to
Armand for his friendship and help with
my computer.

1

A S THE LONG GREY HEARSE PULLED INTO THE YARD, Tanya stood inside the small flower garden, which was enclosed by a weathered picket fence. She glanced upward to see if the mourning dove perched on the roof of the barn was still there. Suddenly, it broke the silence with three long heart-wrenching cries, touching off a note of foreboding within her. A lump formed in her throat. She began to tremble. The bird, in one swift, strong motion, stretched out its wings and flew off. It looked magnificent, its feathers pale golden, shading to soft grey purple. Was it a heavenly messenger bringing them some sorrowful news about Tata? she wondered.

Two days ago, Mama had pointed it out to the family, when she'd first spotted it, sitting motionless as though moulded in clay. Mama's eyes had dilated in fear. "It's come to tell me about death," she'd said, at the same time dissolving into tears.

Tanya, listening to her, felt as though someone had suddenly poured melting hot coals into her stomach. For the rest of the day, she'd walked about the house filled with dread. Now at the sight of the dove, the fear became more intense. Anxiety turned to panic.

Since early morning, she'd listened to Mama whispering to the three older children while crying to herself. And hadn't she burnt an entire pan of eggs after breaking them open? Absent-mindedly, she'd left the stove to stare blindly out the window into the winter-ravaged garden.

Later, several families from the district stopped by to visit, forming small groups in the yard and in the house. It was strange because they rarely had visitors. Aunt Sophie and Uncle Victor, who were Mama's only living relatives in Canada, had been the first to arrive.

Hearing footsteps, Tanya turned to see her mother standing directly behind her.

Natalie Kaplov wiped her eyes on her apron. Her permed, dark hair framed a round, pale face. Her forehead was creased with worry, her green eyes etched with suffering. Somehow, up to this very moment, she'd managed to keep Sam's death a secret from the younger children, though the three stepchildren had already been told.

Verna, the oldest child from Sam's first marriage, was nineteen. She was plain looking and had been endowed with her mother's fiery red hair and freckles.

Once, Tanya had accidently found a matted knot of thick, red hair, similar in color and texture to Verna's, while playing in the attic of the machine shed. Not knowing to whom it belonged, she'd gone to ask Mama about it. Mama had stared at the hair then bellowed out, "Stop asking me stupid questions! Put it back into the shed! And don't let me catch you playing with it!"

She didn't explain her outburst. Later, Tanya and her sisters surmised that it had belonged to Tata's "other wife", ... the one who'd died.

Paul, next in line, was sixteen. He was tall, slim, and he also bore the red hair and freckles. The youngest, John, was fifteen. He was short, stocky, and easy going. He often swore, a habit he'd picked up from his father.

Alisha and Anna, whom Tanya considered to be as close as two peas in a pod, came out to stare at the car and whisper back and forth. Alisha was eleven and Anna nine, while Tanya was only seven.

She wondered what secrets they were sharing? If she was older would they have included her? Their rejection of her had existed from as far back as she could remember.

Thank God for Jip, her collie. She could always depend on him for company, though she still missed being a part of the tight bond that linked her sisters together. At times, she tested herself to prove that she was every bit as good as they were. With Jip at her side, she often engaged in a reckless, daring race across the cow pasture until she dropped to the ground nearly dead from sheer exhaustion. Her satisfaction would have been truly complete had these feats been witnessed by either Alisha or Anna. What a pity that they were never around to see how fast she could run.

One of her favorite haunts was the river. It ran a short distance from the farmhouse and drew her like a magnet. In wild shows of bravado, though her sturdy legs were too short to reach the other side, there were times when she took a chance and leaped across its width.

Once she fell in, landing in water almost waist deep. Shocked to find it ice cold, Tanya managed, only by using all her strength and hanging on to a sinuous willow, to pull herself to the edge.

What a miracle that she didn't drown! The current, in late spring, was very strong, and had nearly swept her away.

Now she turned to look at the funeral director as his assistant opened the back doors of the hearse. He slid a grey coffin onto a trolly and began wheeling it toward the house.

Suddenly, Mama let out an ear piercing cry, shrill and mournful, then ran towards the coffin, sending goose bumps up Tanya's arm. The doleful sound reminded her of the dove that had just flown off. Beside her, Alisha and Anna began to whimper.

Some of their neighbors stopped talking to stare at the scene. Aunt Sophie reached Natalie before she could throw herself over the casket. She frowned. "Natalie! Natalie! Stop! Think of your children!"

Mama let up, momentarily, looking utterly worn out, as the two men unloaded the casket onto two saw horses set up in the bedroom, which doubled for a living room. Aunt Sophie whispered that it was to remain there for three days.

The undertaker opened the casket and Mama began crying again, covering Tata's hands and face with kisses. Once more, Aunt Sophie intervened. "Stop, Natalie! That's enough! Come with me."

With great reluctance, she allowed herself be led away, her face a contortion of grief and pain.

2

SIX WEEKS AGO, WHEN SAM KAPLOV FIRST BECAME SICK, Natalie had been full of hope. "Sam, it's the flu you have. I hear that the Shumaks have it, too. Now get into bed. If you stay quiet, you'll be all right in a few days, I'm sure."

"I can't just lie here. There's work to be done," he'd complained, between coughs.

"Don't argue with me. You can't work if you're sick!"

Sam, brushing aside her worries, had continued with his chores. But several days later, when he hadn't improved, he'd reluctantly taken to his bed, allowing Natalie to administer every tried and "sure to work" home remedy that she could think of. For the next two weeks, the house reeked of garlic and Watkins liniment. But the cough persisted as he'd gradually weakened. At times he swore with impatience when he realized that his strength was failing and there was nothing he could do about it. In all of his fifty-two years, never once had he suffered from any serious type of illness. It was Natalie who had the migraines every month.

Suddenly desperate, Natalie had insisted that they see a doctor in Grand Plains, though Dr. Wong, who practised in Spirit Valley, their home town, was perfectly reliable. However she wanted the best for Sam and had Paul drive him to Grand Plains to see a Dr. George Lyal. He was a good physician and a friend of Sam's that she thought she could trust.

Dr. Lyal had diagnosed pneumonia and had had him hospitalized immediately. Though the doctor had been kind and reassuring to Natalie, and she had faith in him, she was fearful about the separation, their first in the twelve years of married life together. That night, Natalie cried until dawn.

There were days when she thought that he was improving. It buoyed her spirits. She assured the family that he was going to be all right. But, as the days stretched into a month, Natalie was no longer sure of Sam's recovery. The last time that she'd been in to see him, she'd noticed a distinctive weight loss. And he was still coughing.

She'd gone to visit him almost every day; the prognosis must have been bad, for she always cried upon returning home.

Sam passed away on Good Friday, April 19th, 1941.

3

SAM KAPLOV WAS A POLISH IMMIGRANT, a pioneer, and one of the first settlers in Spirit Valley. The town was located in Northern Alberta and in the very heart of the Peace River Country. The land was thickly forested with sturdy poplars, spruce, and willows, their branches pointing skyward in a desperate attempt to reach the sun. Though he found the soil to be rich, he knew that breaking the land wouldn't be easy.

His first house was a log shack with a dirt floor. He'd furnished it with the most necessary essentials that it took to survive. However, in comparison to his home in Poland, he thought it looked like a palace.

Other farmers came to settle on the adjoining farms, clearing the brush and gradually turning the woodland into a prairie.

Sam's first wife had died young, only 21, while giving birth to their fourth child. Some weeks later, the child had also died, from neglect it was assumed. Sam was left with the impossible task of raising three children on his own, while trying to run a farm. Soon after, he'd married Natalie and three more children were born, Alisha, Anna, and Tanya, increasing his family to six.

He'd met Natalie Chernowsky through a mutual friend who'd known her in Poland. An exchange of letters had followed. He'd written telling her that he was a widower and looking for a wife.

Natalie, who'd nearly starved in Poland, thought it was her one opportunity for a better life. She'd accepted Sam's offer without ever setting eyes on him. Since they were both of the same ethnic background, she thought that this common thread would bind them together. Soon after, Sam sent her a one way ticket to Canada.

When she'd first arrived, she was shocked that Sam's children were so young and that Sam even had children. Nothing had been said in his letters about them. Verna was seven, Paul five, and John only three.

Thinking it over, she knew that they'd need a lot of care and wasn't too eager to marry Sam, until he'd threatened to send her back.

Natalie started off the marriage resentful of her ready made family, especially after giving birth to three of her own. Verna, she soon trained to help with the housework and outdoor chores.

The seven year old accepted her role as a maidservant, but she knew that other girls her age lived a far different life from hers. The illness struck Sam at a time w hen he and Natalie had begun to talk about travel and taking things easy.

4

A S SOON AS THE UNDERTAKER LEFT, Verna went to find Alisha and Tanya, who were huddled close to the side of the house.

"Alisha, get inside. Your mother wants to talk to you."

Fearful, Alisha drew back. "What for?"

"I don't know. ... Just go!" Verna insisted.

Tanya went along to see what it was that Mama wanted. As they went past the coffin, Alisha was careful not to look at it. Mama was in the kitchen, surrounded by a circle of women, talking in hushed voices.

"Mama, you wanted to see me?" Alisha asked.

"Yes, and you too, Tanya. Come here! Now listen, both of you.

I want all of you children to take one last look at your father before he's buried. You must say goodbye to him. You'll never, ever, see him again." Her voice broke. "It's only proper."

Mrs. Royko, one of her friends, bobbed her head up and down in agreement.

Alisha blanched. "All right, Mama, we will ... we will." She went immediately upstairs to tell Anna, who sat teary eyed on the bed with her arms locked around her knees. She resembled Alisha; dark hair cut into bangs, slight and frail.

"You better come down. Mama wants us to take one last look at Tata," Alisha told her, sombrely.

"No. Get out of here!"

"Okay, but she's liable to come and get you."

Downstairs, in the bed-sitting room, most of the people were milling about the coffin. Alex Shumak, who owned the farm next to theirs, was crying openly. He was a large, spare man and, because of his size everyone naturally assumed that he had the inner strength to match it; it was odd to see him sniffing and mopping his eyes with a red, polka dotted hanky.

In one corner of the room, a group of men were discussing the current price of wheat. Hitler was embroiled in a war with Europe, and wheat was a precious commodity. Mat Deleny, who owned a dairy farm, held the floor. "I'm sure we'll see wheat go to a dollar a bushel, if not more." The men agreed enthusiastically.

Tanya noticed that as each person entered the house, they went directly to where Tata lay. Their hands folded, they lingered over him with mournful faces. Mrs. Royko's kerchiefed head seemed to be following her every move. Once, she heard her whisper to Mrs. Shumak, "Do you know that not one of Natalie's children has even looked at Sam?"

Verna overheard her and went upstairs to get Anna. She lifted her and brought her down crying and squirming in her arms.

Anna squeezed her eyes shut. "I'm not going to look! You can't make me!"

Verna gave her a swat to settle her down, then hissed into her ear, "In case you don't know it, there are people watching, so stop it and behave yourself!"

Anna opened her eyes a crack. Sure enough, there were some women looking at them. They appeared very interested in what was happening between herself and Verna.

Verna's voice became more coaxing. "Anna, we're in front of Tata. Don't be scared. Open your eyes for just a minute. Don't you want to see Tata one last time?"

Anna slowly turned her head. She knew that Mama wouldn't be as patient with her if she happened to create a scene. For Mama's sake, she looked down on the inert form of what used to be "Tata," beginning at his head and ending with his slippered feet. ... She let out a sob.

Verna lowered her to the floor and led her out, giving Mrs. Royko, who never once allowed her gaze to waver from them, a triumphant look over her shoulder.

Mama's bed-sitting room, where the coffin was placed, was not a room to envy. Mama never cared about having nice things. In one corner of the room was a double bed with a brown steel, tubular headboard. It was covered with a yellow, chenille bedspread and heaped up with some goose down pillows. The rest of the furniture consisted of an oak dresser, a sewing machine, and a cot that doubled as a couch. Behind the dresser were some sepia photos of distant relatives and a calendar with a smiling brunette holding a bouquet of red roses. Cheap, ecru colored lace curtains hung at the sides of the windows. The linoleum was scarred to black in some of the more traveled areas.

It wasn't until the third day that Tanya, unsure of what the fuss was about, decided to have her "last look." She walked slowly toward the coffin, thinking that if Tata was really sleeping, why was he lying down when there was so much company? She tried standing on tiptoe but couldn't see much of him. Frustrated, she ran outside hoping to get a better view from the flower garden. The casket was laid out parallel to the two bedroom windows facing the garden.

Tanya found a dry spot in an ochre labyrinth of dead grass and flowers, wintered from fall. She stepped on top of the pile and bent down to peer through the darkened windows only to be hindered by the reflections from the sky. The glare made it impossible to get more than a faint profile of Tata's head. Slowly, she crept back into the house and came to stand beside the coffin. There was no one in the room. She could see his hands, neatly folded, and a tuft of white hair rising from his forehead. The nails appeared somewhat blue. She noticed that he was wearing a brown suit which seemed new. The only suit that Tata had ever worn was a wool black and grey tweed with a matching cap that he wore slanted at a rakish angle. On workdays, he always put on black and white pinstriped coveralls spotted with grease, a flannel shirt, and ankle length rubber boots.

Tata lay on exquisite white satin. She put up her hand to feel its silky softness. Suddenly, a creepy feeling came over her. She drew back in fear.

Tanya sighed, turned from the coffin, and went into the kitchen where the women were gossiping, while Mama removed large trays of fried chicken from the oven. A meal, buffet style, was being set up in the dining room. She edged closer, hoping to get something to eat without being noticed. One look at Mama convinced her to wait.

After lunch, Reverend MacAllister, from Spirit Valley United, performed a short service, bringing the talk to a respectful hush.

Though they didn't go to church, and he didn't know the Kaplovs, Natalie thought it only proper that a man of the cloth should perform the service even if she wasn't United Church. She had been brought up Greek Orthodox. However, since there were no priests within easy distance in the district, she'd decided that United Church would have to do.

As soon as Reverend MacAllister finished the eulogy, Mama motioned to Paul. "It's time to go to the cemetery. Get the horses hitched to the wagon. And ask some of the pallbearers to help you load on the casket ... it's heavy."

Paul nodded. "Okay. You think the roads are too muddy to take him by truck?"

"I'm afraid of getting stuck. Really, we shouldn't take that chance. ... Verna! Make sure the children have their coats on. There's a strong wind blowing. It's not any too warm."

Verna and John chose to go with the Roykos, who were taking their half-ton truck. Tanya felt it was only right that Tata should ride in the wagon, because he'd spent most of his life with the horses.

She remembered how he'd often tracked bits of manure into the house until Mama, exasperated, would shout, "Sam, look at your shoes. And to think I've just washed the floor! Take them off and leave them on the step, if you please! One would think that I've nothing better to do than to clean up horse manure all day!"

"What manure? I don't see it," he'd say, examining his boots. "Yes, I see it. Damn!" Out he'd go, good-naturedly enough, smiling and chuckling at his stupidity and trying to humour Mama at the same time. Though his manner was coarse, he was kind and gentle.

The casket was hoisted on. The children climbed in. Mama sank into the high wagon seat next to Paul, who drove the team. She held herself erect, while twisting and pulling at a hanky in her lap, occasionally lifting it to her eyes. Behind her, the three girls clung to the back of the seat, while trying to maintain a dignified balance as they bounced and pitched over deep, mud- encrusted ruts.

Tanya wedged herself between her two sisters. Her blonde hair, cut short, framed a child's oval face, brown eyes, and high cheek bones. Suddenly, a gust of wind swept them to the floor. When it stilled, the sun came pouring out from behind a billowy cloud mass, reminding them that it was spring and not uncommon for the hot-cold syndrome to occur. The rolling prairies convoluted for miles in all directions. High above, a V formation of ducks announced their arrival. Small ponds, formed by melting snow, sent forth crystal flashes of light.

"Whoa!" Paul slowed the team, and turned in at the cemetery gate. They rode up a gentle slope where a group of friends and family were waiting beside a freshly dug grave. He jumped down, waving for assistance.

Aunt Sophie, with one arm around Mama, stood guard, determined to see that she remain sane to the end, while Uncle Victor dissolved into tears beside her.

Reverend MacAllister opened his Bible and began reading "The Lord is My Shepherd." He finished with "Ashes to ashes, and dust to dust," as the crowd began to disperse.

Tanya, hearing the first shovelful of dirt hit the coffin, started in alarm, thinking of Tata asleep under the ground. She shuddered, remembering the snows of winter and the rains of summer.

Once home, she felt an emptiness weighing deep within her. That evening, Mama sewed black arm bands onto their coat sleeves.

Hoping to temper her sadness, Tanya came to stand beside her while she worked.

Mama held up a jacket. "As Greek Orthodox, we'll follow the church tradition. You'll wear these bands for six months." No one challenged her.

5

Tata's place remained empty at the head of the table with Natalie sitting, where she usually sat, opposite him. Having survived the first few days, she'd decided to keep the farm going at whatever cost.

It was stupid of Sam not to have left a will, she thought. A Mr. Reed, from the Public Trustee's office, had already called at the house to tell her that if a will couldn't be found, he, as a representative of the Public Trustee, would have to take charge of the estate. The land would have to be sold and the money divided into nine equal shares. A share for each of the six children, two shares for herself, and, for the legal fees, a share would have to go to Mr. Reed. Upon hearing this, Natalie was outraged. How dare they?

Natalie decided to buy the farm outright herself. She planned to use her two shares for the down payment. Thank God that she'd pressured Sam into signing at least one farm over to her. At the time, she'd had to force him to do it. "Marry me, Natalie," he'd said, when she'd first arrived, "and you can have anything you want." She'd told him that she wanted a farm of her own, in her own name. But even after the children were born, Sam kept putting it off. Finally, Natalie threatened to leave him. Only then did he take her seriously. Never did she think that she'd be forced to buy back Sam's farms. However, Mr. Reed had been very firm about it. "We're here to protect the children's rights until they're of legal age, Mrs. Kaplov," he'd informed her.

She seethed inwardly, thinking how unfair of Mr. Reed to take an equal share for himself. It was Sam's sweat that had gone into breaking the land, not his. She sighed, if only Sam had been more astute about legal matters. However, his one interest had been in working the farms that he loved.

After the funeral, Natalie, Paul, and Verna had searched the entire house, going through every scrap of paper, looking for a will.

Now a week had gone by. Natalie was on her knees scrubbing the kitchen floor and complaining to no one in particular. "I'll have to get the crops in. But the machinery! I'm no mechanic. What if something breaks down?" Suddenly, she clutched at her heart; her face twisted in pain. She let out a moan and sobs filled the room. Thankfully, the spasm passed a moment later.

Tanya, watching her, felt a chill go through her. She knew that Mama as a child had been sick with rheumatic fever. The illness had damaged her heart. The next morning, they awoke to find her in bed with a migraine.

"Tanya, quick, a basin. I have to throw up!" Natalie held a hand to her mouth as Tanya ran for the basin. She brought it to her just in time. In the doorway, Alisha, Anna and Verna stood waiting for the retching to stop.

Verna reached for a milk pail. She would have to milk the five cows alone since Mama couldn't help her.

Alisha went into the kitchen and began stoking the fire for Mama's tea. Mama always drank weak tea whenever she had a headache. After it steeped, she carried it to her room with some dry toast.

"How is she?" Tanya whispered, anxiously, when she returned.

"She's sleeping. Maybe she'll be better when she wakes up. Sleep is supposed to be healing."

Tanya nodded. "You know, I've been thinking, I'd like to be a nurse when I grow up ... then, if she got sick, I could help her."

Alisha turned on her, angrily. "Oh Tanya, stop being so stupid!" There was a ring of jealousy in her voice.

"But I'm not stupid. I mean it. I want to be a nurse!"

"Well, you still have a long way to go before you grow up. Now do you want to play house or don't you?"

"Yes, let's."

Tanya came back carrying her "Tootsie", who had once belonged to Alisha. All her dolls were hand-me-downs from her sisters. Mama didn't think it necessary to buy her a new one.

They played until late afternoon. That evening, because her migraine was still with her, Mama left the meal-making up to Verna.

Verna fried bacon, eggs, and some pan fried potatoes. As soon as they finished eating, the two boys got up and left for the bunkhouse.

Long ago, Mama had insisted that they move out of the house. "Sam, there's not enough room for everybody in here! With those two boys in the way, it makes it hard for the girls to dress and undress. How can we even take baths? Besides, I shouldn't have to be watching myself every minute ... or them. They're older. Sam, build them a bunkhouse. We'll put in beds, a heater. I'm sure they won't mind." She'd paused, "You know, one worries more about girls than boys. I wish I'd had three boys instead of girls. With girls you have to be so watchful!" Sam had built the bunkhouse shortly after.

Verna began clearing off the table. "Whose turn to help me wash dishes?" she asked.

Alisha looked at Anna. "It's your's, isn't it?"

"No, because I did them at lunch. It's Tanya's turn. Besides, I don't care, because I'm not doing them anymore today." Anna, in her haughtiest manner, wandered off into the unused dining room.

"But there aren't as many dishes to do at lunch! It's not fair!" Tanya wailed.

"Sh-h-h-h. Be quiet! One more word, and I'm coming out to to strap everybody." Mama's weak voice brought an abrupt end to the argument. They'd forgotten to whisper.

For Mama's sake, Tanya picked up the tea-towel.

At midnight, she awoke and crept downstairs to check on Mama again. Was she breathing? She noticed the quilt moving, ever so slightly. She turned down the wick of the coal oil lamp that Verna had lit earlier that evening, then climbed into bed beside her mother. Snuggling close, she gave her small reassuring pats, content that if Mama should need something, she'd be right there to help her. She felt her stir. "Are you all right?" she whispered.

"Yes, child. I feel a little better. Tanya, why don't you go back to bed? I'll be fine."

"No. Please, Mama, I don't mind. Really, I don't. I'll go soon." She waited until Mama started to doze before leaving her.

Mama didn't know how much she needed to be close to her. She would worry and have a hard time falling asleep if she didn't have these moments with her.

The next morning, the minute she opened her eyes, Tanya still anxious, ran downstairs to find Mama seated at the edge of the bed, already dressed in a blue, cotton house dress. She smiled at her in expectation. "How is your headache?" she asked.

Natalie slowly turned to look at her. A dark mass of hair stuck to the back of her head. She looked drawn and pale. "I'm better."

Tanya looked at her closely to see if she really was. Mama rose to her feet and went into the kitchen, her slippers flopping in rhythm with each step.

The fire had died down; the room was ice cold. Tanya, shivering, drew up a chair and sat down next to the stove.

"Why are you up so early?" Mama wanted to know, annoyed with her. She opened the stove door and put in some kindling.

"I don't know; I couldn't sleep." She couldn't say that she'd been worried about her. Maybe Mama knew it. She was psychic about a lot of things.

Natalie picked up a blackened kettle and filled it with water. "Don't just sit there, set the table before the others come down for breakfast." The crackle of kindling and a faint smell of smoke permeated the room. Alisha, Anna, and Verna came downstairs.

Each child had their assigned chores: the boys tended to feeding the horses and cleaning the barn, Verna to the milking, the younger girls to feeding the chickens, gathering the eggs, and bringing in firewood.

Half an hour later, Verna came in with a pailful of warm milk. She strained it through a clean cloth, then sidled up to the stove, edging Mama out of the way. "You go sit," she said. "I'll finish making the porridge. You don't look too good."

Gratefully, Natalie sat down as Paul and John walked in from the bunk house.

Verna set the porridge on the table. They all took their places. Occasionally, Mama's voice broke through the sound of spoons scraping against bowls. "Alisha, I want you and Anna to do the dishes before you go to school." She took a sip of tea. "I'm still not myself. Paul, I've been thinking, could you teach me how to drive the car?"

Paul, slanting blue eyes at her, looked resentful. Driving was a man's job. He'd learned to drive at age fourteen, just by watching his father. "Yeah, I think I can."

"Good." The 1929 Ford Sedan was twelve years old. These days, only the odd one could be seen on the road driven by someone who couldn't afford anything better.

After school, they came home to find Natalie in better spirits. Her face had lost its pallor and her gait was more brisk.

A low slung Monarch streaked past the house. The three younger girls rushed outside to get a better look. "I wish we had a new car," Alisha remarked.

Anna nodded. "Yeah, me too. Lets go ask Mama if she'll buy a car."

"Mama, that yellow car that just went by, did you see it?" Alisha asked.

"Yes, I did. So what?"

"Can we have one like it? Don't you want a new car? Isn't it about time we got a new one, huh?"

Natalie's eyes hardened. "Dammit Alisha! Shut up about a new car! The Ford will do me just fine. Do you think I want more debts? You think I'm crazy? Don't you know there's a war on? Cars are scarce. And how much do you think a new one costs? Well, let me tell you, they're not free! First, I have to buy a new seeder, pay off the Public Trustee. Somehow, I've got to get through spring seeding ... and on nothing! Do you know what that funeral cost? Close to $500.00! I don't have that kind of money. Sam left me with nothing. And to think he'd worked so hard all his life. ... And so stubborn! He wouldn't listen to anything I said. Do you know, in Poland, if we wanted to go anywhere, we walked. Nobody had such a thing as a car. In fact, we would have been grateful to have had more than one horse!"

Alisha walked quietly into the next room. Mama continued with her tirade. Mama was right about the war and that goods were scarce. Evenings, they sat with their ears glued to the radio for news that the allies had broken through Hitler's lines and that they were winning. But it was always the same, as Hitler's armies kept forging ahead.

After supper, they brought out their homework and spread it on the kitchen table. Tanya opened her Grade Three arithmetic workbook. Almost every page had a red star on it. Pencils, ruler, and eraser went into a neat row at the top of her books.

Anna, seeing the eraser, reached for it.

Tanya was quick to notice and wrenched it free from her hand. "You can't have it without asking. Besides, where's yours?"

Anna's nose went up. "Actually, if you must know, I lost mine, Fatty!"

Tanya blushed red. "Fatty? Fatty? So that's what you think of me!"

Both her sisters teased her with that hateful word. Though Mama often commented that she wasn't fat at all but built muscular like Sam.

Suddenly, Anna's hand shot out and seized the eraser. She went bounding outside with Tanya close behind.

Natalie turned white with anger. Hands on hips, she followed them as far as the front steps. "Come back ... both of you! Dammit! Do you hear me? ... Or you'll be sorry that you didn't!"

Tanya knew that she meant it. But she couldn't stop. She outran Anna a short distance from the house. Her hand shot up. She placed some heavy blows on Anna's back. "Give it back to me or I'll hit you again!"

Anna gave her a disdainful look before she let it fly into the dirt. "There you go. Ha, ha ... you'll have to look for it, won't you? Fatty, fatty, two by four! Can't get through the kitchen door!"

"Stop! Stop! You pig!" Tanya, with tears streaming down her face, found the eraser in the dirt. "I hate you!" she cried. She started back, keeping a lookout for Mama, who hadn't moved from the front steps.

Mama's anger would be at its height. Tanya shuddered, seeing her mouth clenched in a grim line. As soon as she came within reach, Mama hauled her inside by the shoulder.

"Didn't I tell you to stop? Are you deaf? This should teach you a lesson! ... Whack! whack!

Tanya felt the sting of her hand on her bottom.

"You're just like Sam! Stubborn to the core! Only you're worse because you never give me a moment's peace. ... Shame on you!

Whack! ... Whack!

Tanya broke into sobs. "But Mama, Anna took my eraser and ... and, I ... I needed it! And she's always calling me names! Can't you make her stop?"

"Shut up, or you'll get more! Get up to bed! ... Now!"

"But, Mama, my homework. I have to finish it!"

"You heard me! Upstairs!" She turned her attention to Anna, who now stood just outside the screen door. "And as for you ... come in here!"

Anna, stony-faced, uncaring, endured Mama's wrath without a whimper, while she reigned blows on her.

Throughout the ordeal, the noise, Verna sat at the table working on an essay which was due in the morning. She knew that her word with Mama, on any subject, meant nothing.

Finally, Mama's temper abated. She stopped beating Anna. "Up to bed with you! You too, Alisha!"

"But Mama, we haven't even fin ... ."

"You heard me. Go! No talking back! Is that clear?"

As they scurried upstairs, she looked relieved, knowing that she was about to have some peace and quiet.

Stifling sobs, Tanya went to her side of the bedroom that the three girls shared and undressed. She lay down on the single bed and drew the woolen quilt up to her chin. Beneath her, there was a soft rustle of straw. Every spring, Mama refilled the mattress with fresh straw. For a few months after, it was several inches higher before it packed down. Judging from its thickness, it was time for a refill.

A giggle came from the next bed. Were they laughing at her? She sighed. They had each other. She had only her dreams.

Her thoughts centered on Tata, as they did every night since he'd left them. A tear rolled down her cheek. Tata, I miss you. She remembered sitting on his knee while he stroked her head, or sometimes he'd tickle her, making her laugh. With him, she'd always felt warm and secure. Now he was dead. And what about death? What did it feel like? She tried to imagine it, wondering if he was still alive under the ground somewhere?

For a long time the questions clamoured to be answered until she found herself back at the cemetery where she'd last seen him. As she wandered among the crosses, her body felt light as air. She found it astounding that she could leap over everything so easily. Tanya found Tata's plot, although it still didn't have a permanent marker on it. Suddenly she stopped, awestruck, as the earth from the top of his grave began to move and separate, revealing a giant, round cover of steel beneath it. To her utter amazement, the cover began to lift. Was he in there? The next instant, she saw an arm encased in a brown suit, come into full view. Excitement shot through her as a man climbed out. It was Tata! But before she had time to ask him to wait for her, he strode off homeward bound. Joyfully, she started after him, thinking how wonderful that he was alive and well ... as she'd always imagined that he would be. Now what would Mama say when she found out?

It was four-thirty A.M. and still dusk outside. Tanya opened her eyes. A robin chirped in the yard, scrounging for its breakfast. Happily, she bounded out of bed. Mama wouldn't mind her getting up early because all she really wanted was one small peak at Tata. She quickly pulled on a skirt and top over herself, then dashed downstairs to their bedroom to be the first one to greet him.

"Good morning, Tata!" The words came out in a melodic singsong.

Mama stirred and opened her eyes. She squinted at her in confusion. It took a minute for Tanya's greeting to register before alarm spread over her face. She sat up. "Tanya, what are you saying? Who are you talking to? Tata's dead."

Tanya smiled. "No, he's not. I saw him. He's alive, Mama! I tell you he's alive and I saw him!"

For the past week, Tanya had come in at the crack of dawn, awakening her with these very words, behaving as though her father was still living. Exasperated, Natalie dissolved into tears. "Tanya, this nonsense must stop! Your father is dead! Can't you get that through your head? He's never coming back! You're having a dream. Now, go back to bed and stop thinking about him. If you keep this up, I swear, you'll drive me crazy! I can't stand it anymore! Things are bad enough without ... without you making them worse!"

Tanya shook her head. The last thing she wanted was to upset her. Still, she couldn't let go of the hope. "But, Mama, he's alive! I saw him with my very own eyes! I'm going to find him for you. ... He's got to be here ... somewhere!" Suddenly, she brightened. "I know! Wait for me! I'll be right back!"

"Tanya, don't ... go-o-o!"

Tanya bolted through the screen door. The sooner she found him, the sooner she could get back to prove to Mama how wrong she was. The barn would be the most likely place to look. She pushed aside the swinging doors and stood still. A soft whinnying came from one of the stalls. She sighed, disappointed. There was no sign of human life. Undaunted, she thought he might be in the machine shed, and raced full speed towards the shed. She reached the building and came to a stop, panting. She held still to quiet her pounding heart, expecting him to rise up from behind the seeder in the far corner ... or perhaps the tractor? She glanced at the Model A Ford ... then at a rusty hand plough that Tata had used when he'd first started farming. Often, he'd told her stories of his many hardships, as she sat on his knee, hanging on to his every word, while his roughened hand, with the nails permanently blackened, gently stroked her head. Now her eyes swept over the cold lifeless implements in hope. She probed into dim corners stacked high with carelessly placed tools.

"Tata! Tata! If you're in here, answer me! ... Please Tata!" There was no sound from anywhere. Then, touched with despair, her enthusiasm flagging, she walked aimlessly to the edge of the river bank, wondering where else he might be?

"Tata! T-A-T-A-A-A!" Her words echoed back in mock reply from the opposite side of the bank. She remembered the cry of the mourning dove the day they brought him home. A dreadful sadness engulfed her as reality set in.

Below her, the leaves of a black poplar whispered softly as a cool wind nudged its branches. It all looked so tranquil, yet empty and meaningless without him. Could Mama have been right? Shivering, she wrapped her arms around herself. Was it only a dream? Slowly, she turned homeward. It would have been so wonderful! So this was death!

When she returned, Mama tactfully made no mention of the incident, hoping that she'd come to her senses at last. ... In time, the dreams stopped.

6

BY THE MIDDLE OF MAY, a south wind had melted off the rest of the snow and dried out the fields, restoring some of the colour back to the land that the winter had leached out. Bright patches of green grass dressed up the roadways and the cow pasture.

One morning, they came downstairs to find Mama standing in front of the kitchen window, peering through the lace curtains. Her eyes were narrowed on something in the distance.

"Paul, would you come in here. Tell me, is that Mike Anders? Is he plowing his field? I think he's started the spring planting! If it's dry enough for him, then it's dry enough for us." She pointed to a barely discernable figure of a man behind a team of horses engulfed in a cloud of dust.

Paul nodded. "Yeah, that's him all right."

"Paul, just as soon as you get home from school, we'll begin our spring work."

"It might still be a little wet, don't you think?"

"It won't be wet," she snapped.

After school, she was waiting for him. "Paul, gas up the tractor."

He gave her a sullen look. "I gotta change my clothes first."

She ignored his reluctance and went on. "We'll start ploughing that quarter that Sam left to lie fallow last fall. When you get tired, I'll take over."

Paul slammed his homework down on the kitchen table and changed into coveralls then went into the shed. He siphoned purple gas into the tractor, as Mama hovered close by spewing advice.

Deftly, he cranked the tractor into action, obliterating her voice.

She put both hands to her ears. Paul climbed aboard and shifted into gear, the steel lugs digging up chunks of dirt as he rode out of the yard.

Mama nodded approval. She was anxious to get started and try her hand at farming. It was also for the benefit of the neighbours, who, she figured, were waiting to see her fail without Sam to do the work. When Paul came home, it was well after ten. He had no time to get to his books and fell asleep the minute he washed up and ate. After a week of this exhausting schedule, Natalie realized that he was getting behind in his school work and hired someone to help him.

Two weeks later, she was delighted at the sight of tender green shoots springing from the ground, feeling that it was quite an accomplishment for her, especially being a widow.

7

T HAT SUMMER, AS SOON AS THEIR VACATION BEGAN, Mama, anxious
that they preserve their ethnic heritage, enrolled the three younger
girls in "Ukrainian". The lessons were being held in the basement of
the Roman Catholic church.

Tanya was quite happy to hear that her best friend, Dorothy Zidoruk,
would be attending the classes.

As they entered the room, Tanya noticed their instructor, a novice
priest, dressed in a long, black cassock. His unusual apparel caught
her interest. He rose from behind a table at the front of the class,
thumping for silence.

Vera Pawluik leaned toward Tanya to whisper with pride, "That's
Brother Joseph. He's from our church. I know him."

Tanya nodded. Of course she would. The Pawluiks were Catholic.
Brother Joseph's round, pale face was framed with dark black, curly
hair. He appeared young. A cigarette smoldered in an ashtray beside
him, filling the room with an acrid, blue haze.

He smiled. "I'm Brother Joseph. I'm going to teach you how to read
and write in Ukrainian. But first, we'll begin by learning something
about God. Does everyone know who God is?"

Nearly all hands went up, including Alisha's and Anna's.

Tanya kept hers down because she wasn't quite sure, though they'd
read the story of Jesus being born at Christmas time and she knew
most of it by heart.

Brother Joseph nodded. "Uh-h-h, in the beginning ... in the very
beginning, there was God. Even before the world began, He always
existed. That's hard to believe, isn't it? But it's true. He, that is, God,
created the whole world as well as everyone in it. ... He made the
heavens, and He made the angels in heaven. Now, did you know that
we, each of us, have our own special guardian angel? ... Yes, there are

angels ... good and bad angels, all around us at all times. Your own angel, the one that God sent to take care of you from birth, is with you right now, at this very moment. And hopefully will always be with you until you die."

Tanya listened, intrigued. It sounded too good to be true that God was watching over her and caring for her all the time! It was just as hard to believe about the guardian angel. The lesson ended with Brother Joseph giving them a short quiz.

"Now for the second half of this class, we'll learn how to print the Ukrainian alphabet. This is how we print 'Jesus.'" He turned and drew some strange looking letters on the blackboard.

"Write these words in your workbooks."

"Tanya?"

She looked up. Brother Joseph was standing beside her with cigarette in hand.

"Tanya, your printing is excellent. Good work!" A small pat on the head and he moved on in a cloud of smoke.

He's wonderful, she thought. Really wonderful! And absolutely the best teacher I've ever had. Remembering the pat, she gazed after him in outright admiration.

On the way home, she made up her mind to believe in God.

She soon discovered that Brother Joseph, though a chain smoker, was gentle, loving, and generous with his praise and kind words. For the next two weeks, they began with a religious story and ended by being taught the Ukrainian language that Mama expected them to learn. Brother Joseph gave equal time to both.

Meanwhile, Anna took to Catholicism seriously. After school, she often argued that there was no other religion that compared with it. "You know, I'd like to be a Catholic," she said, wistfully. Alisha looked upset. "But you can't be. If Mama found out, she wouldn't let you."

"I know. But still, I'd like to be a Catholic. Mama said we've never been baptized. You have but not Tanya or me." It was true; Mama had neglected to baptize the two younger girls.

The two weeks went by with lightning speed. On the last day at the end of the lesson, Brother Joseph rose from his chair. "Children, indeed, I've enjoyed being your teacher. And, uh-h-h, I'll miss you. However, I sincerely hope that you will continue to learn about Jesus on your own. Don't forget, in times of trouble to ask Him, Jesus, for help. ... I have a special gift for each of you. It's an icon of Christ. A memento to help you remember the time you spent learning your catechism." He held up the icon.

Tanya listened sadly to what he had to say, thinking that she would miss him. Trembling, she walked up to his desk to receive her icon.

He smiled at her. "Ah-h-h, Tanya. You've done well. I'm very proud of you."

"Thank you." She was so overwhelmed by the compliment that she forgot to say goodbye. However, she carried the icon back to her seat in reverence to examine it at her leisure.

It portrayed Jesus in a white robe with a bevy of angels clustered around Him. Her eyes drank in every fine detail, especially the angels. Everything that Brother Joseph had taught them about God being in heaven, and that He knew each and every one by name, and that He could see everything that she and everyone else did on earth, must surely be true, she thought. The icon proved it! Besides, she could never imagine someone as fine a person as Brother Joseph telling a lie!

As soon as she walked into the house, she went upstairs to hide the icon in her "treasure box." The box once held Pot O' Gold chocolates in it. Mama had won them as a door prize for attending a film advertising John Deere machinery. Inside was a red hair bow that Alisha had once owned, a small mirror that Mama had given her, and a silver comb. Now she carefully added the icon of Jesus with the angels to her treasures.

"Tanya! Tanya! Where are you? Come down this minute! I need you!"

She ran down to the kitchen where Mama was waiting. Her mother looked at her sharply. "Do you know what time it is? It's almost milking time. Go get the cows. Where have you been?"

She smiled, eager to be on her way. The chore was a pleasant one. Outside, she whistled for the dog. Jip would do all the work.

They ran together, side by side, with Tanya secure in the knowledge that God was above her and looking out for her. Suddenly she thought it might be nice to sing something to God. But what? Mama always did like the way the French people spoke. For some reason, the language had always fascinated her. I'll sing a song in French, she thought. Though, she didn't know one word of French, a babble of words streamed forth in what she thought was a hymn of praise in French.

As usual, she could count on Jip to listen. He wagged his tail in appreciation when she finished, before he turned the cattle towards home.

8

SINCE MAMA WAS WIDOWED, THE NEWS, having spread to all parts of the district, soon had different suitors knocking at her door proposing marriage to her. She was both flattered and indignant. "It's not me they want, it's my property," she exclaimed. "They must think that Sam left me a fortune. ... Did you know that even Mike Anders asked me to marry him?"

"Mike Anders? Our neighbor?" Alisha's mouth dropped in surprise. "But I thought he liked being a bachelor!"

"I thought so, too. But he tells me he wants to get married."

It was impossible to imagine him marrying anyone. Rumour had it that he'd once been a bank manager who had lost his job when the depression hit and the bank folded. Short, slight of build, he had a wry sense of humour and merry looking eyes. A wad of chewing tobacco bulged in his cheek at all times, which he spewed out whenever he felt like it. He had a few strands of hair which he combed over a bald pate. Yellow skin stretched over a skeletal face. A smile revealed brown, stained teeth. The clothes he wore were of no particular shape or colour.

Newspapers, fly-specked and yellowed with age, lined the walls of the one room log shack he'd built for himself. Tobacco spit browned a wood floor which might never have been washed. The shack smelled of body odor, mildew, dirty dishes and smoke.

Intelligent and obviously well educated, he subscribed to a host of newspapers and magazines. On any given evening, one could observe him through a curtainless window, sitting by a table, absorbed in reading the Financial Post, Life Magazine, or the Winnipeg Free Press.

Mama liked him because he was a good farmer, easy to get along with, and he kept his half section of land virtually weed free.

Mama went on to add, "Did you know that Mat Deleny asked me if

I wanted to sell the property to him?"

Verna looked surprised. "But he owns a dairy. Why would he want our property?"

"Mat thinks that just because I'm widowed, I'm desperate. He probably wants it dirt cheap, that's what. Well, dammit, he can go to hell if he thinks he's going to take advantage of me. I'm not selling to him or to anyone else! This is good land, and I'm going to make it pay!"

Her head shot up in indignation. "This year's crop looks good. ... I think I'll start looking around for someone to run the thresher. The Shumaks, they gave me a name, uh-h-h, a Bill Dansky, he's supposed to be good with machinery. Hm-m-m, Paul, do you think we could drive to Owl Creek to see him this weekend?"

Paul put down The Country Guide. "Yeah, sure."

Natalie went on. "I hear he runs the local store there."

9

BILL DANSKY LIVED IN THE BACK of a small, two-room house with a large front room that served as a dry goods store.

Besides the store, he owned, clear title, eighty acres of land adjacent to it. However, the soil wasn't suited for farming because of the clay and rock content. It irked him that he couldn't even afford a car and had to be dependent on friends and neighbours for rides.

He was six feet tall, handsome, with light brown hair and clear china blue eyes. In his late thirties, still unmarried, he'd spurned more than one girl who'd found him attractive, thinking that with his looks he could find someone with means.

It was through a close friend that he'd heard of Natalie Kaplov and her property. The friend had urged him to get in touch with her. He hadn't rushed into trying to find her. Now, here she was needing his services ... better that she come to him. It was surprising how many of his friends were trying to marry him off! And almost every week it was to someone different.

Natalie Kaplov appealed to him from the very start. He liked her forceful manner and her strength, not to mention the large estate that she owned. But her children ... he hadn't bargained for them. There were six, she'd said. However, children grow up, get married, or leave home. In his family there had been fourteen brothers and sister in all. Being second oldest, he was forced to help care for them. How he'd loathed it!

Once he recalled his mother saying to him: "Billy, I've just put Johnny down for his nap. He's almost asleep; could you rock him for me? ... Billy, you hear me?"

"Yes Ma, I hear. Do I have to?"

"Do as you're told, or I'll tell your father."

He shuddered. His father would be sure to come after him with his shaving strop. Angrily, he'd approached the cradle and had given it a push. In his back pocket, he had a sling shot, newly whittled, that he was longing to try out. Suddenly, the baby came awake and let out a cry. So what was the matter with the kid? Wasn't he supposed to be asleep?

The cradle, the old fashioned type, was suspended from the ceiling by long ropes. His temper rose with the baby's cries. He pushed harder on the swinging bundle. Faster, higher, higher! By now, it was arcing dangerously close to the ceiling. He watched, fascinated, wondering how much higher it could go and if it could really touch the ceiling? Suddenly, the momentum became too much. Horrified, he stood helpless as the baby slid out and, carried aloft, landed on the floor of the adjoining room on some laundry. For a moment, he'd remained as if frozen wondering if Johnny was dead. Then a thin wail broke the silence. He ran and quickly examined the infant. Despite the fall, Johnny was all right. Well, what if something had happened to him? Served him right for screaming. His childhood had been a continuous round of babysitting bouts. He often swore to himself that he'd never have children.

At sixteen, he'd left home in search of the elusive riches that he'd craved all his life. It was the onset of the depression and his parents didn't try to hold him back. He'd drifted from farm to farm doing menial jobs, sometimes earning just enough for board and room.

Some years later, having scraped up a little money, he returned to his home town, built a house, and bought the eighty acres of land that he now lived on. It wasn't much and he certainly couldn't afford any luxuries, but it was his very own, and it gave him a measure of comfort.

10

O N SATURDAY, PAUL AND MAMA SET OUT FOR OWL CREEK, leaving the rest of the family with Verna. When they returned later that evening, Natalie was outwardly excited. "I've hired Bill Dansky to run the thresher," she burst out. "He's the best man for the job, they tell me."

"When's he coming?" Verna asked.

"He'll be here next week to check out the thresher and the other machinery." She started cleaning off the table ... then absentmindedly left it. "He told me his neighbours would take care of his store." She went back to cleaning the table. "Verna, did you see what I did with the dish rag?"

"Yeah, you left it on the window sill."

Natalie, in a euphoric daze, resumed wiping off the table. "Verna, we have a lot of work to do in this house before next week. His place was spotless. He's a bachelor, and yet he's so clean. I want this house cleaned by next Monday. We'll start tomorrow."

11

Two months later, at the end of August, the harvest was in full swing. The large oak table was stretched out as far as it could go. There was a crew of nine men and Mama was up every morning at five. She always made sure that one of her brood was there to help her, before sending Verna to do the milking.

"Alisha, pour the men their coffee. Tanya, take these hot cakes to the table. And be sure that Bill Dansky gets them first." She shoved a loaded plate into her hands.

Tanya went into the dining room and put it down directly in front of Bill Dansky, who paid no attention to her.

As soon as the men left for the fields, she picked up a plate and leisurely entered the dining room to see what was left. Mama always supplied very generous meals during harvest. She'd stocked up on pork and beans, canned salmon, ham, and store bought bread. The three girls fought over the store bought bread for such extravagance was unheard of. Every week, Mama baked at least nine good sized loaves for the family.

Tanya doused some pancakes with syrup, then added bacon, fried eggs, and toast on the side. A cup of coffee, laced with a good dollop of farm cream and several teaspoons of sugar, followed. Mama never allowed them to drink coffee. However, she was far too busy to notice.

With plate in hand, Tanya stepped outside into the flower garden. The crew with their laughter, their coarse jokes, while trooping in and out of the house, broke the monotony of their dull lives and generated a sense of excitement.

All around her was the sound of machinery. In fact, the very air was filled with the fresh smell of wheat.

Once they finished with their farm, the men would help smaller farmers take in their crops, farmers who weren't able to afford the luxury of owning a threshing machine. Paul and John would go back to school, but other hands would take their place.

12

B ILL DANSKY WORKED OUT WELL. Things ran smoothly under his expert guidance. And whenever he was close by, Natalie became transformed. Lately, she seemed absorbed in secret thoughts and secret plans. Sometimes, Tanya caught her smiling to herself. Their farms alone took nearly ten days to thresh. And Mama began sounding like a commanding general.

"Alisha, quick, I want this floor swept, instantly. This house is a mess! Anna, you and Verna clear off the table in the dining room. And no excuses! Tanya, get me some apples. We're going to have apple pies for supper."

They jumped to accommodate her. She rarely made apple pies. Soon flour, lard, and peeled apples littered the table. The three children crowded at her side in eager expectation.

"Verna, make sure the oven is hot enough."

Verna plied the stove with wood. It soon topped 100 degrees in the kitchen. An hour later the pies were out, golden brown and emitting a delicious aroma of cinnamon.

"Can we try one? Can we ple-e-ase, Mama?" Alisha begged.

"No, not until supper, after the men have finished eating. I want to be sure there's enough. ... Away with all of you."

Tanya, her mouth watering, came back in to examine them closer.

Mama gave her a sharp look. "Never mind the pies. They'll keep. Help me load this food into the car. It's coffee time. Verna, start supper without me. Alisha, Anna, you girls set the table. ... Tanya, let's get going."

They loaded the food into the car. Mama drove to the field where the men were working. Her face brightened at the sight of Bill Dansky.

"Let's find some shade. You go round everybody up."

Tanya caught sight of Paul and went running toward him, thinking that he could help spread the news to the other hands about the lunch. He was pitching bundles of wheat into his rack.

Suddenly, he paused with pitchfork in mid-air, as though listening.

"Paul! ... Paul! ... Over here." Bill Dansky was motioning to him.

Paul dropped his pitchfork. "Yeah? Something wrong?"

Bill Dansky turned. "Yeah, something's wrong. I been shouting to you. Didn't you hear me?"

Tanya thought it odd that at times he spoke with a pronounced Ukrainian accent, then at other times the words rolled off his tongue nearly letter perfect.

Paul indicated his ears. "Too much noise."

"God damn pulley broke. Need a new one. You go to Spirit Valley and buy one from the Massey-Harris dealer. You see here how rotten it is?" He kicked at the pulley, which lay on the ground in shreds.

"But I still got my team to take care of."

"Leave the damn team! Get the hell outa here and do like I tell you. ... Your mother hired me to be boss, not you."

Paul's face turned red. He was about to speak but changed his mind and went to tie up the horses instead. Muttering to himself, he ran to get the keys from Mama. He disappeared in a cloud of dust, heading towards Spirit Valley, pressing the Ford to the limits while Mama stood squinting after him.

13

A LIGHT LAYER OF SNOW COVERED THE OPEN AREAS. The children's breath hung heavy in the mid-November day. Walking home, they didn't dawdle as they were wont to do when it was warm. That morning Mama had insisted that they wear their overshoes, because Greenview Elementary and High School was at least three and a half miles away. All six children attended classes in the two room structure where Grades 1 to 12 were taught. Tanya, her feet chilled almost to her knees, began running home.

Breathless, she reached the door and jerked at the knob with Alisha and Anna pounding at her heels. "Ha, ha, I beat you!"

"So what?" Anna flung at her, "how much further did you get, Fatty?"

She flushed. Stop calling me names! ... Even Mama told you not to!" Their laughter infuriated her further, but she calmed down as they walked in.

Tanya, struck by Mama's appearance, stared at her. Mama was certainly dressed up for whatever reason. She had on a very becoming blue crepe dress with a sapphire pin at her throat. Her dark hair, in small tight curls, looked stylish, and there were two spots of rouge on the high part of her cheeks, although it may have been her own color heightened. There was a special glow about her. She looked prettier than usual.

Bill Dansky sat lounging in a kitchen chair, looking handsome in a navy blue suit. His spotless white shirt was offset by a striped red and blue tie.

Natalie smiled and bent down to whisper something into his ear. An intimate exchange took place between them ... then laughter. She turned to the stove, absent-mindedly, to shift some pots about, though it was clear that she wasn't thinking of the pots. Still smiling, Mama turned to Bill Dansky. "Do you think we should tell them now?" she asked.

He nodded. "Yeah, I think so."

Alisha set her books down on the table and started for her room. Mama put out a restraining hand. "Alisha, wait a minute, I want to talk to you."

Alisha paused, dutifully. Curious, Tanya, Anna, and Verna, who were about to disperse, waited as well.

"Yes?"

"Bill and I, we were married this morning!"

The silence was measured by the noisy ticking of an alarm clock before Mama's voice broke in again. "Well?" She smiled broadly, searching each face with delight in an effort to prompt some reaction from them. The children's expressions registered blank amazement. Verna blanched. The door opened and Paul and John walked in from the bunkhouse; having intercepted the charged scene, they stood awkwardly looking at everyone for some explanation.

"They were married today," Verna told them, quietly.

"Married!" Paul's face reddened, no doubt remembering the "to do" in the field with the pulley, while John merely grinned.

Alisha asked, "You were married?"

"Yes, we were married," Mama repeated with pride.

"But why? When? I thought ... well, where did you get married? In Spirit Valley?"

"No, we went to Grand Plains. We were married by a Justice of the Peace this morning. This is your new Dad. Aren't you happy? Huh?"

"Yes, yes, we are happy." Smiling, nodding, they looked at each other to encourage agreement. Though immediately after, Alisha started for the stairs again. Tanya beamed at her new father as she swept past him. He rewarded her with a cold stare. They heard Verna behind them ... her steps measured and slow.

Tanya, sensing something wrong, wondered whether her new Dad would like Verna?

At the top of the stairs, Verna went into her bedroom and shut the door.

"Well, what do you think of him?" Alisha asked, sitting down on the unmade bed.

"I don't know. Maybe he's all right," Anna said.

Tanya remained still, remembering his reserved stare and thinking to herself how handsome he looked. Secretly she hoped, as Anna had voiced, 'that he might be all right'. Then we can be friends, she thought.

"I can't believe it! She only met him two months ago. What does she know about him?" Alisha's voice was tinged with dismay.

Anna nodded. "Yeah, and how come she didn't tell us sooner?"

Alisha indicated the arm bands. "You know, these will have to come off. And so soon after Tata's death! What'll we tell the kids at school? By tomorrow the news will be all over Spirit Valley. Do you know something? At recess, Jimmy Putman asked me if Mama was getting married. So I said, 'of course not' ... shows how much I knew."

Anna looked at her in surprise. "Do you mean to say that he already knew?"

"I guess so. Do you think everybody else did but us?"

"Alisha, Tanya, Anna, Verna ... where did you go? Get back down here! Don't hide yourselves!" Mama's voice put an end to the discussion.

Alisha started. "Now what does she want? ... Yes, okay, we're coming." Tanya was right behind her.

"Yes, Mama?"

Natalie faced her with a determined look. "Alisha, tomorrow at school, I want you to change your name to 'Dansky'. I'm married to Bill. It's only right that you carry his name. Understand?"

Alisha blanched. "But Mama, I really don't see how we can do that. I mean ..." She trailed off weakly. Mama's eyes, flashing anger, stopped her.

"I don't care what you think or don't think; you'll do as I say. Or you'll answer to me for it. Just tell Miss Zaichuk that your new name is Dansky!"

"Yes, okay, I will."

Tanya knew that Alisha only agreed because she was forced to, for soon Mama would lash out with more than words. Their stepfather sat looking somewhat disdainful, his mouth drawn down at the corners, while listening to his new wife carry on. Alisha began taking out the dinner plates. The clatter distracted her mother, who turned her attention back to the pots and supper.

"Tonight we have a nice roast beef. Alisha, mash the potatoes. Tanya, tell Verna to come down. I need some help here."

They sat down, and the meal commenced in silence. At the head of the table, their new Dad assumed a lofty air, his handsome face removed, thoughtful. It was an awkward beginning.

"Is the beef tender?" Mama asked him, smiling.

"Yeah, it's all right."

"Verna, pass Bill the potatoes."

Verna raised the dish to him.

He shook his head, avoiding her eyes. "No, I had enough."

Verna put the bowl close enough for him to reach and resumed eating. As soon as they finished, each child was anxious to get away. The boys to their private bunkhouse, the two older girls running off upstairs, leaving Tanya and Verna with the dishes.

Tanya, because she wanted very much to impress her new stepfather, picked up a tea-towel to help Verna.

Natalie sat down in a chair close to his, her face flushed with pleasure. She talked with animated gestures, while sipping her tea. In no time, she had him laughing.

The next morning, they awoke to the same dreary cold. Because it hadn't abated, Mama insisted that Bill drive them to school.

Tanya, her lunch bag and books in hand, squeezed in between Verna and Alisha in the back seat as "Dad" started the car. She felt embarrassed because no one spoke to him until he stopped to let them off. Then, because Mama would have expected it, they thanked him politely. Only Tanya paused at the door to dazzle him with a smile. "Bye, Dad!"

He turned his head away, intent on getting back, and didn't reply. She stopped, hurt by his indifference. Across the schoolyard, she saw Dorothy Zidoruk talking to some girls and waved to her. She was anxious to be the first to share the sensational news of Mama's marriage. "Hey, Dorothy! ... Girls! ... Girls! Listen everybody! Have I got something to tell you!" Her face beaming, she stopped to catch her breath. "Does ... does ... anyone here know who Bill Dansky is?"

Vera Pawluik leaned forward. "Yeah, I do. What about him?"

Tanya gave her a tolerant look. It wasn't her that she wanted to impress. However, because of her vitriolic tongue, she knew that she couldn't chance having her for an enemy. Drawing herself in, she prepared to grandstand. "Well, my Mom got married to him yesterday."

"What?" Olga Royko's eyes nearly popped. Stefa Hanchuk caught the sleeve of her coat. "She did?"

"Yes. Mama told us as soon as we got home from school. Were we surprised!" She held her breath waiting for their reaction.

Vera Pawluik looked smug. "Tanya, that means that you're related to me, because his brother is married to my cousin."

Tanya drew back. ... "No!"

"I was just thinking that he's also related to the Roykos, ... isn't he, Olga?" Dorothy Zidoruk, exclaimed.

Olga nodded. "Yes. Old man Dansky is my mom's uncle."

Tanya puffed up with importance. "Well, you know, he does come from a big family, so-o, I suppose that makes me related to almost everybody here!" She laughed.

Vera reached out and took her hand. "Come on, Tanya." The giggling girls formed a circle and began running and chanting, ... "related ...

related, we're all re-la-ted."

For Tanya, the moment was a happy one. Lucky for her that Mama had married him. Though deep inside her, a seed of fear had taken root. To the present time, her stepfather hadn't even acknowledged her presence with so much as a nod of his head. The fear remained entrenched for the rest of the day. It clouded her happiness about having someone taking Tata's place. Finally, she pledged that something would have to be done about it.

The rest of the day went by normally enough, and other than a few stares and some whispers behind their backs, nothing was said about the union.

However, back home, Mama was waiting for Alisha to question her about the name change, having sensed her reluctance from the previous day.

"Alisha, did you tell Miss Zaichuk that your new name was Dansky?"

"No-o-o, I didn't. Well, not yet. ... Mama, I don't think we can change it."

"And so tell me why not?"

Thankfully, Paul interrupted her. "We can't change our names just because we want to. It has to be done legally ... through a lawyer."

"Oh." Mama frowned. Lawyers meant expense and money; she let it drop.

Tanya wondered why Mama hadn't said anything to Verna, John, or Paul about changing their names to "Dansky"? Or were they being left out? Certainly it would widen the rift between the two sets of stepchildren even more. What a shame that Mama didn't like her stepchildren.

Alisha picked up a broom and attacked the floor, relieved that the matter had been settled so smoothly.

Natalie turned her thoughts inward, upset that her children couldn't be called Dansky. She wanted her new husband to bond to her children to ensure peace between them.

Just as soon as dinner was finished, Tanya, Alisha and Anna went upstairs. In the empty room next to Verna's, they found Bill Dansky's suitcase. "So what d'you think, shall we open it?" Alisha asked.

Tanya looked at her aghast. "I'm not so sure. What if they find out?"

Anna knelt down, snapped the lock open and lifted the lid.

Her sisters hovered over her. "Well, look at that! All ties! He must have at least fifty of them," Anna ran her hands through the ties. "And only one suit. You'd think he'd have more suits."

Alisha picked up a tie. "Why would he want so many? You know, let's close this suitcase before Mama or Dad come upstairs and find out that we've opened it." Anna snapped it shut. They left the room hurriedly.

14

THEIR NEW DAD HAD BEEN WITH THEM for an entire week before it became apparent to Tanya that he hadn't warmed up to anyone but Mama. Determined to correct the situation, at whatever cost to her, Tanya set her mind to become his favourite child.

She waited until the weekend before deciding on a plan to win him over. All night she could think of nothing else, knowing that she wouldn't be content until they laughed together and he held her on his knee just like Tata used to do. Tata's death had intensified her longing for a father more than anyone would know.

On Saturday, as soon as she awoke, she put on ski pants, a heavy wool sweater and woolen socks before going downstairs for breakfast. Her plan brought a tingle of excitement to the pit of her stomach.

Mama was by the stove frying bacon. Everyone was halfway through the meal. Tanya, with her eyes on her stepfather, rang out with a cheery "good morning."

But he kept eating, and it was Mama who acknowledged her greeting. A bit disappointed, she slipped into her chair and reached for the oatmeal. I'll eat quickly, she thought. I want to be finished when Dad is.

Bill Dansky finished his coffee and pushed back his chair. He walked to the entry to put on his parka and winter boots.

Tanya, seeing him about to leave, dropped her half eaten toast then rushed to get into her outer clothes. Quickly, she donned coat, scarf, and toque. To win him over, she'd decided to help him with the chores.

Outside, she trudged at his heels like a small puppy, in spite of a bitter wind that whipped at her face. Once she thought about going back to the warmth of the kitchen, then changed her mind, thinking that if he knew her better, surely then they would become friends. Mama did say to be nice to him.

But the anxiety that her efforts were being wasted persisted, causing her heart to pound, and at times a feeling of despair engulfed her.

Halfway through the morning, she offered to climb into the loft and throw the hay down to the horses. "I'll save you the trouble, Dad," she told him brightly, scrambling up the ladder before he could refuse. In reply, he grunted something under his breath.

When he began walking toward the chicken coop, Tanya was there first, thinking that she'd feed the chickens.

However, his china blue eyes did no more than glaze over her.

Her spirits waned. An ache caught in her throat. What if I did change my name to Dansky? I'd do it even if Alisha and Anna wouldn't, she thought. By now, her hands were partially frozen. "Where are you going now, Dad?" she asked.

He didn't answer her, but strode towards the shed to the car. The rear tire was flat. Bill jacked up the car and began unscrewing the bolts.

Tanya, ignoring the cold that threatened to numb her entirely, retreated into a corner for shelter. She began moving her feet, thinking that the shed was colder inside than outside. If only he'd talk to me, she thought. After all, they'd been together for three and a half hours.

She saw him struggling with a rusty bolt which held fast in spite of his efforts to unscrew it. Tata had done the same thing but he'd used a different wrench. Tanya found it and held it out to him. "Here Dad, try this."

He took the wrench and applied it to the bolt. It came loose without much effort.

She beamed. "I'm glad it worked!"

She noticed him groping for a lever and sprang forward. "Here, Dad, let me get that for you."

"I see where it is, I can get it myself."

The rebuff sobered her, sending her back into the corner just as Mama showed up. She sighed. Mama made every excuse to be at his side.

"Bill! There you are. I've been looking for you."

His frown changed into a smile. "Yes, what you want?"

"Bill ... at the house, we're nearly out of water. Verna and I, we have washing to do. I was wondering, could you and Paul bring up some water from the river? We have to haul it in barrels, you know."

The smile left his face. "Yeah, I think so."

Suddenly, noticing Tanya, Mama turned on her angrily. "Tanya! What are you doing here? You look frozen. Get back into the house this minute! I have a good mind to spank you!"

She burst into tears and ran from the shed. It was hopeless! Why couldn't he be just a little like Tata?

As soon as she entered the warm kitchen, she took off her coat and boots and slumped down on the floor beside the stove to sob convulsively.

Bill Dansky put away the tools, while Natalie watched him with pride. He had an innate sense for fixing things. "I'll go in and start heating what's left of the water," she told him.

He nodded. "I'll get Paul." His expression looked sullen. He turned and walked toward the bunkhouse. Raising his fist, he pounded several thundering blows on the door, rattling the grey weathered boards before booming out, "Paul, you come out here! Your mother, she wants water. You better show me where it is and how you get it."

Paul came to the door and opened it a crack. Behind his back, he hid a Superman comic book. "Yes?"

His stepfather glared at him. "You come with me. I need you to show me how you get water."

Paul dropped the comic book, dressed quickly, then ran out to the barn to hitch a team of horses to a heavy sled with two steel barrels sitting on it. He took the reins and went down a steep incline to the river's edge. Both barrels were filled to brimming before starting back.

"Geddyap." This time, Bill Dansky picked up the reins, cracking them over the horses flanks to get them moving. The animals began pulling the load, straining with effort at the steepest part of the hill, their nostrils flaring, blowing white mist into the cold air.

"Come on, pull! ... Pull! Son of a bitch, this is a rotten way to get water. What's the matter, didn't you ever hear of a well and a pump?

Should be a well dug here. Then we wouldn't have to sweat like this," he told Paul, sarcastically. "My mother, she got a pump inside the house all her life."

Paul looked upset. "Oh, yeah! Well, we tried digging for a well but never struck any water. Could be we dug in the wrong place."

"Then you should have a dugout," he snapped.

No more was said until they crested the bank and stopped at the front step that led into the kitchen. Paul opened the door and began carrying streaming buckets into the house where Verna and Mama were about to begin washing.

Verna had two large galvanized tubs filled to the brim and heating on the stove.

Natalie turned to her. "Verna, help me get this tub down."

Together, they lowered it to a bench. Verna reached for a glass washboard and began scrubbing all the whites. She worked methodically until the house steamed up, and the smell of lye soap filled the room. Now and then Alisha, hovering close to her, got in the way by playing with the suds.

Exasperated, Verna turned to her. "Alisha, do you want to try washing? Is that it?"

"Yes, yes, let me ... let me!"

Verna stepped aside. She dropped into a chair to rest. Perspiration clung to her face and her hair hung in limp strings. "You think it's easy? It's not easy; it's hard work." Verna's hands were red and chapped right to the elbows.

Lye soap wasn't hand cream. Mama didn't believe in hand cream. "It's for vain, lazy women ... who have nothing better to do than think about their hands. Farm women don't use hand creams," she often scoffed.

Alisha put her arms into the suds and pulled out a bed sheet. She began scrubbing it back and forth, imitating Verna. Soon her rhythmic motions slowed to a crawl. She stopped, puffing.

"Had enough? Want me to finish?" Verna asked.

"No, it's okay. I'll do it." She soaped the sheet again and scrubbed with what little strength she had left, as Tanya and Anna looked on. By the time she finished, her enthusiasm was as damp as the sheet.

Mama's voice cut through the talk. "Verna, are you going to sit there all day, or are you going to work?"

"Alisha wanted to try washing."

"If she does, you'll be at it all day. Away you go Alisha! Let Verna finish!"

Alisha wrung out the sheet and dropped it into the rinse tub. "There. You do have to be strong to wash, don't you, Verna?"

"Verna, these tea-towels are positively grey. Can't you get them any cleaner? Here, let me try. Nothing gets done right unless I do it myself." Natalie took a tea-towel and began scrubbing with firm, vigorous strokes.

"I think it's because of that river water. How can a person get anything clean, washing in rusty water?" Verna dried her face on a towel and pushed back her hair, which only sprang out again.

Mama pointed to the clothes waiting to be hung with a soapy finger. "Verna, don't just stand there like you have nothing to do! Of all the lazy good-for-nothing ... get these things out on the line to dry before it gets dark!"

Verna said no more but hurried to put on a wool sweater, and tucking a pair of woolen gloves into her pockets, she picked up the tub of wet clothes and opened the door. A cold gust swept into the humid kitchen.

"Damn it! Shut that door! Do you want me to catch cold? Is that what you want?" Natalie carried on even with Verna out of sight.

Shivering, Verna slipped on her gloves before attempting to throw the wet soggy sheets over the wire clothes line, which stiffened to pieces of cardboard in just minutes. By the time she finished, her gloves were nearly frozen to her fingers. She ran back to the house, banging her hands against her sides to keep them from freezing completely, where Mama waited for her with another load.

"Verna, I'm done. While you're still dressed, empty this water for me. It's so dirty, I swear it looks thick."

Verna nodded. Though her hands were numb, she grasped both handles and with the tub held fast in front of her, weaving precariously like some drunken stick man, she let fly the contents into the snow. She looked tired, her strength sapped from the push, pull of too much work.

"Verna! Vern-a-a! Come back inside. How long does it take to empty out water?" Mama gave her an angry look.

Verna came back in with the tub. "What did you want?"

"What do you think I want? Hang up the rest of these things, then scrub down the kitchen floor while I get supper. It looks like a pigsty in here." Mama brought out a pot of soup left over from the day before and put it on the stove to warm. She took a pail and opened a trap door in the kitchen floor. Carefully, she lowered herself down a ladder into the root cellar where the root vegetables were stored during the long winter months. She picked through the potatoes choosing the larger ones, then came back up.

"Alisha, while I'm peeling these, set the table. Tanya, put another stick of wood into the stove, and Anna, you run out and bring in more kindling. Tanya, you might try helping Anna as soon as you're done."

They did as they were told. With Mama's energy running short, her temper would soon be the same.

Natalie set the potatoes to fry just as Verna came back with the empty clothes basket. "Verna, when you finish washing the floor, you can help me milk the cows." Natalie put on a heavy coat, ski pants and wool scarf. With milk pail in hand, she turned to give them one last warning. "Alisha, see to it that those potatoes don't burn."

Alisha found the turner and stood in front of the stove, determined to be watchful. The door opened to let in Tanya with an armload of firewood.

Since early childhood, it was "Verna do this," and "Verna do that!" Her knees were as chapped and as red as her hands. Yet, Verna had talent. Once, Tanya remembered seeing a pencil drawing of Tata wearing his pinstriped coveralls and the rubber shoes that laced up. She'd drawn a remarkable likeness! Amazed, Tanya had exclaimed, "Why Verna, this looks exactly like Tata! Here, let me show it to Mama. I'm sure she'll love it." She'd taken it to her with pride.

At first, Natalie seemed interested, then at the mention of Verna her face hardened. "H-m-m-m, yes, it does looks like Sam all right. So what? It's nothing. Give it back to her."

Ashamed of Mama's outright rejection of the sketch, Tanya had remarked, "Verna. I really like it. We don't have any pictures of Tata, do we?"

"No, it's nothing. Give it here," Verna said, crushing the drawing in her hand.

Tanya's face fell. "Oh, Verna! Why did you do that? It was so like him."

But Verna, deaf to her comments, merely walked away.

15

DURING FEBRUARY, THE FROST COMPLETELY COVERED the single pane windows of the farmhouse. One day, Tanya stood scratching and blowing at the ice on a corner of the glass, having every intention of putting her tongue to it. Suddenly, she let out a scream.

Mama turned and looked positively exasperated. "I knew this would happen. You've got your tongue stuck. Well, good for you. Here, don't pull it too hard, or you'll rip it off. Slowly, pull it off slowly, I said!"

But as Tanya's head snapped back, her tongue came painfully free. She let out a wail, making Mama all the more furious.

"I hope this has taught you a lesson!" Two whacks followed in close succession. "If you even come close to those windows again, you'll get more!"

Tanya ran off into the dining room, crying and holding on to her mouth.

A minute later, Mama appeared in the doorway, blind to her tears. She pointed to a brimming pail where they emptied their leftovers and dishwater. "Stop bawling, and take out these slops to the pigs!"

Tanya looked aghast at the pail. "But what about Alisha? ... Can't she? Or Anna? ... Yes, Mama."

Unhappily, she reached for her heavy clothes. After Mama finished putting a scarf on her, she could barely see and was nearly suffocating.

"Here." Mama shoved the pail into her hand and pointed her out the door.

She stumbled into the biting cold, the hard packed snow crunching under her feet. Steadying the bucket, she carefully held it slightly away from herself, trying not to spill any of the greasy, smelly liquid onto her ski pants.

As she came closer to the barn, she could hear her stepfather and John arguing. Her stomach took a turn. She set the pail into the snow, then went running to the stable. John had a bad temper and he'd never back down, even if proven wrong.

Her stepfather stood with clenched fists. "God damn you, for the last time, I said I want the barn cleaned every day!"

John's answer came back, defiant. "I can't. I got lots a homework to do. No damn way ... can't do it."

"You gonna do like I say! It would be better for you guys if you did. You gonna find that out!"

Bill Dansky's voice sent a shiver up her back.

A smirk touched John's face. "I ain't cleaning no shit out everyday. You can't make me."

"You lazy bastard! You good for nothing!" He bent down, and picked up a long piece of leather harness, letting it fly at John.

It struck his arm with a sharp crack. "Oh, hell!" John lost his balance and fell backward into a pile of manure.

Tanya, horrified, watched her stepfather raise his hand to strike him. "Don't do that!" she cried out without thinking.

Bill turned at the sound of her voice, giving John time to get away. He took some quick steps after him ... then changed his mind. "You son of a bitch! You bitch sucker! You wait till tomorrow when you want a ride to school. I hope you freeze off your nuts! Stubborn son of a bitch! You not gonna talk back to me and get away with it! ... Tanya, what do you want?"

Sick at heart, she turned and ran to pick up the slops where she'd left them. She jerked along toward the pigpen, no longer bothering to be careful. She emptied the pail into a trough and returned home, saying nothing of the incident to Mama, thinking that she'd find out soon enough.

At supper time, the two boys came into the house laughing, while Tanya was setting the table. She gave John an anxious look. He seemed unconcerned. Her stepfather hadn't come in yet. Another minute went by before she heard his step at the door. She tensed, fearful for John.

Bill Dansky's face turned a slow purple when he saw them. "What you doing in here? You said you had a school work to do? Why you not doing it?"

"I finished." John answered, sarcastically.

"Bastard! Liar! This time I'm gonna give it to you like you deserve," he said, pulling off his jacket.

Mama's mouth dropped. Her eyes narrowed. "Bill, what are you doing?"

He paid no attention to her and started towards John, his head lowered.

Suddenly John, with Paul behind him, leaped up and ran for the back window. He gave it a shove upwards. It creaked and opened wide enough for both boys to dive into the snow outside just as Bill reached them.

"God damn bastards! Go to hell, both of you!" he roared, lowering the window with a bang.

"Bill, what's happened?" Mama asked.

"You know what that rotten son of a bitch done to me today?"

Mama looked upset. "No! What?"

"He tried to fight me, that's what! He likes talking back to me and fighting me! I'm not putting up with that kind of crap from him. I asked him to clean out the barn and he said he had some kinda homework to do!" He shook his head. "No siree! I'm not taking no shit from no snot nosed bastard. If he never gonna listen to me, why should I feed him?"

Tanya recoiled. What did this mean?

Mama drew herself in. She took on the same indignant look as Bill. "Oh, you don't say? ... The nerve of him!"

Tanya could no longer hold back. "But Mama, it's not true! ... None of it! ... I saw what happened when I was taking out the slops. John didn't do anything! Dad hit him. Please, don't be mad at John! ... Please! And Paul, he didn't do anything, either!"

Mama, enraged, rewarded her with a stinging slap. "Tanya, shut up! Do you hear me? I didn't ask you for advice. How much more can I take of this? Stop sniveling and get out of my way. This is none of your affair! Get to the table, sit down and eat. We're going to have our meal with or without them." She noticed Alisha and Anna by the door, ready to flee. "Well, don't just stand there, go tell Verna to come down!"

Still sobbing, Tanya didn't move. "But Mama, what about them? The boys? Aren't they going to eat? ... Do you want them to starve?"

Bill's voice cut in, putting an end to her queries. "Sit down, before I knock you down. Do you hear me? You ... you ... pout face! What do you know about it? For the last time, all of yous, sit down!"

Anna sat down and edged a large bowl of soup closer to her stepfather, anxious that he have the first helping.

Bill Dansky poured some into his dish and picked up a spoon just as Alisha walked in with Verna. He directed a mean look at them. "Verna, you shouldn't be loafing in your room."

Verna lowered her head and said nothing.

Mama gave her a sidewise look. "I'm not surprised. John had it coming! ... He's like his Dad. Stubborn fool! Nothing will change him. So what am I supposed to do about it? I tried my best to be a good mother to him. Where did it get me? ... I tell you this, from now on I don't care what he does." She looked at everyone in frustration. "One does his best for their children and what happens? They get kicked in the teeth by their own flesh and blood. Is there any point to having a family? I wish I didn't have any children. Most of the time it means trouble. And expense!" She shook her head. "Is it worth it, to have children? Why in Poland we couldn't talk back. We had to listen to our parents ... no matter what!"

As soon as they finished eating and cleared off the table, Mama cornered Tanya in the dining room.

"Tanya, what do you mean by talking back to me in front of your father? Huh? Those children aren't mine! Why should I care about what happens to them? Huh? ... Go! Get out of my sight! I have a mind to spank you for being so mouthy."

Tanya fled to her room upstairs. She found her treasure box, and took out her picture of Jesus with the angels. Her attempts to win over her stepfather had failed miserably. What about John and Paul? What about them? A tear came rolling down her cheek. Could anything be resolved between her stepfather and stepbrothers?

Maybe with Paul, but never with John. Then, remembering how Dad had called her "pouty," she lay down on the quilt and wept.

16

"ALISHA, ANNA, WAKE UP! TANYA YOU TOO! I want everybody down here this minute! ... Be sure to put on your underwear and ski pants. Do you hear me? And don't bother coming down unless you do. It's 38 degrees below zero and very cold. Hurry! Bill is driving you to school in the sled."

Tanya shivered as her feet touched the ice cold floor. She noticed a layer of frost in the corner of the bedroom.

Alisha threw off the covers and sat up. "I hate winter!"

Half asleep, Anna groped for her stockings.

"Did you hear me? I said hurry!" Mama's voice carried a warning. They dressed and ran downstairs to wash.

"Get a move on! You still have your lunches to make." Mama kept prodding them, while piling potato pancakes onto a plate.

Tanya poured herself a glass of milk and took some of the pancakes. With sinking heart, she noticed that John wasn't at his place. "Has John come in yet?" she asked.

Natalie looked at her angrily. "No! And don't ask me where he is. I can't keep track of everybody. I have enough to do without worrying about him. You heard what your Dad said. If you ask me, he has to learn to be more obedient."

Verna, her face a stony mask, got up from the table and refilled the milk pitcher just as the outside door opened, letting Paul in.

Tanya glanced at him in dismay. Should he have chanced it? She looked at her stepfather who sat as if alone and didn't look up. She sighed, thinking it must be all right between them.

Paul pulled up a chair, and helped himself to the pancakes. No one mentioned John. Everybody ate in silence.

"What's for sandwiches?" Tanya asked.

Mama pulled out a loaf of home made bread from the cupboard. "Bread, here. And ... h-m-m-m, I don't know. Uh-h-h, peanut butter and plum jam. That's about it. It'll have to do. I'm out of bologna."

"Isn't there anything else?" Alisha asked in exasperation. Mama hardly ever kept anything on hand, and the bologna never lasted any length of time ... whenever she remembered to buy some.

Tanya took a knife and cut off two slices. The bread felt dry. "Is there any butter?" she asked.

"We're out of butter," Verna said. "I haven't had time to churn it. Maybe today." At Mama's suggestion, Verna had dropped out of school, though she was a very good student. However, with Mama insisting that she'd be better off at home, she just gave in.

Tanya spread peanut butter over the bread and smeared it with plum jam before slipping it into her lunch bucket together with an apple.

Bill Dansky finished eating and pushed back his plate. He put on his heavy parka then went outside.

Mama hurried to the window to see where he'd gone. "Are you girls ready? Quick! He shouldn't have to wait for you. Get your coats on. Hurry! ... Tanya, let me tie that scarf." She yanked it off and retied it to suit herself. "Quickly! You know how he hates waiting. Everybody out! Out!" She shoved them into the cold as the horse drawn sled drew up to the door.

The morning had begun though the sky was still littered with stars.

Mama came after them with some heated blankets to put over their heads. "Get inside the sled. I've warmed these. Bill wait! I've heated a stone in the oven for their feet."

"Then get it," he snapped, reining in the horses. She brought the stone out covered with a cloth, and laid it on the floor of the sled. They pranced off with a resounding snap of the reins.

Paul sat across from his stepsisters with his back to the horses. He declined any covers when Tanya offered one of the blankets to him, preferring to ride with his face exposed to the bitter cold. Mama hadn't thought of providing him with a blanket.

Forty-five minutes later, the sun began making its ascent. The sky took on a lighter shade of blue. By now, a heavy coat of hoar frost covered the horses' manes and nostrils.

The trip was uneventful, until Tanya noticed a familiar figure striding ahead of them. "Look Dad! Isn't that John?" she asked, her voice rising with excitement.

Next to her, Alisha and Anna removed the covers to see for themselves. Paul, who had been sitting slumped over, came alive, his eyes darting anxiously between his brother and stepfather.

"Yeah, that's him. And look, he's not even wearing a hat!" Anna exclaimed.

Her stepfather turned to look at him. "Uh-h-h, yeah. It's him all right."

Tanya, unable to restrain herself, cried out in exasperation, "Dad, stop! Let's give him a ride! He's not even carrying any lunch. And he's, he's ... he's not dressed very warm! ... Well?"

"Stop? You say stop! For what? That bastard? God damn him!" He flicked the reins, urging the horses to a faster trot.

"But, Dad ... why not? It's so cold walking like that. He'll freeze!"

"Let him freeze. Serves him right! And you shut up. I don't want you telling me what to do!"

They went past him without slowing down. Paul turned his head making it impossible to see how he felt. And though they passed very close, John didn't seem to notice.

Looking back, Tanya felt a lump blocking her throat. Why couldn't he even ride on the runner? she wondered. But a look at her stepfather's face changed her mind about asking the question. John's hair was covered with hoar frost.

Bill Dansky snapped the reins over the horses. "He thinks he's tough. Well, we'll see how tough he is."

Tanya saw him later at school. He looked through her, beyond her, but not at her, considering her part and parcel of the enemy.

Five days passed. John didn't show up for any meals. Tanya wondered what he was eating. On the morning of the sixth day, Paul came in to breakfast alone, as usual.

Mama was waiting for him. "Paul, where's John? What does he think he's doing? How long is he going to keep this up?" Six slices of bread lay toasting on a wire grid on top of the stove.

She deftly turned each piece as it browned and slathered it with home churned butter. "Stubborn! Damn stubborn fool! Verna, there's no cream on the table. Go get some!"

Tanya turned to Mama, surprised that she had actually inquired about John.

Paul slumped down into a chair by the table. He looked haggard. He lowered his head and spoke in a high-pitched voice.

"Well, you don't have to worry about John no more. He's left." Then, unable to hold back, he sobbed out, "He said to tell you he was never coming back. He said he had enough!"

Tanya felt a tear roll down her cheek.

"What do you mean "left"? Has he run away?" Mama asked, sombrely.

Bill Dansky put down his fork.

Paul nodded. "Yeah, he's gone for good. He didn't know where to, for sure. ... He said he might head towards Calgary. He was gonna go looking for work."

Bill Dansky, looking righteously indignant, nodded. "Good for him! I'm not sorry. Let the bastard go!"

Tears poured down Mama's face. She dropped heavily into a chair. "But what will he do? He's barely fourteen!"

It left Tanya wondering why was she shedding tears when she'd never shown him any love or kindness? Verna pushed back her chair, and walked to the window to stare out of the frozen pane. Though she kept her back turned to them, Tanya noticed that she was trembling before she slipped into the unused dining room.

"Did he say why he was leaving?" Mama asked.

"No. He just said it was time to go." They knew why he'd left.

Tanya rose from her chair and, since the bedrooms upstairs were too cold, she sat down on the landing. She thought about the swear words, the anger, the hatred that they were exposed to every day. Sadly, she knew that this was wrong. It was evil. This knowledge was stronger than anything that was done to her or happening around her. But what could she, one lone person, do to stop it? Forgetting the cold, she went up to her room to look at her icon of Jesus.

Nobody bothered to find out what had happened to John, though he was still under age and should, by law, be attending school. He had no money. He'd have to wait until he was twenty-one for his inheritance from the Public Trustee. How would he live? Tanya wondered.

A year later, Paul, when he realized that there was no future for him on the farm, left as well. Bill offered to keep him on as a labourer for $1.00 an hour. It was hardly enough to buy socks.

17

APRIL WAS NEARLY OVER, and an occasional gust of cool wind whistled through the trees along the river bank. There was still snow on the ground, for it hadn't been a warm spring. However, because it was a Sunday, and Mama was in a good mood, she'd given them permission to invite the Hanchuk girls. Stefa Hanchuk was in Tanya's class and Edie was in Alisha's.

It wasn't often that Mama allowed them to have anyone over. They spent the afternoon playing hide and seek before the two girls decided to leave for home.

Tanya and her sisters trudged to the top of the hill and stopped. A team of horses and a buggy were tied to a fence post in the yard. "Someone's here!" Tanya exclaimed. She opened the door. They walked quietly into the kitchen, surprised to see a young man sitting by the table, drinking tea and visiting with their stepfather and Mama. He had medium brown hair, deep-set brown eyes, and thick eyebrows that very nearly touched. Two creases, etched between his eyes, gave him a perpetually worried look. He was of average build and height and rather handsome in a rugged way.

Verna wore a polka-dotted, white and blue rayon dress. Tanya felt that his visit had something to do with her.

Alisha started for the stairs but Mama cut her off.

"Alisha, Tanya, Anna! Girls come in here. This is Fred Belinko. These are my three children, Fred."

"Hello." He grinned at them, shyly. His dress was rather formal: brown pinstriped suit, brown tie, spanking clean white shirt. The crease in his pants was razor sharp.

"Alisha, come with me. Fred is staying for supper." Alisha followed

Mama outside.

"Supper? But why? Who is he?" she asked, as soon as they were out of earshot.

"Never mind. He's come to see Verna. I think he's going to ask her to marry him."

"Ask her to marry him? But she doesn't even know him! Who is he? Where is he from?"

"It's none of your business. He's from Owl Creek. She said they met several times at a dance."

"But why does he want Verna?"

"Because he thinks that she's decent, hard-working, and would make him a good wife, that's why. However, little does he know that she's lazy! He owns a half-section of land, cleared. He even owns his own house. Pretty good, don't you think? And Verna, she's lucky to find someone as good-looking as Fred. Verna's no beauty. In fact, she's downright ugly! Myself, I'm surprised at him. You'd think he'd want someone prettier. Now stop talking, and help me catch one of those roosters for supper. I haven't got all day. There, that one!" She pointed to an elegant, white Plymouth Rock, strutting proudly about while keeping his distance from them.

Alisha started chasing after him as Tanya and Anna joined in. It sounded as if Mama was angry because Fred was reasonably well-off and good-looking. Verna was anything but lazy. They caught the rooster and Mama took over.

18

"MAY I PLEASE HAVE MORE CHICKEN?" TANYA ASKED. She was using her best table manners. Mama was very critical about their manners whenever they had company. However, she didn't take into account how they "really" lived without so much as a "please or a thank you" to be heard, ever.

Verna smiled as she passed it to her.

"Thank you."

"You're welcome!"

The roast chicken was a hit. There were mashed potatoes, dressing, and boiled carrots. Natalie had baked a rhubarb bread pudding, covered with a sweet wine sauce and served it with thick, fresh cream. Every crumb was eaten. She didn't always give so much thought to making the meals tasty.

Tanya held up the wishbone. "Who wants to make a wish? All eyes turned to Verna. ... "Verna?"

It snapped apart. Verna held up her half. "I won! See, I won!" She turned a bright red.

Alisha giggled. "What did you wish for?"

Verna only smiled.

"Uh-h-h, where did you go to school, Fred?" Mama wanted to know.

"Elk River. I finished High School. I have my diploma." He had a soft, quiet way of speaking. It was hard to imagine him ever angry.

Verna stared at him. Their eyes met. She quickly lowered hers. Tonight, she looked different. Her thick red hair was drawn back and tied with a blue ribbon. Her skin, peppered with freckles, had a glow to it. There was a hidden sparkle in her light blue eyes.

Tanya wondered if she was going to marry Fred and leave them? She noticed her stepfather was being quite civil to Verna's prospective suitor.

"Bill, why don't you give Fred more wine?" Mama urged. "And some to Verna, as well."

"More wine Fred?" Bill held out a gallon of sweet Australian port to him.

"No, thank you, I still have some."

Natalie took note that Fred was a man of temperance!

Tanya took a small sip of her wine which she thought tasted very sweet. Mama had poured about an inch into each of their glasses. Even the tiny bit she had made her head spin.

"Verna? How about you? More wine?" Ordinarily, Bill spoke to Verna only through Mama.

Taken by surprise. Verna was slow in replying. "Actually, I still have some, but thank you."

Thinking back, Tanya recalled the last time they "spoke." Her stepfather had pointed to a comb with some of Verna's red hair still clinging to it. "Natalie, you tell Verna not to leave her hair on the comb so somebody else could use it," he'd commented angrily, though Verna was but three steps away from him.

Mama had struck her across the back with the open palm of her hand. "Verna, get your own comb. Do you hear me?"

Verna's shoulders had drooped. She had merely nodded.

The meal carried on for some time. Tanya's eyes grew heavy from the warmth in the kitchen. Mama made a rapid clock check. "Oh my! Is it ten already? Girls, off to bed with you!"

"Aw-w-w, can't we stay just a little longer."

She relented only because she didn't want to appear too rigid in front of company.

At ten-forty five they said "good night" and went upstairs. A full moon shone through the window. Tanya lay down and pulled up the quilt, feeling sad at the thought of Verna marrying and leaving them. Ever since she could remember, Verna had always been there.

Two months later, her fears materialized when Fred proposed to Verna and she accepted. During their courtship, he'd come at least once a week to see her. Sometimes they went to a movie and sometimes he took her out for a meal to a restaurant in Spirit Valley. Once, he borrowed a friend's car and they drove to Grand Plains where he bought her an engagement ring. For Verna, it was the beginning of a new life.

Mama began talking about a reception as soon as she saw the ring. "You know, Verna, with you and Fred setting the date for next week, it doesn't give us much time to prepare anything."

Verna looked at her evenly. "It doesn't matter to me none. I'm not fussy ... as you well know. And Fred wants to keep it quiet."

"Maybe we can have the reception here in the house? Huh? We'll serve a lunch. I'll pick up some sausage and ham from the butcher shop. Maybe make some squares, or cakes. ... I'll invite your Godmother, and Mrs. Royko, of course. She still talks about Sam. We'll have to think about cleaning this house. ... For sure, something will have to be done about the walls and the windows. My, look at this linoleum! I hadn't noticed how torn it was. Verna, we have a lot of work to do by next week."

"I'll help all I can."

"Good. I'm glad you're sensible about having it at home. It'll cut the cost. After all Verna, you don't have a single friend your age that we could invite, do you?"

"It's okay by me. If we don't have many people coming, why bother?"

"Because it's your wedding, that's why."

Verna didn't have any friends because Mama didn't allow them into the house. And she didn't complain because she knew that it would be useless.

At the end of June, Verna and Fred drove to Grand Plains and were married by a Justice of the Peace with Mama and Bill Dansky as witnesses. The three younger girls weren't allowed to attend. Natalie didn't want her children getting in the way.

"Can I see your ring?" Tanya asked as soon as they came back, married.

"Sure." She held out her hand.

What a disappointment! Just a plain gold band! Mine will be a diamond solitaire, she thought. One whole karat! No less! "Uh-h-h, it looks nice, Verna." She ran off to tell Alisha.

Later, Verna baked her own wedding cake for the reception. A simple white cake iced with a seven minute frosting and sprinkled all over with coconut. With the cake out of the way, she went upstairs to see about the sleeping arrangements.

Half an hour later, they heard the sound of furniture being moved. Tanya, her curiosity piqued, went up to check. Verna was in her room kneeling on the floor next to two twin cots.

Tanya looked puzzled. "What are you doing?"

"I'm trying to get these beds tied together if I'm to sleep next to my husband tonight."

"I see." Poor Verna. She even had to find a way of being with her husband on their very first night. Somehow Verna managed to get them tied together and after the covers were on, they didn't look that bad.

The next morning they awoke to the creak of the oven door opening and closing. Tanya opened her eyes to see Alisha standing by the window as Mama's voice floated up to them. "Alisha, get up! Girls, get down here and help me in the kitchen!"

"Yes, Mama, we'll be right there," Alisha answered in frustration. "But we're still dressing."

Suddenly, Tanya sat bolt upright. "Alisha, those look like my anklets. Are they mine?"

"Yes, I hope you don't mind. I can't seem to find any."

"I do mind! Take them off! I washed them yesterday so I could have something to wear today. You can't have them. Get them off." Her voice rose in panic.

"Honestly, Tanya. I don't have any socks. Nothing! Not a thing! I've got to wear something!"

"Alisha, you and Anna, you're always doing this to me because you're too lazy to wash your own clothes. Well I'm not! Last week, you even took a pair of my panties! Don't think I didn't know about it. Take off those socks, I need them!"

"But, I ..."

Furious, Tanya jumped up and flew at her. Alisha hit her across the back with a clenched fist and taking a handful of hair, she pulled hard. Tanya screamed in pain, alerting Mama who came flying up the stairs.

"Mama, Alisha's got my anklets on, and she won't give them back to me. She even pulled my hair!"

"Then find some others to wear, can't you? This is no time to start fighting. Either you come downstairs, both of you, or I'm going to start hitting." Mama left with Alisha at her heels.

Tanya felt a slow anger burn within her. Was there nothing she could count on as her own? Was she to be stripped naked of not only her feelings but the paltry bit of clothing that she owned? She walked to the closet in despair and began to sort through a pile of shriveled up, soiled socks lying on the floor. She found the cleanest of the lot and turned her attention to something appropriate that she might wear. There wasn't much. Mama had made some of her dresses, but she was no seamstress. The other things were mostly hand-me-downs from Alisha and Anna. Not one thing was nice. She found a pale yellow, taffeta dress with puffed sleeves which she thought might do. Mama had sewn this one herself. It was the only dressy thing that she had. For Verna's sake, today she wanted to look nice.

"Anna ... Tanya, get down here! Didn't you hear me? We don't have much time." Mama's voice sounded threatening.

Tanya subdued her dejection. "Come on, Anna, let's go."

Downstairs Mama, her face flushed, was loading a ham into the oven. "Tanya, I'm sure there'll be some people coming early. You and Anna set the dishes in the dining room then help me clean up this mess in the kitchen. But first, go back upstairs and change that dress. Put on something you can work in. For heavens sakes, you can't work in yellow taffeta!"

"Yes, Mama, silly of me." Disappointed, she ran back upstairs to change; with Mama being so touchy, there was no point in arguing.

"Hurry!"

They needed Verna. But as of yesterday, Mama no longer had any claim to her. Tanya came down in a faded, blue cotton dress that had once belonged to Anna.

She bolted down a doughnut and swallowed a glass of milk as fast as she could. When she finished, she looked up to see Fred and Verna coming downstairs. Verna looked the same except for trying to keep a straight face in concealing her happiness from Mama. Fearing, no doubt, that if Mama ever got wind of it, she'd find a way to stem it. She wore white shoes, a white, pique cotton dress, sewn coat-style with a row of red buttons down the front and a narrow red belt at the waist. It looked perfect for a bride's reception.

"Good morning, Verna ... Fred. Did you sleep well?" Mama asked. Then, not waiting for their reply, she went on, "Verna, I hate to ask but, could you cut up the squares for me?" Mama would have to be desperate to ask Verna to help her on the very first day of her married life, Tanya thought.

"Yes, as soon as I find a knife."

"Fred, there's coffee on the stove and some doughnuts on that table. I'm sorry, I was just too busy to prepare anything fancy. ... Tanya, Anna, have you finished in the dining room?"

At eleven o'clock, Verna, with Alisha's help, began putting out the sliced ham, fried chicken, rolls, pickles, ham sausage, and baked beans. Then she really made Mama happy by cleaning the kitchen.

As Mama flew past the window, she stopped to peer outside. "Verna, come here, quick! Your Godmother, Irene, she's here! You know, I could have used another hour but ..." She whisked off her apron, and patted her hair into place. "Well, did you see their fancy car? Tanya, don't you look ragged. Run upstairs and change your dress. Flustered, she turned to Alisha. "Do I look all right?"

"Yes, Mama, you look fine."

"I hope so." She composed herself, then rushed outside, with outstretched arms to greet her guests. "Irene, it's so nice to see you! And Raymond! Why don't you ever come to see us, anymore? Verna, look who's here! It's Irene!"

Vaguely, Tanya recalled some scenes from childhood: of splashing in bath water, of piles of ironing and laundry, and Mama laughing with Irene. Mama had hired her to help out during the depression when money was scarce; Irene had been more than willing to work for just her room and board. Later, she'd left them and married. Judging from the car and their clothes, she had done well for herself.

Mrs. Royko walked in, bearing something loosely wrapped in brown paper. She kissed Verna on the cheek. "This is for you Verna. Your Dad, God rest his soul, if he was still alive, would be so happy for you." She dabbed at her eyes with a lace hanky.

Verna smiled and tore open the package, exposing a heavy white, wool blanket. Tears welled in her eyes as she tried to find words to express her gratitude. She couldn't fathom that someone would find her worthy enough to go to the trouble of buying her something. "Thank you."

Verna had never developed any social graces. Sometimes, when company found its way to the house, she simply sprinted away to her room and shut the door. She'd lived most of her life in Mama's shadow, and was totally unprepared for the attention lavished on her by the reception.

"Verna, I'm so happy for you. We heard about it last week from your mother." Tanya looked up to see Matilda and Matt Delany standing in the doorway. Behind them were Dora and Alex Shumak. Matilda's tall, angular form was ablaze in a printed sheath of mauve, pink, and purple. "We'd like you to have this ... from Matt and myself." She handed Verna a large box wrapped in flowered gift paper. "And this must be Fred. How nice to meet you," she exclaimed, smiling and shaking his hand.

Verna removed the paper, exposing a set of aluminum pots. It was surprising to find the neighbours not as standoffish as Mama had led herself and her family to believe.

Sadly enough, her own sisters gave her nothing. Mama had assumed that her gift would include them, and having no money of their own, they had no means of buying her anything.

The reception continued late into the afternoon with Mama and the three girls exhausted from doing dishes and serving food.

Irene Lalonde and her husband were the first to leave, expressing a desire to visit friends in the district. The Shumaks left last.

Wearily, Mama waved to them, shut the screen door, and went into her bedroom. "Verna, could you come in here a minute?" she called.

Verna walked into the room, with the younger siblings trailing behind her. Tanya's stomach took a turn in predictable dread.

"Before you go, I'd like to give you something." Mama said, sounding flustered and unsure of herself, while Verna stood looking at the floor, her roughened hands held tightly in front of her.

"I have these for you." She shoved some goose down pillows and a wool quilt at her. "I think they'll come in handy."

Verna nodded, letting them slide to the floor. A heavy silence followed. Tanya's heart started to pound, thinking that this was goodbye and, since Verna knew very well how Mama felt about her, she was not likely to return or ever want to see them again.

"We're also giving you a hundred dollars. A gift from Bill and me. I hope it's enough." Suddenly, tears began staining her face. "Good-bye Verna," she choked out.

Verna lowered her head and started to cry as Mama's arms embraced her. They stood crying together, and for the first time in her life, Mama kissed and held her stepdaughter.

"Good bye, Mama." Her shoulders convulsed. The words came out in a whisper.

Mama's arms loosened. Verna wiped her eyes. If she had any last words to say to her, they remained unsaid; the farewell had rendered her speechless, for she was unable to utter more than a sob that tore its way out of the depths of her being.

In the doorway, all three sisters stood crying in sorrow, giving vent to the sadness that had taken root from the very first day when her intended had come to call. They had known how it would end.

Verna bent down, gathered up her quilt and the down pillows and turned to leave. She looked up to see Anna sobbing in the doorway. "Good-bye, Anna," she said patting her head. Anna had always been her favourite.

They looked on in silence, their love for her covered over by the constraints of propriety set by Mama, who had long ago discouraged any overt show of kindness or affection.

Outside, Fred had already loaded the gifts into the buggy and stood talking with Bill Dansky. Their raucous laughter, untainted by any sorrow or gloom, could be heard clear to the house.

Verna stowed away her endowments, then climbed into the buggy as Fred shook hands with everybody. "Thanks for the wedding gifts, Mrs. Dansky ... Bill!" He climbed in beside Verna and, clucking to the horses, they began to move.

"Good bye, Verna." Tanya ran after them for a short distance, waving, and wondering whether her new husband would treat her kindly so that she could soon forget her tortuous past.

"Come children, we have supper to prepare." Mama motioned for them to follow. "I'll be better off without her. It's not easy when there's so many mouths to feed. The more children, the more work. Come inside. Help me get this mess cleaned up."

"But Mama, she helped. She did work." Tanya came to her defense, reluctant to lay blemish on her memory so soon.

Mama's lips narrowed. "Never mind that. And don't talk back to me. I know what I'm talking about when I say that children mean work. You don't. Go get the cows; it's milking time. Alisha, Anna, start washing that pile of dishes."

Tanya whistled for Jip, grateful for the short reprieve from the chores in the house. She reached out to stroke the dog's head, her only living consolation.

That night, before going to bed, she brought out her icon from the treasure box and gazed upon it with a heavy heart. Tonight, she needed very much to be comforted. After a time, she put it away and went to bed with Verna on her mind, wondering how she'd ever managed to keep all her feelings bottled up so well, even in the most trying moments!

In the morning when she awoke, everywhere she turned, there was a reminder of Verna. The rest of the week went by in leaden monotony.

Whether Mama admitted it or not, Verna had been a very integral part of their lives.

19

AUGUST BROUGHT WITH IT MORE HOT, DRY DAYS. The rain held back for nearly a month, and every time a car went by, a grey curtain of dust hung over the gravel road. As the kitchen became hotter and more unbearable, Natalie became more irritable.

Tanya spent the time outdoors, in the garden, or roaming over the fields with Jip. The peas were at their peak, and she took to sampling them almost every day.

One day, as she sat in the middle of the pea patch, Mama suddenly appeared out of nowhere. At the sight of her, Tanya started. The general rule was that no one was allowed to raid the garden.

"And what are you doing here?" she snapped.

"Why ... I ... I'm eating some ... peas." Her voice dwindled down to a whisper.

"You know you're not supposed to be in here. How many times do I have to tell you to stay out of the garden?" She leaned down and hauled her to her feet. Tanya let out shriek after shriek as Mama pummeled her with the palm of her hand.

"There, and there! Next time I say something, you obey me! ... You're getting more like Sam, every day. Damn it! It's disgusting. Further more, you're beginning to act like him. This attitude of yours will have to end." Her rage quelled, she let her go and tramped back to the house.

Tanya went sobbing to the machine shed to sit in the shade, her seat burning tender, thinking that Mama never did do anything with the peas. She simply allowed them to dry out after they'd ripened. She hated canning.

Beside her she became aware of Jip, standing with his wet nose in her hair. She let out a cry and draped herself over him, while her tears fell into his fur. Finally, her crying wound down. She rose to her feet and went back inside the house, going directly to her room.

Alisha and Anna were already there. Alisha was lying flat on the bed with Anna sitting beside her. Tanya started in disbelief! In one hand, Alisha held, upended, Tanya's piggy bank. With her other hand she was prying the coins out with a bobby pin. Nickles, dimes, and quarters, were scattered over the bed that Tanya had saved. Mama often paid them for extra work done around the house.

Tanya let out a scream and dived for the bed. "What are you doing? That's my money! Give it back to me!"

Alisha dropped the piggy bank, scrambled out of the way, and went thumping down the stairs with Anna flying after her. They rushed out the screen door and down the path; at the gate, the two girls took to the open road with Tanya close at their heels, determined to catch up. She caught up to Alisha as soon as she became winded. Tanya could feel shooting pains in her own side. However, the added adrenaline pumping through her body brought one thought to mind: to get even! They had no right to violate her, especially since this wasn't the first time that she'd caught them robbing her!

Alisha and Anna suddenly stopped to confront her together, their sharp elbows digging into each side of her. Tanya hit out with both fists at the same time, uncaring where the blows landed, concerned only that she feel some appeasement within.

"Don't you dare touch my money! It's mine! I worked for it. And I don't steal yours!"

"Stingy! That's because you're stingy, that's why! ... You don't share anything because you're selfish! Isn't that so?"

"I don't care! You're not supposed to steal from me. That money doesn't belong to you! Don't you dare touch anything of mine!"

She fought until she was sure that they'd both felt her blows before letting up. As she walked away, behind her their mocking laughter rekindled her anger. One thing was certain. A different place would have to be found for the money.

Tanya went upstairs, gathered up the change from the bed and took the piggy bank to the river. She found a hollowed tree and put it inside. Later, I'll look for something more permanent, she thought.

The next day after lunch, she whistled for Jip thinking that she'd have to resign herself to being a loner. With both sisters intent on undermining her how could she trust them?

As she walked along, she searched the ground for wild mushrooms. However, today her search proved fruitless and she returned home empty-handed.

Alisha was standing by the table swishing a dish rag through a pan of unwashed dishes when she walked in. "Did you find any mushrooms? I saw you in the field just now."

"No. Not even one. It might be too dry or maybe too early."

"Dad's splitting wood, you know."

"Yes, I saw him. Where's Mama?"

"I don't know. Probably in some field."

Suddenly, the screen door opened and their stepfather, his face streaming sweat, confronted them.

At the sight of him, they both stopped talking. Lately, there was no pleasing him. Sometimes, late at night, they heard him quarreling with Mama about their disobedience to his petty rules.

"Tanya! You! I want to talk to you."

"Me?"

"Me?" He mimicked her tone. "Yes, you! I told you this morning that I wanted you to stack the wood for me in rows. Remember? Just now, I saw you in the pasture. What were you doing?"

She stared at him, stricken. "I was looking for mushrooms. I didn't know you wanted me to stack the wood. I'm sorry."

"You sorry! I don't care that you sorry! Instead of sorry, why don't you do the work? I think it's because you lazy, huh?" He came closer.

She shrank back. "But, Dad, I'll still do it," she said faintly.

"You God damn right you will! I'm not gonna do it. The whole damn bunch of you is lazy." Suddenly, his right foot shot out and he landed a blow to her ankle.

Tanya dropped the tea towel and limped outside, crying in pain with Bill striding after her.

"You God damn pout face! Come back here. Never mind your crying. I want you back in five minutes. You hear me?"

Tanya went running across the road towards the river. She could hear the dog pounding at her heels. Suddenly, before she could stop herself, she turned and landed a swift kick to his rear. The dog, yelping in pain, made an about face and veered off in a different direction. She stopped, aghast at her actions, instantly sorry.

It was senseless to kick Jip just because she'd been kicked. "Jip, come back! Jip! I'm sorry, I didn't mean it. I need you." She ran after him until she caught him. Then, throwing her arms around his neck, she held fast. Jip, sensing her change of heart, stood still, panting warm breath into her face, to withstand yet another bout of sobbing.

"It's okay, Jip. I'm sorry. I have to go now or Dad will be coming after me. You wanna come? Good Boy. I love you. You know, you're all I've got, don't you? Seems they all hate me because I look like Tata. Or so Mama says. Funny thing, I don't even remember what he looked like anymore, or what I'm supposed to do about it."

She stood up and walked towards the woodpile, keeping a close watch on her stepfather, who kept chopping the wood without a glance in her direction.

Back at the house, Alisha finished wiping the dishes and cleaning off the table. She carried the dishwater outside to throw into the garden. Mama came up the path with a hoe.

"Did your Dad come in for coffee?" she asked.

"No, I don't think he wanted any. Though he did come in for a while, but he didn't say anything about coffee."

"I just saw Tanya. She's stacking the wood." Mama smiled. "That's nice. Why don't you go help her? I think I'll have a bite to eat."

At supper time, it was obvious that Bill was still angry. He glanced around the table. "Natalie, I think everybody in this house is lazy but me. ... Me! I'm the only one who works. Natalie, you spoiled your daughters. Look at them. What do they do around here? ... Especially Tanya. I never seen nobody so crabby in my life. Always walking around with that, that ... pout on her face." He turned down his mouth and stuck out his lips to imitate her. "She needs training! You know today, I had to tell her two times to stack the wood. Do you believe that? Two times! When all I should have to do is look at her, and she should know by herself what needs to be done. Seems to me she's like her bastard brother John."

Mama nodded, absently, half-heartedly agreeing with him. "Yes, you may be right."

They left the table quickly the minute the meal was finished,

Tanya headed for the barn to find solace with Jip and the cat. As she was crossing the yard, she stopped dead in her tracks. A grey mass, something like a large mudball, was moving slowly across the yard. "Tommy? ... Is that you?" She ran closer. Sure enough, it was the cat, so thoroughly mud encrusted that he was hardly recognizable. Between the heavy folds of dirt, two shiny dots, where his eyes should have been, focused on her. "Tommy, what happened? Did you fall into something? ... Okay, don't move, I'll be right back."

She returned with soap and a basin of warm water. Then, ever so gently, she washed, disentangled, and smoothed out his fur until he was clean again. "Tommy, since I'm going to be a nurse, this is good practice for me." She stood up to check him over before taking him with her to the barn.

Tanya scaled a ladder leading to the loft, and sank down into a loose bale of straw. She withdrew a small diary from her pocket and unlocked the cover. Her last entry was dated July 14, 1945. It read: "Dear Diary, today I caught Alisha stealing my savings from my piggy bank. I really gave it to her and Anna too for helping her. I think I taught them both a lesson. Last night I cried because I don't think that Dad will ever even like me. And I don't know what's come over Alisha because when I awoke in the morning she was going through my clothes again looking for something of mine to wear. We had an awful fight. Mama had to come upstairs to separate us. As usual she took Alisha's side and not mine although she was to blame. Mama never listens to me." Suddenly, she sat bolt upright. There was a note scrawled at the bottom of the page in Alisha's handwriting. ... Ha, ha, ha. You don't really think that anyone will believe this crap, do you?

She turned bright red. A wild urge for revenge seized her. Why would Alisha want to read her personal and private diary? She thought about "having it out" with her then changed her mind. If she told Mama, Mama would, no doubt, absolve Alisha. Like the piggy bank, now I'll have to find some place to hide the diary, she thought.

The next morning when they awoke, Mama was dressed in a pair of men's pants and shirt ready to leave the house.

"Your Dad and I are picking roots in that south quarter we just bought. Alisha, you and Anna have something ready for us to eat when we get home."

"Yes, Mama, we will."

Mama's eyes came to rest on Tanya, who sat crying on the floor next to the stove. A look of exasperation crossed her face. "Tanya, you look terrible. If you don't stop bawling, I swear, I'll give you something to bawl about. Are you listening to me? No wonder everybody calls you "pout face." There must be some work you can do instead." She looked here and there. "Help Alisha with the lunch."

Tanya nodded.

"Get up, wash your face, and smile. No more pouting for today. Your Dad hates it when you pout." She sighed, reaching for her straw hat. "I'm leaving. We'll both be back at noon."

Tanya resumed her crying, as Alisha picked up a broom and swept a circle around her. It was Friday. Alisha was planning to ask Bill Dansky to drive them into town to see the latest movie playing at the community hall. Sometimes, if caught in the right mood, he obliged them and took Mama along as well.

However at noon, Bill walked in alone.

"Where's Mama?" Alisha asked, keeping her voice unnaturally cheerful.

"She be coming soon."

The door opened and Tanya came into the house. Alisha glanced nervously at him ... at her. It was obvious to everyone that he couldn't stand the sight of her.

However, he gave her no more than a glance, and after washing his face, he blindly groped for a towel. "Alisha, for God's sake, where's the God damn towel? Get me a towel! How do you expect me to dry myself?"

"Yes!" She hurried into the bedroom and pulled out a clean towel from a pile of unironed and unfolded laundry. She noticed Tanya and thrust it at her. "Here, you give it to him. Quick!"

He snatched it from her, causing her to break into tears. For a minute, it looked as though he was going to hit her, but he held back.

Just then Mama, blackened with dust, walked into the kitchen. Anna trailed after her carrying the cat in one hand and her doll in the other.

"Where did Tanya go?" Mama asked.

Alisha looked up. "I don't know. I think outside."

"I noticed her crying as I came up the walk. Why is she always crying?" She looked at Bill. "I did speak to her about it today. I told her directly: no more crying." She sighed. "It seems it didn't do any good. I hate to admit it, but she cries every morning. I have no idea why!"

That night, Tanya lay in bed straining to hear the argument between her stepfather and Mama downstairs. The quarrel seemed to be about the three of them.

"Natalie, I can do it. You're not strict enough. Can't you see Tanya does nothing all day but cry? She got too much time on her hands."

She sat up, wondering what he meant by "Tanya does nothing?"

What right did he have to criticise her? She strained to hear more.

"I can't say for sure. Maybe you're right. They are lazy. Maybe I haven't been strict enough with them. Maybe I'll have to do something about it. But I can't say exactly what," Mama answered.

"Natalie, you're only making it worse by putting it off."

The screen door opened and their voices faded out.

Wide awake now, Tanya lay wondering what her stepfather was pressuring Mama to agree to? The next morning the question still very much with her, remained in a tight knot at the pit of her stomach.

At breakfast, nobody spoke. Tanya sat down trying to read their faces. Mama's looked pale and Dad appeared angry. Alisha and Anna were already at the table. Alisha was serving him breakfast.

"Tanya!" He boomed out.

She jumped. "Yes?"

Mama became still and turned white. She gave him a stern look.

Suddenly, he threw down his knife and fork with a clatter. "Get the salt!"

Tanya found the salt and pepper shakers and set them as close to him as she dared. She breathed easier when he finished eating and left the house.

All that morning, Mama seemed preoccupied with something on her mind. At lunch time, they received the same cold reception from Bill Dansky as before.

Mama picked up the bread knife and cut off a thin slice of bread. Her face looked drawn as she broke the silence. "Bill, I've been thinking about what you said to me last night. You said you wanted to beat my children! I can't allow you to do that. You're their stepfather. I know you, you'll have no mercy on them."

His face turned purple. He glared at her. "They're lazy. The whole damn bunch is lazy, I swear."

"Just the same, I don't want you laying a hand on them." She clenched the knife and leaned forward. "You're to leave them alone. They're mine, not yours. Is that understood? This is my house, not yours. And whatever I say goes! Lay a hand on them, and I'll kill you."

His eyes bulged in the heat of the moment. "How you gonna make something outa them?"

"That's my business and my responsibility. ... I'll discipline them in my own way. If you don't like it, you can go. You came to live here, to my house, with no more than a paper suitcase filled with ties. All this property is mine. Take your suitcase, your ties, and leave!" She gestured with the tip of the knife. "There's the door!"

His mouth dropped open in disbelief. Suddenly, he jumped to his feet. The chair clattered behind him. His face looked a picture of rage as he strode purposefully out the door, slamming it shut.

Mama put down the knife and went to the window. Alisha began stacking the dishes very carefully, with Tanya and Anna helping her. They looked as sombre-faced as mourners. Then Mama turned and left the house too.

Bill stayed away for three days. No one knew where he'd been. On the third day, he returned with Natalie at his side, holding hands and laughing. It seemed that all was well between them.

Outside, Tanya, with Jip beside her, her blond hair waving in the wind, walked parallel along the river bank. The tall timothy grass reached past her waist. The three days had been a peaceful reprieve for her.

In all probability, he never expected his wife to disagree with him. But after due consideration, he decided that she did have the upper hand in the situation after all.

That night, Tanya brought out her icon and knelt down to pray. She prayed that someone would love her, and that her stepfather could accept her just the way she was. In the next bed, she heard her sisters whispering. ... "Dear Lord, and them too, especially them!"

20

TANYA ADJUSTED HER BOOKS UNDER HER ARM and ran outside to the waiting school bus. The previous year, the school trustees of Greenview Public School had amalgamated with the Spirit Valley Elementary and High School. The country school had closed down, and the children from the surrounding district were being bussed into Spirit Valley.

She climbed the steps of the bus and sat down next to Dorothy Zidoruk, taking note of Alisha and Anna at the back. "Hi," she said. "Sorry, I'm late. Robert Danieve, you know, he took my French book, and he just wouldn't give it back to me. We had an awful fight! What nerve!"

"He did?"

Tanya thought she noticed envy on Dorothy's face, and laughed. "Yes, and I mean an actual fist fight!"

Dorothy observed her through dark brown eyes. She was built spare with a strong body and bone structure. Her thick, chestnut- brown hair set off plain features in an unblemished but sallow complexion.

Rarely did Tanya see her with make-up on, giving her good reason to envy her, her own face having recently broken out in a rash of pimples. Each night, she swabbed it faithfully with calamine lotion, looking for signs of improvement in the morning.

Dorothy's quiet, stoic manner drew Tanya like a magnet as she herself searched for this elusive quality. It amazed her that though her friend's grade standing was barely average, she never let it bother her, and neither of her parents ever badgered her about it, accepting her as she was, whether her grades were good or bad. Tanya came to the conclusion that Mrs. Zidoruk had been so grateful to have had a girl, after giving birth to three boys, that she never allowed her daughter's lack of ambition to stand in the way of her love for her.

Tanya shifted the pile of books to her knees, thinking that the assignments, if she was lucky, would take well into the night to complete. She grimaced, remembering that having turned twelve on the 11th of November, Mama had had the presumption to present her with a doll for her birthday. Her first!

The gift had come as a shock. She was an honors student in Grade Seven and felt too grown-up for the doll.

"I thought it was time you had one of your own," Mama had said, seemingly satisfied with her choice.

As soon as she'd left the room, Tanya had propped her up on her dresser, for decorative purposes only, while trying to recall exactly when the desire for a doll had left her. Something in clothes would have been a better choice.

The crowd at Spirit Valley Junior High were more clothes–conscious and more sophisticated than anyone had been in Greenview, as each girl strove to present a striking appearance. And nobody would be caught dead coming barefoot to this school as they'd done in Greenview!

Mama spent almost nothing on her wardrobe, still adamant that she wear Alisha's or Anna's old things, thinking she was too young to be worrying about styles. Even Stefa Hanchuk was better-dressed. She wondered how Mrs. Hanchuk could afford it, when she had to "make do" on a widow's pension and cleaned houses for extra income. However, with several of the the local families donating their cast offs to them, Mrs. Hanchuk always managed, in a clever way, to restyle the clothes to fit one of her girls, coming up with something original and different.

Meanwhile, she'd found out that her stepfather and Mama were planning to build a new house in the spring. Every night they sat at the kitchen table, poring over the plans, with Mama listening intently, while her stepfather carefully explained the details to her. The blue-prints had been ordered through an ad in the paper advertising prefabricated homes.

Mr. Henry shut the doors of the vehicle and started the bus rolling. Dorothy glanced sideways at her. "Tanya, be honest, is there something going on between you and Robert Danieve?"

"Me and Robert? Don't be silly. We're just friends, that's all. He sits behind me and likes to tease me, so we fight a lot. He's such a nuisance; don't jump to any conclusions." However, it pleased her to have his name linked with hers.

"Didn't I see him passing you a note during math period? I'm not blind. And he's always pulling your hair. I'd say he likes you."

"You mean just because he pulls my hair he likes me? I don't think he likes me one bit. ... Oh, the note? ... Uh-h-h, it was about math, we were comparing answers."

"He's really intelligent, isn't he? And so is his brother."

"Yeah, I know. Can you imagine him asking me for answers?" Robert was French and the ethnic difference made him all the more intriguing to her. She liked him. And though they rivaled for top marks, she thought it a good thing; it spurred her to study harder. The one thing that bothered her was that recently she'd grown a shade taller. She was afraid that he might lose interest in her if, by some twist of fate, she happened to outgrow him. Ideally, it looked best if the woman was the shorter.

Each morning, she looked forward to seeing his scrubbed face, his glistening brown hair combed neatly back, and his shining brown eyes which seemed to conceal hidden laughter.

If things weren't right at home, the very sight of Robert was enough to set her heart pounding. She sighed, already imagining herself in love with him, going so far as to think that maybe, someday, they would marry. It was exciting and scary.

The bus stopped to let her off. "See you tomorrow." She ran to catch up to her sisters.

As soon as they entered the house, both Alisha and Anna disappeared upstairs. Tanya rid herself of her books and went to the mirror to examine her face. She filled a wash basin with warm water from the stove reservoir. The pimples were a real concern. If only there was some magical cream that could make them clear up.

"Tanya, what are you doing?"

Her stepfather's voice came from behind her. He flustered her, but she tried not to show it. "I'm washing my face. Dr. Wong said I'm supposed to wash off the calamine lotion after school."

"Washing, you always washing. You know how hard it is to get the water. Don't you have something else to do? I don't want you using so much water alla time. You hear me? Get outa here."

She nodded, giving herself a final splash, thinking that getting the water out of the dugout, which was but a short distance from the house, wasn't as much work as he made out.

Mama reinforced his words. "Tanya, finish up and go. You heard your Dad. Hurry!"

She wiped the soap ring from the basin before she left. Lately, she'd been forced to take her baths in her room, sneaking the water up in a galvanized pail when he wasn't around. Though she was sparing with the water, he still used the excuse to pick on her. Even her clothes had to be laundered in secret, since Mama was still sporadic about doing the wash, she found it best to rinse out whatever she needed by hand.

The next morning, she went quietly downstairs before her stepfather awoke, before the water in the reservoir had time to heat and doused herself with a cold rinse, while listening furtively for his step. She unscrewed the top of the antiseptic smelling calamine lotion and hurriedly dredged it over her skin. Then she passed a brush through her thick blond hair and applied a faint coat of pale lipstick, being careful to blot it because Mama might get nasty about her wearing it. She could tell her that every girl in the school wore lipstick, but it wouldn't do any good.

That morning, her first class began with French 1. Tanya sat down and thumbed through her text to the correct chapter.

"Quiet, please." Mrs. Du Lac, her French teacher, a thin, slight woman, walked up to the front of the room.

Tanya noticed that more than once she turned in her direction, seeming compelled to stare at her. Finally, she spoke. "Tanya, please tell me, what is it that you've put on your face? ... My dear, it does look a little like flour."

Someone behind her giggled. Blushing, her hand went to her cheek. She hunched down, her brown eyes two dark pools staring out of the geisha girl make-up. "Oh, I ... I ... well, actually, it's only calamine lotion, Mrs. Du Lac. I guess I put a little too much on."

"It would seem so to me. ... I think I'd tone it down a bit, if I were you. Uh-h-h, you might inquire if it comes in a darker shade. Now, let's get on with the lesson. By the way, tomorrow, we'll have an exam on what we've covered so far." Everybody groaned.

The swift change of subject brought some relief. For the rest of the period Tanya bent low hardly able to endure the ordeal until the lesson ended only to rush madly for the bathroom when it was over.

One glimpse in the mirror and she gasped. What must Robert be thinking of her? In her morning rush, she'd applied the lotion on too thick, causing the skin to draw together and pucker in some places. Even the pale lipstick had taken on more brilliance than it should.

No wonder Mrs. Du Lac said it looked like flour! She groped for some toilet paper. Wetting a small piece, she sloughed off as much as she dared, at the same time afraid to expose the inflamed mounds underneath, before hurrying to her next class.

That evening, in preparation for the exam, she studied late into the night. Because of Robert, she took more than a keen interest in the subject, thinking that what if someday she should become Mrs. Robert Danieve? It would be nice to know how to speak French to her mother-in-law. She smiled, remembering that Mrs. Du Lac had even complimented her on her diction.

The following day, the teacher returned their exam papers as they were about to leave for home. Tanya was scanning the sheet for her mark, when she felt Robert's tap on her shoulder.

"Hey Kaplov, what did you get?"

"Uh-h-h, one wrong. I got a 97%. How about you?"

His face broke into a grin. "Well, whaddya know ... I got a measly 89%. And to think I'm French. How come you got more'n me?"

She laughed. "Because I'm smarter, what else?"

"Okay, so maybe you are. See you tomorrow." He swaggered off.

She found school a pleasure. It was a place where her stepfather and Mama couldn't reach her. Where she could rely on her intelligence to carry her through from day to day even though her self image was at rock bottom. She was sorry when the term ended and the summer holidays began, dreading to face the inevitable turmoil once she was home.

That summer, her parents purchased another half section of land from a neighbour, Paddy McBride, who had decided to sell out and move his family to British Columbia. He left behind a run down old building on the property.

One morning, Tanya finished her chores and decided that the old house would be the ideal place to spend the day. She wrapped up a quick snack of cold pancakes, spread them with strawberry jam, and hurried out.

The rooms were littered with debris. She curled her nose at the musty odor inside. Tanya lifted up a tattered oil cloth to discover a pile of "Macleans" and "Saturday Evening Post" magazines. Scooping them up, she went outside to read them in the fresh air.

There was an article on good health and nutrition which stressed washing one's face and eating a balanced diet. Tanya, who worried that her face would remain pimpled forever, read every word religiously.

She took note of the broomstick thin models in crisp, tailored, pinstriped suits with wide lapels and long tunics. Peek-a-boo pumps and pert hats were very much "in."

The day passed quickly. Eventually, she had to tear herself away. But, before leaving, she tucked the magazines safely back under the oilcloth thinking that tomorrow, she'd return to read the rest.

However, the next morning she came downstairs to hear Mama, already dressed for work, giving Alisha the day's instructions.

"Your Dad and I will be on the McBride property today. Uh-h-h, stooking the wheat. ... So-o-o, I expect you and Anna to do the cooking." She turned to Tanya. "And as for you, you come with me. We weren't able to hire anybody. It seems every able bodied man has been called into the army." Mentally, she appraised the two older girls, who she figured were too thin and frail to be of much use in the fields. Tanya, being the stronger of the three was the favoured choice.

Tanya put the magazines out of mind and changed into a long sleeved, cotton blouse and faded slacks before leaving.

The sky above was of the brightest blue and swept entirely free of clouds; however, on the way to the field, they were forced to buck a fierce wind. When she arrived, she noticed that her stepfather had already started setting up the bundles into the familiar pyramid shapes. One sure thing about him, he was a serious minded worker. She sighed. In the back of her mind, she still nurtured the hope of winning his admiration and respect, somehow.

Mama motioned her closer. "I don't expect you to stook like me or your father. The stooks, they're really too heavy for you, and ... and you're not tall enough. But you can rake up what's loose, or bring the bundles closer to me. It'll make my job easier."

Tanya picked up a sheaf of wheat and dragged it to her mother, wondering whether Dad was watching. However, he appeared bent on getting the work done, and paid no attention to her.

The sun climbed higher; it grew hotter. The wind remained strong, tugging at her hair and forcing her to taste an occasional mouthful of grit.

At mid morning, Mama, covered with sweat and dirt, paused long enough to pour herself a drink of water. "Tanya, why don't you run home, and ask Alisha to fix us some coffee and sandwiches? We could use a break."

She nodded, more than willing to leave. Dropping her rake, she went running through the open field to the river bank, then downhill and over a log bridge which, years ago, Tata had put into place. Even from a long way off, she could smell baking. With Mama out of the way, her sisters would be experimenting with different recipes.

She opened the screen door and walked in. "Alisha, why have you got it so hot in here? Why it's ... it's almost to boiling! What are you doing? Why is the kitchen is so messy?"

Alisha turned on her, furious. "Can't you see? I'm trying to bake some cookies, that's what! And if it's messy, it's because I haven't had a minute to clean it. Honestly, Mama never keeps anything around. We're out of vanilla, and nuts, and every recipe calls for vanilla." With a harried look, she opened the oven door a crack.

"Uh-h-h, do you have anything baked?"

"Yeah, try these. They're not too bad ... but not perfect, either." She frowned as she passed her a plateful of oatmeal cookies. "Mom coming home soon?"

"No. Actually, I'm supposed to take them some lunch. Can you make some coffee and sandwiches?"

Angrily, Alisha snatched up the coffee pot. "I suppose she wants me to drop everything just for that? You know, you'll have to wait for at least an hour."

"I've got time." Tanya moved towards the staircase to check on her treasure box. Sometimes they snooped into her things. The box came out from under the bed. Everything was intact. She shoved it back and rose to her feet. The heat in the room was impossible. Her hand brushed against the chimney as she was leaving. She drew back in alarm. It was burning hot to the touch! Suddenly, a thunderous roar burst out. Tanya found herself rushing madly down the steps.

"Alisha ... Alisha, the house is on fire! Do something! Let's go! ...

Get Anna! ... Get out of here!"

A look of shock swept over Alisha's face. "You're right! It is on fire! Quick, what can we do? Outside ... get outside! ... Anna, Anna, out! Out! ... Get out!"

They rushed through the screen door, their eyes on the roof. Tanya gasped. Flames were shooting up six feet into the air, sending showers of sparks over the wooden shingles. If one caught, ... the house would go down like a pile of straw. Next to her, Alisha was standing shaking and wringing her hands. Tanya grimaced. "Oh God, what are we going to do?"

"Don't ask me, I just don't know. Maybe, if we put the fire out in the stove. ... Yes, maybe, that would help." Alisha rushed back inside.

Mama had neglected to clean out the chimney. Now the accumulated soot, with help from the wind, had caught fire. Anna came to watch from the doorway as Alisha doused the flames again and again with water. A hiss, then a burst of white ash rose up in a cloud from the open burner. "Anna ... quick! The salt! Have you seen it?"

"Yeah, it's right there in front of you."

Alisha snatched up the half empty bag and went outside. "I'm going to try and get some into the chimney. I heard Mama say it's supposed to put out fires."

"Alisha, I'm going back to the field to tell her and Dad." Tanya went running, wondering how Alisha would possibly get over her fear of heights in such a short space of time. Once she looked back to see her climbing up towards the burning chimney with the bag of salt in one hand, while clinging to the rungs with the other, as a gust of wind lifted up her skirt. Below her, Anna stood hanging on to the ladder. It looked dangerous.

Thudding along, her heart pounding, she pushed herself to the limits, until a sharp pain in her abdomen slowed her down. Alisha would be the one they'd punish for causing the fire.

She reached the outskirts of the farm, looking for Mama. She saw her in the middle of the field with nearly a third of the sheaves stooked. Using her last bit of energy to close the gap, she waved to her frantically, before stopping dead in front of her.

Tanya, her breath coming in short, painful gasps, opened her mouth to speak. To her horror, she found that though her mouth was moving, she wasn't making a sound. Now wild with anxiety, she gestured towards the house.

Mama's eyes narrowed. "What's wrong? ... Tanya, tell me what's wrong?"

Once more, she tried to explain but couldn't.

"Tanya ... Tanya ... what's the matter? Here, sit down. Tell me, what is it?"

She slumped down onto a stook and fixed her eyes on Mama's face.

Mama motioned to her stepfather. He came running to where Tanya sat and stood looking at her, frowning. ... "Well?"

Mama reached out and placed her hand firmly on her shoulder. "It's all right. I don't know what's happened, but don't worry. It's all right! Tanya, listen to me. Whatever's happened, I don't care. Relax a minute."

Tanya, totally taken aback by her consoling attitude, suddenly let go, breaking the awful spell. "H--h--hou-se ... bur-ning." She slumped back. The words were out.

Mama repeated her words, calmly. "House burning? ... It's all right. Let it burn. You sit and catch your breath. It's okay." She kept patting her shoulder and made no move to leave.

Tanya's breathing gradually evened out. "But Mama, I just told you that the house was burning, didn't you hear me? It's the soot, it's burning in the chimney."

"Yes, I heard what you said. ... Bill, should we go and check?"

He shrugged. "Might as well." He bent down and picked up the water cooler. They began walking homeward at a brisk but unhurried gait, while keeping up a running conversation between themselves.

Tanya, overwrought with panic, leaped to her feet. She started ahead of them, looking back many times to see whether they'd speeded up. But their pace remained the same. Finally, topping the crest of the hill, and fully expecting to see everything leveled, she stopped. A smile spread across her face. "It's out. The fire is out. Look Mama! ... Look, it's out!" There was a blackened telltale streak over one side of the shingles, but the fire had, somehow, been smothered.

Mama nodded. "So it is. Thank goodness!"

Alex Shumak stood talking to Alisha and Anna in the driveway. He raised a hand to them. "Bill, Natalie, you had a chimney fire! We put it out. I could see the damn thing burning from where I was working. So I left my tractor and came on the double. Your girls, they were trying to put salt into the chimney when I got here. It was the soot! You should keep it cleaned out, you know. It burned off and quit. I'd say you were lucky this time."

Mama smiled. "Thanks for helping. We appreciate it."

"Gotta go. Left my tractor. See you folks."

Tanya followed them inside. She went up to her room to remember and ponder over Mama's strange reaction in the field. For some reason Mama had considered her temporary loss of speech to be more important than the house burning down! A warm, comforting feeling spread through her insides as she reached for her icon of Jesus.

21

TANYA TURNED FOURTEEN IN THE FALL OF 1948. She had grown taller, and having lost some of her stockiness, her figure took on a more proportioned look. A perm added maturity to her tender years and anyone looking at her would guess her age at closer to sixteen.

The spark between herself and Robert hadn't died out. On her part it never would, but in the back of her mind there was the fear that since they were far from grown up, someone more alluring would come along and snatch him away from her.

The year passed with nothing out of the ordinary happening. At the end of the term, Tanya couldn't believe that she had scored several points higher than Robert in her Grade Nine Departmentals.

Often, she entertained a favorite day-dream about him ...with her and Robert together ... Robert already a graduate accountant ... he seemed to be heading in that direction ... and coming home at night to her where she waited, eager for his embrace, his love, his kisses. There would be children. ...

The summer holidays began. She spent time tending to the animals, doing whatever chores needed doing, taking an occasional stroll to the Zidoruk's to call on Dorothy, and already missing Robert, as she waited impatiently for fall classes to start.

Alisha was in Grade twelve, Anna in Grade eleven. Her older sister found a bookkeeping job at the local hotel and had moved out of the house. Now she only came home on weekends, if it suited her.

The new house had been built. A sunny three bedroom bungalow with running water, electricity, and indoor plumbing. Throughout, shiny hardwood floors glistened with the look of fresh wax. A large picture window in the L shaped living and dining room faced west. Sometimes, Tanya watched the sun spew out its last rays of light before darkness set in. If only Mama would take the time to enjoy it!

Mama bought a new chesterfield suite in a dull turquoise. Though comfortable, it did nothing to enhance the room; however, it was understandable since she never had a sense of color or cared about any kind of decor.

Tanya went back to school in September. Happily, she and Robert managed to sit within close proximity of each other in their home room.

On a fine weekend in October, Mama suggested that they drive to Grand Plains to do some pre-Christmas shopping.

Tanya was ecstatic! There was a Christmas concert and dance coming up in December, and she was hoping that Mama would buy her something new to wear. Alisha, as soon as she found out about it, decided to come along as well.

Early Saturday morning, Mama, dressed in a black, velvet pillbox hat, and checkered black and white coat, led the way outside to the Ford.

Alisha got in first and secured a seat by the window. "Excuse me, since I get car sick, I really can't sit in the middle."

Anna scrambled to the other side. "Well, then, don't expect me to, either!"

Tanya looked at them angrily. "Wouldn't it be nice if you'd let me sit by the window, just once? Huh? More fair, too. I always end up in the middle."

Her stepfather turned to glare at her. "Tanya, if I hear one more word from you, you gonna stay home. Shut your mouth and keep quiet!"

Silenced by his cruel rebuff, she sat between her sisters, careful not to touch either one.

As soon as they reached Grand Plains, Mama got out and headed for the "The Bay." It was the largest retail store in town. She checked through a reduced rack of clothing and turned away, disappointed. "One has to be a millionaire to afford these clothes. Girls, let's try Sally's." Sally's Smart Fashions, a small, exclusive dress shop, was known to be more reasonably priced.

Again, Mama zeroed in on the sale clothing. Suddenly, Tanya pulled out a shimmering taffeta dress in a turquoise green and black plaid. "Mama, look at this one! Should I try it on, Mama? Huh? It's reduced you know, to ... uh-h-h, only $15.00!"

Mama nodded.

Tanya came out of the fitting room and made a slow turn. The dress looked stunning on her. "It's perfect, don't you think?" she asked, her eyes positively glowing.

Alisha nodded. "Tanya, you do look lovely!"

The dress had a square neckline, delicate puff sleeves trimmed with black velvet piping, and a dropped waistline which came down in a V at the front. There was a wide belt that tied into a bow at the back. The skirt was gathered and swayed out gently. No question that it suited her.

"Yeah, it looks nice on you," Anna agreed.

Mama nodded. "That's a very nice dress ... and the price isn't bad. ... We'll take it."

She felt a burst of joy, imagining Robert's admiration when he saw her in it.

After the shops closed, they had dinner at the Royal Hotel and took in a movie before coming home at 1:30 A.M.

Tanya ran into the house with the dress and switched on the light, compelled to look at it again. She pressed it to her face. The material smelled wonderfully new. She repacked it, carefully, and slipped the box under her bed.

On Monday after school, she lured Dorothy in to show it to her. As they came around the corner of the house, she kept a cautious eye out for her stepfather until she caught sight of him in the living room and made a snap decision to go in through the back door. "Follow me," she whispered. She opened the door to the kitchen and tiptoed down the hall to her room.

Trembling with excitement, she opened the box and lifted out the dress. "Well, what do you think? Do you like it?"

"Why ... why ... it's beautiful."

"But do you really like it?"

"Well, who wouldn't? It's very pretty. I wish I had something nice to wear like that. Why don't you try it on?"

She needed no prompting and hurried to change, remembering with a pang of guilt that Dorothy's folks were by no means wealthy and had little enough to eat let alone the money to buy her frivolous dresses.

She came out and waited for Dorothy's reaction. "Well?"

"It's lovely. You're so lucky! It's really beautiful." Dorothy sighed, then looked at her watch. "I think I'd better be going. Mom doesn't know I'm here."

"Okay. I'll get this off and walk you part way home. Oh, by the way, there's a dance this Friday. Are you going? Anyway, I can't go because Mama won't let me."

"Me neither."

Tanya put her clothes back on and guided her out.

On the following Friday, Alisha surprised her two sisters by coming home with them on the bus. As soon as they were let off, she caught up to Tanya. "Uh-h-h, how is everyone at home?"

"Oh, all right, I guess."

Alisha turned full face and smiled at her. "Tanya, you know about the dance tonight, don't you?"

"Yes. So what?"

"Are you going?"

"No, Mama won't let me."

"Well, I was thinking, would you mind, awfully ... if I wore your new dress?"

"What!" She stopped in horror. "No, certainly not! Besides, Mama bought it for me."

"But Tanya, everybody's going to that dance. I've got to wear something nice. Can't I wear it for just tonight, huh?"

"No, you can't! It's mine! Mine!"

Ahead of them, Anna stopped to listen. "I told you she wouldn't let you. Why would you even bother to ask her?"

Tanya's anger flared. "Oh, shut up Anna! I don't want her to wear it because I'm saving it for the Christmas concert, that's why!" She ran

to her room and sat down on the bed in case Alisha tried to take it by
force. As she'd expected, she soon heard her at the door.

"Tanya, if you won't let me wear it, I'm going to tell Mama, and then
we'll see what happens."

"Don't you dare, you stupid pig! She bought it for me. Me! And get
away from my door. ... You have no right to ask me for it!"

"Tanya, please. I've tried it on and it fits just perfect."

Tanya gasped. "You tried on my dress? Without asking me? Why
you ... you ... stupid cow! How dare you touch it? When have I ever
taken anything of yours without your permission?"

"Tanya, please ... just for the one night? Can't I wear it?"

"No!"

"Okay, but you'll be sorry."

A moment later, Tanya heard her talking to Mama.

Her heart pounding, she jumped up, wondering where to hide the
dress. Suddenly, the door burst open and Mama, with Alisha behind
her, glared at her, her face white with indignation. She held out her
hand. "Give me the dress. Now!"

A sick feeling went through her "But Mama, it's mine! ... It's mine!
You bought it for me! You said it was mine. Please don't give it to her!
... Please, Mama! It's the only nice thing I've ever had. ... She'll ruin it!
... Please, Mama, please don't!" Tears streamed down her cheeks as she
pleaded with her. "Please, why can't she wear something of Anna's?
Please, I haven't had a chance to wear it myself! ... Ple-a-se!"

"Let me have it!"

"But Mama ...!" Before reaching under the bed, she gave Alisha one
last look of hatred. Sobbing uncontrollably, she resigned herself to the
inevitable and passed it on to her mother. Mama promptly handed it to
Alisha and walked out without another word.

"Thanks, Tanya," Alisha said, trying to conceal her triumph. "I'll be
real careful with it, you don't have to worry."

"Get out! Out! You've got what you want. Now get out! I want to
be alone." She slammed the door shut after her. Then, lying face down
on the bed, she began pounding it with her fists, hoping to beat her
feelings into submission, thinking that it was the most despicable thing
that Alisha had ever done. And of Mama to take her side. Why would
she buy it for me then give it to her? she asked herself. She cried until

her fury waned. Then, saddened, she sat up to stare out the window. She could hear Mama padding about in the kitchen and Alisha getting dressed. The door opened a crack, and Mama looked in.

"Tanya, stop pouting and come and eat. Supper's ready."

"I'm not hungry."

Mama sighed. "All right, have it your way." She went back to the kitchen.

"Ah, Poutface, is she still at it?" Tanya heard her stepfather ask. Then Mama's laughter. Her heart sank to a new low. Slowly, she stood up, and walked to the closet to put on boots, hat, and coat.

Outside, she whistled for the dog, who came leaping at the sight of her. "Hi, Jip. Did you miss me? Let's go for a walk."

They trudged through the snow until she tired herself, bringing temporary relief to the pain within. Above her, the sky was already in darkness and a silvery moon threaded its way through the clouds. She shivered, though in her present state, the cold was most welcome.

Ahead of her, she noticed a car had stopped at the house. That would be Alisha's ride. There was the sound of laughter before it sped away. Only then did she return to her room.

Heartbroken, unable to concentrate on her homework, she lay down on her bed to toss and turn in helpless wrath, mulling over the events, remembering them, yet trying not to.

Inside her lay the dread that somehow Alisha would ruin it. The awful part was that the next time she, herself, wore the dress, it would seem like another "hand me down."

Last summer there had been a similar incident which involved a yellow coat. Alisha had come across it at "The Bay" in Grand Plains. She'd held it up to exclaim, "Look Tanya, I think this coat would look really nice on you. It's your color. Try it on. We have to buy it, it's been marked down to $5.00."

The coat did suit her. And what a bargain! The fit was perfect; Mama had approved it, and had paid for it. However the next morning, Alisha, after giving it some thought, had changed her mind. ... "Tanya, you know the coat Mama bought you yesterday? I'd like it back. You know, when I said to buy it, I really had it in mind for myself. ... I hope you don't mind," she'd said.

She'd cried to Mama. But it did no good, and couldn't believe it when

Mama actually forced her to relinquish it and had given it to Alisha, though Alisha had a perfectly good fall coat, while she desperately needed a new one. Was there no limit to her selfishness? Reliving the memory only brought on another bout of sobbing.

She lay awake as long as she could, waiting with impatience for Alisha to return. Finally her eyelids shut and she dozed off.

She awakened at dawn, instantly remembering. Then, throwing back the covers, she tiptoed into her sisters' bedroom.

They were both asleep. Tanya began to search for the dress. She found it crumpled on the floor where Alisha had shed it. Her hands trembling, she reached for it and shook it loose. There were some long creases at the back that would have to be pressed out. Other than that ...? Suddenly, frowning, she stifled a moan. Under each sleeve two large circles of perspiration stained the dress. Even from this distance, it smelled.

She rushed back to her room with the dress, withholding a strong urge to cry all over again. Her beautiful dress, as she had predicted, was ruined. It would never be the same again. Never! Never!

She lay tossing, turning, waiting for morning to break, wondering how Alisha could be so cruel?

Tanya pressed and wore the dress to the Christmas concert with the stains imbedded into the material, because Mama, after considering the cost, had refused to have it dry cleaned. Its magic was lost.

But apart from Alisha having worn it first, it was Robert who was the greater disappointment. She had hopes the dress would attract him, hold him spellbound. But he behaved in his usual manner ... blithe, carefree, barely acknowledging her presence. He was surrounded by a circle of his friends paying court to him, laughing at his ready wit and ready supply of jokes. They made a fine barrier for him, making her realize that even if she'd worn the crown jewels, it wouldn't have made any difference to him.

22

ALISHA FINISHED GRADE 12 but remained for a time in Spirit Valley. Sometimes she came home for a visit, though not as often as before, preferring her life in town. Anna, with her Grade twelve diploma in hand, left for Edmonton just as soon as she received the results from her exams.

Tanya was about to enter Grade 11. With one more year left, she still clung to her dreams of Robert, though up to the moment he remained noncommittal. She willingly excused him, thinking that he needed time to grow up, to mature. Still, it worried her that in the four years that she'd known him, there had never been any mention of any formal dating between them. Not even so much as a movie together! There were other couples at the school steady dating. It wasn't uncommon. But she couldn't let go of him, because her dreams were the antidote she needed to counteract the constant upheavals at home. And she needed them.

The year passed. She finished Grade 11 with honors. Would Robert be impressed?

It was the last day of the semester. Tomorrow was the school picnic. After tomorrow, they might never see each other. Her heart tugged in her throat as she gathered her books to leave. The picnic, held in the romantic setting of the Dunvegan hills, might prove exciting. Perhaps, just perhaps, an opportunity could arise for her and Robert to talk. Many times, she'd imagined it happening. Tomorrow, he might insist that they "talk". He might even want to sit beside her on the bus to the picnic. It was a desperate hope.

After school, she rushed home to put together an outfit. The yellow blouse that Alisha had left her and a red flowered skirt of Anna's was a close enough match. And, in case it turned cold, a red sweater.

She waited until Bill Dansky went outside, then she washed and pressed everything. He still complained about the water.

After supper, she washed her hair and drew a bath, remembering, as she stepped in, how she'd fought with her sisters about who should be first into the galvanized tub of hot water that Mama prepared for them every Saturday night when they were children. She'd hated being last. Hated the tepid water that had cooled considerably by the time it was her turn. And hated getting into a tub with scum floating on top, making her wonder whether they really did "pee" into it. Their teasing had driven her wild. Not once did Mama give in to her cries and let her bathe first. Natalie's one concern had been to get the bathing over and done with for another week.

It was late when she finally went to bed. Sleep didn't come with ease as a nagging thought kept recurring: she could count on the fingers of one hand the number of times that she'd danced with Robert at the school functions. Those few dances meant the world to her. Did they mean anything to him? Staring into the darkness, she longed for something more.

Recently, Tim Branden, a boy from Greenview, whose father had been Principal there, had attached himself to Robert. What a twist of fate that it should be a boy and not a girl that was the problem!

She noticed Tim hanging around Robert at the beginning of the year as he tried to emulate his gestures, his mannerisms, ready and willing to laugh at anything and everything Robert said. Now, every time she saw them together, jealousy gnawed at her. She felt Tim guarding Robert, keeping them apart by his very presence.

At Greenview, Tim had been shy and awkward with girls, blushing if a girl so much as spoke to him. He had been a nobody in Greenview, and he was a nobody in Spirit Valley. It was obvious that he was sticking close to Robert in the hope of becoming like him, likeable and popular with everybody. It was annoying to be constantly bumping into Tim whenever she wanted to speak to Robert.

In the morning, as she was about to leave, she paused to look at herself in the hallway mirror ... blonde hair, brown eyes set well apart, full lips, high cheek bones and lightly tanned skin. Slim and well proportioned. It raised her confidence, knowing that she was quite pretty.

As soon as the roll call was taken, the students poured outside to the waiting buses. Her eyes strayed to Robert, trailed by Tim, boarding a different bus from hers; disappointed, she searched for Dorothy who'd found a seat directly behind the bus driver.

Behind them, Luke Hanson and Jean Blake sat side by side, with Luke's arm around Jean. With a pang, Tanya wondered what it would feel like to have Robert's arm around her?

"Don't you hate the noise in here?" Dorothy asked. She loved silence.

Tanya laughed. "Yeah. You can sure tell it's our last day."

Thirteen miles out and the flat prairie changed to rugged hill country with steep banks and cliffs dropping sharply downward. Mr. Henry geared the vehicle to a crawl and began the winding descent to the river's edge. It was always a thrill to see the river, nearly a half mile wide, flowing placid and serene.

She giggled. "Dorothy, don't turn around. You know, I just saw Luke Hanson kiss Jean Blake."

"Oh. That's nothing new."

"It is if it's done in public."

The bus took another turn, and the full expanse of the river came into view. The ferry was on their side and they wouldn't have to wait to get to the other side.

As soon as they were ferried across, Mr. Henry drove to a secluded grove of maples and let everybody off.

"Dorothy, you haven't seen Robert, have you?" Tanya asked.

"Yeah, right now he's climbing Little Mountain with a bunch of boys."

Tanya looked up at a steep hill that everyone referred to as "Little Mountain." Sure enough, a group of boys were swarming over it. Each year, the challenge was to see who could make it to the top the quickest.

To pass the time until Robert came back, she and Dorothy walked to a Catholic church, entirely hand built and now used as a museum.

When they returned there was a fire going in one of the stone pits. A wiener roast was in progress. Robert saw her and broke away from his friends. He extended a sharpened willow to her. "Kaplov, wanna use my stick?"

Tanya's heart beat faster. Behind him, she noticed Tim with a disapproving frown on his face.

"Yes, thanks, Robert." She took the stick and skewered a wiener onto its tip. She looked up to see Stefa Hanchuk watching them. Stefa's hair looked almost blue black against the white of her peasant blouse. "Uh-h-h, Robert ... if you want your stick back, just let me know." She smiled at him, wanting the moment to last and not knowing what else to say.

"Naw, you can keep it."

"Uh-h-h, thanks, anyway."

He turned and walked away with Tim following.

The afternoon lengthened. Tanya made every excuse to seek him out in the hope that he, too, would be trying to seek her out. There were moments when they could have been together; however, Tim was never far off. It worried her to think that they would have ended up a threesome, had the right moment been found.

An ideal time occurred when Robert went for a canoe ride. He was alone in the boat while she stood on the shore looking on. Their eyes met; the message in hers was clear ... but he chose to look away and signaled to Tim, instead. "Hey Tim, care for a ride?"

Tim leaped into the boat, grinning at Tanya over his shoulder.

Anger welled inside her. She slumped down next to Dorothy who sat sunning herself on the pebbly beach. The day had passed too quickly. It pained her that she was no further ahead with Robert. She knew that he'd deliberately shunned every opportunity to be together, and each opportunity had vanished like a wave on the sea.

At five o'clock they lined up at the busses to go home. Tanya couldn't keep her eyes from straying to see where he was. Her breath caught in her throat as she noticed Robert step into line in front of her, directly behind Stefa Hanchuk. He placed one hand casually on Stefa's shoulder.

Stefa smiled at something he said to her. Tanya tore her eyes away and climbed in after them. She suffered another shock when she heard Robert gallantly offer the window seat to Stefa, before sitting down beside her. They looked like the perfect couple with the petite Stefa the perfect height for him. ... It hurt.

She slipped in beside Dorothy, who'd chosen to sit directly in front of them. If only she was on a different bus! If only she didn't have to endure his presence so near to her! Unable to stop herself from listening to their conversation, she heard every word that passed between them painfully clearly, the jokes, the laughter, the teasing, despite the noise.

Behind Robert and Stefa, Tim sat by himself.

"It was a lovely day, wasn't it? Dorothy remarked.

She nodded.

"Tanya, do you see who's sitting behind us?"

With great effort, she reigned in her grief and jealousy."Oh, you mean Robert? Well, of course, I do. He can sit anywhere he likes. I really don't care."

"I'd say that we all had a good time. Wouldn't you?"

"Of course! ... Wonderful! ... Just wonderful! And such fine weather, too," she said, wishing with all her heart that Dorothy would shut up.

They began to move. Tanya thanked God. She acknowledged Dorothy's inane comments with a frozen smile and a nod of the head, adding nothing of her own. All her senses were directed behind her, though she tried in vain to shut out their voices.

After an eternity, Mr. Henry let her off at her stop. She sprang up, giving Dorothy a casual wave, while keeping in check the torrent of emotion.

Then, when the bus was well out of sight, she let out a sob, and began running home. Thinking that Mama would be in the kitchen with her stepfather, she went in through the front door.

Mama came into the hallway as soon as she heard her. "Tanya, is that you?"

She brushed past her, her head bent, and only nodded.

"Did you have a nice time?"

"Yes ... yes," she said, impatient to get into her room and shut herself off.

"I have supper ready. Would you like something to eat?"

"No, thanks, we ate." She turned the knob, went inside, pausing long enough to see whether Mama would follow. A moment later, she heard her talking to her stepfather. Tanya flung off her sweater, threw herself down on the bed and cried until her eyes nearly shut. Sorrowing that there was no one to confide in, no one to comfort her ... no one who cared about her. It was clear that Robert didn't have the same feelings for her that she had for him. She'd built her hopes on a dream ... an illusion, out of a desperate need to be loved.

23

IN THE FALL, SHE RETURNED TO SCHOOL, braced to accept Robert's change of heart. It was immediately noticeable. His cool indifference cut into her. She watched helplessly as his interest in Stefa picked up. What would they have in common, she wondered? She had always regarded Stefa as haughty and somewhat arrogant. Perhaps being poor, she'd learned how to protect herself by building up a proud exterior?

Tim, she noticed, was once more doggedly hanging on to Robert, making her wonder if he was to blame? Had he spread some malicious rumor about her to Robert? Or had he discouraged him in a different way? Tanya began to hate him.

Regardless, she forced Robert out of her mind, turning to her studies, while putting on a dignified and nonchalant air, fearful lest he find out how much her heart really longed for him. At night, when he came creeping into her thoughts, only then did she allow herself to dream of their making up ... and how happy they could be.

Shortly after, another change occurred in Tanya's life. One day, while vacuuming the house, her stepfather stopped but an arm's length away from her. She had on a pair of white shorts and a skimpy halter top. Reaching out, he ran his fingertips over her bare shoulder.

Startled, she moved away, her face scarlet, thinking that somehow, it felt like a caress.

"You need any help?" he asked, his smile flirtatious.

"No, Dad, you know I can manage by myself."

He hung around a moment longer before going outside. Tanya finished cleaning, sobered by the realization of this new transition in him. At the same time, she pacified herself that his touching her could have been purely innocent. However, she noticed that now, every time he came near her, his face had that certain smile. No longer was he angry whenever she spoke to him as he had been when she was a child.

Instead, his eyes sought hers. She was always first to look away.

Unconsciously, to draw the attention away from herself, Tanya began wearing the most shapeless, colourless clothes she could find. Moving like a ghost from room to room, she hoped that he wouldn't possibly want to be bothered with her. Even his complaints about her had dwindled down. Now he was deliberately being nice to her. Tanya began spending more time in her room with her books.

At school, she maintained a very disciplined attitude towards Robert. By the end of June, having endured ten months of misery, she considered herself fortunate to have had the fortitude to keep her feelings under control, for though she was feeling crushed, her pride was undamaged, despite the hurt.

She turned her thoughts to graduation and the formal banquet and dance to be held in honor of the Grade 12 graduates at the Spirit Valley Community Hall.

To save Mama the expense of a grad dress, she consulted Alisha about sewing a dress. She chose a peasant style, ankle-length gown in a white sheer organdy. It had a wide, gathered, double collar, which could be worn on or off the shoulder. The dress, fitted at the waist, had an A-line skirt. The look was romantic. And Tanya, though she wouldn't admit it, had Robert in mind when she'd picked the style.

To deal with her inner pain, she threw herself into helping Mama around the house. Jip had long since passed on, and a black and white mongrel, "Spot," had taken his place. But, whenever she hugged him, she still had Jip in mind.

On the weekends, Alisha came home to work on Tanya's dress, using Mama's old Singer treadle. After many fittings and many adjustments, it was finished. Tanya slipped into the gown for Alisha's final inspection.

"I think I'll make a white satin belt for it. It looks lovely on you. Your banquet? Next Friday, isn't it?"

"Yes. You did a good job. Thank you, Alisha."

Her stepfather came into the room to stare at her. "Tanya, you look pretty good. Do you have a date?"

She stiffened and shook her head,. "No. I'm going stag." She felt uncomfortable until he left the room. Tanya sighed. She wanted a father, a father who cared about her in a paternal way, nothing more.

Tanya led the way into the banquet hall, which was filling up quickly. She sat down at a long table next to Mama and her stepfather. Mama looked ill at ease with the educated and scholarly around her. Her stepfather kept aloof and silent, maybe jealous of them, she thought.

Tanya felt that having worked very hard, she had the right to be there, to drink in the accolades, to enjoy the evening.

Mrs. Hartley, their principal, walked up to the podium. The grey haired, elderly woman had been witness to many graduating classes.

Now she tapped for silence. "Ladies, gentlemen, parents, teachers and students! It is my distinct pleasure to welcome you, and also my pleasure to propose a toast to the graduating class of 1950. It's been my privilege to be your teacher as well as your principal. Let's rise and drink a toast to the new graduates!"

Tanya felt her throat constrict. Across from her, Robert sat at a different table beside his parents. Stefa, she noticed, sat next to her mother and away from Robert.

Raising her glass, she silently toasted him. As soon as the banquet ended, Mama and her stepfather went home.

It was too early for the dance. Not knowing where to go, Tanya decided to visit Alisha at her apartment before the dancing began. She felt glamorous in the gown. She climbed the flight of stairs to Alisha's apartment and knocked on the door.

Alisha's pale face appeared. "Tanya! Don't you look nice! Come on in."

"Thanks." She walked in and stopped in surprise. Robert sat lounging on Alisha's day bed. He looked handsome in a dark, charcoal suit. Tim sat close by in a straight backed chair.

Bewildered, she stammered, "But ... but ... what are you doing here?"

"I'm waiting for the dance to begin, same as you," he commented, nonchalantly. He leaned back, trying in vain to reach a rose satin cushion propped up against the wall.

Tanya turned to Alisha to explain. "Uh-h-h, I thought I'd come up and wait here a while ... if you don't mind?"

"You're welcome to stay as long as you like. In fact, I'm glad you're here. I have to leave. Mirna Roginsky wants me to go to the dance with her. We're going stag, you know. Now isn't that something? You come to see me, and I'm rushing off. Would you lock up for me?" Alisha picked up her purse and went out the door.

Tim stood up, looking out of place and uncomfortable. "Gotta go to the can."

Tanya silently applauded as he left the room. She glanced at Robert, just an arm's reach away, feeling at that moment how very romantic and sexy it was to be alone with him. Then, remembering that dead silence was awful, she hurriedly put in, "Well, what did you think of the banquet?"

He half smiled. "I guess it was okay as far as banquets go."

"Do you know what time the dance starts?"

"Yeah, nine. I like your earrings."

She blushed. "Thanks." All too soon, Tim returned.

Robert glanced at his watch. "Well Tim, maybe we should go check out the pool hall before the dance? Think we have time for a game?" He rose to his feet. "See you at the dance, Tanya."

"Yes, see you." She wondered why he hadn't asked Stefa?

At nine o'clock, Tanya walked to the community hall by herself. She waved to Dorothy at the far end of the room. But as soon as the lights dimmed and the music began, she looked for Robert. There was a group of boys around him. He was smiling.

Several of them even asked her to dance. She accepted, thinking that it was better to be dancing with somebody than waiting for "Mr. Perfect."

After the intermission, it was then she looked up to see Robert standing before her.

"Dance?"

Her heart leaped. "Yes, Robert." He took her hand as the orchestra started up a waltz. Tanya, finding herself tongue-tied, did no more than follow his steps. He held her lightly and slightly away from himself. For one impulsive, wild moment ... in the short space of time that they were together ... she thought of making it known to him how she really felt, but restrained herself. Regrettably, the dance ended. He returned her to her seat, making her feel both glad and sad that she'd kept her tongue in line and hadn't burst out with any foolishness.

He bowed slightly. "Thanks. It was a pleasure, Tanya." He didn't ask her again, making her wonder if he was only being polite by asking her at all. Nor did she see him dancing with anyone else. At the end of the evening, she went home with Dorothy.

She shut the door to her bedroom and brought out her icon of Jesus and the Angels that night. She thought that the image of Christ had grown somewhat fainter. Opening her diary, she slipped the icon in between the pages and closed it.

24

"TANYA, DO YOU KNOW THAT ANNA'S WRITTEN TO ME that she wants me to come to Edmonton. I think I'll go. ... What about you? You've graduated. What are you going to do?" Alisha asked, waving a letter from Anna in her hand.

"Honestly, I don't know." They sat on the turquoise chesterfield, staring at the sunset. The sky was a garish kaleidoscope of florescent pink and purple. It was nice to be alone; the parents, having gone to Grand Plains, still hadn't returned.

"You aren't thinking about staying here, are you?" Alisha asked.

"Staying here? I don't know. What'll I do here? I don't have a job. Actually, I think that I'd like to get some training in secretarial work. ... I just don't know."

She stopped talking, overcome by sorrow, remembering her dream of wanting to be a nurse. She'd mentioned it to Mama who had immediately ridiculed her. ... "Tanya, do you really want to make a living carrying bedpans? Is that what you want to do with your life? Surely, you're not serious?"

When she needed it most, the support wasn't there. And she wasn't strong enough to fight for it. From Mama, it would take money as well as support. Alisha, as usual, brushed it aside whenever she brought it up. She was no match for them and stood helpless as her dream eroded and fell apart.

About leaving home ... she would miss Mama ... the animals. She was only sixteen. Was it time to go? The future was uncertain. She sat brooding, feeling the weight of the problem fully upon her.

Alisha left for the city on the 15th of July. In mid-August, Tanya received a letter from her, saying that she had a job in a bank and was living with Anna in a small housekeeping room. Anna was employed as a switchboard operator with Sunland Finance. They seemed to be having loads of fun. They mentioned dates with different men.

The letter only threw her into further confusion and doubt. In her search for enlightenment, she brought up the subject to her mother. "Mama, listen, I've been thinking ... now that Alisha's gone, do you think, maybe, I should go too? Or should I stay?" The question was asked with the hope that Mama would encourage her to stay. Perhaps she needed someone to keep her from being lonely?

Mama suddenly became busy with cleaning off the kitchen counter. Her face took on a determined look. "Tanya, it's your life. I wouldn't stop you, if you want to leave."

"But Mama, I don't really know what I want. I could get a job in town and come home weekends to visit you and Dad."

"Listen, Tanya, if you've set your heart on going, then go. After all, you are sixteen and of legal age to do whatever it is you want to do."

It dawned on Tanya that being "of age," she could be a threat to Mama because of her stepfather. There might be trouble with him further down the road. Perhaps Mama could foresee it and didn't want her in the way. There were times she sensed it herself. Other than the touch on her shoulder, he hadn't tried to make any further moves. ... Yet, one could never be sure about such things. To test Mama further, she went on. ... "Uh-h-h, I think I'll write to the girls that I'm coming."

Natalie nodded. "I think that's a good idea. A very good idea. Uh-h-h, how soon will that be?"

"I thought at the end of the week." Inside her, the child that she still was screamed out ... but Mama, I'm still not ready. I need just a little more time with you.

A faint smile lit up Natalie's face. She nodded her approval. "Yes."

That evening Tanya began packing her suitcase.

She had been brave with Mama when saying goodbye, but later on the train, she sat glassy-eyed, remembering how broken up Mama had been when they parted. The train went past Prestview where Robert lived, and as hope of a life with him had already started to dim, she forced him out of her mind.

25

A S SHE ENTERED THE CNR STATION ROTUNDA, she spotted Alisha and Anna, looking glamorous and worldly. ... Alisha in a two piece, navy blue suit with striped red and white blouse, Anna in something pale blue.

"Tanya! ... Tanya! Over here." Alisha was calling.

"Hi. Well, don't you two look nice." she said, self conscious of her wrinkled white, cotton shift and scruffy sandals.

Alisha examined her. "Hi, you look tired."

"Of course I'm tired. I didn't sleep a wink on that train!"

Anna picked up her shabby, brown suitcase and a shopping bag stuffed full of clothes. "We'll have to take a cab home, the bus driver won't let us on the bus with a suitcase."

In no time they were home and Anna was paying the taxi.

Alisha brought in her luggage and unlocked the door.

Tanya glanced around her. Her face fell. It was a garage converted into a suite. The inside was far from opulent, though it looked clean enough. There was a sink with a cupboard over it, a small counter, gas stove, and a sofa bed in the living area. A door led to a bedroom just off the kitchen. She noticed only a toilet and sink in the bathroom.

She turned to Alisha. "Where's the bathtub?"

"Uh-h-h, you have to go inside to the main house. There's a shower in the basement. You remember Mrs. Hollowach from Spirit Valley? Well, she owns this place. ... Really, it's not that bad, and it's only $35.00 a month."

"Where am I going to sleep?"

Alisha pointed to the bedroom. "Well, for right now, you can sleep in there. I'll sleep on the coach."

Anna, with her purse in hand, interrupted. "I think you two can decide who sleeps where by yourselves. I'm leaving. See you."

Suddenly, Tanya felt tired. "Alisha, if you don't mind, I'd like to lie down. Uh-h-h, just as soon as I can, I'm going to find my own place."

She reached into the shopping bag and pulled out a nightgown. The trip was exhausting. She changed and collapsed on top of the covers while Alisha went to find a blanket.

The next morning, Tanya awoke at seven even though it was a Sunday and she could have slept longer. Alisha was making breakfast while Anna still slept. The day looked gloriously sunny.

By the time Tanya finished washing, Anna awoke, waived breakfast, washed, dressed, and quickly left the house.

Tanya turned to ask Alisha, "Where did she go?"

"Probably to meet a friend for coffee. She doesn't tell me." Alisha frowned. "You really don't have much in the way of clothes, do you?"

"No. I couldn't afford them."

"Well, how about tomorrow at noon we meet at Eaton's during my lunch break? Maybe we can find something on sale for you."

"But Mama didn't give me much for spending money ... only a $100.00. ... And I have to live on that, too."

Alisha nodded, remembering that Mama had given her only $35.00 when she'd left.

Alisha arrived at noon at the store as promised. "Hi. We can't waste time, I have less than an hour."

Tanya lowered her head to conceal her face. After they'd left for work, the homesickness had hit hard, making her realize more than ever that emotionally she wasn't prepared to cope with the outside world. Mama's rejection hurt like an open wound in her heart. She began crying the minute the door closed behind them. For one solid hour she couldn't stop. When she noticed the time, somehow, through bursts of tears, she'd managed to dress and make it to the store before Alisha.

She noticed Alisha taking in her puffy eyes at a glance. A look of distress swept over her face. Alisha turned her attention to some skirts, pretending to examine them. "Here's something you might like! Isn't this pretty?" There was a hint of concern in her voice as she held up the skirt.

Tanya went to try it on, thinking that the one thing she didn't need from Alisha was her pity. Though, it looked as if Alisha was about to cry herself.

She returned with the skirt to find her still fumbling through the racks. She held up a dress in a dark green plaid. "How about this?"

It reminded her of the turquoise, green taffeta which Alisha had ruined for her. Why should she trust her? She shook her head. "No, I don't feel like trying it on."

Alisha stopped. "Tanya, if there's anything you need just ask me or Anna."

"No, thanks, there's nothing I need from you or anybody. Maybe my own place ... which I can't afford right now." She sighed. "I've decided to take a secretarial course at Alberta College. Have to make a living, you know." She sighed. "Guess you'll have to put up with me for a while longer."

"Tanya, you can stay with us as long as you like. There's no rush. Really! Uh-h-h, sorry, I have to get back to work. We'll talk tonight."

Longing to be independent, Tanya enrolled at the college the very next day. The course started at the end of September and ran for eight months. There was no time to be homesick.

She established a routine for studying and practicing shorthand. Since Mama had paid for the tuition, she was determined to do her best.

The following Saturday, she awoke to find her sisters having breakfast and making plans to go dancing to the Silver Ballroom.

"I told Mirna I'd meet her there," Anna said. Mirna Rodginski had been her best friend in Spirit Valley. "Uh-h-h, Tanya, would you like to come with us?"

"I think so. Why not? I have nothing else to do."

Anna went on. "You'd be surprised how many girls I've seen there from Spirit Valley."

"What about clothes, what'll I wear?"

"Take something of mine, or Alisha's."

As the afternoon waned, the dressing took on a more serious note. Alisha, wrapped in a pink house coat, was preparing to have a shower. Tanya looked in awe as they went through their clothes for just the right outfit, combed their hair into the most becoming style, and applied makeup for that flawless look. "Can I wear your black dress, Alisha?" she asked.

"Yes, take it."

Anna began sifting through everything on top of the dresser. "I'm meeting Mirna at eight, so we better be out of here by seven thirty at the latest."

At 7:25 they caught the Number five bus, with each girl a touch heavy on makeup, but looking very glamorous.

As soon as they entered the dance hall, Anna waved to Mirna and left them.

Alisha found two chairs by the wall and they sat down. Tanya thought the soft light in the room enhanced everyone's looks. Did she look all right or did the black dress make her look dowdy? Her cheeks felt hot. Alisha went into the dressing room just as the band started to play a fast jive. The room came alive with swaying, spinning bodies. She broke into a sweat, remembering that she didn't know how to jive and started for the bathroom after Alisha.

"Care to dance?"

A blond, young man in a black suit stood squarely in front of her. Her heart started to pound. Out of the corner of her eye, she caught sight of Alisha dancing. Should she say "no"? ... "Yes, I'd love to."

They began to shuffle in time to the music. Tanya glued her eyes to his feet, attempting to imitate and co-ordinate her steps with his while trying to stay in rhythm. "Sorry."

"My fault," he said, spinning her around.

She came back out of beat and out of step. "Sorry."

This time, he said nothing. The music played on. Tanya looked with envy at the other dancers. They looked so expert. If she could only dance half as well ... one quarter. ... "Sorry." It was close; she nearly tripped. ... Still, they kept going. Would it never end? Finally the music stopped, and he led her back. Thinking "how awful" she thought she would burst from embarrassment.

He inclined his head. "Thank you."

Thank goodness the next dance was a waltz. She waited eagerly for someone, anyone, to dance with and was disappointed that no one asked her. After the waltz came another jive number. This time, she bolted for the powder room.

It was midnight before she caught sight of Anna and Mirna.

"Do you girls need a ride home?" Mirna wanted to know. "Ronnie," she indicated a young man beside her, "he'll drive you."

Alisha smiled. "Yes, thank you, we'd love a ride."

Grateful that they didn't have to take a bus, Tanya sank into the back seat of the sedan between Alisha and Anna, thinking that she'd have to practice jiving with one of them.

26

EACH MONTH, MAMA SENT A LITTLE EXTRA FOR ROOM AND BOARD. The paltry sum tempted Tanya into getting a part time job typing for an insurance company after school. However, it left her too exhausted to study, and she had to quit.

At the end of May, with her course finished, Tanya, desperate for money, went job hunting on the very afternoon that she received her diploma. She was down to counting pennies and most anxious to get started.

The employment agency made an appointment for her to see a Mr. Swenson for an interview, the manager of All Weather Roofing. Tanya, who didn't expect to be hired, thought that she'd give herself at least a week to find a job.

However, Mr. Swenson, as soon as he read through her records, looked up smiling. "Miss Kaplov, your diploma and qualifications are very impressive. I assume you can type?"

"Yes, Mr. Swenson, about sixty words a minute without mistakes. I also take shorthand."

"Wonderful! We can use you. In fact, we're short handed at this very moment. Uh-h-h, the building business is booming, I'm happy to say. We need someone that's competent. Now about your salary, let's say we start you off at $150.00 a month. How's that?"

"I'll take it, Mr. Swenson, thank you. ... Thank you, very much."

"Uh-h-h, Miss Kaplov, can you start today? I mean right now!"

She could scarcely believe that he was asking her to start this soon, feeling that she would have preferred to have a few days to herself. "Yes, yes, I think I can," she assured him.

"Good! I'll introduce you to Stella Brownlee. She runs the office for us. She'll be happy to know that we've hired you. Poor girl, she's the one who needs the help."

He led her down a corridor into an office packed tight with metal filing cabinets, files, accounting books, ledgers, and invoices, with barely enough room for a person to walk through.

"Tanya, what you're looking at here is the guts. All the work is done in this office." He pointed to an attractive, blonde, young woman in a light grey suit and hot pink blouse. "Uh-h-h, Stella, this is Tanya Kaplov. We've just hired her. Honour student in her class! She'll be your new assistant. I'm sure you two will get along just fine."

Tanya smiled. "How do you do." One of the first things taught at Alberta College were the rules of etiquette.

Stella's desk was a clutter of papers and files. She held out her hand. "Tanya, I'm glad he's hired you." Suddenly her phone rang. "All Weather Roofing, may I help you?"

Mr. Swenson turned to go. "I'll leave you with Stella. She'll inform you about your job."

"Thank you, Mr. Swenson, and thank you for hiring me."

She began searching for a place to hang her coat. Tanya squeezed past a filing cabinet, set her purse down on an empty desk in a corner of the room, then waited for Stella's conversation to end, which seemed endless.

The speed with which she was hired made her feel strange and unreal. Close by, a phone began to ring. How was that possible with Stella still talking? she wondered.

Stella put her hand over the mouthpiece and motioned to her. "Answer it," she whispered.

Tanya looked blank. "Pardon me?"

Stella pointed to the desk. "Answer the phone, it's under the file."

"Oh, sorry!" It rang again as she lifted off the file, startling her. "Hello? ... Hello?" She turned to Stella, bewildered. "But, but, there's no one there!"

"Just a moment, please." Stella put down the receiver and walked to her desk. She disengaged the phone from Tanya's clammy hand and turned it around. "Wrong end!" she said, pointing to the mouthpiece.

Tanya flushed. "Sorry." What would Stella think of her "excellent qualifications" now? she wondered. And what would Stella say if she knew this was the very first time that she'd ever used a telephone? Suddenly, remembering the call, she hurriedly said, "Hello?"

"What's going on there? Have I been cut off?" This is Bert Swenson." Stella, are you there?"

Tanya froze. "No, Mr. Swenson, this is Tanya. Stella's still on the other phone."

"Put her on right away."

"Yes, yes, of course. Uh-h-h, Stella, it's Mr. Swenson."

Stella got up and took the receiver from her. "Yes?"

Tanya, feeling her ignorance inexcusable, felt herself shrink. Would she tell on her? She listened with bated breath to what was being said.

Stella ended the conversation and went back to her desk. She pointed to some files. "Would you straighten these for me. Alphabetical order, please."

She relaxed. "Yes, of course."

She went home feeling a genuine liking for Stella, thinking that she was a real lady. Not one word had she uttered to Mr. Swenson about her obvious blunders, neither had she laughed when Tanya tried to speak into the wrong end of the phone.

27

TANYA LOOKED SUSPICIOUSLY AT ALISHA. Her hair was set into pincurls, and though it was a Saturday and already six thirty P.M., no one had said anything about going to the Silver Ballroom. "You and Anna, have you any plans for tonight?" she asked, trying to sound unconcerned.

"Uh-h-h, yes, Mirna invited us to a party."

"But what about me? Didn't she include me?"

"Well, she really didn't say. Maybe I should have asked her if you could come?"

She bristled. "It's a little late for that now, isn't it? You know, I don't think that I'll stay home either. I'm going to call Dorothy Zidoruk, and if she's free we'll go dancing. I don't need you or Anna to get me there. Yes, I think I'll do that."

Dorothy had recently moved into the city and their friendship had resumed.

"Tanya, I'm so glad. That sounds okay. Sorry that you're not coming with us."

"Yes, I'm sure you are." She snatched up a magazine and slouched back into a pillow. It was painful to watch them dress. She felt hurt that they were still excluding her from their plans.

As soon as they left she threw down the magazine and wandered outside into the sultry, night air. It was extremely hot for June. What a shame to waste the evening cooped up in this horrid room! Within her, she felt a strong pull to be a part of the flow of life. She liked the faster pace in the city. It was never dull or boring. Tonight, she wanted desperately to be somewhere independent of her sisters.

She went back inside to put the call through to Dorothy. They arranged to meet at the Royal Gardens at eight-thirty. Though she'd never been there before, she remembered someone telling her that it was a very popular place. She'd picked the spot because it was only twelve blocks away and, to save bus fare, she could easily walk the distance.

Quickly, she bathed and changed into a sheer, flowered blouse and slim black skirt. She glanced at her watch as she clipped on gold earrings. Nearly eight-fifteen. She outlined her lips in bright red lipstick. Tanya slipped on a pair of high heeled, black patent shoes, and was out the door by eight-twenty five.

She'd gone only four blocks when she noticed that the people on the street looked different. She was shocked to see vagrants drinking from whisky bottles half concealed in paper bags. Some even lounged unashamedly on the sidewalk. Others leaned against buildings. She began to walk faster.

Directly ahead, there was a large group of men in front of a pool hall talking in garrulous tones, their number spilling across her path and onto the road. She gave them wide berth, and setting her mouth into a grim line, skirted around them. A man made a grab at her sleeve. He laughed as she shrugged free and began running.

Hot with anxiety, she was spurred on by catcalls and wolf whistles from all sides.

"Hey baby, wat's your hurry? Take me wit ya, huh?"

"Yeeow! Dig dat crazy skirt! Not so fast. ... Come'er."

Tanya was about to panic. The only other female on the street was a woman in a tight dress and spike heels who stopped to stare at her, her hands akimbo on her slim hips. Tanya, who wasn't aware that she was a street walker, wondered why she was glaring at her with such anger?

Suddenly, a man blocked her flight. He'd stepped out of the shadows and now stood squarely in front of her. She noticed his dark, leathery skin, deeply furrowed brow, and rheumy eyes. She started to tremble. A lock of hair lay in a greasy clump over black, bushy eyebrows.

"Hey Blondie, wanna make a dollar?"

Though her fear nearly did her in, she managed to scream out in anger, "No! Outa my way!" When he didn't budge, she stepped off the sidewalk and walked around him as quickly as possible thinking, thank God it was still light! He was too drunk to follow.

By the time she made out "The Royal Gardens" sign, in bright red lights, her breath was coming in short gasps. One final push before she reached the building, opened the door, and stumbled inside. At last, she thought, breathing hard, I'm here, I'm safe.

She stood still, trying to calm down. A dim bulb in the ceiling high above her revealed a steep staircase leading to another door at the top where a Country and Western band was playing.

She felt better, but still apprehensive. Slowly, she started upwards, noticing that the steps were blackened, scarred, and scuffed. Dust and small clumps of dirt lay unswept in corners.

It was disheartening to see the cement walls heavily crayoned with graffiti. The surroundings were deplorable and nothing like The Silver Ballroom. Her footsteps lagged, as some of her anxiety returned. Had it been wise to come here by herself? It was too late to turn back. She reached for the handle and pushed the steel door open.

As she stepped inside, sudden panic engulfed her. The room was in total darkness. Except for several spotlights that glanced off the dancing couples, she felt, rather than saw, the floor tight with bodies. She couldn't move for fear of stumbling into someone, and tried in vain to see through the thick blackness, wondering how she'd ever find Dorothy?

The music ground to a halt. Someone flicked on a switch. Tanya blinked. In contrast to the dark, the room was now totally drenched in white light. She looked around her, astounded to see that here too, the walls were smudged with grease and defiled with obscenities, making a mockery of her attempt to appear respectable.

Around her, bottles flashed out of sight and were slipped into pockets to be sipped from in secret during the next dance, which was about to begin. Everywhere, there was the smell of stale beer, hard liquor, smoke and sweat. It was amazing to see such an odd mix of races that she identified as Indian, Chinese, Italian, Portuguese, European, and other mixed breeds that she couldn't place. Every one seemed in good spirits and intermingled freely with each other.

She noticed fat men in shiny silk, tailor-made suits with slicked down mustaches. Lounging on chairs against the wall, they appraised each and every female who happened to be within debatable range. There were young men in business suits as well as men in jeans and cowboy hats. The sound was ear splitting.

Tanya walked around the room once, hoping to find Dorothy. Her search ended when the band began to play and someone cut the switch. Once more, the room flicked into darkness.

She saw a large group of women massed together at the front of the dance hall and made a snap decision to join them. It felt awkward not knowing anyone. Why not pretend to be one of a group? she thought, sidling closer.

Next to her stood a dark haired, Chinese woman. She had on a black, satin dress with a mandarin collar, heavily embroidered. A side slit went halfway up her thigh, exposing a shapely leg. Tanya felt embarrassed for her. Had Dorothy, after seeing what a dive it was, fled the premises?

The orchestra began a pounding, exciting tango. The music was embracing, and reverberated to all corners of the room.

"Dance, lady?"

A slight, dark haired man, wearing a three piece, black suit stood before her. He only came to her chin. Italian, she thought, catching the gleam of gold cuff links in the spot light. "Yes. I'd love to."

He smiled, his teeth flashing white. As soon as her eyes became better adjusted, she saw that he was good looking.

They walked to the dance floor, with his arm at her waist. He pulled her forward. Suddenly, his grip tightened, expelling all the air from her lungs, leaving her breathless. Tanya, fighting for breath, tried to back away from him, but he wouldn't loosen his hold. She gasped as a pungent odor of garlic hit her full in the face, nearly suffocating her. For a moment, she thought she would faint.

Then, desperate for air, she put both elbows in front of her as a shield to force a small space between them should his grasp get any tighter. He took no notice.

She'd never danced a tango before and wondered if she could fake it? They began moving slowly, with deadly precision, as one body. Tanya felt herself riveted to him, hip to hip, toe to toe. Strangely enough, she could follow his every move perfectly.

Occasionally, when she missed a step, his foot came crunching painfully down on her toes, causing her to grimace in pain; but these instances were rare.

There was no exchange of conversation, making her suspect that he was a recent immigrant with a limited vocabulary. It's no business of mine, she thought. The music, torrid and heady, had a mesmerizing effect on her. She felt an urge to dance on and on. When, finally, it beat to a stop, and the lights blazed on again, she was sorry that it had ended.

He led her back, holding her hand upraised in queenly style. He smiled, bowed, "Thanka you."

"You're most welcome!" My, but could he dance!

Later, she danced with some of his friends. She was positive that some were married. At times, she noticed a wedding ring. However, she was treated with the utmost respect and courtesy and thoroughly enjoyed herself. She wondered about their wives? Did they mind being left at home with families while their husbands were out dancing with strange women? How humiliating to say the least! She had a variety of partners and hardly missed a dance; however, when the dial on her watch read twelve-thirty A.M., she realized that she had come alone and was about to leave alone. She thought about making her way through the gauntlet of men, and shuddered. At this hour it would be risky. The lights flicked off. The orchestra began playing "Home Sweet Home." Tanya looked desperately around the room for someone that she might know even remotely!

"May I have this dance?"

"Yes." The man was tall with a pale complexion, dark hair, and handsome. She sniffed. There was a peculiar odor about him that she couldn't quite place. Couples started vacating the premises and the worry about getting home returned.

"Mind if I drive you home?" he asked, as if in answer to her thoughts.

Though her heart leaped, she demurred. "Uh-h-h, I'm not sure. I'll think about it." How could she say yes? But she needed a ride! Somehow, it didn't feel proper. Nice girls didn't go home with strangers, at least not at a moment's notice. She didn't even know his name! She thought of the hands grabbing for her, the crazies lying in wait. It tipped the balance in his favor. For the sake of propriety, she should at least find out his name. "Uh-h-h, you know, I don't even know your name."

He smiled. "My name? ... Art Henderson. What's yours?"

"I'm Tanya Kaplov. Uh-h-h-h ... Art, where do you work?"

"I'm with Diamond Drilling. We're drilling for oil about 300 miles north of here."

"That wouldn't be around Grand Plains, would it?" she asked, eagerly.

"Why yes, as a matter of fact, it is. How did you know?"

"I come from there." At least they shared something in common. That, in itself, bespoke trust, she consoled herself.

The dance ended. Under the strong fluorescents, she noticed that his clothes were oil stained and worn, explaining the odor. Had he come straight from the field to the dance? she wondered.

He put his arm casually around her waist. Smiling, he steered her toward the door. "Well Tanya, what say we get out of here? My truck's in the parking lot."

He seemed harmless enough, polite, friendly. If she didn't like him, she needn't ever see him again. Her one concern was a ride home.

They approached a beat-up half ton. Art opened the door, first leaning into the cab to push aside a pile of tools which lay in a tangle on the seat.

Tanya stood back, wondering how to scale the first step in her tight skirt and still maintain a ladylike stance. In the next moment, she felt his hands encircle her waist and, with no apparent effort, he hoisted her up.

"Thank you," she said, astonished at the strength she felt in his grip.
"You're light as a feather."

"Art, this is so very nice of you. You don't know how much I appreciate it. But, really, I hate to be such a bother."

He grinned. "No bother, Tanya. Didn't I offer to drive you home? Where do you live?"

She gave him the address, assuring him that it wasn't far. With all the tools beside her, she was fearful of getting grease on her clothes and didn't dare lean back.

He touched the starter. The motor drowned out any hope of a conversation. She noticed his hands on the steering wheel, large, the fingers square, with each nail rimmed in black. How could she have been so foolish as to accept a ride from a perfect stranger on the precept of his having worked on an oil rig near Grand Plains? And what must he be thinking about a last minute pick-up? That was stupid of me, she thought.

She sighed and rolled down the window hoping that the fresh air would counteract the musty smell of oil, which was intolerable inside the cab. A cool breeze whipped at her face, making her wish that she was already home and safely in her own bed. There was still the matter of having to say "good night" to him that she wasn't looking forward to.

"Did you say you were from out of town?" he asked.

"Yes, Spirit Valley, it's north of Grand Plains."

"I know ... I know ... I've been to Spirit Valley."

"Have you really?"

"Yeah. Lots of exploration going on in them parts. You'd be surprised how many other oil rigs are drilling there. Nice country."

"Yes, isn't it?"

They had reached the residential area that was so familiar to her. It would be a pleasure to get away from him and his greasy truck. Now, I wonder if he knows where to let me off? ... It seems, no, he doesn't. "Art! ... Oh Art!" ... She reached over, tugged at his sleeve, then shouted, "That was my place! You just went past it."

He seemed unperturbed and not one bit surprised. "I did? ... Well, don't worry. I know a different route. We'll still end up the same."

"But why not just go around the block or back up, whichever is easiest for you."

He paid no attention to her and speeded up, driving further away from her street.

A warning bell went off in her head. Was he crazy? Or did he think she was? With each passing block, her panic mounted. What if he had other plans for her? She looked at his hands, remembering his strength, and shuddered.

"Art! ... Art! Please stop and let me off. Right now! I'll walk from here. I mean stop this minute! ... I'm not going with you any further. Do you hear me?"

He glanced at her sideways. "And what if I don't? What are you gonna to do about it? ... Just sit tight and be calm. I'll let you off when I'm good and ready."

"Stop! Let me out!" His determination to keep her prisoner only enhanced her determination to escape.

He kept driving, ignoring her cries.

Tanya's hand strayed to the door handle. She started to jimmy it back and forth. "If you're not going to stop, I'm going to jump."

He threw her an incredulous look. "Don't be a fool. ... You'll kill yourself ... sure as hell. Don't do anything stupid!"

But he let up on the gas and the truck slowed. "Don't open that damn door! It's liable to break off!"

"If you don't stop, I am going to open it and jump. Stop the truck! I mean it! ... Stop!" Her heart began to pound. Suddenly, she couldn't wait and pulled back on the door handle.

"I said to leave it alone! ... No, don't do that! You can't! Christ! Not when I'm driving!"

It was too late. The door was already open; it swung precariously in the breeze. As she edged toward it, she heard him swear. Anxious that the door not fly off, he slowed the vehicle down, giving her the break she was waiting for.

Tanya closed her eyes, and with a prayer on her lips, hurled herself into the street. She landed in one painful thud in the middle of the road, her hip hitting the pavement. Dazed, she tested to see if anything was broken, then swayed to her feet. One knee was skinned and bleeding badly. Her arm was bruised. There was a gaping hole in her nylons and her skirt was split. Thank God, there weren't any cars coming toward her or she might have been run down.

Hurriedly, she started toward the sidewalk. Bits of gravel, sticking to her knee, sent sharp pains up her leg. Trembling, she turned to check where Art was.

His truck was parked by the curb with the motor running. Tanya watched in horror as he began moving in reverse in her direction. Was he coming after her again? She quickly hobbled to the other side of the street and began walking home against the traffic. Half running, half limping, her one thought was to put some distance between them.

A block down, she dared another look over her shoulder. The truck was still parked by the curb. She kept going. After some time, she heard the sound of grinding gears as he drove off. Tears mingled with relief flowed down her face. Art had driven her at least twenty-five blocks out of her way. Never again, on any account, would she ever accept a ride from a stranger. He would surely have raped her if she'd stayed in the truck. Her instincts didn't lie. Of course, he'd think she was easy! No respectable girl would allow a stranger to take her home after one dance! Bedraggled, exhausted, Tanya limped into the suite at two A.M..

Luckily, Alisha and Anna still hadn't come home. An hour later, when they did come in, she pretended to be asleep, knowing that it would only upset them if she told them what had happened.

In the morning, she was the first one awake and went out to buy the Sunday paper. Determined to move out as soon as possible, she scanned the ads.

She spent the next week checking out different suites. Alisha urged her to stay out of concern, but Tanya didn't let up on her desire to be on her own.

One evening, she found just what she was looking for. A one bedroom housekeeping room in a basement suite, only three blocks away from where her sisters lived. The rent was $30.00 a month. It fulfilled her expectations perfectly. At the end of the week, she moved out.

28

"Y OU KNOW, I QUIT MY JOB AT ALL WEATHER ROOFING. I'm now working for the Federal Government of Canada." Tanya came to tell Alisha the news as soon as the position was finalized.

"Have you really? Does it pay more?"

"Yes. One more thing, I'm head of the steno pool. And there's all kinds of fringe benefits that I'm entitled to." She sighed "But the job, it's not so easy. I work very hard for my paycheck."

"I'm sure you do." Alisha placed a kettle on a burner. "Would you like some tea and a slice of chocolate cake?" she asked. Tanya loved chocolate.

"Yes, I wouldn't mind."

"Have you written home to tell Mama?"

"Yes, but, so far they haven't answered."

The door opened and Anna walked in. "Hi. She smiled at them. I'll have some of that tea, Alisha."

As Tanya explained about the job, Alisha filled three cups. Anna reached for the sugar. She stirred the tea and picked up the teacup, her hands shaking. The cup clattered against the saucer, the amber liquid spilling over. Anna had to use both hands to steady it, before taking a sip. "D'you see my hands? I can't even hold a cup without shaking. ... It gets worse when someone's watching, and I wouldn't dare try drinking it, because I couldn't."

Alisha looked upset. "Why not?"

"Do you remember when we were small how Dad used to yell at us? Well, the shaking started then. And that goes for my writing too. If I have to write something, anything, my hands... they shake."

Tanya nodded. "Yes, I do remember," she said, thinking that Anna had been traumatized as well.

Tanya wrote home often, describing her life in the city. Since Mama wasn't able to write, it was her stepfather who answered her letters.

A year went by. Fall approached and the leaves started to turn; Tanya knew that the harvest would be in full swing. A distant voice from the past, which would not be stilled, prodded her into action and she found herself, along with Alisha, taking the train home to help Mama with the harvest.

29

At Anna's insistence, Tanya joined her at Roy's Super Bowl, a well known hangout for the youth of her generation. They sat down in a booth with a good view of the bowling lanes and ordered a couple of cokes.

Smiling, Anna surveyed the room then leaned across the table toward her. "Try not to look, but do you see that guy over there? The tall, dark one? He's really thin. The one with the curly, black hair. Uh-h-h, watch him, he's about to throw the ball."

"Yes, I see him. What about him? Who is he?"

"His name is Lou Hagen."

"He's awfully good-looking, don't you think?"

Anna smiled. "Yes, he often comes here to bowl. And what a bowler! I'm sure he could be professional if he wanted to."

"Really? He looks as if he might be Italian or something."

"No, Mirna said his father was native Indian and his mother white. Mirna was here yesterday and introduced me to him."

"Where does he work?"

"Well, right now, he's unemployed. ... Uh-h-h, I think he was slinging beer at the Grand Hotel when they laid him off. Or something like that.

Have you finished your coke? Let's go over there."

"What?" Tanya's hand flew to her face. "Yes, I guess I have."

Between plays, Anna caught his attention. "Hey Lou, how are you? I want you to meet somebody. ... Lou, my sister, Tanya."

Lou turned to look at her. "Hi."

Tanya, feeling herself drawn to him, became nervous. His eyes were the closest to black that she'd ever seen. His face portrayed strong, even features. She noticed his jet black hair and jet black eyebrows. There was no denying that he was handsome, but close up, she detected a hardness under the good looks. A cigarette dangled loosely between long fingers; a half smile lit up his face. He looked poised, sensual. She sensed him to be exciting and found herself wanting to know him better.

"Lou, Tanya and I, uh-h-h, we were watching you play. Nearly all strikes, huh? You're some bowler!" Anna spoke with genuine admiration.

"Thanks. You girls wanna bowl?" His eyes bore into Tanya's.

She blushed, then laughed nervously. She'd never bowled in her life. "I'd like to but I'm not really good at it. Uh-h-h, don't we need bowling shoes or something?"

"Yeah. The girl at the desk will fix you up with a pair. Anna, you bowling, too?"

"Yes. Count me in. You make it look so easy. Come on, Tanya, let's get the shoes and give it a try."

Tanya lagged behind with her heart doing flip flops. "Anna, wait! I can't bowl! What am I going to tell him?"

"Don't worry, you'll learn. It's fun."

When they returned, Lou introduced them to Howie Frasier, a young boy who bowled on his team. "Like me, he's crazy about bowling," he explained. "Tanya, I got you down next."

She hesitated. She was perspiring. "Lou, really, wait! I hate to spoil it for everybody, but I've never bowled before."

He laughed. "Oh, that's okay. I'll be your instructor. Here, put your fingers into these holes. See the pins at the end? Aim a little to one side of the middle one. You're sure to get a strike every time." Taking her hand, he guided her through the play.

She wondered how he could be so patient, so kind, with a beginner like herself? Though she tried very hard, the ball nearly always ended up in the gutter. "Sorry, I'm hopeless, I think!"

Lou merely laughed. "It's okay, everybody does that when they first start. ... Don't worry, try again, we got all night."

Lou, to her delight, flirted with her throughout the entire game. He joked, he teased her about her blunders, and praised her when she got her first strike. She realized that not only was he good looking, but he was fun to be with.

At the close of the second round, her score was better.

However, Anna suggested that they leave, since it was nearly midnight.

Reluctantly, she bent down to unlace her bowling shoes, thinking that she really wanted to stay. "Lou, I'm sorry I wasn't better competition for you. ... Maybe, next time? ... Uh-h-h, Anna's waiting for me. I work tomorrow."

His smile revealed white, even teeth. "Tanya, wait a sec. Can I walk you home?"

Her heart jumped, knowing that she couldn't pass up such an opportunity. "Yes, Lou, that would be nice."

"Do you live close by? I don't have a car."

"That's okay. My place isn't far from here. We can easily walk," she said, thinking that if he'd asked her to, she'd walk to the moon with him. Anna waved and went home alone.

Once outside, Tanya felt awestruck and inhibited. Lou's touch on the back of her elbow sent tiny shivers up her spine. Everywhere was the smell of spring. She felt the moment was pure magic. She tried to think of something original to say to liven up their time together. ... In the end, she blurted out what she thought he might like to hear. "Lou, your bowling, it's phenomenal. How do you get a strike every time? In fact, you're the best I've ever seen. How do you do it?"

"Well, I get lotsa practice. Crise, it all depends on your delivery. If you practiced like me you'd be good at it, too. Tanya, what do you do? ... I mean for a living?"

"I'm a secretary for the Federal Government. Actually, I'm head of the steno pool. It's really no great honour, just a lot of extra work."

"Yeah? Well, me, I'm looking for work. Between jobs, right now."

"Oh! Sorry to hear that."

"Aw-w-w, I'm not worried. I'll get a job ... somewhere. Always have."

They turned in at the gate of her residence. "This is my place. It's not much ... just a basement suite. But it's home to me."

"Tell me about it. I happen to live in one just like it." He laughed. "Hell, wouldn't you know, it's only a couple of blocks from here."

"Lou, really? What a coincidence!" She unlocked her door and turned towards him. "Good night, Lou. I had a great time, I really did!"

"Yeah, me too, Tanya."

Unexpectedly, he put his arms around her waist and, pulling her close, kissed her hard on the mouth. "G'night, baby. Thanks for letting me walk you home. Wanna give me your phone number? Might wanna call you, sometime."

"Lou, really? Why, yes ... yes." Weak with emotion, she began a wild scramble through her purse looking for something to write on. "Oh, here ... here's something. I hope you don't mind an O'Henry wrapper?"

He laughed. "Naw, it's okay. Got a pen?"

After searching for a pen, she giggled out, "Then how about eyebrow pencil to write with?"

"As long as it writes. ... Thanks." He folded the wrapper neatly into a square and tucked it into his shirt pocket. Taking her hand, he raised it to his lips and kissed it, while she looked on in disbelief. "I'll see you."

Tanya walked into the suite in a daze and turned on the light still unable to fathom why he'd want to kiss her? No man had ever kissed her before! Someone like Lou would have many girl friends.

Later in bed, she tried to sleep, but the events of the evening kept circling in her mind and wouldn't go away. It always ended up with Lou kissing her. Longing for more, the thought kept her awake.

The next day, she heard the telephone ringing in the hallway as she was coming in from work. She scrambled to unlock the door then rushed in to answer it. "Hello?"

"Tanya?"

Her heart began to pound. It was Lou. "Yes."

"How are you?"

"Fine. I'm just fine, Lou, thank you."

"I was wondering, how about a movie? I think there's something good playing at the Rialto. Have you seen "River of No Return"?"

"No, I haven't ... but it sounds wonderful! I'd love to see it."

"Okay. Uh-h-h, be ready around eight. We'll catch the late show."

"Thank you, Lou. ... Yes, thank you. I'll be ready. See you at eight." Tanya hung up and ran to turn on a bath. She had a date! Tonight, she would not be alone. Her hand went through her hair. It needed washing. ... Too bad there wasn't time.

An hour later, freshly bathed, perfumed, and wearing a simple cut navy, linen dress, she was ready and waiting when she heard his knock. Lou looked very handsome in a dark jacket and tan colored pants. He grinned. It was amazing how much her feelings for him had intensified since only yesterday.

"Hi, baby. You look great," he said, handing her a gift wrapped box. "For you."

"Thank you, Lou. But you shouldn't have!" She sheared off the paper. "Oh, Lou, Laura Secord chocolates! How delicious! But why?"

He smiled. "Aw-w-w, it's nuthin. This your coat?" He picked it up and slipped it over her shoulders, kissing the back of her neck at the same time. "Miss me?"

She flushed with delight. "I'm not saying."

"I bet you did. Come on, we'll talk about it after the movie."

Hand in hand, they raced up the steps to the bus stop, Tanya thrilling to every moment with him.

There was a lineup at the theatre. She stepped deliberately in front of him as he was about to buy their tickets. "I hope you don't mind, but this one's on me."

Grinning, he whispered into her ear, "Not if you don't."

"I'm glad. Two please."

During the movie, she couldn't keep her eyes off him, eager to catch his laugh, noting the shape of his mouth and jaw, and the small wrinkles that formed at the corner of his eyes when he smiled. Their being together was just too good to be true. Lou sat with his arm draped casually around her. At the end of the show they followed the crowd outside, with Lou behind her, his hands at her waist.

The evening had been perfect! Why not make it last a little longer? "Lou, how about a chocolate soda? Would you like a soda? My treat, of course!"

He tapped out a cigarette and struck a match. "Yeah, why not? Wanna try the Silk Hat?"

"Sounds okay to me. I think they have booths there, don't they?"

"Yeah, they do."

"Good!" She wanted privacy, a booth would provide that. The Silk Hat was a restaurant patronized mostly by business people, young executives, and the after theatre crowd.

A hostess showed them to their table and took their order.

Tanya leaned back and focused on Lou. The bright light in the cafe brought out the small wrinkles in his face, making him look older.

"Lou, your family, do they live in town?" she asked, thinking how much she wanted to know all there was to know about him.

"Yeah, my Mom and my old man live here, so do most of my brothers and sisters."

"Brothers and sisters? How many do you have?"

"Hm-m-m, let's see ... Jeez, at last count, there was seven of us," he answered, grinning.

The waitress brought their sodas. She was blonde, young, pretty, and wore a tight fitting, pink uniform. Very slowly, very deliberately, Lou's eyes went over every inch of her. Tanya felt a pang of jealousy reverberate through her.

As soon as the girl left, she was prompted to ask him something that had been bothering her from the day before. "Lou, I don't know if it's any of my business, but are you going steady with anyone?" She blushed. "I mean a girl friend, or someone like that?"

"Steady? Are you kidding? What for? When I can play the field? Shit, no way!"

Surely, he didn't mean this last admission! "Lou, I'm serious!"

"Me too. I'm dead serious!"

She looked away, wondering whether anyone had ever tried to change his mind? Could she do it?

After their drinks, she paid the cashier before catching the bus home. When they reached her door, she turned to him in anticipation. "Lou, would you care to come in for a while?"

"Yeah, baby."

She was ashamed that her suite was furnished cheap and shabby. A table, three wooden chairs, an old sofa, a gas stove, and fridge. There was a small window over a stained, white porcelain sink. Some of the walls were wood paneled in light amber. They looked most dreary in the winter when the daylight hours were shortened and the wood panels took on a darker look. There was a separate bedroom and bath.

She shed her coat and reached for the kettle, having decided to make coffee. Lou followed her to the stove and put his arms around her. "Crise, baby, come'ere. You know, you're driving me crazy."

Tanya, after the second kiss, started to tremble. Breathless, she broke away from him. "No, Lou, don't! You can't do that." She pushed her hair back into place. "Lou, I must tell you, right now, that I believe in saving that kind of love for marriage. ... The kettle's boiling, I'll make the coffee."

He loosened his arms. "I thought you liked me."

"Don't get me wrong, I do. But I'm not ... that kind. I'm not... you know ... easy." Besides, what would people say if she got pregnant? Or brought disgrace to Mama? With someone like Lou, it wouldn't take much to give in to her natural desires.

"Would you like some cookies to go with your coffee?"

He laughed and lit a cigarette. "Cookies? Yeah. By all means. Pass me some cookies! I gotta have something."

Tanya filled two cups with instant coffee as Lou reached for the sugar. "I like it sweet ... just like my women." He winked at her, while pouring four generous teaspoonfuls into his cup.

She laughed. "Then how do you manage to stay so thin?"

"With this." He waved his cigarette under her nose. "You oughta try it. Best reducing medicine ever. It cuts out your appetite."

"No, thanks. I'll stick to a diet." It was remarkable how easy she found him to talk to. In a sincere desire to be open, she told him about the farm. He told her about his sister, "Marylou". "She's married to an Italian. They got five kids."

They finished their coffee. Lou came around the table and reached for her. This time, too weak to resist, they collapsed together on the couch, with Tanya clinging to him, thrilling to each kiss ... thinking that the rapture she felt at the moment was something she'd never experienced before in her entire life.

At one A.M., she broke free and rose unsteadily to her feet. "Lou, I'm sorry, but you'll have to go. It's late and one of the rules is that all guests leave by eleven. It's well past that. Lou, uh-h-h, will I see you tomorrow?"

"Yeah, sure, baby, see you tomorrow." Lou produced a comb from his pocket and ran it through his hair.

She locked the door after he left and went to bed with her head in a spin. Lying awake, restless, she tossed until dawn broke, knowing it was him that she wanted.

The next day after work, she ate hastily, dressed, and waited for Lou until midnight, pacing the floor with impatience while listening for his step. He didn't show up. In despair, she washed off her make-up and prepared for bed, wondering what could possibly have kept him from coming?

A week slipped by, a desperate week of waiting and hoping for Lou to call. In the end, she decided to call Anna hoping to somehow make contact with him. "Would you like to go bowling with me tonight? I feel like a game," she said, wondering if Anna would suspect her real reason for calling? She hadn't told her about her date with Lou.

Anna hesitated. "Hm-m-m, maybe. I'll check with Anton and let you know. Oh, by the way, have you heard from Lou?"

"Uh-h-h, once."

"Almost every night he's at the bowling alley, you know."

"Yes, I know. Anna what about tonight? Find out if Anton wants to go there tonight?"

Anton Moroz was Anna's current interest. A quiet, handsome, young man in his thirties. He was well mannered, and exactly the catalyst that Anna needed to counteract her demanding nature.

Tanya put the phone down, having decided that, with or without Anna, she would go to the bowling alley by herself, thinking, I must see him again.

Anna called back to say that she and Anton would meet her in the cafeteria at eight, giving her less than an hour to dress.

Tanya rushed to the closet to appraise her clothes. She chose a skirt in a good quality cotton sheen with pale yellow roses printed over a black background. There was a matching top in yellow, trimmed with the same black print as the skirt. It looked perfect for bowling.

Quickly she bathed, combed her hair into a casual style, dusted on face powder, and rouged the high part of her cheeks. Her hand shook visibly as she applied lipstick. One final look in the mirror, and she rushed out.

At the bowling alley, she hastily examined the booths. Anna and Anton were nowhere in sight. Tanya headed for the lanes, looking carefully at each player until she saw Lou. Her heart picked up momentum at the sight of him. How should she approach him without seeming obvious? She paused to watch him deliver a strike.

"Excuse me!" Oblivious to everyone but herself, she didn't realize that she was standing in the busiest part of the room and blocking traffic. She moved aside. On second thought, why hide herself? Hadn't she come specifically to see him? Her heart began to hammer as she forced her steps in his direction. "Hi, Lou."

He looked up and grinned when he saw her. "Hi Tanya. How've you been? I just delivered a strike, did you see it?"

She nodded, brightly. "Yes, it was great, Lou. Really great! Mind if I watch?"

"I ain't gonna stop you whether you do or don't," he answered, laughing. He turned to a couple that seemed to be with him. "Tanya, this is my friend Bob McFee, his wife Donna, and you remember Howie?"

"Yes, yes, nice to meet you." Relief flowed through her, realizing that they were a married couple, and that Lou hadn't brought a date. She shivered. "Oh Lou, there's Anna and Anton. Do you mind if they sit here, too?"

"No." He threw another ball. The pins shattered leaving one still standing. He glared at her. "Damn! That's what happens if I don't concentrate. Hell!"

She felt guilty, knowing that she was distracting him. "Lou, I'm so sorry." Tanya turned to Anna. "Do you two want to play? Lou said you could."

"No thanks," Anna answered, having sensed Lou's coolness. "We'll watch. We looked for you in the cafe, then I figured you'd be here ... didn't I, Anton?" She, playfully, nudged him in the ribs.

Smiling, Anton nodded. "Right." His dark hair was smoothed back to a professional slickness. He was a meticulous dresser. Since meeting each other, he and Anna were inseparable, making Tanya wonder if it would lead to something.

Lou started another game with the McFees and Howie Frasier, while Tanya sat looking on. The game began with Lou ringing up strike after strike. She looked on amazed, spell-bound. Behind her, a gallery of spectators had gathered.

"Lou, you're positively wonderful! How do you do it?" someone behind her remarked.

He laughed with glee, enjoying the attention. "You should see my trophies! Hell, I came in first at the last tournament in Calgary."

"Great game! ... Best bowling I ever saw!"

It ended late. Anna suggested that they go for coffee to the cafeteria. Lou, in a euphoric state, nodded eagerly. He was anxious to discuss the pros and cons with an appreciative audience. Tanya followed, thinking it would give her a chance to find out why he hadn't called.

They found a booth and she slid in first, patting the space next to her. "Lou, there's room here."

He seemed to hesitate, but in the next instant he was beside her. It was dull talk, centering on where and when the next tournament was to be held. At twelve-thirty A.M., Anna and Anton left for home.

 Bob McFee, tall, thin, with a mop of mouse colored hair, stood up, pulling up his dark haired wife at the same time. "We gotta go, honey. Sorry, Lou, we have a sitter looking after the kids, and it's costing us money. Good night, you two. Nice meeting you, Tanya."

Smiling, she nodded. "Hope to see you both again."

Lou rose to his feet. Alarm shot through her. "Lou!"

He looked at her, coolly. "You want me to walk you home?" There was a note of exasperation in his tone that she managed to overlook. Playing the role of the helpless coquette, Tanya answered in a small voice, "Oh Lou, if you wouldn't mind. I came alone. It's kind of scary to even think of going home alone at this hour, don't you agree?"

He nodded stiffly, steering her out the door without comment.

She felt that he wasn't the playful charmer he'd been the first night, making her wonder if she'd done something to upset him? There were so many things that she wanted to ask him. However, sensing his change of mood, and being content just to have him beside her, she kept still.

At her door, she raised her face up to his, eagerly, knowing that she'd been longing for this moment the entire evening. He laughed and pulled her to himself. She wriggled closer, uncaring that he read her emotions, because it was so wonderful to be in his arms again. "Shall we go inside?" she asked, slipping him the key.

Something had changed, she thought, tonight he had other things on his mind. After half an hour of her kisses, which she showered on him without restraint, he pushed her aside and stood up. "Gotta go."

She looked up in alarm. "Lou, so soon? Will I see you again, Lou?"

"Yeah, sure. Maybe, tomorrow. I'll see. G'night."

"Lou, wait. What happened to you last week? Why didn't you call?"

"Last week? Hell, I can't remember that far back! Come on, Tanya, grow up!"

"But Lou, you said ..."

"Look, I said I gotta go." He strode to the door. "If I have time, I'll be by tomorrow. ... I'll see."

Did he really mean it? "Yes, why don't you come right after work? I'll be home about five-thirty."

"G'night, baby."

"Good night, Lou." She closed the door behind him. The main thing was that he'd come back. But how to keep him? It was obvious that something was amiss. Was there someone else? She broke into a sweat, just imagining such a possibility. That night, again she lay sleepless.

The next day, as she came rushing home from work, she was relieved to see him waiting for her on the front steps of her rooming house.

He grinned at her. "I got good news! I'm employed. I got a job setting pins at Roy's. Now I can pay my rent."

"Oh, Lou, that's wonderful! I'm so happy for you. Come inside."

"Yeah! It don't pay much, but it's a job."

"Shall we celebrate with a bottle of wine?"

"Hell, no, I don't like wine. Let's go some place for a beer."

For the next several months, though Tanya didn't always see him on weekends, Lou called on her sporadically during the week.

She despaired at having to spend three days alone in misery, when most couples were together. However, she refused to question him about it, thinking that it might end the relationship if she did. It was better to see him some of the time than not at all.

There were times when she caught him lying about his whereabouts and was convinced that he was dating behind her back. Yet, she couldn't give him up. For her, no other man would do. Secretly, she admitted to herself that she'd fallen in love with him. A desperate, hopeless, kind of love. She even practiced saying the words to him. "Lou, my dearest, I love you. ... Lou, I love you. Lou, I ..." If he'd only say them to her!

But Lou, guarded in his feelings, remained noncommittal and free-spirited.

A year slipped by with the romance at a stalemate. Tanya, after taking stock of the situation, felt that she was no better off than she'd been when they'd first met. Perhaps, she was worse off. Lately, he was staying away for longer periods ... sometimes for as long as two weeks at a stretch before getting in touch with her.

One day, she realized that an entire month had passed and Lou had neither phoned her nor shown up at the suite. Still, she waited, subduing the panic within, telling herself not to worry, while spending nights trying to figure out where he might be.

In desperation, she called Marylou, his sister. Once Lou had taken her there for dinner. She was dark, slim, attractive, with the same laid back attitude that Lou had. She'd confessed to Tanya that she and a girlfriend often met for drinks in a bar, driving her Italian husband, "Julio" to the brink of insanity with jealousy. "He said he'd kill any man who touched me," Marylou, laughingly bragged to her.

Tanya had been thrilled to meet some of Lou's family and entertained the possibility that Lou might be contemplating marriage.

Now she dialed her number. "Marylou? This is Tanya."

"Tanya? What a surprise! Nice to hear from you. How've you been?"

"Fine, Marylou, just fine! It's nice that the weather is holding out so well, don't you think? April can be so uncertain. Uh-h-h, Marylou, I'll get right to the point. I'm calling about Lou; would you happen to know where he is? I haven't heard from him lately; is he all right? ... Do you know?"

"No-o-o, he hasn't called here, either. You could try Bob McFee. Lou likes to go over there quite a lot."

"I already have. Bob, he said he has no idea where Lou is. Well, thanks, anyway. ... It seems strange that he'd disappear without telling anyone. Especially, since he just got that job at Roy's. You'd think that if he was quitting, he'd have let them know, wouldn't you?"

"Yes. Haven't they heard from him?"

"No, they haven't. Yesterday, when I called to ask whether he was still working there, his boss sounded quite angry. He said Lou hadn't phoned or told anyone that he'd be away. Marylou, if you happen to hear from him, would you please ask him to call me?"

"Sure will. Oh, and Tanya?"

"Yes?"

"Do me a favor and relax. Don't be so serious about it. You're far too serious. And don't worry about Lou. He'll turn up when he's good and ready."

"Maybe, you're right. Thanks for the advice."

She hung up, disillusioned. Marylou was behaving as though she was sure that Lou was all right. On the other hand, she was a lot like Lou, preferring to take things lightly. Must run in the family, she thought.

Step by step, Tanya tried to recount each small detail of the last time they'd been together. He'd been in a petulant mood. She'd had to coax him out for a hamburger and coffee. They'd returned to the suite. He'd had several beers. Shortly after, Anna and Anton had showed up, and Lou had started an argument with Anna over some trivial bowling rule. However, since drink usually drove him to quarreling, she'd thought nothing of it. He'd left the suite in a huff. It hadn't worried her, because sooner or later he'd always come back ... until now.

She'd called his place at different times, but to no avail. And neither Bob McFee nor any of his bowling friends seemed to know where he was. However, she'd noticed that Bob McFee did appear somewhat evasive, making her wonder if he knew more than he was telling her. Had Lou found someone else? And why would he maintain his room and not live there? What if ... she never saw him again? She started to tremble.

Just to be sure, tonight, just as soon as it gets dark, I'll go check his place, she thought.

It was nine P.M. and semi-dark when she started out. There were some patches of snow still visible, and the streets had a drab, dusty look to them.

As she came closer, her heart began to beat faster. His suite was much like hers: a basement housekeeping room with its own private entrance, except that she considered his to be on the bleak side.

She ran down the six steps and knocked on the door. When no sound could be heard, she pressed her ear to the wood. After a second knock, she gave up and went back up.

Where could he be? The question burned inside her. On impulse, she first looked to see if anyone was watching, then stepped to the side of the building and crouched down to peer through the basement window, trying to pierce the gloom. Inside the suite, everything looked dark. Sheepishly, she straightened up. What if someone should see her?

She felt lost without him. Her life empty. A void gnawed within her. It seemed that all her life she'd been looking for love. Now, having found it, once more it had been snatched away.

Tanya returned home, undressed, and went to bed, tossing about all sorts of possibilities before coming to the conclusion that it would be best to forget him.

She went to work the next morning determined to keep her resolve. In an effort to keep her mind off Lou, she put in a very intense day.

At five, she left the stuffy office. The day was balmy, warm, and a soft wind had reduced yesterday's paltry mounds to watery puddles. Instead of taking a bus, she decided to walk home.

Disregarding her high heels, she started out. Her feet began aching within a half mile of her place. She slowed her steps, her eyes longingly searching for the gate. Thank God, she was nearly there!

As she came closer, she saw someone leaning against the stucco siding. Lou? Could it be? Her heart leaped. A smile spread over her face. ... Yes, yes, it was him! She began to run. It was like a dream come true, and her happiness lay in the reality that she wasn't dreaming. The ache in her feet was forgotten.

His lean form etched clean cut against the grey surroundings. "Lou! Lou!" She sang out his name, then threw herself into his arms, pulling his head down to hers, covering his face with kisses.

"Hey, Tanya, hold on."

"Lou, where have you been? I've missed you so, Lou! Don't you know that?" She clung to him fiercely, possessively. He laughed, holding her casually loose. What would he think if he knew that because of him, only yesterday, she had resorted to becoming a peeping Tom? She cringed, remembering. How could she stoop so low? This, she'd have to keep to herself.

He smiled at her, and though his smile seemed cool, calculated, he seemed pleased at the excitement he'd generated in her. "Aw-w-w, I was out. You know ... away. The city gets to me, sometime. Crise, I needed time to think."

"But where did you go? I called your boss. He's very angry at you. You know, I think you're fired."

He disengaged himself. "Damn, I knew it! But what the hell, it only paid minimum. I can't be a ruddy pin boy all my life! It ain't a career."

"Guess not." They went inside. Tanya brought out a bottle of beer from the fridge and popping the cap she set it on the table in front of him. "Here, have one." She'd kept it especially for him.

"Thanks." He took a sip and leaned back in his chair, stretching out his long legs and yawning audibly; his eyes looked bloodshot. The lines seemed more noticeable.

"Lou, you look tired. Are you sure you're all right? Now tell me, where did you go? You have no idea how I missed you!" After what she'd been through, she felt that he owed her an explanation.

"Tanya, for Crise sake, don't ask me no more. I ain't married to you, and I ain't accountable to you or anyone else, for that matter. If you really wanna know, I went camping. What the hell? You got no claim on me!"

"Yes, Lou. Sorry." His rebuke silenced her. He was right on all counts. Wherever he'd been, it apparently angered him to talk about it. So why should she complain since he was back and in her very own apartment? Still, many questions demanded to be answered.

Lou changed the subject. "Oh, by the way, I went to see Roger. He's having a party at his place Saturday, and he wants me to come. Wanna go?"

Roger Wilis set pins at Roy's, part time. He was going to be a doctor. He and Lou often worked together.

"Yes, I'd love to go." Uh-h-h-h, would you like to stay for supper? I've got some left over roast."

"Yeah, sounds good."

At nine o'clock, Lou got to his feet and stretched. "Jeez, I'm bushed. I gotta get some sleep. G'night baby. I'm going to hit the sack."

"But, Lou, you just got here. Must you leave so soon?" He gave her a sharp look.

"All right, Lou, all right. Good night. You do look tired." She walked him to the sidewalk, anxious to ask him if she'd see him again, yet unable to do so.

Would a time come when he'd feel a fraction for her what she felt for him? If he liked her, as she thought he did, why did he make her feel so unnecessary? The question would not go away. Of course, she was going to see him again; they were going to Rogers' on Saturday, so why worry?

Tanya bought an off white dress in cotton eyelet, trimmed with lace. It enhanced her coloring. Would he like it? She kept her makeup subdued to create a soft, romantic look.

Lou arrived at eight dressed in a dark, navy blue suit, white shirt, and navy velvet bow tie. His eyes appraised her. "Hey baby, like your dress."

She blushed. "Thank you. And don't you look handsome!"

"Uh-h-h, we better get a move on, Bob and Donna are waiting for us in their car."

"I'll get my shawl." She frowned, annoyed that he'd never saved enough money to buy a car of his own. Even a battered, second hand vehicle would have been better than having to impose on friends all the time.

Roger's house was packed to overflowing. Lou introduced her to some of the couples that he knew, then stood awkwardly at her side.

Tanya immediately sensed his impatience to get away. It didn't surprise her when he motioned towards the other room. "Uh-h-h, I'm gonna talk to Howie, d'you mind?"

"No, by all means, go talk to Howie." She wondered if he was bored with her. She sighed, wondering who she could talk to. She noticed Donna McFee, standing alone and reluctantly began to edge towards her, knowing that spending time with Donna would be very dull. "Hi, Donna. Great party, isn't it?"

Donna nodded. "Yeah."

"Where's Bob?"

"He's in the next room. I think most of the men are in there."

"So is Lou. ... Uh-h-h, how's your family?"

"My family? Fine. I have three children. Bob Jr., he's five..."

Tanya stifled a yawn. At ten-thirty she excused herself and went to look for Lou. Odd, he hadn't been around all evening. She went from room to room, wondering if he'd gone home without her. There was music coming from the rumpus room in the basement, and she went down to check.

Tanya entered the room and froze. Lou, who couldn't dance a step, had his arms around a very attractive brunette. They were, supposedly, dancing. Moving slowly to the music, they were oblivious to everyone but themselves. The young girl looked stunning! Her complexion was satin smooth. She had naturally curly brown hair that offset a perfectly oval face. Her slight figure was clad in a sheer, black dress, her long legs in black, sheer stockings.

She pressed against Lou in a close, intimate embrace. They're not dancing, Tanya thought, they're making love! The music stopped.

Lou held on to her. Suddenly, a strong wave of jealousy swept through her. Enraged, she marched swiftly across the floor and stopped dead in front of Lou.

Lou, surprised, opened his mouth to say something.

Involuntarily, her hand flew up, and she struck him a stinging slap across his face. Turning, she ran to get her wrap with Lou pounding after her.

"Tanya! Tanya, baby! ... Hey, wait a minute!"

"No, go back to her! Don't worry about me, I'll take a cab home."

"Tanya, I didn't mean it. Honest, baby! She's nothing to me. Honest! Baby, believe me, Tanya! ... Wait, dammit!"

He caught her by the shoulder and spun her around. Her anger dissolved into tears. She melted against him as his arms went around her.

"Sorry, baby. I didn't mean to upset you. She's nobody, I swear. It'll never happen again. Never!"

"It's all right, Lou." She laughed, nervously. "I'm the one who should be apologizing. I don't know what came over me to slap you like that. Jealousy, I guess."

"Wait here, baby. I'll phone for a cab."

They spent the evening making up in each others' arms. To Tanya, it was pure heaven. Though questions and serious doubts raised themselves, she pushed them aside and, unable to resolve anything, put an end to her worries by telling herself that if he loved her, he would be more than willing to change for her, reminding herself that he'd been very concerned and responded quickly enough when she'd slapped him.

30

TANYA AND LOU DRIFTED FROM ONE DATE TO THE NEXt for the next three years, with Lou more than content to keep the relationship going on a purely casual basis. But Tanya, longing for fulfillment, despaired. Though she loved him, she feared a future with him. Would anything serious come of it, she wondered. They'd known each other for four years. She felt it was time to spur him into some kind of action. She was twenty-one and old enough to marry and settle down.

Alisha had found a young man, Allen Semco, a law student, and had made Mama very happy by getting married. They now had a four month old child. From the looks of her, she couldn't be more content. And Anna had just announced her engagement to Anton. Tanya envied them.

One evening, she sat next to Lou on the couch, miserable, and wondering if he was coming to see her purely out of habit? His weekly visits were becoming less frequent. Was it his financial state that was keeping them apart? Lou, being broke most of the time, might be hesitant about proposing marriage. Was he aware that she had a good job and brought home a decent paycheck? If need be, I can easily support the both of us, she thought.

She put down her coffee cup. "Lou, I've been thinking. Did you know that I've got almost $4,000.00 in my savings account?"

He jerked his head to look at her. "You do? Where did you get it?"

"I worked for it and saved it, silly! Where d'you think? Every time I get paid, I always put something away for a rainy day, don't you?"

He laughed. "Hell, no, I spend mine. Besides, you know how much I make. It's peanuts. I can't save nuthin."

"Yes, I know, Lou."

He looked at her with interest, "$4,000.00? Hm-m-m, you know, that ain't bad for a damn woman."

She nodded, happily. "I know, my job pays well. I like to save."

"Yeah. Damn well!"

The change in Lou was immediate; he became more attentive. The next week, he came to see her every night. At first, she didn't give it too much thought, yet something warned her that it wasn't right. At the same time, she basked in his rekindled interest.

One day, he took her on one of his fishing excursions, patiently explaining how to hold the rod and how to cast out, exclaiming with surprise when she landed her first fish. To Tanya, it refreshed the memory of their first meeting and his attention then. She began to feel content as the courtship progressed.

"Tanya, tonight, come watch me bowl," he urged.

"Oh, Lou, you know I can't play a decent game, especially against someone like yourself. I get anxious."

"Even if you don't play, I'd like you there to cheer me on."

She nodded, more than satisfied to comply.

Lou took her to see some of the best acclaimed movies. In the privacy of the darkened theatre, he sat with his arm possessively around her, occasionally stealing a kiss. To Tanya, it was the most wonderful time of her life. She relaxed, satisfied that at long last, she'd found someone who really and truly loved her as much as she loved him.

One evening, Lou quit bowling early and steered her to the cafeteria towards a booth. "Let's have a coffee, okay? I nearly had all strikes that first game. Did you see? I tell you, Tanya, if I had more time to practice, I could make a living at it. I'm a lot better than just good. I can beat all the guys on my team. In fact, I keep that damn team going."

"Yes, I know you do, Lou. You always come out with the highest score, don't you?" Tonight, he seemed nervous about something. It was so unlike him, she thought.

Now he leaned across the table and covered her hand with his, looking intently into her eyes. "Tanya, I've been meaning to ask you something."

"What is it, Lou?"

"It's just that ... Crise, I don't know how to say this. Well, here goes. Tanya, will you marry me?"

Her spoon clattered to the table; her heart started to race. "Lou, do you mean that? Lou, I didn't know that you loved me! Lou, those were the very words I've always wanted to hear you say! Oh, Lou, you've made me so happy! I'd be honoured to marry you! Yes, yes, more than honoured!"

"Crise, Tanya, I don't know that you should be so happy, because I gotta ask you something else, and you might not be so thrilled when you hear it. First, promise that you won't get mad at me?"

"What? What is it? Of course I'm not going to get mad at you! You don't have to be afraid of me. You can ask me anything, Lou, anything! You must know that I'm crazy about you. Besides, we should have no secrets between us, if we're going to be married."

"Dammit, shut up and listen, because this ain't easy to say. First, I want to say that I'm real sorry about this. Tanya ... honey ... you're so understanding about everything, I didn't think you'd mind. You see, it's like this. I'm between jobs right now, and I'm a little short on cash. I wondered if you wouldn't mind lending me some money. ... Uh-h-h, it's for your ring. ... And don't worry because I ain't gonna forget about it. I mean to pay you back just as soon as I get a decent job. Every red cent of it! ... I promise! I mean it! Honest!"

Her delight dulled a little. But she firmly reminded herself that if she really and truly loved him, it shouldn't matter who paid for the ring. "Silly! Of course, I don't mind. We'll go to Irving Jewelers tomorrow, and I'll give you a hint about which one I want. I'll bring my cheque book."

"Thanks, honey. That's just great! You've made me the damn happiest guy in the whole damn world. Now, let's go someplace and celebrate with a beer, okay?"

"Yes, Lou, whatever you say. That sounds real nice."

They found a bar close by and toasted each other with brimming glasses, while Tanya's head began to fill with plans for the wedding. Though she kept hers to one glass, Lou downed several bottles, before walking her back to her suite. Tanya told herself that since he was going to be her husband, she didn't mind paying for the beer and a pack of cigarettes, as well. After all, what could she expect if he was out of work?

After a lengthy good night in each others' arms, Lou promised to see her the next day right after work.

Tanya went to bed the minute he left, feeling restless and perturbed. Something was not right. Though the man of her dreams had proposed, and she had accepted, there was something amiss. She ran over the scene in her mind. Suddenly, she sat bolt upright. Never once did he say that he loved me, she thought. I said it to him, but he made no such statement to me. Never once! What am I supposed to believe? She lay back disoriented and nearly frantic. Was he conning her? Perhaps she shouldn't marry him? Was it a mistake?

The next day, she phoned Alisha to let her in on the good news, at the same time dreading it, remembering that Alisha had never approved of Lou. She started off on a bright note. "Alisha, guess what? Lou proposed to me last night, and we're engaged to be married."

There was an audible gasp at the other end. "You're what? Oh, Tanya, don't do it! You're making a mistake. Lou's no good, he's a bum!"

Anger shot through her. "No, you're wrong. He loves me. And... and, besides, it's none of your business. You're supposed to congratulate me, not break us up. ... What do you mean I can't marry him?"

"Tanya, please, please, don't marry him."

"What? How dare you?"

"Tanya, it's just that I think that you're too good for him. ... And too young. You still have plenty of time to find someone decent. You're only twenty-one. He's already thirty-three. That's quite an age difference, you know. He's been around, you haven't. Please, Tanya, you should wait."

How stupid of her. "Oh, do you think so? Well, let me tell you what I think! You don't like him. You never have. And you don't want me to marry him for that very reason!"

"Are you going to live in your basement suite after?"

"Yes, we are. What's wrong with that? I didn't see you living in a palace after you married Allen. In fact, you lived with his folks for a while. Besides, we can't afford a palace!"

"Tanya, don't marry him. Ple-e-e-ase! Did Anna tell you that he spent time in jail? She said he'd forged some cheques or something like that. I think he got a year. So, on top of everything else, he's even got a criminal record!"

"Actually, it was three years. So what? Yes, he told me that himself. And he didn't try to hide it. I'm going to marry him whether you like it or not. Besides, it's none of your business, so leave me alone!"

"Oh Tanya! He's cruel, he's mean. You can tell by his eyes. He doesn't love you. He doesn't love anyone but himself!"

"It doesn't matter, I'm going to marry him! You can't stop me! So stop trying!" She slammed the phone down, feeling very discouraged. After he'd proposed, Lou had confessed about the jail term to her: 'Tanya, I was out of a job. I had no money. I had to do something or starve. So I made up a fictitious name and wrote a cheque. And you wanna know something? The stupid clerk at the grocery store, she cashed it. So I wrote another one, and she cashed that one, too. You know why? Because she liked me, that's why. I coulda got away with it, but her damn boss caught on. Then he made her tell him who it was writing the cheques."

His face had sobered at the recollection. "I'll tell you something else, from now on baby, I'm going straight. I ain't gonna end up in no jail. You can bet your last dollar on that one! The jail term ... I'll never forget it. Would you believe those bastards raped me? But hell, I got even. I got one of those guys alone that did it to me, and," ... his face took on a mischievous glow, "I did it to him."

"Lou! How could you?"

A look of fear flooded his face. "Hell, I had to ... to protect myself."

"Oh, Lou! You poor thing! You must have suffered terribly!"

"Hell, yeah, I did."

Despite Alisha's warning, she went right ahead with the wedding, making two lists of everything they had to do. "Lou, here's your list, and this one's mine. ... I can't do this by myself. I don't have the time. I work."

Lou, after he read his, became silent and moody.

She was quick to sense it. "Lou, what's wrong?"

"You can't expect me to go everywhere on the bus to do all this stuff. ... Get wedding license. ... Pick up flowers. ... Talk to minister. ... Hell, I need a car, or I ain't gonna bother. Do it yourself, for all I care." He threw down his list.

"Oh Lou! You're right, we do need a car! Look, do you think you can find us a car? Nothing too expensive. It can't be new. I can't afford new. But maybe a good used car. Huh?"

He jumped to his feet, smiling. "Now you're talking. Leave it to me, baby. I already got one in mind. Get your coat, I'll show you."

They caught a bus to Chevron Motors where Lou pointed out a two door, second hand, 1943 Chevrolet to her. The sign read $700.00.

"Do you really think it's okay?" she asked, "You know, I can't complain about the price."

"Crise, yeah, I do. So, what d'you think? Are you gonna buy it or you gonna hang on to your money? It would uncomplicate our lives a helluva lot, you know. The deal is that you can either pay cash, or get a loan, whichever you figure is best for you."

She nodded. He'd convinced her. "I don't want to spend every dime I've got in my account. So-o-o, I think I'll give them $400.00 in cash and put the rest on payments. What do you think?"

"It's your money. Sounds good to me." He turned to the salesman. "We'll take this one."

Lou, who had never driven before, insisted on driving the car home. After some hasty instructions from the dealer, he slid in behind the wheel. Tanya got in beside him. He turned on the ignition and began to experiment with the gear shift, swearing as they jerked out of the lot.

Tanya froze when he narrowly missed an oncoming car. "Lou, don't you think you should have some lessons?"

"No, dammit! Shut up, and let me concentrate on steering this damn car!"

Sighing, she resigned herself to being silent. With the wedding date drawing closer, an edgy, moody side to him had emerged. Now, every time they got together, he made her nervous.

That evening, Tanya breathed easier when Bob McFee came over to show Lou how to run the car properly.

31

SUNSHINE STREAMED IN THROUGH THE STAINED GLASS WINDOWS of St. Luke's United Church. The day, June 13th, 1954, turned out to be bright, the sky a luminous blue, and wonderfully warm.

Alisha commented that it might have been nice if Mama had been there. However, Tanya thought no. Mama was totally against mixed marriages, refusing to contend with the popular belief that love conquered all. Better that she not witness it; she could easily ruin the blissful occasion and might even have put a stop to it.

Alisha sat on the bride's side of the church. Some of Lou's family were present. Earlier, Alisha told Anna that she didn't approve of Lou. However, since it was Anna who'd introduced Tanya to him, she totally disagreed with her.

Lou stood at the altar with Anton, his best man, exchanging smiles and small talk with the minister. His white shirt and tie gave his skin an olive cast.

Suddenly, the organist switched to, Wagner's "Wedding March." They all stood up. Anna, who was maid of honor, came out first. Tanya walked behind her, escorted by Allen.

She looked radiant, her eyes brighter than usual as she went smiling past them. The light, streaming in from the stained glass windows, touched briefly on her hair, turning it to gold. A wisp of a veil floated back from her head. Her gown was made of white, sheer organza with a sweetheart neckline, elbow-length sleeves, and a gently flowing skirt. Her jewelry, a simple strand of pearls and pearl earrings. Streams of white satin ribbon cascaded from a bouquet of dark red sweetheart roses mixed with white stephanotis.

Since Lou was still looking for work, this was all she could afford.

Allen brought her as far as the altar then came to sit next to Alisha as the minister started the intonation of the vows.

"Dearly beloved, we are gathered here today to witness the union between Tanya and Lou. Marriage is a sacred trust which we endow to one another. It must never be taken lightly. When two people are joined together, in the eyes of God, they become one flesh, one person. Love is the basic ingredient in binding them together. Love is patient, forgives all, is never quarrelsome, and never demands its own way ..." He proceeded smoothly to the end. "Is there anyone present who has just cause as to why this couple should not marry, let him speak now or forever hold his peace." There was total silence.

Alisha stifled a sob, but sat unmoving. The moment passed.

"... and do you Lou, take Tanya, to love her, honour her, comfort her, in sickness and in health, and to keep her so long as you both shall live, until death do you part?"

"I do."

When it was over, Alisha, though she fought back tears, came forward to congratulate them. "Tanya, I hope you'll be very happy," she exclaimed, looking mournful.

A small reception followed in a Chinese restaurant. Tanya had arranged a week's honeymoon in Banff. She was looking forward to their time together in a rented cottage, anticipating long walks with Lou, conversations with Lou, within the natural splendour of the mountains. It would be so romantic!

The reception ended. They drove to her suite so that she could change into a beige suit.

Lou turned to her with impatience. "Hey, I want to get there before dark, so be quick."

She flushed, excited, and ran in. She came out, carrying a suitcase. Snuggling close beside him, she wondered if he was going to be more civil to her now that they were married and the pressure of the wedding was behind them? Sometimes couples fought because of the tension.

Several hours later, they were well within the folds of the mountains. Suddenly, a shower drenched the road expunging the scene from view. Lou slowed the car and set the windshield wipers into motion. She tensed, straining to see through the rain. Ten minutes later, it let up.

"Lou, look! A rainbow! Isn't it beautiful? It's a good sign, don't you think?"

"Yeah, real nice, ain't it! Did you remember to bring the beer?"

"No, Lou, I'm sorry, I forgot. Uh-h-h, we can buy some at the liquor store."

"Yeah, guess you're right. The town is just ahead." He turned off the main road and drove through a residential area, before pulling up in front of a brown, stucco bungalow. "This is it." He shut off the motor and got out.

Tanya, who'd seen to all the arrangements, went to the front door to check with the owner about the key. Now they were inside and alone. She turned to him, playfully. "Well, Lou, aren't you going to give Mrs. Lou Hagen a kiss?"

He laughed, kissed her on her mouth, and turned to leave. "See you later, baby."

She looked at him in confusion. "Lou, where are you going? It's already nine-thirty. The stores will be closed."

"Not the liquor store. It's open till eleven. I want a beer, and I ain't got all night."

"Oh!" Disappointed, she went to unpack, thinking that though her married life had just begun, there was an unfamiliar emptiness at the pit of her stomach.

She shook out a white, satin night gown and slipped it on. The soft material clung to her slender form. It hadn't been cheap. After all the bills had been paid, she'd given in and bought it. Now, she brushed out her hair and retouched her make-up, then arranged herself on the pillows to wait for Lou.

An hour later, he was back, lugging a case of beer under his arm. "You in bed already?"

"Yes, Lou, it's almost eleven."

"Yeah, so I see." Lou ripped open the case and reached for a bottle, gurgling it down in a hurry, leaving the empty on the floor when he finished. He stretched, removed his clothes, belched, and throwing back the covers slid in next to her.

She turned away from the acrid smell of beer on his breath, thinking that tonight should be special. "Lou, where did you go, it's been over an hour?"

He slipped his arm around her. "Not now, baby."

"Lou, wait! There's something bothering me. It's important that I know ... it really is."

"Yeah, what?"

"Lou, do you love me? I mean really love me?" The words sounded strange, and made her heart pound as if her very life depended on his answer.

"Yeah, sure, I do." His face covered hers with impatience. Her arms encircled him. She wanted to say more, but couldn't. Unspoken questions whirled in her mind. "Lou ..."

"Sh-h-h, shut up, baby!"

She complied, sensing his urgency, and tried to meet his need, straining to feel some response within her. Where were the crashing cymbals? From Lou, there were no caresses, no kisses, no talk. It was purely physical, lustful. Strangely, she felt herself performing, play acting, going through the motions. She wanted desperately to cry, even with his arms around her. Yesterday, a secret had revealed itself. Now it came back to taunt her. As she was about to retire for the night, a small voice within her had confirmed that she didn't love Lou. She'd tried to still it. But it was true. Saddened, she resigned herself to the role that she was destined to play. A role, forced upon her, from this day on.

Lou, having satisfied himself, lay back. "G'night, baby."

Is this all there was to it? Did I keep myself chaste for this? Where was the tenderness, the giving? Where was the love that she'd anticipated from him? She remembered how desperately she'd fought for it. A tear rolled silently down her cheek. She wiped it away with the back of her hand. Their marriage was a mistake. Even standing before the minister she'd had second thoughts. She turned to look at Lou, who was already asleep.

It was strange to awaken in the morning and find him lying next to her, confirming that yesterday had not been a dream and that she really was married to Lou. Her heart felt heavy, empty, as she realized that she would have to spend all her time with him no matter how she felt. It was too late.

In between the proposal and the wedding, Lou's attitude had become cold, distant. She'd bought the car thinking that it would make a difference. However, there wasn't the slightest bit of gratitude from him. Before she could stop it, the actual date of the wedding was upon them, giving her no time to change her mind.

She sighed. Last night had confirmed that Lou felt nothing for her. Now she wondered why, out of the great number of love struck- females who he'd bragged had chased after him, had he chosen to marry her?

She rose from the bed and walked to the window. The brightness of the day and cheery chorus of birds in the pines outside intensified her remorse. Then, remembering her vows, she pushed aside her feelings. Her eyes strayed to the bed.

Lou turned and opened his eyes.

"Good morning." She forced a smile and went to the stove to fill a kettle with water for coffee.

He coughed, a raspy smoker's cough, bronchial and loose. "Got anything to eat in this joint?"

"Yes. I brought some bacon and eggs with me. You know how

expensive Banff is at this time of year." She pulled out a frying pan and turned on a gas burner, mentally chastising herself for being so practical, thinking that on this one occasion, they could have eaten out even though Lou was counting on her to pay for it.

The coffee began to sputter. "Lou, coffee's ready."

He swung his legs over the edge of the bed, lit a cigarette and took a long puff in silence. After his smoke, he showered, shaved, and came out fully dressed in a black and white, checkered shirt and black dress pants.

"Lou, I hope you're hungry." She filled his plate with bacon, eggs, toast, and set it on the table, thinking that the lengthy silence was making her nervous.

Lou ignored her searching eyes and began to devour his food while Tanya sat watching him. He had a unique way of eating. Neither savouring nor taking pleasure in the taste, as he wolfed everything down in big, hungry bites, leaving a small piece of toast when he was full. Then he tilted back his chair and struck up another cigarette, drawing on it long and deep before exhaling.

Suddenly Tanya, who couldn't stand the silence, burst out,

"Lou, is something wrong? Was it all right? I mean last night? Was I ... was I ... all right?"

"Nothing's wrong. Crise, you're a nag! ... Don't talk to me about last night." He rose to his feet. "I'm going to get some air. The smell in here is killing me. Shit!" He strode out, slamming the door behind him.

She sat still, too stunned to move. Why was this happening? Was it her fault? She got up, sobbing, and fell across the unmade bed.

At eleven, Lou came back with a magazine. He ignored her tear- stained face and pulled up a chair to read a copy of "Playboy," occasionally letting out a laugh.

She dried her eyes, knowing that having been deprived of the attention that she'd imagined her tears would solicit, she was on the verge of hysteria. Slowly, she rose to her feet and went into the kitchen, reminding herself that there was lunch to be made.

Lou put down the magazine and picked up the car keys.

She felt a sickening crunch go through her. "Lou, where are you going? This is supposed to be our honeymoon!"

"Well, damn the honeymoon! I'm not hanging around here with you bawling all day. I'm going bowling. You can do what you like."

She rushed to the bed to collapse on the covers. She wanted to be loved, comforted, reassured! Nothing was going right! This time, she cried until dark. Finally, when Lou did come in he slept on the couch, leaving her the bed.

As the week went by, it became clear that he wasn't going to change. Tanya spent many hours alone, crying, with Lou behaving as if she wasn't there. It was a relief to return to the city.

She called Alisha to let her know that they were back, parrying her questions with vague answers, reluctant to give anything away.

Her first day at work, she worried all day that her marriage, though barely a week old, was already suffering. Something will have to be done, she thought ... and very soon. We'll talk about it as soon as I come home tonight. We'll talk.

At five-thirty sharp, she walked into the suite to find Lou stretched out on the sagging couch. "Hi, Lou, I'm home. What did you do all day? ... Any mail?"

"Yeah, some bills came." He blew a smoke ring and watched it dissipate. "I didn't do much. About the same as right now."

He smokes too much, she thought. During their courtship it hadn't bothered her. And when they'd first met, she'd thought it made him look sophisticated. Now she noticed the foul odour of stale cigarette smoke on her clothes and in the suite.

"Did you go job hunting?"

"Naw, what for? There's nothing out there! I tried two weeks ago. Geez, how many times do I have to tell you that?"

"You know, Lou, you should go back to the Employment Agency more than once. If it was me, I would. I'd go every day. New jobs are coming up all the time. You might land something." She wondered why it didn't bother him to be out of work? It didn't seem right that he was so willing to do nothing and accept her charity so readily.

She flipped through the mail. "What's this? Here's a letter from Gilt Finance. I don't remember having anything to do with Gilt Finance." She opened the envelope and gasped. "Lou, according to this letter, we owe them a payment of $30.00. There must be some mistake! Lou? ..."

"Oh, for Crise sake! Don't you remember? How dumb are you? How do you think we got the Chevy? You didn't wanna part with the cash, so we had to finance some of it. Remember? Tanya, sometime, you piss me off."

"Sorry, Lou. Yes, I do remember. We did finance it. It's just that for a minute, the name didn't register." She put the letter down and went into the kitchen to prepare supper. I'll bring up "the problem" after we eat, she thought. The phone rang when the meal was about ready. "Lou, honey, could you get that for me?"

"Yeah." He slid off the couch and picked up the receiver. "Hello? ... Yeah. She's fine. ... Uh-h-h, about eight okay? ... Yeah. See you." He went back to the couch and lay down.

She waited for him to speak then burst out! "Lou, for goodness sake, who was that? Can't you tell me by yourself? Why do I have to ask?"

He smiled. "Bob McFee. He wants me to play poker with him. Him and some other guys. You don't mind, do you?"

"Uh-h-h, actually, I'd like to talk to you about something really important, Lou."

"Can't it wait?"

"I suppose so." She wondered whether he was meeting any of the men he'd done time with in jail? "Lou, do you really have to go tonight?"

"Yeah, I said I would, so I'm going."

He downed his meal and rushed off to the McFees. Tanya washed the dishes and sat down with a magazine, thinking that she'd wait up for him. At one A.M. she gave in and went to bed, wondering what had happened. Had he been in an accident? Was he lying hurt somewhere?

It was two-thirty when Lou came in. She smiled to herself with relief. "Lou, is that you?"

"It ain't Santa Claus!"

"Lou, it's late, I was worried. I thought you might have had an accident or something."

His shoe came down with a thud.

"Lou, you could at least have phoned me."

"Yeah, yeah, do I have to report to you like some kid? Well, I ain't a kid, and you ain't my mother. Shit! We played cards. Are you satisfied? I lost eight dollars." He slid under the covers. She moved closer, needing comfort. She caught a faint hint of perfume. Lilac, she thought. She consoled herself thinking that perhaps it was his after-shave.

"Leave me alone, I'm tired."

His rejection hurt. She closed her eyes, forcing herself to sleep, knowing that she couldn't put in a full day's work in the morning with no rest.

On the following Wednesday, Tanya came home to find Lou fully dressed and ready to go out. Her heart sank! "Lou, are you going somewhere?"

He ignored her question, as he adjusted his tie.

Anger urged her on. "Lou, where do you think you're going? Don't you ever want to stay home with me? ... Huh? ... Lou, answer me!"

Furious, he turned on her. "You know damn well where I'm going. I bowl Mondays, Wednesdays, and Fridays. For Crise sake, stop bitching! Get off my back, willya? You know my schedule. It's the same as before. It ain't a secret."

"Yes, yes, I know. I'm sorry if I'm crabby. The work at the office, I'm so tired. Sometimes, I say things I don't mean. But Lou, I would really appreciate it if, sometimes, you stayed home with me, Lou. Just sometimes ... please?"

"Well, tonight, I can't, so don't be such a bitch about it."

She went weak. It seemed he had little regard for the rules of marriage. Why was he going out every day? Nothing she did or said enticed him to stay home. Nights, she was losing sleep, trying to overlook the fact that he was coming in later and later, looking bedraggled and haggard. What had become routine to him was a bitter pill for her to swallow.

One evening, she came home to find him already gone. She waited for several hours, then picked up the phone to call Bob McFee, wondering if there was a card game at his place.

"Bob, Lou's not home. Is he over there?"

"Uh-h-h, sorry, Tanya, no. I haven't seen him. But I'm sure he'll be back soon. Give him a couple of hours."

"Bob, if you know something, please tell me. Tonight isn't his bowling night, you know."

"Uh-h-h, no, sorry, Tanya. ... Uh-h-h, I couldn't. Uh-h-h, I mean, I don't have a clue."

"Bob, please be honest with me, do you know where he might be? ... Please!"

"Tanya, I don't think you wanna know."

She stiffened. "What do you mean? ... Bob, don't keep me in the dark! Tell me where he is!"

"I hate to be the one to tell you. I'm supposed to be his best friend, remember?"

"Tell me what? You're talking in riddles. Bob, aren't you my friend, too? ... Well, aren't you?"

"Yes ... yes, uh-h-h, I am ... both."

"Then where is he? If you know, please tell me! Don't keep me dangling!"

He sighed. "Okay, Tanya, okay. ... Right now, he's on the south side with a friend."

"What do you mean "a friend"? You don't mean a woman, do you? ... You can't mean it."

"Yes, a woman."

"Bob, could you take me there? Now? ... Please!"

"Uh-h-h, I'll be over in about fifteen minutes. Is that too soon for you?"

"No, no, it's not too soon. I'll be waiting."

She rushed out when he honked his horn.

"Tanya, I swear, I feel like a traitor ratting on him like this."

"It's all right, Bob, you're not ratting on him. Remember I'm his wife."

They drove to a residential area on the south side. Bob turned into a quiet street and shut off the motor. She tensed, unable to fathom what to expect. Her watch read nine P.M., she noticed it was getting dusk.

He turned to her. "Tanya, isn't that your car up ahead?"

She saw the Chevy half a block away. "Yes, that's it. Thank you, Bob. Uh-h-h, you can go home now. It's all right, Lou will drive me back."

She opened the door, slid out, and began running towards the car, her heart pounding as she drew nearer. The window was slightly open. Lou was half lying on top of a young, dark haired woman, his mouth on hers, her arms were around his neck. Her blouse was undone. Lou had his pants down.

Tanya's fury mounted. She jerked the door open, thinking if she had a gun she would kill him. "Lou, what are you doing?"

Lou jerked up. "Who? ... What the God damned are you doing here?"

The girl, her lipstick smeared, her clothes undone, looked at her in disbelief. "Lou, who is she? Is she crazy or something?"

"I'm his wife, that's who!" Tanya screamed at her.

Her mouth dropped. Wildly, she scrambled to do up her blouse. Only half dressed, she reached for the door.

"Audry, don't go. It's all right. Wait Audry! ... I'll handle it." He put a restraining hand on her arm. Audry! ... It's all right! ... Wait! ... Audry!"

The girl flung open the door and jumped out. She looked terrified. She ran a few steps and disappeared into a house close by.

Lou turned to Tanya who was pounding him with her fists. "Stop that! Stop it, I said! ... Lay off!"

Tanya, unable to stop, kept beating him. "You dog! You ... you, slime! ... How could you do this to me? Where is your decency? You bastard!" She punched, she slapped, she clawed. He put up his arm to ward off her blows.

Suddenly, he caught her wrists. "Okay, okay, that's enough, for Crise sake!"

"Let go of me! You're taking me home. This is my car, I paid for it. I want to go home, now!" She sagged.

Lou let go of her. Tanya walked to the passenger side and got inside. "What were you doing with her?"

"That's none of your God damned business!" he roared, turning on the ignition and gunning the motor.

"Yes, it is my business. I'm your wife! So it is my business!"

He drove home sullen, fuming, letting her off at the gate in front. Tanya opened the door and climbed out. Suddenly, without warning, he sped off with the squeal of tires and spurt of gravel, the stones hitting her legs in stinging bites.

"Lou! ... Lou! Come back!" It was no use. Sobbing, she returned to the suite alone, thinking that he had no right, no right to be so cruel. In a fit of anger, she went to the closet, gathered his belongings and threw them outside on the lawn, then locked and bolted the door.

She picked up the receiver and dialed Bob McFee's number.

"Bob? If you see Lou, you tell him from me that he better find someplace else to live. ... You tell him his things are outside on the lawn. ... And, I don't want him coming back!"

"Uh-h-h, sorry to hear that, Tanya. But, yes, I'll tell him. You bet I will."

"And Bob, thanks for helping me!"

That night, she cried herself to sleep, knowing that she could never, never trust him again. There would always be the doubt and the awful scene of Lou making love to that woman.

A week passed before Lou called her. "Tanya?"

"What do you want?"

"Baby, I want to come back! Can I? Huh? Please?"

"Lou, what about that ... that woman? You didn't want her to leave ... even with me there!"

"Her? She's nothing! She doesn't mean a pinch, I swear. Tanya, you're the only one that really means anything to me. Honest, baby! Can I come home? It's real lonesome without you, baby."

She thought a minute. She, too, was lonely. "Oh, all right, Lou. But this must never, ever, happen again! Is that clear?"

"It ain't gonna, baby! It ain't gonna, I swear!"

She took him back; they made up.

32

SEVERAL MONTHS PASSED WITH LOU NO BETTER THAN BEFORE. One morning, Tanya sat alone in the suite unable to concentrate, unable to eat. Her worries had intensified. Lou had gone out Friday night to bowl. It was now Saturday morning, and he still hadn't come home. He'd never done this before. No telling where he might be or when he'd be back. The thought brought on a tremor. She rose and reached for the phone, wondering if she should call Marylou? On second thought, what would be the use? She'd only preach about how she should be more relaxed about it.

The laundry, cleaning, and grocery shopping had piled up. No sense in moping; it would only make her feel worse. She went into the bedroom and changed the sheets. It was best to keep working and never give in to the depression.

The day ended. She expected Lou to be home at any moment, or calling her soon. Every time the phone rang, she jumped. She waited for him long into the night, not knowing whether she could sleep without him.

She propped herself up on pillows and tried to read. At times, the words made no sense, but she read and reread the lines, struggling to keep her mind focused on the plot and not on Lou.

At three A.M. she awoke with a start. She'd dozed off and the book had slipped from her grasp. Lou was still missing. Sighing, Tanya turned off the light and closed her eyes.

Early Sunday morning, she awoke to find that he still hadn't returned. Anger replaced anxiety. Anger that Lou could be so irresponsible! So thoughtless! This time, I'll make him tell me where he went, she vowed. I won't listen to any of his excuses.

She did some ironing, then cleaned out the kitchen cupboards. Once, she caught sight of her face in the mirror and was shocked to see that her eyes had sunken in and her face looked utterly ghastly.

After supper, she sat down to sew a hemline into place. Suddenly, the door opened and Lou walked in. She stared at him, unbelieving, her anger draining away. She felt lighter; her breathing suddenly came easier.

"Lou, where have you been? Do you realize how worried I've been? I was wondering ... "

"Cut the shit! I was out ... fishing, okay?"

She stared at him. He was holding a fishing rod and net which he immediately propped up in a corner. He shed his boots, jacket, and shirt, then went into the bathroom and shut the door. A moment later, she heard him whistling and the shower running.

Lou came out dressed in a royal blue, terry cloth robe, his black hair smoothed back and still wet with droplets of water clinging to it. Tanya watched closely as he collapsed onto the couch, lay back with a half smile, and promptly went to sleep.

She subdued her anger. In sleep, his face looked relaxed, vulnerable. Her head began to spin thinking, "he's driving me crazy! We might as well be roommates."

At work the next day, she began thinking that what Lou really needed was a job. She picked up the phone and called Brenda Martin, a friend she knew at the Employment Agency. "Brenda, I know someone who needs a job. Uh-h-h, here's the bad part, he doesn't have much experience or skills in anything. Would you know of something?" She could not bring herself to say that it was Lou.

"Sure, Tanya. I'll look into it and get right back to you."

Mid-morning, Brenda called her back. "Tanya, I think I have something. It's at the Army Base. They need someone to run the supply store. ... Doesn't pay much. But your friend won't starve, either. Tell him to get right on it, okay?"

"Thanks, Brenda, I will." She hung up and called Lou.

His voice sounded croaky, making her wonder if he'd been sleeping. She told him about the job as briefly as possible.

Lou perked up. "That sounds okay. Yeah, baby, thanks."

His enthusiasm surprised her; she thought he might balk at the prospect of work.

Later in the afternoon, he called back. "I got the job! I start tomorrow. Crise, today, they already gave me some training. Baby, I got the job!"

Secretly, she thanked Brenda. "Wonderful, Lou! I knew you would. Lou, you can fill me in when I get home." She tried to imagine the changes his working would make to their lives and envisioned him spending some time with her. That evening, to celebrate his success, they ate out.

Surprisingly, Lou liked his job. A week later, as Tanya was preparing dinner, he walked in and peeled off his jacket, flipping it onto a chair. "Hi, honey. What's to eat?"

He hadn't called her honey in a long time. "I've got a steak. How did it go today?"

"Great. It's easy work. Mostly women coming in. They buy everything. Would you believe some woman came on to me today?"

Tanya stiffened, knowing that he'd like that. "Really? How?" He reminded her of a school boy, bragging about how well he was doing in class. She set two plates on the table and ran to check the steak under the broiler.

Lou sat down. "Tanya, I dunno what it is about me, but women just go nuts over me. And to tell you the truth, sure as hell, there's nuthin I can do about it. They just act crazy when they're around me." He stretched out his long legs, his face full of self-love.

She put french fries and a salad before him, then brought the steak to the table. "Shall we eat?" Though it hurt, she wanted to hear more. "So what makes you so irresistible? How do you do it? Come on Lou, admit it, don't you flirt with them just a little?"

He smirked. "You know, it's all in the way I present myself. I trained myself. You might say I practiced. I practiced in front of a mirror ... like this." He stood up, took a long puff on his cigarette, then, leaning against the wall, he drew on a half smile.

Tanya remembered that look when they'd first met. Had he been play-acting then so he could appear exciting and mysterious?

Lou sat down and picked up his fork. "As for women, I tell em anything ... any kind of a lie I can think off, and they always believe me. And," he laughed to himself, "they eat it up and want to hear more. ... Baby, it's so easy! Didn't you notice that when we first started going out I never chased you, but you kept coming after me?"

She tensed. "Lou, stop that! I've heard enough." It was true, she had been drawn to him and had to admit to pursuing him; however, at this point in time, she had no wish to be reminded of her foolishness. She sighed. Had he conned her too?

"Oh, by the way," Lou continued, "this might interest you. The other day, I waited on this babe who came in to buy a purse. Well, we started talking and she said she was from Spirit Valley. So I told her you were from there, too. And ... uh-h-h, it turns out that she knows you!"

Tanya noticed a lewd glint in his eyes. Was there something he wasn't telling her? "Really? Who was she?"

"I think she said her name was Jenny Mariak. Know her?"

"Is she tall, brunette, slim built?"

"Yeah, that's her."

"Uh-h-h, I went to school with Jenny." She looked at him closely, trying to second-guess what really took place between them. It would be so easy to meet someone after five when the store closed.

"Yeah, well, we got to talking, and she told me she knows your whole family. ... She's some gal! Tanya, women are all alike. They all wanna hear the same things. Like, how pretty they are ... how sexy. You know, stuff like that. Shit, they'll eat out of your hand once they get hooked. And all you gotta do is appear halfway sincere ... like you really mean it when you sympathize with their problems." He smiled in satisfaction. "They buy it every time."

"Yes Lou, I'm sure, they do." Tanya, tormented by his blatant, devious admission, put down her fork and glared at him.

"Aw-w-w, come on, baby! I didn't mean you. Did you think I did? I tease some of 'em now and then, but that's all. It never goes beyond that. Honest! Relax, eat your steak."

"Lou, that's wrong. You shouldn't lead a person on."

"Well if that's the way you're gonna be about it, I shoulda kept my mouth shut. Shit!" He pushed his chair back. Hooking his jacket by the collar, he strode out.

"Lou, I didn't mean ..." Should she have been so hard on him? Though he'd bragged about it, he'd been quick to assure her that it hadn't gone beyond that. She carried their plates to the sink, thinking how short lived her contentment had been. Only a week.

That night, frustration kept her awake as she desperately tried to relax and let go.

She was awakened by a pounding on the door. She tensed and lay still. The clock beside the bed read five after four. The knocking grew louder.

"Tanya, Tanya, let me in. ... Tanya, I forgot my key. For Crise sake, let me in."

She started to rise, then slumped back. No, no, let him knock, she thought. He had his nerve coming in at four in the morning. I'll say I was asleep and didn't hear him, she thought. Do him good to stand there and suffer some of the anxiety that he made her suffer each and every day since their marriage.

"Tanya, it's me, Lou. For Crise sake, open the door."

She waited until he'd been outside a full ten minutes, knocking and pleading, before getting up to let him in.

His face grim, he brushed past her in an obvious rage. "You took a mighty long time to open up, didn't you? Crise, I must have stood out there at least a half hour."

"I'm sorry, Lou. It's after four. I was sound asleep. I really didn't hear you. Where were you?" She shuffled back to bed. He ignored her question, undressed in the dark, and lay down.

Friday night, when she came home from work, Lou was already getting dressed to go out and stayed locked in the bathroom for almost an hour before he emerged looking impeccably polished.

Her stomach churned. "Lou, why so dressed up? Are you going somewhere special?" she asked, frowning.

"Yeah, this is my bowling night, remember? I'm in a tournament at the Parkland Hotel. We're competing in the Provincials."

He picked up a small overnight bag and disappeared with it into the bedroom. She heard the sound of dresser drawers opening and closing. Fifteen minutes later, he reappeared with bag in hand.

Her mouth sagged. "Lou, I hope you're not planning to stay the weekend again."

"Why shouldn't I? You didn't let me in the last time I came in late. God damn it, Tanya, it's your own fault! Just what do you expect me to do? Huh? ... Uh-h-h, I'll eat dinner over there, so don't bother cooking anything." He put on his suit jacket, ran a comb through his hair, and with bowling kit in one hand and overnight case in the other, he strode out of the suite.

Tanya, resigning herself to the inevitable, emptied a can of soup into a pot and set one bowl on the table. The upheaval didn't give her much of an appetite, but she ate the soup, then sat down to watch television before dozing off. At midnight she stirred, and only half awake groped her way to the bed, grateful that she'd trained herself to fall asleep with or without Lou. Burrowing under the covers, she fell into a deep slumber.

Suddenly, for no apparent reason, she awoke with a start and sat bolt upright. The clock read three-thirty A.M. How strange, that at this very moment, she had the distinct feeling that Lou was with another woman.

She threw back the quilt and ran to the phone. Lou had the "Parkland" hotel number listed in their personal directory. She dialed it with shaking fingers.

"Parkland Hotel, how may I help you?"

She calmed herself as best she could. "Could you please tell me if Lou Hagen is registered there? Could you dial his room number for me, please!"

Her request was followed by a long pause. "I'm sorry ma'am but we're not allowed to give out that information about our guests. Sorry!"

"But, but, he's my husband! He's with his bowling team. They're playing there. ... Surely I'm entitled to speak to my husband!"

"It's rather late. Sorry, ma'am."

Trembling, she put down the receiver and went back to bed. There was no doubt in her mind that Lou was with someone else. An urgency to grieve, to cry, came over her. She stifled it, knowing that it would only make her feel worse. It took some time for her heart to quiet down. By then, dawn was starting to break.

The weekend slipped by with no sign of Lou. When she awoke Monday morning, he still hadn't shown up. However, when she came home from work, he was waiting for her in the suite, dressed in his work clothes. "Hi."

"Hi." He picked up his overnight bag and went to the bedroom to unpack.

She wanted to ask him where he'd been but changed her mind and busied herself with getting the meal on the table. "Lou, supper's ready."

He sat down, helped himself to some chili, and ignored her probing eyes.

Tanya suppressed her depression, reassuring herself that he still needed her. After all, who would pay the bills if not her? She stuck to a rigid routine whether Lou was present or not. If he was home, she cooked for two, if not, she ate alone.

33

A YEAR LATER, ANNA MARRIED ANTON MOROZ. The ceremony took place in the United Church at Grand Plains.

It was Mama's first meeting with Lou. Tanya, who was apprehensive about the outcome, introduced them. One look at Lou and Mama's face went dead white. She recoiled, taking a step back, much to Tanya's embarrassment.

"Tanya ... this man is ... is ... Indian ... isn't he?"

"Mama, please!"

Mama looked at her, alarmed. "Why did you marry him?"

Lou took it in stride, simply shrugging his shoulders and keeping a poker face, while Mama spent some time crying to herself. Later, realizing that what was done was done, she behaved more civilly towards her new son-in-law. To Tanya's surprise, Lou magnanimously overlooked her mother's rude behavior, displaying a patience she didn't think he had in him.

Her stepfather, cold and disdainful, after shaking Lou's hand, avoided him.

A small reception was held for Anna at the farmhouse. Mama, having appraised Anton critically, called Tanya to one side. "What does Anton do for a living?" she asked, for Anna hadn't said much about him ... only that Anton was of Ukrainian descent and that his mother was of the Greek Orthodox faith.

Tanya looked surprised. "Didn't she tell you? He drives a truck for Alberta Poultry."

Mama frowned.

"Don't worry, Mama, it's steady work. He'll be all right."

"I'm not so sure. But you can tell her that if she expects to live on love to forget it, because she'll have a hard time of it. Why even in Poland, if a man didn't have a trade, he was counted less than nothing. But, I suppose, it's none of my business. Well, she makes her bed, she sleeps in it." Sigh.

34

FORCING ITS WAY THROUGH THE BASEMENT WINDOW, a patch of sunlight warmed her face. If only there was some way that she could save enough for a house! She knew if it were left up to Lou, he wouldn't care if they lived in a tent. Tanya thought it could be done provided they both pooled their incomes. However, since Lou spent all his salary on himself, she was compelled to keep up the payments on his most recent car, the groceries, rent, her clothes.

Small wonder she could save any money at all. But it didn't hurt to dream.

She jerked her head around as footsteps approached. The door opened and Lou walked in.

"Hi, you're home early. It's only five-thirty."

"Hi." He threw his jacket over a chair, lit a cigarette, opened the fridge for a beer and turned on the television, rebounding onto the couch. Drawing heavily, he let out a cloud of smoke and stared at the ceiling, while waiting for the picture to come into focus.

She looked at him, exasperated. Their communication had dwindled down to very few words. Sometimes, several days went by without Lou acknowledging that she was even in the room. She sighed. It was his loss. The phone rang just as Tanya was about to start the meal. "Lou, could you? ... Well, never mind, since you're watching television ... hello?"

A slight hesitation then a woman's voice asked, "May I speak to Lou, please?"

"Who shall I say is calling?"

"This is Rene."

She held the receiver out to him. "It's Rene."

"Thanks."

"Hi Rene. How're you doin'?" He stretched, yawned, and dangled his free arm over his head. ... "Great! Uh-huh. ... Well, how bout seven? Is that okay? ... Fine by me. I'll pick you up." He put the phone down and turned to Tanya. "Rene's on my bowling team. She wants a ride."

She had the feeling that it was more than just a ride.

"Uh-h-h, I gotta go. Don't bother with supper for me." Lou hurried into the bathroom to shower. Lately, she'd noticed he'd changed to a more daring openness, presumably to see how much he could get away with. At the same time, she felt herself slipping away from him.

She shut her eyes, took a deep breath, letting it out slowly, conscious of a floating feeling at the pit of her stomach. She knew it was brought on by Lou's abuse. Was she losing touch? Inside her, she could literally feel a string being cut each time she had to face some shocking revelation. At the present, she felt there was little enough left to anchor her down with. Oh, Lord, will I be all right? Must keep a tighter grip. Barely a half hour slipped by before Lou left the suite.

She went to the phone and called Alisha to talk, thinking it might help to get her mind off the depression. "Hi, how are you?" she asked.

"I'm fine. And you?"

"Fine. Is Allen all right, and the children? ... Dan? ... Is Dan all right?" Dan, their son, was their pride and joy.

"Dan's fine. How's Lou?"

"He's okay. He bought another car. Uh-h-h, I think it's a Pontiac."

"Well, that's nice. When are you two coming to see us?"

"I don't know, but we'll surprise you one of these days."

The conversation was aimless since nothing pertinent was discussed. She couldn't bring herself to share any of her misery with either one of her sisters. Within her, she felt an urgency to keep her life a secret, a trait carried over from childhood. She said "good bye" and hung up more determined than ever to keep silent.

35

THE LEAVES ON THE MAPLE TREE OUTSIDe the suite were at their ultimate splendor in late September. Later, coming home from work, Tanya was surprised to see the tree nearly stripped bare. She paused to examine it. Then, reminding herself that Lou had suggested an early movie at the Strand, she hurried on. It had been some time since they'd been out together.

Lou walked in just as she was setting the table. "Hi. I hope you don't mind soup and sandwiches?"

"Okay by me. Be there soon's I wash up."

They finished eating in fifteen minutes. Tanya left the dishes in the sink then went to touch up her make-up. Lou was already dressed and waiting for her by the door, impatient to get going. "Come on, Tanya, hell, the picture will be half over if we don't get a move on."

"Yes, you're right."

He started ahead of her; she hurried to catch up. By the time she tugged the car door open, Lou had the motor running. She shut it just as

Lou slammed on the gas pedal, throwing her back. She frowned. "We still have half an hour before it starts, you know."

Lou's profile looked grim. "That's not a helluva lot of time."

He drove to the main part of town. It took a while to find a parking place. He got out of the car, and took up a fast pace, his long steps making it impossible for her to keep up. Suddenly she froze, as Lou stopped to admire two very attractive girls walking in front of them. He let out a long wolf whistle. They looked back at him and giggled.

Tanya curbed the urge to say something cutting just as Lou got behind the line-up to buy tickets. She noticed the cashier, very blond, very pretty. In a flash Lou became transformed while Tanya stood by in hopeless agony, expecting the inevitable.

"Two, please."

"Here you are, sir."

He winked at her, grinning in open admiration, as she blushed prettily. "Baby, you are special!"

Behind him, Tanya felt her panic mount as she felt another string cut loose. Jealousy exploded inside her. Why couldn't he make time with the girl when he was on his own?

"This way, please." The usherette led them to front and centre.

Tanya slumped into her seat and tried to concentrate on the picture, though the evening was already spoiled. His flirting was something that she could never accept. Now she waited with impatience for the movie to end. When it finished, they got up and began to move out with the crowd.

Lou turned to her. "Wanna get something to eat? Maybe a burger?"

She almost said "yes", but then, he'd probably make a pass at the waitress. "No, I don't feel like eating."

"Aw-w-w, what a bitch!"

Tanya blocked out the words and sat silent in the car until they got to the suite. She noticed that Lou kept the motor running while he let her off. She turned to shut the door. Without warning, Lou accelerated and drove away. She raised her hand in utter disbelief. ... "Lou, where ...?" Tears stung her eyes as she made her way into the darkened basement alone.

At week's end, Friday, she braced herself to spend the next three days without him. As expected, Lou came home, polished his shoes, showered, doused himself with after shave, then dressed in just the right shirt and tie without so much as a glance at her.

Tanya sighed, then turned to prepare her meal. She was half finished eating a hamburger when he walked out of the bedroom fumbling with a pair of gold cuff links. She stared at them. They had been a gift from her on their wedding day! "Going somewhere?" she asked.

"Yeah, out." He smiled at her, picked up the car keys and left.

"Out" had become his standard answer to her queries.

In exasperation, she pushed her plate away, quietly raging within as she wandered aimlessly from bedroom to sitting room, chafing with discontent. She picked up a copy of the "The Bulletin," lying on the coffee table. Absentmindedly, her eyes focused on an ad. ... 'Why not put the fun back into your life? You, too, can be the life of the party! Sign up for ARTHUR MURRAY dance lessons today!' There was an address and phone number at the bottom of the page.

She read it again, thinking that it must feel gratifying to be a good dancer. She'd always been intrigued with someone who could dance well. Most psychologists considered dancing good mental therapy. ... What if she started disappearing nights? It might give Lou something to worry about! ... There would be men there.

She went to the phone, wondering if she should call? Not to commit herself, of course ... but only to get more information. Astounded by her daring, her heart picked up a faster rhythm.

"Arthur Murray Dance Studio. May I help you?"

"Uh-h-h, do you give dance lessons?"

"Yes, we certainly do."

"Uh-h-h, could I come by just to try? I mean, I'm not really sure I even want to ..."

"You're welcome to come and watch us instruct, if you like. How about Thursday? Thursdays, we have open house ... and you can bring a friend. It won't cost you anything. The lessons start at eight P.M."

"Thursday? Hm-m-m, yes, that might be all right. Yes, I think I can make it. ... Uh-h-h, I'll think it over. Thank you."

She hung up, trying to place Lou on a Thursday night. It didn't matter. Other than the lies, he never confided in her. If he asks, I'll say I'm going "out."

On the following Thursday, Tanya didn't have to worry about Lou;

he was long gone before eight. She showered, dressed, and made it to the studio on time. Climbing the stairs, the very idea sent shivers up her spine. However, having come this far, she wasn't about to turn back.

At the top of the second floor, there was a glass door with "Arthur Murray Dance Studio" printed in gold letters. She took a deep breath and opened it.

The room was large and mirrored. It was tastefully decorated in Italian Provincial. She felt a lift. Small groups of men and women stood talking and drinking coffee. They were well dressed and appeared to be at different age levels.

"Hi! May I help you?" A tall, blond man, good-looking, young, held out his hand to her. "My name is Brent Styles. I'm the manager. This is my wife Shirley."

Tanya nodded at his wife but shrank away from him, thinking of her clammy palms. Reluctantly, she touched his hand only briefly. "Hi, I'm Tanya Hagen. I was wondering if I could try some lessons ... Uh-h-h, do you teach modern jive?"

"My dear, we teach everything. Seems everybody these days wants to learn modern jive. ... Come, let's introduce you to the other students. How would you like to be my partner for tonight?"

Smiling, he tucked her hand under his arm.

She felt herself blushing. "Oh, that would be wonderful!" She sensed a warmth about him. "How much do the lessons cost?" she asked, wondering if they were affordable.

"We give group instruction. They're not expensive. Four lessons will cost you only $15.00. How's that?"

She relaxed. "Actually, it sounds very reasonable."

He flashed a smile at her. Good, she thought, that's exactly what I need. Lately, she'd been feeling shaky. The lessons might bring her back onto solid footing. Brent led the way to a group of men.

"Tanya, I'd like you to meet Jerry Holton, John Reed, Louis Mouton. Gentlemen, Tanya Hagen. ... She'll be joining us."

Trembling, she smiled at them, wondering what Lou would say if he knew where she was. Brent led her to another group of men.

"You'll be dancing with all of them before the lessons are finished," he remarked. Suddenly, loud music filled the room.

Brent turned to her and bowed. "Shall we? ... A one, a two, a three

..." They whirled away.

He was amazingly light on his feet. With a partner such as him, I'll have no trouble learning, she thought.

Her spirits lifted by the music, she forgot about Lou. She felt mildly stimulated and more normal then she'd been in a long time. The time seemed to fly; it was fun. Some of the men even flirted with her. She found herself flirting back.

At ten, she went home, still unsure of what to say if Lou should ask where she'd been. The bus let her off; she flew to the suite. Breathless, she flung open the door. Lou was still out! Her mood flagged, making her wonder where he'd gone and the worry and the old feelings came back.

She washed her face, brushed her teeth, and went to sleep, curling up in a corner of their double bed, grateful to have had a short reprieve from the dull, abhorrent life that she endured from day to day with Lou.

The next Thursday she went again. This time her partner was Jerry Holton. Jerry was tall, slim, and dark haired. He had a small mustache and could be considered handsome. She felt that he was as nervous as she was. She could feel his palm, wet and sticky through the sheer, violet blouse she wore.

"Hey, you're doing good," he remarked nervously.

She nodded. "Thank you, and so are you. ... Ouch!" She only mouthed the word when his foot crushed down on her sandaled toes.

He looked dismayed. "Sorry! Did I hurt you?"

"No, no, not at all," she assured him, quickly testing it. The pain began to subside.

"Tanya?" His hand tensed at her waist.

"Yes?"

"May I drive you home?"

"Uh-h-h," she floundered. She was married. But why not accept? Wasn't she here to teach Lou a lesson? "Yes, thank you. That would be fine."

As she was about to get into his beat-up Buick, he reminded her of Lou during their courtship, opening doors, helping her on with her coat. ... He started the motor.

"Where do you work, Jerry?"

"I go to University. I'm a law student. This is my third year. What about you?"

"I work for the Federal Government. Actually, I'm the supervisor of a steno pool." She stopped, afraid to say more, reminding herself that it would only create problems should he attempt to get in touch with her.

"Are you enjoying the dance lessons?" he asked.

"Yes, very much. Brent is a good instructor." They were almost at her suite before she felt a twinge of fear intermingled with guilt. The question of Lou reared its ugly head. "Jerry, stop! Please stop! Uh-h-h, do you think you could let me off here? Actually, I'd like to walk the rest of the way. I love the month of June, and really, it's such a lovely night." What if, heaven forbid, Lou should see her in this strange man's car?

"Are you sure? We don't have much further to go." However, he slowed the car and stopped. Taking her hand, he gave it a squeeze.

She recoiled. Then, thinking that she mustn't risk encouraging him any further, she withdrew her hand.

"See you next week?" he asked.

"Yes, see you next week. Thanks, Jerry." She jumped out and waved him on. Though she liked him, and she was sure that he liked her, it didn't seem right. No matter how badly Lou treated her, it didn't make it right! Nothing made it right. Even if Lou was cheating on her, it would still be wrong.

She walked home, upset, angry, knowing that Jerry Holton wasn't anything like Lou. It would be so easy to fall in love with someone like him ... to have a decent life ...

She opened the door and walked in to find Lou already home. He sat turned away from her, with the phone pressed to his ear. Her heart gave a jump. Would he notice that she was dressed up? Surely, he'd be curious?

"Okay, Bob. Yeah. See you tomorrow." Lou put down the receiver and switched channels on the T.V. before lying back on the sofa. He merely glanced at her.

Tanya gave him a searching look, then went into the bedroom, upset that he wasn't the least bit interested.

However, on the following Thursday, she deliberately chose a different partner, knowing that it wouldn't be fair to Jerry Holton to be led on by a married woman. At times, she caught him looking at her and forced herself to look away.

The lesson ended. Tanya went out the door as quickly as possible, knowing that as long as she was married to Lou, she would remain faithful to Lou.

After work the next day, she decided to do the laundry. Since Lou was going out, it was good to have something to do other than think and wonder about him. She picked up the laundry basket and began sorting the whites from the darks. He was in the bathroom, getting dressed. "Lou, do you have anything that you want me to wash?" she asked.

"Nuthin."

She reached down for one of his white shirts then stiffened, noticing a red mark on the collar. It looked like lipstick! Her heart began a rapid pounding. Hurriedly, she scrambled through the other shirts. All his dress shirts had the same telltale marks! The shorts she found to be sticky with semen. She snatched up a handful of his clothes and marched to the bathroom.

Lou was busy filing his long nails which he kept tapered to perfection.

"Lou, what's this?"

"What's what?" he asked, poised and unconcerned. He looked suave, with a silver tie knotted at his throat and patent shoes polished to a mirror finish. Was he off to a rendezvous with someone? "What's this?" Tanya pointed to the lipstick marks. She threw down a pair of shorts at his feet. "How did this happen? Where do you go every night? Answer me! Damn it! Are you having an affair with someone?"

The nail file was carefully tucked into his pocket. Suddenly, she noticed his face coming closer ... then a sudden blur before everything went black. When she came to, she was lying on the floor dazed, confused. Strangely, she couldn't remember falling. Slowly, her head cleared. She saw Lou, towering above her, shaking with rage, his hands clenched, his knuckles white.

"It's none of your God damn business where I go. I'll come and go as I like. And, by Crise, don't you try to stop me! Keep on nagging and you'll get more!"

She lay quivering with fear, not daring to move, threatened by a feeling that he would surely kill her should she rise. She started to sit up. "I'll leave, if that's the way you feel!"

His lips curled back into a sneer. "What d'you mean, slut? You'll leave?" He laughed. "No, you won't. Hell, I'll find you, and I'll kill you. Remember, I've got a gun." He snapped his fingers. "I'll make it look like you cracked up and committed suicide. Simple as that. Don't think you can screw me and get away with it!"

Horrified, she remained on the floor ... just in case he tried hitting her again.

Lou whipped out a pack of cigarettes and lit one. Taking a long pull, he muttered, "God damn, bitch!" before striding out of the suite.

Slowly, she pulled herself to her feet. It was difficult to keep her balance. She opened her mouth, testing her jaw where it hurt. Suddenly it dawned on her that Lou had knocked her out. A feeling of despair rocked through her. It was all wrong. He was the one cheating on her ... yet he was behaving as if she had no right to question him about it. How could they go on living together? She collapsed onto the couch, breaking into sobs, remembering that the very day they'd returned from their honeymoon he'd phoned some woman then immediately left the suite. He was having the time of his life, while she was providing him with all the comforts of home and living on the hope that he'd soon realize his mistakes and become a decent husband. Could she leave him? Remembering his threats, she knew that she had reason to doubt that she could. Fear, like bile, rose within her, haunted by his words, 'I'll kill you'!

Tanya threw herself into her work, her suffering dulled only by the passage of time as one day followed the next, while Lou kept on with the dating game.

Fearing for her safety, she decided to let things pass and overlook his wayward life. It took all her will power to patch things up between them and act as if nothing unusual had happened.

36

DOMINION DAY, JULY 1ST, DAWNED. The long weekend always brought on a celebration with fireworks and a parade down Main Street.

Though it was a holiday, Tanya, who awakened early, was surprised to find Lou still home. Their third anniversary had just passed and he'd made no mention of it to her. That weekend, as usual, he'd left the suite returning home on the following Monday after work. It was just as well, she thought, when one considered the kind of marriage they had.

However, today he was home. I'll make the day special, she thought. I'll bake a chocolate cake for dinner. Lou had a weakness for chocolate. Inside her was a longing for a stable home life, unmarred by emotional swings. Outside, the day was rapidly warming. She picked out a mix and poured the contents into a bowl, wondering if Nora and Ron had already moved into their new apartment, at the same time reminding herself that she'd promised to help Nora arrange her furniture after the move. Nora had no sense of home decor.

The couple were Lou's friends. Nora O'Reilly and Ron Brandon lived together common-law. An arrangement that Tanya didn't care about. People gossiped and there were questions from anyone who found out. At present, Ron was unemployed and looking for work, while Nora waitressed at "The Pancake House."

Now, half-way through the mix, the phone rang. "Lou, will you get that? If it's Nora, tell her I'll be over just as soon as I'm finished baking this cake. Uh-h-h, tell her in about an hour."

Lou put down his coffee and picked up the receiver. "Hello? ... No, she's busy, baking a cake or something. ... Yeah, she'll be over later. ..." He smiled. "He's not? ... Why not come here? Uh-huh. Nora, give me a minute, okay? I'll come getchya. ... Hey, I could do that for you. ... Aw-w-w, come on, sure I can. I'm every bit as good as Tanya. It ain't no trouble, honest. Okay, see you in a while." He hung up and turned toward Tanya. "I'm going to Ron's to get Nora. You don't mind, do you? Ron's out someplace."

She turned off the mixer. "Fine, if that's what she wants."

"Okay, be back in a little while." Lou flipped a comb through his hair as he passed a mirror. He appeared quite energized and went bounding up the basement steps two at a time.

She paused, feeling uncomfortable thinking about the two of them alone. Nora was the kind of girl most men dreamed about. She had flowing, raven black hair, a voluptuous figure, deep blue eyes, and a complexion like cream. However, since Lou was Ron's best friend, it wasn't likely he'd fool with his girlfriend.

She slid the cake into the oven, washed the dishes and straightened up the suite. Half an hour later, she set the cake on the counter to cool, wondering what had happened to Lou? The new apartment was only a ten minute walk down the street. Both she and Nora had rejoiced about this fact.

Another two hours went by with still no sign of Lou or Nora. She began to feel edgy as she poked about from room to room, suspecting the worst. By the time she heard their voices, her stomach was in knots. She was ready to cry at any given moment. Tanya turned to watch them enter, wondering whether her suspicions were correct and if Lou really had ...?

Lou gallantly held the door open for Nora to let her in. Perspiration, like dew, glistened on his forehead. There was a self satisfied contentment about him.

Nora's cheeks were flushed, her hair slightly tangled, her face aglow. Tanya pretended not to notice the secret exchange that passed between them.

Nora looked at Tanya and smiled. "Hi, how are you?"

Sick at heart, Tanya turned away from her. How was she supposed to react to someone who'd just had sex with her husband? She started to shake. "Uh-h-h, fine, just fine, Nora. Did Lou help you move your furniture? You were gone a long time, Lou," she probed, her tone dull.

Lou smiled, sat down on the chesterfield, and lit a cigarette.

Nora gave him a lingering look. "Oh yeah, Lou helped me an awful lot. I could never have moved all those heavy pieces by myself." "Uh-h-h, I forgot to say "thanks," Lou. You were wonderful." She went to the couch and rumpled his black hair with long, red tipped nails.

Laughing, he playfully caught her by the wrists. "Hey, kid, watch that stuff. Besides, it was a-a-ll my pleasure."

Tanya bit her tongue in despair, thinking, I'll bet it was! She curbed the urge to shout at them that she knew, curbed the urge to lash out in anger that they weren't fooling her.

Lou, smiling, turned towards her. "Uh-h-h, I forgot to tell you, I asked Nora and Ron for supper. Do we have enough to feed them?"

"Yes, I think so." She grimaced, and busied herself at the counter, unable to meet Nora's eyes when she came to see what she was doing.

"Hm-m-m, chocolate cake, my very favorite! Mind if I have a taste?"

The friendliness seemed overdone! Stupid girl! Why didn't she shut up? Didn't she realize that she'd just been used? ... "Yes, of course. Here's a knife. Let me cut you a piece. It happens to be Lou's favorite, too." She threw him a sideways glance before slicing into it. "Lou, would you like some cake?"

"No, thanks. Maybe later."

Nora took her plate to the couch and sat down beside Lou to eat it. Their charade continued until Ron walked in.

At eleven o'clock, the couple went home. Tanya, who'd had to cook the meal and serve them, felt tortured.

As soon as they were gone, Lou stretched, yawned, and flopped down on the couch. "I tell ya baby, I've had one helluva day."

"I know what you mean, Lou, I have too." There was a weight on her chest. She finished the dishes an hour later and put away the tea-towel, then went into the bedroom to put on her nightgown.

Suddenly, in despair, she slid to her knees beside the bed and covered her face with her hands. "Dear Lord, please, please, change things for me. I don't know how much longer I can stand this. I don't even know if I can keep sane. Please, Lord, change it for me!"

She wept quietly, rocking back and forth, thinking that nothing, but nothing, had improved for her and that Lou would never change.

37

TANYA SHARPENED HER PENCIL FOR THE THIRD TIME before going over the figures once more. "Lou, I've checked the bank balance three times and, you know, there's just a little over $1200.00 left in the bank. What's happened to all the money? You know, I deposit nearly my entire salary into that account. ... I buy very little. Where's the money going to?" Anger, intermixed with futility, made her fidgety and nervous.

"Search me. How should I know? You do all the bankin'." Lou lay on the couch, his eyes half closed, drawing on a cigarette.

"Lou, we're spending far too much money. We've got to cut back. If an emergency comes up, we'll have nothing to tide us over. What's more, we'll never get ahead. I'm trying to save enough for a house. I hate this suite. I hate living here."

"What emergency? Ain't nothing wrong with the suite. You worry too much. That's the trouble with your kind. You're always worrying. Shit!"

He put down the cigarette and stretched lazily, reminding her of a cat in warm sunshine. Seeing him unmindful, unconcerned, her temper got the upper hand. "What's my kind, Lou? Just because I want something more than this dungeon, I'm being criticized?"

"Well, look at your whole family. Crise, all they ever think about is money. My family don't. Did you ever see me worrying? Never! Relax! Enjoy! Hell, a house ain't gonna help none. You were brought up with the wrong kinda philosophy."

She reigned in her rage and turned her attention to the bills at hand thinking, who could she blame but herself? Shortly after they were married, blinded by love, she'd changed her savings account into a joint account that included Lou. It had been a stupid thing to do! He could very well twitter away every dime that she made, spending both their salaries! Never once did he put in one cent of his paycheck into the account, though she'd often suggested that it wouldn't hurt to have him contribute at least $50.00 a month. He'd always refused, pointing out that he needed it for gas and bowling fees.

Lou opened his eyes a slit. "I thought I should let you know the Dodge is acting up. Yesterday morning, I couldn't get the damn thing started. And, baby, I tried."

Her fury returned, rekindled. "But you just bought the Dodge! Can't it be fixed? Lou, we can't afford a new car. If that's what you've got in mind, forget it!" In the three and a half years that they were married, Lou had traded off eight different vehicles.

"Well, I'm not so sure that it can be fixed. ... Okay, tomorrow, after work, I'll take it to Watson Motors ... if I have the time." He dozed off.

Tanya knew the signs: the none too subtle hint about the "car acting up" could only mean that he'd found something sportier. By the end of the week, he'd have it traded. Her reward? ... A ride to the grocery store. Lou never bothered to repair anything.

At eleven o'clock, she put the bills away, seething that it was her and not Lou who paid for everything. If he kept on, her dream of owning a house would remain just that, a dream. Suddenly, overcome by an empty, desolate feeling, she went into the bedroom and knelt down. She'd come to depend on the prayers and the peace that they brought her. She remembered her icon, and brought it out. "Oh Lord, please help me. Can't you see, Lord, that I'm barely hanging on? I can see nothing but heartache in my life. Please, Lord, there's got to be more!" The prayers always strengthened her. ... Strangely, the strength had been granted to her the very day that she'd found out about Lou and Nora. The day she thought she couldn't live through.

Later, when Lou came to bed, she pretended to be asleep. The mattress creaked under his weight as he stretched out to full length. Tanya waited until his breathing evened out. Though her head ached, she wanted to think.

Ben Hagen, Lou's father, came to mind. At sixty he was a vital and still very handsome man. Whereas Lou's mother, who was only fifty-two, looked ninety. Ben, smiling, affable, gracious, had had the nerve to make a pass at her shortly after Lou had introduced them. Small wonder that his son was doing the same thing. Would she look ninety when she was fifty-two? Tanya sensed that the poor woman must have had a hard life. It was near morning and dawn was almost breaking before she resigned herself to sleep.

At six A.M. she awakened with a full blown migraine, wondering how she could endure working the entire day. "Lou, are you up?" she asked, running the water full force into the bathtub. Sometimes, a hot bath helped.

"Yeah," he croaked.

In a few minutes she smelled the acrid smoke from his cigarette. She grimaced, feeling nauseous.

Mornings were always the same because Lou never spoke unless forced to. What did people talk about in the morning? The weather? The news? She got out of the tub and dried herself off.

"Lou, do you want bacon for breakfast?"

"Yeah." He ate quickly, never once lifting his head to look at her.

At work, the migraine didn't let up as she found herself battling with Lou's spending habits. What if he didn't stop until every dime was gone? With his lust for cars, it could very well happen. She gulped down two aspirin and forced herself to concentrate on a letter that she was typing.

Louise, her co-worker, caught her attention. "Coming for lunch, Tanya?"

"Uh-h-h, no, not today. I think I'll eat right here at my desk."

"Hey, aren't you feeling well?" She bent down to examine her. "You have shadows under your eyes. You look beat!"

"No ... no, I'm all right. I had a late night."

"Okay. I'll be in the lunch room, if you change your mind."

Tanya worked through the lunch hour, keeping a check on the time. She was dying to get home ... and dreading it. Some things had to be ironed out with Lou. On the other hand, with her head still aching, she wanted to lie down and rest.

She was homeward bound the minute the clock struck five, wondering how to approach him and what his reaction would be? Her stomach convulsed at the thought, knowing that she'd have to tell him "no more cars," and that was final!

On the ride home, she began planning her strategy. There would surely be a fight. She got off the bus, taking note that the car was nowhere in sight.

Tanya unlocked the door to the suite and stepped inside, pausing to adjust to the dimness. Her eyes swept over the room, suddenly aware that something was not right. She looked everywhere at once, wondering what had happened to Lou's jacket? His coats? The hooks were empty! She ran to the bedroom and flung open the closet door. His side was bare; his clothes gone! All that remained were some wire hangers. Lou was gone! He had left her! A weight lifted off her chest. She walked to the couch, slumped down, and began to cry.

38

"LOU LEFT YOU?" Alisha echoed her words. "When?"

"Yesterday."

"Do you know where he went?"

"To Banff with some girl. Bob McFee told me when I phoned him to ask where Lou was. He knew that Lou was cheating on me. Lou didn't try to hide it from him. He even told him that he'd married me for my money. Imagine that!"

"So he took off with a another woman ... to Banff? Well, you just pack up your stuff and get over here. You can stay with us for a while. I'll have to check with Allen first, of course. To tell you the truth, I'm glad. Now you can divorce him. You know, I always thought he was no good. And I never changed my mind about that."

"Yes, I know."

That evening, Allen Semco moved Tanya and her meagre possessions into their house. Tanya knew that with the recent birth of their third child, Gloria, the bedrooms were filled to capacity. By coincidence Anna had also given birth to a baby girl about the same time. She wondered what kind of a father Lou would have been if they'd had a child? She willed the thought away.

"Do you mind sharing a room with Maria?" Alisha asked.

"Are you kidding? I'd sleep on the floor if I had to. You know what else I did?"

"No, what?"

"I closed our joint account and took all the money out. Won't Lou be surprised?"

The sisters smiled at each other. "Yeah, won't he?"

"Tanya, you should ask Allen about a lawyer. Lou has certainly given you good grounds for a divorce. You don't want him back, do you?"

"No, I don't! Alisha, you haven't heard the half of it."

"Well, you know, I always had the feeling that something was wrong. What bothers me is why you didn't leave him sooner?"

"I don't know! Don't ask! ... Fear, I guess."

39

Charles Stinton's secretary ushered Tanya into the lawyer's inner office. After the introductions, she left them alone.

The tall, portly man with thinning grey hair looked about fifty. Allen had assured her that he was the best divorce lawyer in town. She sat down across from him, feeling on edge, her nerves frayed.

"Now, Mrs. Hagen, what seems to be the problem?"

"Mr. Stinton, I, uh-h-h, want to divorce Lou, my husband. Sorry, I'm quite nervous. I, uh-h-h, don't know where to begin."

"No need to be nervous, Mrs. Hagen. Please, tell me everything. Everything you say will be kept strictly confidential ... I assure you."

"Please call me Tanya."

He smiled. "Tanya. ... And, I'm Charles, call me Charles. I've always found it best to operate on a casual basis. Makes for better communication."

"Thank you, Charles. ... Uh-h-h, Lou and I have been married for only three and a half years ... ." Gradually, she led him along the horror path of her marriage. It was painful. She choked with emotion and stopped to wipe away tears as she poured out the secrets of her life. Tanya finished her story, unable to remember how long it had taken her. She sighed, thinking how the rendition had left her with a feeling of being cleansed.

Charles Stinton shook his head. "It sounds as if you've had a hard life. I must say, yours is an extreme case, no doubt about it. Definitely, you got yourself a lemon, honey. However, I know how to handle his type. First, we'll have you both come in to see me. Then we'll see what he's willing to admit to on his own. Leave it to me, and don't worry about a thing. I've handled worse than him ... believe me." Smiling, he checked through an appointment book. "Uh-h-h, how about three weeks from today, July 24th, at one P.M..?"

"Yes, that will be fine with me. I'll take the time off from work. I don't know about Lou, but I'll check. There's one more thing I must know. Uh-h-h, how much will it cost? I'll have to foot the bill myself, Lou has no money." She was beginning to feel more secure about cutting the strings from him.

"Well, depending on how much investigative work we have to do, ... roughly around $500.00. ... My dear, I would strongly advise the divorce, at whatever cost to you; it will be well worth your trouble to be rid of him!"

"You're right, of course."

"Get in touch with Lou and let me know if he can be here on that day. And please, other than that, no contact with him whatsoever."

As soon as Lou returned from his Banff vacation, Tanya phoned to let him know about the date that Charles Stinton had set for them. Lou merely drawled, "If that's the way you want it, okay baby."

The phone rang while they were having dinner. Alisha, who was feeding Gloria, handed the child to Tanya. "Here, take her for a minute."

It was Lou. "May I speak to Tanya?"

"Just a moment, please." Alisha turned to Allen to whisper,

"It's Lou! What shall I say to him? He wants to speak to Tanya."

Tanya sat motionless, remembering Charles Stinton's last words to her. "Please, no contact ... whatsoever!"

Allen held out his hand. "Let me have it. Once they're separated, they're separated, he has no legal rights to demand anything. Hello? ... No, she doesn't want to talk to you. ... Yes, that's right. She has nothing to say to you." He hung up. "That should spell it out for him."

Lou called several more times that week, hoping that Tanya would answer. Each time Alisha took the calls, assuring him that Tanya was out even though she was standing but a few feet away.

The next Saturday, Lou surprised them by driving to the house to speak to her.

Alisha saw him coming up the walk and motioned to Allen. "Allen, it's Lou, would you please answer the door."

He put down his paper and turned to Tanya. "You keep out of sight. I'll handle this. He's not gonna push me around." Allen walked to the front door and glared at Lou. "Yes, what do you want?"

Lou looked grim. "I want to see my wife."

"Well, she doesn't want to see you."

"She's still my wife, I have a right to see her if I want to, don't I?"

"No you don't! This happens to be my property. Get off my property! And get off the step!"

"But I ..."

"You heard me, I said beat it."

Lou turned white and started to walk away. He wasn't prepared to deal with Allen's anger.

"And don't try coming back. I don't want to see your face here again." Allen locked the door behind him. "He's not gonna play any mind games with me. Tell Tanya she can come out now." He picked up the newspaper and sat down.

However, later that week Lou phoned again. This time, it was Tanya who picked up the receiver.

"Crise, Tanya, am I glad it's you that answered. For a minute, you had me worried. Don't you ever wanna talk to me again?"

She felt a slight shock go through her. "No, Lou, I don't. It's over between us."

"But Tanya, I still love you, baby! Come back to me. We can still make a go of it. Honest! Listen, honey, I'll reform! I'll change. I'll change for you, baby. You gotta believe me!"

"No, Lou! ... We can talk in the lawyer's office. Did you get Charles Stinton's letter? ... Yes? ... Good! If you want to say something, be in his office at one o'clock on Wednesday. Is that date okay with you? ... Lou? ... Lou? Are you still there, Lou?"

"I won't do it. I won't give you the divorce. You got no proof of anything."

"No proof? Lou, we both knew what was going on! You didn't keep it a secret."

"Yeah? ... Okay, I'll make a deal with you. I'll give you the divorce on one condition."

"What condition, Lou?"

"You pay me $1200.00 and you can have the divorce."

"$1200.00? Lou! You want the rest of the money that I have in the bank, don't you? ... Make sure you're at Charles' office on the 24th! That's all I have to say." She hung up, her stomach churning, thinking that this was sure proof that he'd married her for the pittance that she'd saved up. He had his nerve!

40

TANYA, PALE, THINNER, WITH HER MOUTH SET INTO A SOMBRE LINE, walked into the reception room with Charles Stinton. Lou sat hunched over, nervously chain smoking. He looked up and instantly mashed his cigarette into an ashtray.

She averted her eyes from the look of pleading that he sent her.

The lawyer nodded to Lou. "Mr. Hagen, I presume?"

"Yeah."

"This way, please." They filed into his inner office. "Sit down, Mr. Hagen."

Tanya sat down next to Charles, facing Lou.

"Mr. Hagen, we're here to discuss your divorce."

"Well ... ah-h-h, yeah, she told me. You can't pin nothing on me, I never did nothing." His lips curved into a cold smile.

Charles Stinton leaned forward. A thick folder lay in front of him. He placed his right hand on the file with his fingers resting lightly on top. "Mr. Hagen, adultery is the only admissible grounds for a divorce in a court of law. In this file, I assure you, we have definite proof of adultery." He tapped lightly on the edge of the cover. "Need I go any further? You see, a "Miss Rose Bennit" is willing to testify on our behalf. ... I'm sure you remember her. ... However, just to refresh your memory, she was the young lady you spent a weekend with in Banff at the Sleep Tight Motel. The date, uh-h-h, May 5th, 6th, and 7th, 1959. Mr. Hagen, it's only fair to warn you that the divorce will be granted whether you sign these papers or not. So you see, it doesn't make any difference, because we have the proof. Furthermore, Mr. Hagen, you may not have been aware of this, but for the past three weeks, we've had a detective on your trail. He's been gathering evidence for us." With deliberate care, Charles Stinton began turning the pages of the file.

Lou looked alarmed.

"All the proof we need is in here, Mr. Hagen. We have dates, places, names! It's all in here!"

Lou threw Tanya a despairing look. "I didn't do nothing! I swear, Tanya, I didn't! ... D'you believe all this crap?"

"Now, Mr. Hagen, be reasonable. You can't ignore undeniable proof! The judge will grant the divorce on factual and indisputable proof of adultery. That's all we need."

Suddenly, Lou covered his face with his hands. Tanya was shocked to see big, round tears come rolling down his cheeks. The hard facade crumbled and a side of him that she'd never seen before revealed itself.

"It's true. It's all true. You're right. I'm sorry, Tanya, I was with Rose on that day. Yeah, we did spend the weekend together. But it was nothing! Just a, a, fling, believe me Tanya! That's all it was. You ... you understand, don't you, honey?" His eyes bore into hers, begging forgiveness.

She stared at him as a shock, as distinct as a jolt of electricity, went through her. All the time that they were together, she'd blocked out the true facts, facts she couldn't face and didn't want to. His admission only brought out the painful reality.

"I gotta tell you some more. I've gotta tell it all to you. Everything. Before Rose, there were others. I'm telling you now, because I wanna make a clean breast of it. There was Rene Boisvert. She used to call to the house for a ride. ... She was on my bowling team. I ... we spent a coupla nights at the Parkland Hotel. You remember I told you that women liked me? Hell, she chased me. It was her, not me, that wanted the affair. Uh-h-h, I spent a weekend with Sue Melford. You wouldn't know her. ... Jenny Mariak, you know Jenny." Lou looked directly at Tanya. "She was your school pal. Honey, I'm sorry, I went to bed with her, too. ... And ...and ... Nora O'Reilly. You remember Nora, don't you, honey?"

Tanya steadied herself at each appalling revelation.

"It happened the weekend that I helped her move her stuff. I ... I mean we ... uh-h-h, did it that day. ..." Lou couldn't seem to stop. The confession poured out between bursts of sobbing as he named names of women that she'd never heard off. Knowing her penchant for honesty, he believed his only chance to win her back was to be openly repentant.

Once she opened her mouth to tell him to stop, that she'd heard enough. Everything within her longed for him to stop. She wondered why he'd go on verifying her suspicions by tearing her apart inside? Weren't some things best kept secret?

But Lou went on. ..."Then there was Mary Black. You don't know her. She helped out at the store sometimes when we were busy. ... Most weekends, we ended up in her apartment." He uncovered his face long enough for her to see his cheeks drenching wet. "But honey, I just gotta tell you, I love you, and I'm real sorry if I ever hurt you. How can I make it up to you? Tell me now, whatever you want ... it's yours! Tanya, take me back! Please, please, Tanya, take me back, I'll make it up to you. Lets start again. I ..."

Listening to his pleas, the coldness around her heart began to melt. Did he really mean it? Was he serious this time? Would he change? A part of her wanted to embrace him, to wipe away his tears, to comfort him.

Charles Stinton's eyes darted toward her. "That'll be enough Mr. Hagen. We have enough evidence, thank you." Suddenly, he leaped out of his chair, gripped Tanya's arms and forced her out of her seat. "I'm sorry to have to do this, but you don't have to listen to him. Please, step into the other room. I'll handle it from here on ... my way."

Lou's confession tapered off.

Her heart took flight. Lou's words staggered her. Words that she'd been waiting to hear since she'd married him. His confession revealed a deep love for her. Never had he uttered those words in all the time they'd been together ... or even whispered them to her in their most intimate moments. Second thoughts crept in. Now, in the presence of a witness, he wanted her back. The mother in her, the caretaker, longed to say, "yes, yes, let's try again. Lou dearest, you're right, we can make it work this time. Let's go home and start over." She opened her mouth to say those magic words to him, to put an end to his pain, his suffering ... and most important of all, to end her own pain. Suddenly, she felt an invisible power, a firm, invisible power, a power so strong that she couldn't explain. It took control of her. It deliberately turned her head, against her very own will, away from Lou towards the wall. She was aware of obeying Charles Stinton, of leaving the room, closing the door behind her, and shutting Lou out of her life.

During the trial, Rose Bennit testified to having spent the weekend with Lou in Banff. Tanya was struck by her classy good looks, making her wonder why she'd stoop to something so sordid. She wore a soft wool, navy blue coat, and high heeled patent shoes. Her blond hair was cut in a simple, classic style. Rose took the stand, looking very nervous and on the verge of tears. By her speech, Tanya surmised that she was well educated. It made her wonder how Lou could have convinced her to go on a weekend fling with him?

After the trial, they returned to Charles' office. He put away his brief case and sat down. "Tanya, consider yourself very lucky that you'll have another chance. You're young. You'll meet someone else." He grinned sheepishly. "By the way, the file I threatened Lou with was the appointment book. There was no evidence in it. His guilt made him confess."

She smiled. "Really? ... Charles, thank you for your kindness and your help. ... I don't know what I would have done without you. I might even have gone back to him." She held out her hand. "You might think I'm awful, but I hope we never see each other again. ... At least not professionally. You know what I mean!"

He laughed. "And rightly so. Good luck to you, Tanya!"

"Thank you."

Three months later, the court granted Tanya a divorce on the grounds of uncontested adultery. She gladly paid Charles Stinton the $500.00, as well as the court costs, grateful that she'd resisted Lou when he'd emotionally implored her to come back to him.

Tanya turned her thoughts to the future thinking, I've learned a lesson from Lou. Next time, I'll make sure that whoever I meet loves me, and that he loves me for me.

41

TANYA CHECKED THE NUMBER ON THE HOUSE to confirm the address that she held in her hand. She opened the door and entered a reception room, then waited for her eyes to adjust to the light. A middle-aged woman sat at a typewriter.

Tanya, her heart pounding in her ears, and still unsure that she'd made the right move, approached the desk. "Excuse me, I'm Tanya Hagen. I have an appointment with Dr. Carlsten at one-thirty."

The woman smiled and glanced at an open book in front of her. "Yes, Mrs. Hagen, I have you down for one-thirty. Dr. Carlsten is with another patient at the moment. Please have a seat, I'll let you know when it's time."

"Thank you."

She sank into a wicker chair. Soft light filtered in through a tall window facing the street, softening the shadows. An elegant, gilt-framed mirror hung over a gold settee. A chandelier, suspended from the ceiling, dripped brass and crystal.

She sat uneasy and filled with doubt, wondering if she should have come to see the psychiatrist? Fear had driven her to make the decision. Lou had been a controlling, destructive influence in her life. She'd had to maintain a firm grip on herself to keep from falling apart. The depression had set in right after the divorce. Tanya was faced with having to resolve the problems that she'd tried so hard to cover over during their marriage. She'd survived only by pretending that they didn't exist. For a short space of time, she'd imagined that she was someone else. If only she could let go and be herself. Each night, as soon as her eyes closed in sleep, the nightmares began, leaving her shattered and on shaky ground in the morning.

"Mrs. Hagen, this way, please."

She stood up and followed the receptionist into the next room.

"Doctor Carlsten ... this is Mrs. Hagen."

A middle-aged man rose from behind a large, oak desk which, by its size, seemed to eclipse the room. He was of average height and weight with light brown hair, very blue eyes, and a round cherubic face. He extended his hand, while assessing her over a pair of metal rimmed glasses.

"Mrs. Hagen?"

She shook his hand. "If you don't mind, please call me Tanya."

"Yes, Tanya, how can I help you?"

She sensed an innate kindness behind the words. She hoped that he'd be right for her. ... "Uh-h-h, it's about my ex-husband, Dr. Carlsten. We divorced recently. You see, since the divorce, I find it hard to carry on from day to day. I'm alone and I have to make a living, uh-h-h, that is, I have to work. I'm turning into a wreck, thinking that somehow I'll break down. And if I break down, I won't be able to look after myself. It's become a real worry. This feeling, it's so destructive. I thought you might be able to help me get over it."

The tears started to form behind her eyes. There was so much to tell, yet how could she talk when there was a storm building inside her?

He appeared unimpressed. "Why should it be so difficult? I know lots of women who are divorced, and they manage quite nicely."

"Well, my husband, Lou ... he said he would kill me if I left him. I'm still afraid that he will."

"But if you're divorced, how can he hurt you?. ... Your divorce ... tell me about it."

"Uh-h-h, we met in a bowling alley. Lou was a great bowler. My sister Anna, she introduced us, and ..." She got no further as the dam inside her let loose. She covered her face with her hands and began to sob.

The doctor handed her a box of kleenex. "It's all right, take your time. It's best to get it out gradually. There, there ... tell me just a little more."

"Thank you. You see Lou, he ..." The memory brought on a fresh flood of tears. She fought for control. "Well, Lou had all these women in his life that he had sex with, and though I knew about them, he didn't care!"

Sentence after painful sentence wrenched itself from her. A heap of crumpled tissues began piling up in her lap. ... "I ... his friend told me that he'd married me for my money, though it wasn't very much. All the time, I felt as if Lou hated me. You're not going to believe this, but he used me like a slave. We had a joint bank account. I worked, I put all the money in, I paid all the bills ... and I must tell you that Lou bought eight different cars in the four years that we were married. He needed the cars to impress the women he dated. And though he had a job, he kept his money in a separate account so he could spend it on himself."

"At first, I thought I could handle it. ... I thought I'd be all right; but right after the divorce, I got really scared."

"What exactly frightened you?"

Another sob broke through. "Because ... because ... I noticed that there were empty spaces beginning to form in my head, because of all the things I wanted to block out. I couldn't face what he had done to me ... so, I created voids in my mind. Oh, Dr. Carlsten ... now I can't remember anything that took place during those voids. It was the only way I could handle it. ... I don't want to go crazy. Do you think I'm going crazy?" Her eyes took on a look of terror.

"Tanya, you're not crazy. You're far from it. Your body had to protect itself."

His reassurance felt soothing. She relaxed. "Dr. Carlsten, I've been having terrible nightmares about him since we separated. I can't tell you how they've worried me."

"Tell me about them."

"That's another reason I came here today. I want to get rid of them. They're so ... very ... so frightening!" She leaned forward. "Since the divorce, I've had this awful dream about Lou each night. ... I dream that I'm in a strange hotel room, and I'm lying on a bed. ... It looks like a metal four poster. In some of the dreams, I'm lying naked and in others I have just a slip on. For some reason, I'm always tied up and helpless. The door to the room is locked."

"Suddenly, Lou bursts in. I'm not sure how he gets in through a locked door, but he gets in. My heart starts to hammer. He's furious. At first he just stands there looking at me, his face dead white, full of hatred and anger. ... His eyebrows are arched up and flare back. There's a cigarette hanging from the side of his mouth. His lips look twisted and cruel. Lou is dressed in black, everything he has on is black." She took a deep breath. "My heart starts beating even faster than before. I twist, I turn ... I try to free myself. It feels so real! And I ask myself what am I doing lying half-naked like ... like ... some kind of a prostitute. He starts towards me and begins shouting, 'I said I'd find you! ... I'm going to kill you! I'm not letting you go! ... You're not getting away from me that easy.' ... I must tell you that when I was married to him, he did threaten to kill me. He lifts his hand to strike me, and there's no doubt in my mind that he's going to kill me. I just lie there cowering, and thank God, that's when the dream ends. I've had this same dream over and over and over. It's driving me crazy! Lately, I'm afraid to go to sleep." She trembled, visibly. "What am I going to do, Doctor?"

He cleared his throat. "Tanya, I think that the dream is normal enough under the circumstances. Especially, since your husband was so abusive to you. You're right, he was using you as a slave, and in the dream, you're reliving the worst parts of your life with him. Don't worry, it'll all go away when you've calmed down. Give yourself a chance to forget. ... Time has a way of healing. H-m-m-m, I wonder how you'd do in group therapy? I think that might be the answer. For the next couple of sessions, I'll take you privately, because I want to hear more of your history, then I'll put you in with a group of people who've had experiences similar to yours. We meet here in my office the first and last Tuesday of every month. I think what you need is to interrelate with some of them. Actually, you help each other." He looked at the clock. "Tell Mrs. Tompkins I want to see you next week." He held out his hand. "Tanya, don't worry, you're going to be fine, just fine."

Buoyed by his encouragement, she felt calmer. "Dr. Carlsten, thank you so much."

At the end of October, as soon as Allen Semco returned to university, demanding perfect quiet from his family, she moved into Anna's house. Occasionally, she wondered how Alisha could stand it, ... living like a mouse, afraid to let even the children cry, while Allen spent long hours going through his law books.

Anna had a bedroom in the basement that she rented to her for a small fee. With the assurance of privacy and freedom, it made it worthwhile.

42

THE BUS LET HER OFF IN FRONT OF A RAMBLING, WOODEN STRUCTURE, and though it was a warm night for August, Tanya brought a summer coat, just in case.

Earlier in the week, she and Iris Newman had arranged to go dancing at the Elks Temple. She'd met Iris at a party and the friendship had taken root when they discovered their common goal was to meet someone and get married. Sometimes, they got together for coffee to discuss any progress and exchange ideas.

A year had already passed since her divorce from Lou. Dr. Carlsten had been right about the nightmares, for they'd gradually stopped.

Tanya entered the building, thinking that she'd been cooped up far too long. Tonight, should the opportunity arise, I'll free myself of my inhibitions. It's time to kick up my heels, to live, to have a ball. It's time to enjoy life. Yes, tonight, I'll do just that, I'm going to have a good time.

The log structure had a massive, cathedral style ceiling, providing good acoustics for the country and western band on the stage. Long wooden benches lined the walls. She noticed a throng of men standing by the door. Some wore cowboy shirts and jeans and some looked like business executives in three piece suits. A girl from the steno pool had told her that one shouldn't be surprised to see doctors, dentists, and lawyers there. She'd referred to the dance hall as 'the hot spot of the down town crowd'!

Cigarette smoke hung in a thick haze over the dance hall. She coughed slightly as she elbowed her way through the horde. Tanya stared at the women who were pressed against the walls and swarming around the stage. They were dressed to the teeth in velvets, satins, and sequined blouses, beautifully bedecked and ready at a moment's notice, to entice, attract, and beguile. And such exotic hairdos she'd never seen!

The strains of a waltz floated through the room.

She saw Iris, standing close to the orchestra, and reached out to touch her. "Nice crowd, isn't it?"

Iris smiled. "Yes, and the men, aren't they good looking? I'm so glad we came."

"Yes, me too. Your dress, it's lovely, Iris."

"Thank you."

She resembled Elizabeth Taylor with her flowing black hair done up in a romantic beehive. Her fair skin, blue eyes, and fine features looked especially alluring in the violet print she wore.

A tall, well-dressed man in a grey suit approached them, holding out his hand to Iris, ending the conversation.

Tanya's eyes swept over him, wishing he'd asked her to dance instead of Iris. Iris's beauty was not your regular drug store kind. She always attracted the best-dressed and best-looking men around her.

Tanya found herself squeezed between a woman in black taffeta and a buxom blonde. Before coming, she'd agonized about what to wear. Her final choice was a two piece cotton suit. The skirt was a black sheath. The blouse, in kelly green, had a small standup collar, three quarter length sleeves and a nipped in waistline.

She was disappointed that with the evening half over, she still hadn't found anyone whom she would consider even remotely interesting. However, there was still time.

The orchestra announced a break at 11:30. She looked for Iris to find her standing beside the man in grey.

Someone tugged at her sleeve from behind. A male voice said, "Hi." She turned to look. A young man with blue eyes and carrot red hair stood grinning at her. He was nice-looking. She sensed an aggressive excitement about him as his arm boldly encircled her waist.

"Like to dance?"

She smiled. "I'd love to, but haven't you noticed there's no music?"

He started to whistle. "Like the tune?" They swayed back and forth in rhythm. She flushed.

"I'm Brad Stewart." He put his face close to hers. "And who may you be?"

"My name is Tanya Hagen."

"Tanya! That has an exotic ring to it. Are you Irish?"

"Of course not!"

He broke into laughter. "I didn't think so. Well, I'd say this is your lucky night, Tanya."

"Why?

"Because you ran into me."

"I think that statement works both ways."

"With your looks, I'd have to agree with that."

The band began to play again.

"Wanna dance?" he asked.

She nodded, ever grateful for the dancing lessons and that she didn't miss a step.

"Tanya, I gotta hand it to you, you're a great little dancer."

"Thank you."

"How would you like to live dangerously?"

"Uh-h-h, in what way?"

"I know where there's a party tonight. How about it? You and me ... wanna go?"

She hesitated. "Well, maybe ... yes."

He stopped dancing but held on to her wrist. "Okay, let's go."

"Not so fast, I have to tell my girlfriend that I'm leaving. I didn't come here alone."

She found Iris with the same partner. "Iris ... would you believe that I met this guy, Brad, and we're going to a party? I'll call you tomorrow and fill you in. ... Bye, now."

"Oh, Tanya, that's just great! Have a good time!"

Brad's car, a dark blue Oldsmobile sedan, looked brand new. He opened the door and she slid in, appraising the expensive interior. "Brad, where do you work?"

"Actually, I work for myself, you might say." He laughed. "I sell pots and pans door to door."

Tanya, surprised at this open admission, threw him a second look to see if her really meant it. Somehow, he didn't look the type! However, business must be good from the looks of his car. His suit looked tailor made. "I bet you meet a lot of interesting people in your job."

"Yeah, love my work ... and you?"

"I work for the government, ... Federal, that is. I'm a secretary." At this point, there was no need to tell him that she was newly divorced.

Most men considered her fair game once they found out. "By the way, where is this party we're going to?"

"A friend's house. You'll like it. I promise you a good time ... and I assure you, I never disappoint a lady!" He winked at her, ... "especially someone pretty."

"Thank you." She checked her watch. The dial read eleven-fifty five. "Don't you think it's kind of late for a party?"

Laughing, he tramped on the gas. The car squealed out of the parking lot. "Hell no! The night is young. Tanya ... you and I, we're going to enjoy it!"

He drove to a house located on the south side of the city. A string of cars lined both sides of the street, forcing him to park nearly a block away. "Damn it! Listen to that racket! It's coming from Lorenzo's house!" He got out and opened her door. "Come on, let's go. Sounds like they've started without us."

"I wonder if the neighbours mind?"

"I wouldn't worry about the neighbours, they've probably been invited."

He led her to a brown stucco house and down a flight of stairs. The room was noisy and crowded. There were comfortable lounges and chairs throughout. A smoked glass mirror reflected a bar at the far end; the lighting was a dim glow.

From their dress, Tanya surmised that the crowd was upper class. Several couples were dancing in a tiny space provided in the middle.

Brad waved to a beautiful, auburn-haired woman with hair that cascaded down to her waist. She broke away and came towards them, smiling. "Brad! I see you were able to make it."

"Loretta! Come here, my darling. ... Tanya, this is Loretta Lorenzo ... the woman I'm currently in love with." He put both arms around her and kissed her.

She pushed him away. "Sorry Brad, my husband is watching!"

Tanya felt embarrassed for her.

"Loretta flashed her a smile. "Brad, help yourselves to a drink. I must run." She waved to some people who had just come in and left them.

"Thought you'd never ask," he muttered, steering Tanya towards the bar. He reached for the shaker. "How about a martini?"

"Yes, fine," she answered. Though she'd never tasted one in her life, she was determined to try it.

He mixed the drinks and poured them into two glasses. "Here's to us!" Raising his, he downed it in one draught.

"To us." Tanya echoed, taking a small sip.

He winked at her and poured another, quaffing it down as quickly as the first. Two more followed in quick succession. Tanya noticed that he was swaying as he gripped her arm.

"Wannadance?"

She recoiled, her smile fading. "No." Was he drunk already?

In one hand he held a glass streaming drops of liquor to the floor, with the other he held on to her. Just then, she heard a phone ring.

"Hey, Brad!" Loretta's voice topped the noise. "It's for you! It's your wife."

Tanya stiffened. His wife! He didn't say anything about a wife! She put down her glass, her mind racing, as he went to answer the phone.

"Yeah? ... Whatd'ya want? What the hell? No! ... No, I'm not coming home, bitch! Screw you! ... Hell, cause I don't wanna! ... What d'ya say? ... Fer that, ya can go ta hell, fer'all I care! ... Listen to me, bitch, and listen good. ... Shit, nobody tells me wat ta do. Ya hear me? Rememer, I'm gonna kill ya, jus as soon's I get home. ... I'm gonna knock your God damn block off. Sides ... who tole you to phone me here? ... Ya got no right to meddle in my fairs! ... Tha's too damn bad. Jus' wait till I get my hands on ya. I'll wring your bloody chicken neck ... an it'll be a real pleasure, ... bitch!"

His voice carried several decibels above the racket. Tanya cringed in horror, both unsettled and fearful for the person at the other end. Heads turned to listen.

Suddenly, all her instincts went into action, telling her to get out of there. She grabbed her coat. Brad slammed down the phone and came lurching after her, his face mean, angry.

"Bitch, come'er, bitch."

She froze. He had no right to call her names! She wasn't his wife!

"Yore all alike. I'm gonna teach ya ... teach ya ... ya'll never forge-t ..."

She rushed towards the stairs.

Quick as lightening, he grabbed her wrist, twisting it behind her.

"Not so fas! Were you thin you goin?"

She winced as pain shot up her arm. "Stop! Please, stop!" she begged, imploring him with her eyes. Suddenly, she shrank back. There was a dangerous, disturbing look about him. "Let me go! I'm nothing to you. You have a wife! You don't even know me!"

He twisted harder. "I don't care, bitch. Know sumthin? Yore a whore, nuthin but a whore s'far as I'm concerned."

She remembered Lou. With fear as her master, breaking loose became paramount. Tanya relaxed. As soon as he felt her go limp, he loosened his hold.

She broke free and leaped forward. Hiking up her sheath skirt, she made a dash for the stairs, conscious that he was running after her. Once outside, the high heels were kicked off as she took to the middle of the road in her stockinged feet. A glance over her shoulder pinpointed him racing towards his car.

It wasn't long before she noticed headlights behind her. Thinking to protect herself, she ran for the sidewalk and began running against the traffic.

He swerved the car to her side and kept pace calling out, "Bitch! Whore! Stop, bitch, I wanna get my hands on yore bloody neck!"

The obscenities brought chills to her. Tanya, afraid that he might try running into her placed herself well behind the parking meters, reckoning that he wasn't likely to damage his expensive car. She was terrified that her strength might give out and kept a look out for some type of hideout or shelter.

Sure enough, soon her lungs felt as if they would burst. At the end of a long block, breathing hard, she began to slacken.

The car squealed to a stop. "Hold it, right there, ya God damn whore."

Tanya doubled over as a sharp pain stabbed at her side. She clamped a hand over it. ... "Oh God, help me! Save me! Please, don't let me die!" Her eyes darted everywhere at once in desperation. Suddenly, beaming at her, directly across the street, she noticed a red neon sign, "Mohawk Car Repair and Service Garage ... Open 24 Hours". She leaped off the sidewalk, her feet hardly touching the concrete, and flew to the other side. The car lurched forward, barely missing her.

She stumbled to the door. Gasping, she clawed it open and collapsed into the arms of a surprised attendant. "Help me! ... Please ... help me! ... Don't leave me! ... Please, please, stay here with me!" Heaving uncontrollably, she clung to him, her pupils dilated in terror.

"What's wrong, miss? What's happened?"

She pointed to the street. "Look out there. Tell me, d'you ... d'you ... a man in a, a, blue Oldsmobile, is he still there? He's... he's ... trying to kill me!"

The attendant glanced toward the street. "Yeah, there's a guy in a blue Olds by the curb."

"Call the police! Call them right now! He's trying to kill me! Oh God, I'm so scared! ... Please, help me! ... You've got to help me get away from him!"

The attendant started towards the phone ... then stopped, hearing the sound of a motor being gunned and the squeal of tires.

"I think he's gone, miss. Do you still want me to call the police?"

She went down to her knees. She'd been spared. "No, it's all right! Just call a taxi. I want to go home."

"You bet, I will. You sure you're okay?"

She nodded.

"Come, sit in this chair and rest while I phone for a cab."

As the full impact of her narrow escape hit her, she broke into a fit of sobbing.

The cabbie let her off at Anna's at four-thirty in the morning. The fare was $10.00. She had to wake Anna to lend her the money to pay the driver. He'd been kind enough to stop and buy her a cup of coffee, after hearing of her narrow escape.

Weary, shaken, Tanya related the dreadful details to Anna.

Anna looked shocked when she finished. "You just never know about people, do you?" she commented, dryly. "I think you need a drink." She poured some brandy into a glass and handed it to her.

"It'll help you sleep."

"Thank you." Tanya slept until noon the next day. When she awoke, she felt giddy and somewhat lighter. To her surprise, she'd lost eight pounds. Alisha and Allen came by in the afternoon.

Again she was obliged to repeat her tale of horror to them.

Allen shook his head in disbelief. "Tanya, there's only one thing I can say ... and I say this seriously ... if you keep this up, I think that

one of these days we'll be reading about you in the front page of The
Bulletin. You know, it's very likely that someone will kill you."

"Allen, I should hope not!"

"Well, think about it. In the first place, you don't know anything
about these guys that you pick up, and in the second place ... why do
you do it?"

"I don't do it deliberately."

"Then why do it at all? I don't understand!"

"I don't know," she said, wondering why herself.

Later in the afternoon, she went to visit Elana Benson. She thought
that Elana might know Brad Stewart. After her divorce from Lou, Elana
had generously offered to share an apartment with her.

Tanya had moved in for just three months, then returned to Anna's
when she realized that the rent was higher than she'd been prepared to
pay. Elana was a private nurse. Her job was to care for patients either
seriously ill or dying. Usually, after a difficult case, she told Tanya that
the patient had "expired."

She was strikingly beautiful, with a crown of lush red hair that
attracted men to her like flies. She knew a lot of men, and it was a sure
bet that she either knew Brad, or of someone who would know him.

"Tanya! What a surprise! ... Come in." Elana was wrapped in a pure
silk, azure blue kimono, with a red dragon embroidered on the back.
The apartment was decorated in white and looked very elegant.

"Your place looks lovely, Elana."

"Yes, I've had it redone. ... Here, try the sofa. Care for coffee or
maybe a drink?"

"Coffee will be fine, thanks."

Tanya leaned back into a white damask covered coach. "Elana, do
you know a Brad Stewart? He sells pots and pans door to door ... or so
he said."

Elana burst out laughing. "Brad Stewart? Did he really tell you that
he sells pots and pans door to door?"

"Yes, he said that."

"And you believed him? Tanya, you're so naive!"

"What was I supposed to believe? So what does he do?"

"Ha, ha, well, to start with, he happens to be a friend of my ex-
husbands', Mel. ... Mel will tell you that his line of work is not that

mundane. Tanya, Brad Stewart is a hit man for the Mafia. How do you know him?"

She gasped. "Yesterday, I met him at the Elks dance hall, and he nearly killed me." She went on to describe what happened. "Elana, tell me, what's wrong with me, why can't I meet somebody decent? Other girls do! My friend, Dorothy Zidoruk, she met some guy at the Silver Ballroom the very first time she went there. She's married to him now. It turns out that he's really nice. And Brad, he was ten times worse than Lou. If I hadn't gotten away from him, I'd be dead today."

"You were lucky. He doesn't need to be drunk to kill." Elana's face looked grim.

"I never would have guessed that he did anything like that. He started out by being ... well, fun!"

"Yeah, I bet he did! He's got a nice wife. I know her. They're as different as night and day."

"I wish that he'd told me that he was married. ... Elana, after last night, from now on, I'm going to be more careful with men."

43

TANYA WALKED INTO DR. CARLSTEN'S INNER OFFICE AND SAT DOWN. Usually seven or eight people came to the group. They had become like family to her. Dr. Carlsten she regarded as a surrogate father. It was touching that while in his care, he tried to make everyone feel safe, secure, encouraging them to discuss their most consuming problems.

At her very worst moments, when she'd cried while talking about her fears, there had been someone to comfort her. She felt that they understood and cared about what happened to her. She was beginning to feel more confident about herself.

As usual, Dr. Carlsten sat to one side of the group, smoking his pipe, while listening to their grievances and occasionally interjecting with advice.

Laurie Schmidt sat next to Tanya. Only nineteen, she was young, beautiful, and gangling. At the moment, she had the floor.

"Last Thursday, I went out with a med student. He was really good looking. I even thought that maybe it could turn into something, but then I came to the conclusion that he didn't really turn me on. He called again this morning and wanted to take me out. I said "no." I thought what was the use? Besides, on weekends, I'm seeing this older man. Actually, we're having an affair."

Tanya looked at her in a ho-hum way. Nothing the girl said shocked her anymore. She was uninhibited, her affairs were numerous and purely physical. Though her bed partners were many and varied, she was devoid of any emotional attachment to them. Easily bored, she tired of them quickly. Tanya wondered whether she worried about venereal disease?

She glanced at Pierre Sutton. Everybody in the group knew that Pierre was bisexual, freely dating both men and women. Tall, youthful, lean waisted, with brown, wavy hair, he was extremely handsome. She could tell by his clothes which way he leaned on any given day. The homosexual brought out the flamboyant, the open shirt to the waist, a colorful silk scarf at the throat, skin tight leather pants. He often described one of his benders: "We partied all weekend. It was non-stop! I'd say there were twenty or maybe twenty-five of us." He'd laughed at their shocked looks. "I never got a wink of sleep." His meaning was clear.

Sometimes, he was straight and apt to be dressed in a classy suit with matching tie and white shirt. He made his living as a dance instructor and was skilled in everything from ballet to tap.

Next to him sat Caroline Hall. She worked as a secretary for an oil company. Petite, blonde, she was endowed with deep aqua-blue eyes and perfect skin. She wore clothes that were always perfectly coordinated. Tanya thought that she was beautiful enough to be a movie star, and that she could have had almost any man she wanted. Though many men courted her, none of them attracted her enough to marry. Strangely, it was Pierre that she fell in love with ... a choice as wrong as wrong could be. Pierre had too many personal tangles of his own. After several dates, the relationship came to a halt. Caroline, who was very level-headed, had had the insight to put a stop to it. Tanya admired her greatly, picturing her in the role as some rich man's wife.

Occasionally, Lucy Woloshin, a law clerk, joined them. She had rich, chestnut colored hair and looked very attractive. Lucy avoided all close ties. Yet, she often bragged about having several relationships going on at the same time with different men. Relationships that dragged on for as long as eight or nine years; meanwhile she had a passionate mistrust of all men.

Joyce Huntman was employed as a secretary for the Gas Company. She had large, spare features and was mean and insulting to those close to her. Not one person in the group escaped her barbed tongue. Once during a heated argument, Tanya had flicked her hand lightly across her face then lived to regret it when she threatened to take her to court. Dr. Carlsten had come to Tanya's defence. "Joyce, I don't think she meant to hurt you," he'd told her evenly.

"But Doctor, she slapped me so hard she pushed my teeth over to one side!"

"Now Joyce, we all know that's an exaggeration. Let's drop it."

Tanya had been most grateful for his help. Fearing Joyce's threats and the court case, she hadn't slept a wink for two solid weeks! She gave her wide clearance after that.

Sometimes Lea Thompson showed up. Lea kept everything bottled up and hardly shared anything of her past life with anyone. Tanya liked her because she felt they had something in common. Sometimes, after a session, she had coffee with Lea.

There were others who joined them whenever it was convenient. As a whole, they shared one problem in common: the inability to relate to anyone on a close, personal basis.

Now Dr. Carlsten turned to Tanya. "Tanya, do you have anything that you want to discuss?"

"Well, yes, I do. I want to tell you about a horrible experience I had this last Saturday. I met this man at the Elks Temple, and he asked me to go to a party with him. I thought it might be fun so I said "yes." Actually, I'd decided that being free from Lou, it was time to start enjoying myself. Well, let me tell you about what happened. ..." When she finished talking, no one spoke.

Dr. Carlsten stared at her in disbelief. She caught a hint of anger on his face. "Tanya, I don't understand you. You're deliberately playing with fire! Don't you care about what happens to you? Before you go and do it again next week, I'd consider the consequences first."

"Yes, I know, Dr. Carlsten. I must be a poor judge of character. But I don't want to end up alone, either. How am I supposed to meet someone? Sometimes I feel like a half person, ... always in search of the other half." She sighed.

"Then you'll have to learn to be more discerning."

"Yes, of course, you're right."

44

IN LATE JULY, SHE READ AN AD IN THE PAPER which seemed to be the answer to the days that she spent at home when she wasn't going dancing. She thought it might stem her loneliness. Temporarily, she was staying at Iris Newman's apartment while the girl was away in Europe visiting relatives.

The ad was sponsored by "The Edmonton Civic Opera Society." They wanted singers and dancers to audition for Cole Porter's musical, "Can Can." It would be an exciting diversion to offset the monotony of the steno pool. She loved both singing and dancing.

The next day after work, Tanya auditioned before Dean Winfield, the director of the musical. Surprisingly, he accompanied her on the piano while she sang. When she finished, he gave her an approving look. "Good! You can be in the chorus. I'm looking for someone to play the countess. It's only one line, but I think you might be right for it. We'll see."

"Thank you. And thank you for the part, Mr. Winfield." She walked away, her feet treading air. He was actually giving her something to say. Just one line, to be sure, but still something. She knew that some of the big time stars got their start that way.

Tanya hadn't expected to see so many "would-be stars" at the audition. The room was teaming with people. As soon as the auditions ended, they were told to report for rehearsals on the following Wednesday at six P.M. sharp. "Please be on time. The show goes on stage at the

Jubilee Auditorium three months from today and runs from November 27th through to the 30th. Four days."

She arrived early for the rehearsal. There were ten girls in the chorus line as well as a group of professional dancers. A tall, thin, Swedish girl, Lorna Sorenson, stood next to her. She was shy, soft spoken, and sang alto.

Victor Lansburg, a velvety baritone, had been given the lead part. Though he only came to Tanya's chin, his singing was so superb, so grand, he completely captivated her and everyone else in the cast. Michele Daniels, a soprano, was chosen to be the leading lady. She was only eighteen and very beautiful. Both were single.

The secondary lead roles went to Nell Wilson and Gary McGovern. Nell sang in a rich contralto. In her private life, she was a housewife who was married to a policeman. Her features were strong boned, and her chestnut brown hair hung in a long, silky cloud around her shoulders.

Gary McGovern sang baritone. He was a tall, handsome Irishman and the supervisor of a school. His hair was knotted into tight, black curls, and every girl in the room fell in love with him. It was disappointing to find out that he was married with a trio of young ones at home.

They were given a large notebook with their parts in the musical marked off. Dean Winfield was a brilliant director. Tanya loved to listen to him talk. He was humorous, kind, and everyone was bent on pleasing him. He was in his early fifties, Catholic, and a devoted father to six daughters. The production wasn't his first, but considering the large cast he had to deal with, it was an ambitious undertaking. Tanya and Lorna discussed the clever way he dealt with the varied personalities, especially since Michele Daniels and Victor Lansburg weren't getting along.

Tanya faithfully attended all rehearsals twice a week, looking forward to the warmth and camaraderie of the group. Unfortunately, they'd had an early snowfall at the beginning of November, and it became difficult to get to and from practice; even so, she wouldn't allow herself to miss any.

One snowy evening she shed her winter wear and walked in on a charged scene between Michele and Victor. Michele, angry and defiant, with her hands on her hips, had the stage. "Well, what am I supposed to do? Kiss him first or shall I throw myself into his arms first, then kiss him? I'm only asking because I'm not sure that I want to, or care to do either. ... Sorry, but that's the way he makes me feel!"

"If you want the plain truth, that works both ways!" Victor bellowed back at her. As usual, the two stars were quarreling.

The director's face turned red. "Stop it! I don't want one word of that ... that ... anger coming through. Keep your personal differences to yourself! ... Let's start from the beginning. ... Michele, you first."

One grew weary listening to them. It was a different story with Nell Wilson and Gary McGovern. They sang solo, held hands, while gazing into each other's eyes, enraptured. The scene ended with a long kiss. For amateurs, they carried it off superbly well. Almost too well. Everyone in the cast sensed the chemistry between them.

Two weeks before they were scheduled to go on stage, the costumes arrived from New York in large, wooden trunks. Tanya thought they looked stunning. Each girl was handed a different coloured dress. She examined hers. Low cut, short, the material an iridescent green taffeta with a black underskirt and a waist so small that she couldn't imagine how she'd fit into it. Black fishnet stockings gave her a seductive, alluring look.

The stage manager announced that the rehearsal was to be in full dress. Tanya repeated her one line and mouthed the words to the song, as she struggled to squeeze into the outfit. ... "We are maidens typical of France. ... In a convent educated ..."

"Gladys Fenton, the musical's professional cosmetic artist, turned to her. "Tanya, you're next."

Tanya nodded. "Gladys, could you please help me get into this dress? Are you sure it's my size? It feels very tight."

"Take a deep breath while I zip you up. ... There! You see, it fits."

"Gladys, I can hardly breathe. ... And I don't consider myself to be fat."

"It looks good on you. Now sit down so I can make you beautiful."

When Gladys finished with her make-up, Tanya stood up. She glanced into the mirror. She looked beautiful. A tremor of excitement went through her. At the same time, the costume did look risque. The flounce, the frills, the heightened color in her face added to the look. Strange, that she felt uneasy about wearing it. She paused to reflect "why?" Deep inside, the small voice that had been her guide throughout her life demanded to know what she was doing there?

The director shouted, "Places, everybody!"

Tanya went on stage, sure that no one else felt that way but her.

She stepped into line next to Lorna and pushed her thoughts out of the way.

The rehearsal went very well. Dean Winfield was enthusiastic and beaming when they finished. Even Michele and Victor seemed to be on better terms. However, riding home on the bus that night, she reflected on the true meaning of the play, trying to understand why it should bother her. The musical was about a woman who ran a laundry during the day. However, at night, the girls who worked for her did the "Can Can," a naughty dance which had been outlawed by the respectable citizens of Paris.

It seemed harmless enough. Still, she was nagged by a feeling that she was doing something wrong.

On the day of the live performance, Tanya decided to throw a towel over her conscience. It's only a play. It was meant to make people laugh, she consoled herself. Remembering how tight the dress fit, she decided not to eat anything. On second thought, it would be foolish not to, since it took energy to dance, to sing, to perform. God forbid that she should faint. She could never forgive herself for spoiling it for everyone else. She ate a small sandwich, drank a glass of milk, then hurried to the elevator.

As she opened the outer door of the apartment and stepped outside, she was pushed back by a ferocious gale. It was barely five o'clock, but the sky was already darkening. The horizon was a deep purple with streaks of fiery red painted over it. Overhead, plump, cushiony, grey clouds scurried by. Should I take a bus or walk, she wondered? The theatre was about two miles away and it meant that she'd have to cross the High Level bridge to get there.

It was still early. I'll walk, she thought. She assumed a moderate pace, enjoying the mild warmth of the evening. However, on approaching the bridge, she had to go through a short tunnel. Once inside, fear began to pulsate as blackness closed in on her. Tanya groped her way through the dark, telling herself not to panic, wondering why the city didn't provide some kind of lighting for safety's sake? It could prove dangerous if someone happened to be lurking inside the tunnel! She relaxed only when she emerged at the other end.

Urged on by the dinner hour, there was a steady stream of cars on the bridge next to her. She felt grateful that a sidewalk for pedestrians spanned the full length of the bridge, and there was no need to worry about being run down.

Suddenly, a rush of air pinned her flat against the railing. Tanya clung to the iron bar until it passed. She looked down into the cold, murky blackness of the North Saskatchewan River flowing beneath her and shivered. The wind seemed strongest at this point. With quickening heart, she realized that only by hanging on and pulling herself forward would she make it safely across because it didn't let up.

Walking nearly doubled over her progress was slow, hampered by showers of flying dust and gravel. It hit her relentlessly with each blast of wind. At last she set foot on the other side, and, leaning against a cement wall, she thanked God for her safety.

The crossing had taken longer than she'd anticipated. Now, to make up for lost time, she began to run.

She reached the steps of The Jubilee and sat down to rest, gulping down quick breaths of air to slow the rapid pounding of her heart before going into the building and running downstairs to the washroom.

She stared at her face in the mirror in disbelief. It was a grey mask of dust and dirt! Dismayed, Tanya quickly groped for paper towels, hot water, soap. She scrubbed every inch of her skin that was visible, before joining the rest of the cast in the main dressing room.

The room, a fevered pitch of movement, was packed with women in every stage of undress. Tanya put aside her modesty and began shedding her clothes. Someone with clammy, ice cold fingers touched her on the shoulder. She turned to see Lorna Sorenson already in costume. "Tanya, I'm so nervous! How about you?"

"Well, me too, Lorna!" A quick hug and they separated. There was no time to tell her about the wind that she'd had to fight.

Exhausted, she sat down to have her face made up. The harrowing walk to the theatre had utterly drained her. It seemed but minutes before Gladys transformed her into a glamour queen. As soon as she finished with her face, Tanya stood up and confronted a full length mirror. Outside, she looked wonderful, inside she felt unreal, unsure.

Qualms of guilt assailed her once more, while waiting backstage for her signal to go on. However, this time the guilt only reinforced her determination to do a good job.

The director gave them their cue while urging everyone to "Give it all you've got!"

The dancers, the girls from the chorus line, swarmed onto the stage. The curtain went up. Tanya, the countess, turned toward the audience with pounding heart. Beyond the stage, everything looked black. It was a sell-out crowd and though she couldn't see anyone, she sensed their friendliness and expectation. ... But those lights, what heat!

A rustle of taffeta behind her brought her up short. Her part in the musical! This was where she came in. What was it that she had to say? Stage-struck, her mind had gone blank! Suddenly, a whisper from the wings restored her memory. It was the director!

She raised her arms, waved to the dancers and ran it in as quickly as possible. "Now, let's line up! Come on girls!" It wasn't quite right, she was supposed to have said it the other way around. Too late! Thank God for the prompter!

As each act was completed the applause thundered through the house. When it was over, she was conscious of a strong high that lingered inside her, making her wonder how the lead actors must feel after a successful run. She came off stage exhausted and found herself covered with perspiration.

At the end of the show they joined hands and took a bow before the appreciative audience. To Tanya, the applause felt like strong wine. As they walked off stage, someone mentioned a champagne party downstairs.

Still in their costumes, she ran down with Lorna. There were dancers and singers standing in groups. The lead actors were taking acclaims. A critic was present. Everyone who was somebody was there. Tanya recognized some well known actors from television and the movies. "They must have flown in from Toronto for the opening," she remarked to Lorna. Most of the women wore lavish floor length gowns. It was all black tie for the men.

Thank God that she had her stage dress on! She couldn't imagine coming out in the shabby cords she'd come in. Holding on to their champagne glasses, the two girls stood together, hugging the sidelines, not daring to venture in any further, and trying to remember the names of the celebrities. Tanya was awestruck by their importance. It was an uppity crowd. They kissed, they hugged, they called each other "darling," just like in the movies.

After the party, Dean Winfield, concerned about the lateness of the hour, drove both her and Lorna home.

The next day she felt slightly drained but in good spirits. A young man from Estate Tax stopped by her desk. "Uh-h-h, didn't I see you in "Can Can" at the Jubilee last night? Wasn't that you?"

She blushed. "Yes, it was."

"Thought so. I thought you looked gorgeous! My wife and I really liked the show. Congratulations!"

"Thank you." A warmth spread through her. She felt like a star. There were others who'd recognized her. What a let down on the fourth day when it ended!

However, soon after, Dean Winfield accepted an invitation to take the show to Calgary, which sent her and Lorna into another frenzy. Since the play was scheduled for only one night, they took a chartered bus to the city. Not one seat in the theatre was empty. By now, Tanya had no trouble remembering her one line. The show was a resounding success! Again, when it ended, she found herself both exhausted and exhilarated.

After making their final bows, she and Lorna changed into street clothes and ran for the bus. She noticed Nell Wilson and Gary McGovern in the seat in front of them. The couple seemed to have grown very fond of each other. More than once, between acts, she'd noticed them holding hands. And each time that he'd kissed her during the play, it was utterly believable!

The bus driver dimmed the lights inside the vehicle and started north. Lorna turned to her. "I wonder if Dean has anything in mind for another show?"

"I wouldn't begin to guess," Tanya answered, remembering that before they left, once more she'd been assaulted by guilt. On the one hand, she knew that she was attracted to the glamour of the stage like a bee to pollen. On the other hand, she kept asking herself, was it right?

Now she watched in shock as Gary and Nell shrank down and melded into an embrace that seemed never to end. Oblivious to everyone but themselves, they kissed wildly, passionately.

Tanya sighed. "Lorna, do you see what's going on between those two?

... They're supposed to be stable, upright people. How can Nell do this when she's got children and a husband at home? Do you think they've mixed up acting with reality? ... Or has the show gone to their heads?"

"I think it's both."

The love-making continued all the way home. Five minutes before the bus rode into the depot, the couple pulled apart. Nell smoothed her clothes, retouched her lipstick and ran a comb through her long hair.

They rolled to a stop. Tanya watched in disbelief as they rushed to their individual partners. Gary's wife, short and fat, with a scrubbed look about her, had her trio of toddlers, all under five, standing in a row beside her. It was touching to see them holding hands. Smiling, Gary ran to her, put his arms around his wife and kissed her on the lips.

To the left, Nell was being embraced by a tall man in a policeman's uniform. Tanya looked away in disgust. It seemed that, due to the show, their fragile egos had taken off. A person would have to be strong, be morally watchful and in tune with oneself if this kind of attraction was to be avoided. Even if their intentions were honourable, it was so easy to get swept into the mood. A let-down feeling went through her. Dear Lord, how can I ever trust anyone?

She stayed on to take part in several more plays before she stopped; the guilt, instead of diminishing had intensified, and she no longer felt good about performing.

45

THE TRAFFIC LIGHT TURNED GREEN. The lunch hour crowd surged forward, rushing to get to the other side of the street. Tanya, on her way back to the office, started after them. Halfway through the intersection, she looked up and stopped cold. Weakness swept over her as she stared at the red-haired man on the sidewalk opposite her. Brad Stewart stood absorbed talking to some men. The light flashed red. She floundered, still in the middle of the street. Someone blew their horn. "Look lady, make up your mind, I don't have all day!"

Quaking with fear, Tanya turned and ran back, thinking that she couldn't face him. She remembered the dreadful evening when he'd tried to kill her. She reached the curb and walked a block further, to eliminate any chance of running into him.

46

As she walked home from the bus, Tanya noticed the sun still blazing high in the heavens, though her watch read only five-thirty P.M.. Not unusual for this time of year. It was the spring equinox, June 21st, the beginning of summer.

For Tanya, another year had passed. She was still safely ensconced at Anna's. Living there she could coast and not have to worry, knowing that as the days slipped one into another, it would be easy to stay hidden in that basement room for the remainder of her life.

She went in through the kitchen door as two year old Laura, to date Anna's only offspring, came to greet her, her hair splayed out like fine gold thread, her baby face a picture of trust and innocence. She had Anna's large blue eyes. "Mummy, Tante's here," she announced.

Tanya smiled, holding out her arms. "Come, Laurie. Let's go upie." The child beamed and surrendered herself willingly, giggling with delight as Tanya swooped her up and carried her inside.

"Look what I found," she said to Anna, thinking how the child always brought out the best in her no matter how heavyhearted or tired she felt.

Anna turned from the table, her face somber. "We just had a call from Dad. Mom's in the hospital in Spirit Valley. Dad wants us all to come home ... tonight."

She felt a shock. "What's wrong with her?"

"He said she's dying. It's her heart. We're going with Alisha and Allen in their car."

Tanya lowered the child to the floor. A feeling of alarm spread through her. "I'll go pack some clothes." It would be a dreaded six hour drive, she thought, wondering if she should eat something, though hunger had fled.

Allen came for them promptly at nine. Tanya got into the back seat next to Anna and Anton. Would they make it in time? The car began to move. Anxiety gnawed at her insides. "Alisha, did Dad say if Mama was still alive?" she asked.

"Yes, she is."

"Thank God."

For a time they kept up a running conversation between themselves, but as the hours went by and the light of day turned to semi-dusk, followed by near darkness at midnight, each lapsed into silence ... their heads lolling against the seat, propped up in the most comfortable position that the cramped space allowed.

Several hours later, the sun was already beginning to show a faint glow on the horizon when Allen drove into the farmyard at 3:30 in the morning, setting off two mongrel dogs to barking.

Lights blazed inside the farmhouse and Bill Dansky came out with a flashlight. "I didn't expect yous so soon. I'm sure glad you got here."

"How's Mama?" Tanya asked.

"Well, she's okay. But she not gonna live ... her doctor said."

A tremor went through her. She picked up her suitcase and followed her stepfather and the others into the house, thinking about getting some sleep and how bone weary she felt.

It was eight when she awoke. The exhaustion was still with her.

Alisha, in a rush to get started, hurried everybody through breakfast and into the car. Tanya kept silent, anxious that they get there as soon as possible. She tried to imagine what Mama would be doing at this moment, and her reaction when she saw all of them.

They tiptoed into the room. Mama was awake, staring at the ceiling. Tanya came close to the bed and put a hand on her arm. Alisha and Anna, their faces creased with worry, filed in beside her.She hadn't touched her breakfast and the note on her tray read, "liquids only."

"Mama, how are you?"

Her familiar face turned to them. She smiled wanly in recognition, reminding Tanya of years past when she'd crawled into her bed to reassure her of her love.

"Why, it's, it's ... Tanya! ... You're all here!" She acted surprised as though she couldn't believe that they would actually take the time to come to see her. Tears formed at the corners of her eyes.

Tanya felt a lump in her throat. "How are you, Mama?"

"Not good, child."

"Does anything hurt?"

A hand fluttered to her left side. "Here, it hurts here. My heart. The doctor said ... my heart, it's enlarged. I have no strength. ... My feet hurt."

Alisha lifted the covers and began to massage them.

Her face grimaced with pain. "Alisha, stop! Hurts too much."

Alisha, her face distressed, stopped. "But Mama, your feet are ice cold. ... And your breakfast, why didn't you eat it? It's only juice and jello."

"I can't! I just can't! ... I'm glad you came. It's good to see everybody."

Tanya stroked her head. "Mama, we want you to get better ... and come home ... soon."

Bill Dansky came to her side. "Natalie, would you like to go home?" he asked.

She gave him a searching look. "Home? Yes, I would like that, I really would." Her face crumpled. "But, I can't, it's not time."

Tanya stood, pondering what "home" she was referring to? Mama reached out and took her hand. She looked searchingly into Tanya's face. Then she smiled and whispered only loud enough for her to hear. "Bye bye, my sweetheart."

As her meaning sank in, Tanya tried to return the smile but couldn't. She freed her hand to disappear into the bathroom as a rush of tears blinded her. She leaned over the sink, crying broken-heartedly until she remembered that for Mama's sake alone she would have to be brave and bear it. With great effort, she composed herself and returned to her bedside.

There was an unsettled look about her stepfather when she re-entered. He paced nervously about the room, occasionally glancing at his wife, as if he had some worry that had to be dealt with.

"I'm glad you all here," he blurted out. "She won't sign her will without you." He withdrew a long, brown envelope from his jacket pocket and gave it to Allen.

So that was it. He wanted them home so Mama would sign the will!

Natalie, with the help of Allen and Anton, was raised up to a half sitting position. The effort was totally exhausting for her. She turned to look at her children. "You must understand that I gave Bill the biggest share of the property. I've given a farm to each of you. Alisha, you have a family, your farm is the biggest. Anna's is a bit smaller, and Tanya, who has no family, will get the smallest piece of land."

"Bill worked the land. ... He spent his days on that noisy tractor, eating dust, working late when the weather was good. It wasn't easy. He's had years of it. Now he wants it ... and he's entitled to it," she explained, coming to his defense.

They began to understand why she wanted them present. She'd always said that her share of the property would belong to them some day. Now she wanted to tell her children face to face why she'd changed her mind. To make peace between them and herself, just in case they should harbor any hard feelings toward her after she died. The unequal division of the property hadn't come without some guilt on her part.

The sisters exchanged looks, but said nothing, though their share was only a token of their stepfather's.

Mama's eyes begged them to tell her that she had done right.

She looked at her oldest, Alisha.

Alisha nodded. "It's all right, Mama, sign the will."

Allen read the will to her, then gave her a pen. She began writing each letter laboriously ... straining to make it as perfect as her weakness would allow, upset that her condition was interfering with her ability to make the signature more legible. Long ago, she'd insisted on learning to write her name instead of making just an "x", taking pride even in this small accomplishment.

Suddenly, she stopped and frowned at Bill Dansky. "Wait. I won't sign it ... not unless you promise me something."

"What? Yes, I'll promise," he said with impatience, without waiting to hear what it was she wanted.

"You must promise to leave the property to my girls when you die."

He looked at her in dismay.

She put down the pen. "Then I won't sign it."

"All right. Okay ... have it your way, I promise. Now, sign the will."

Mama glanced at Allen. "I want Allen to be my witness." She picked up the pen again. The signature ended in a scrawl as her strength gave out. Gasping for breath, she slumped back and began to cry.

Tanya came to her side. "Mama, what's wrong?"

"I have nothing left. Once, I had the farms. They used to be mine. Today, I signed them away! Everything's gone!"

Tanya remembered that she'd always equated her property with financial security. "Mama, that's silly! As long as you're alive, legally the farms are still yours. ... That's what the will says. Ask Allen, if you don't believe me."

"No, everything I've worked for is gone. Mark my words, your Dad, he's no business head. He'll twitter everything away before you know it. That money will fly from his fingers like feathers in the wind." She dabbed at her tears as Bill Dansky tucked the will back into the envelope, looking much relieved.

Tanya thought it strange that she should be so concerned about what he'd do with the farms after she was gone. It was nobody's business but his.

Her will power still strong, Natalie strained to live. Alisha wrung her hands, anxious that she not suffer. Anna quietly shed tears.

At one P.M., Dr. Reed, a slight man wearing a pair of heavy rimmed glasses, came into the room.

Mama's breathing had become more laboured, her eyes had darkened, and her skin had taken on a grey-white color. The doctor reached for his stethoscope.

Tanya turned to ask, "How is she, doctor?"

He motioned them into the corridor. "I'm sorry, your mother is dying. I'm surprised she's lasted this long. You see, though her heart is enlarged, and one of her valves isn't functioning properly, the heart muscle is still strong ... it's still working, and she's a fighter." He sighed. . ... "I'll see that she gets something for pain."

Thankfully, Mama drifted off to sleep as soon as the nurse gave her the injection, relieving their anxiety while she slept.

Tanya paced the corridor outside her room, making numerous trips to the bathroom to mourn in private.

At midnight, they went home after the nurse assured them that she would phone if there was any change.

Tanya undressed and lay down, determined to relax. Suddenly, she started to tremble. She pulled the covers tightly over her head, hoping that the warmth would calm her. However, she remained as rigid as a board with her heart hammering in her ears. Soon she was covered with perspiration and every part of her became dripping wet. Shock, fear and insecurity engulfed her. If she didn't unwind, she'd be nothing but a quivering mass of nerves in the morning.

It took hours. Finally when sleep did come, it did so on its own, and for a short space of time it brought relief, blocking out the cares and worries of the previous day.

She awoke to the sound of voices coming from the kitchen. She sat bolt upright and honed her ears to find out some news about Mama. ... "We got there just before she died. Your Dad, he was with her at the end," she heard Allen say.

A shock vibrated through her.

"What time did she die?" Alisha asked.

"I think about half past four this morning."

Tanya slowly fell back and curled up into a tight ball. "Oh Mama, Mama ... do you know how much I love you? Do you know that I really cared about you? I did, Mama, I really did!" She rocked back and forth, mourning the loss of a mother who'd showed her no affection from the very day that she was born. Yet she knew, in some strange way, that whatever kind of relationship it might have been, there must have been love at its nucleus. And Mama, who she really and truly loved, had loved her in return. Embracing this thought, she cried without restraint.

The funeral was scheduled to be held at two P.M. at the Spirit Valley United Church. It was filled to capacity. Mama's few relatives were there as well as some of Bill Dansky's family.

Reverend MacAllister, who'd served at Sam's funeral, now served at Natalie's. His hair was nearly snow white. The years had rendered him more gaunt. He was dressed in sombre black and began the service with reverence. He motioned everyone up for a hymn.

Tanya reached for the hymnal, her heart heavy from the weight of her sorrow. In front of her Allen had his arm around Alisha.

Anna was holding on to Anton's arm. They each had someone to lean on. Tanya's eyes welled, then spilled tears. However, adamant not to break down, she began to sing: ... "Through many dangers, toils and snares ... I have already come ...His grace has brought me safe thus far

... And His grace will lead me home ..." The words brought a feeling of peace to her. They commenced the second chorus: "The Lord has promised good to me ..."

Suddenly, both Alisha and Anna turned to look at her at the same time. Alisha frowned. "Sh-sh-sh-sh, you're not supposed to be singing," she hissed.

Her voice died out. Of course, she'd forgotten that it was unseemly for the bereaved to sing. But she couldn't deny that she felt better singing, and the hymn had eased her grief. Keeping her book open, she followed along in silence, saying the words to herself.

As they were about to leave for the cemetery, a cloudburst showered them with a sudden deluge of rain. However, it soon stopped and by the time they reached the plot on the hill the sun was shining again.

At the gravesite, Reverend MacAllister continued on with the burial. ... "Dear brethren, let us not grieve for Natalie. Instead, let us remember that it is in dying that we are born to eternal life. And the Lord shall call everyone of us to fulfill this promise. For Natalie, this day is a most joyous occasion. So let us not grieve for Natalie, but let us celebrate her heavenly life!"

Tanya, her heart aching, absorbed into her being the inspirational words, hoping that it was truly so for Mama and that she was happy.

After the burial, they extended an invitation for everyone to come to the house for coffee and sandwiches. Though Mama had never endeared herself to anyone, it was surprising how many of the neighbors turned up.

47

NOT LONG AFTER NATALIE'S DEATH, Bill Dansky wrote to say that he'd sold the property, as well as the farms inherited by the three sisters, to a neighbour. He'd had enough of farming, and a big auction sale would be held at the end of July.

The three girls met for coffee to discuss this sudden decision. Alisha held up her letter from him. "He says he's having a house built in Grand

Plains. And do you know that he's building two apartment blocks? Well, I suppose they won't be as hard to keep up as the farms were. It'll give him a steady income, too."

Anna sighed. "If Mama had lived, she'd never have consented to selling anything. She'd never have moved. She loved those farms too much."

At the end of July, they made the trek to Spirit Valley in Allen's car to help with the sale.

It was well attended. Hoping to get a bargain, some farmers had come from fifty miles away.

After the sale they went through Natalie's personal belongings. Tanya, still battling with her grief, didn't relish the chore. It brought back too many memories.

Alisha opened the closet doors of the master bedroom and stepped back. "You won't believe how much stuff there is in here. I have a feeling we might not get finished today."

Anna came to look. "She spent too much money on clothes. And she never gave one thing away or threw anything out. Do you know that there's five plastic garment bags full in the basement?"

Alisha began taking the clothes out of the closet. "Let's get a move on, Allen has to be at work tomorrow."

"And so does Anton! So what do we do with everything?"

"We'll give what's good to the Salvation Army. Uh-h-h, and the rest, well, I don't know."

Tanya chose the closet next to Mama's bedroom, which was also packed full. She worked quietly, while listening to Alisha and Anna chatter, thinking that in a subtle way they were still excluding her. She felt a dull ache around her heart as she opened a drawer stuffed with under-things.

The piles began to grow. One with clothing that was still salvageable, and one with clothing that was beyond saving. Some of it eaten out by perspiration stains, gave off an acrid odor and would have to be disposed of. Some things were brand new and still had price tags attached to them.

Alisha pulled out a beautiful blue crepe dress. "Isn't this her wedding dress? Hardly any wear in it. I hate to part with it. Too bad it's not my size." She threw it into the pile for the Salvation Army. "Why would she need so many things? She never went anywhere. Well ... maybe into town, sometimes. Such extravagance! You know, she always wanted us to be so thrifty."

When they finished, they went into the basement to unzip the plastic garment bags, spilling their contents onto the cement floor. Tanya went to look under the stairwell. "There's piles of shoes, boots, old stockings, purses, you name it."

Anna came to help her. "We'll have to get rid off these. Think about it ... who wants to wear somebody's old shoes?"

In the afternoon, Bill Dansky loaded the clothes onto a truck to take to the Salvation Army.

Alisha took stock of what was left. "It'll have to be burned. What else can we do with it?" She picked up an armful of shoes. By three o'clock they'd carried everything out to the middle of the garden.

Tanya thought about how hard Mama had labored for this collection of rags. This was an accumulation of a lifetime of clothes. Mama had been lavish and wasteful. Sooner then have a dress dry cleaned, she'd thrown it aside and bought a new one, never giving the cost a second thought. Was this what she'd worked for? A lump rose in her throat as Alisha touched a match to the mound.

They stood watching. The flames became a roar, sending up sparks and thick, black smoke into the air. Had it been worthwhile to deprive her children of her love so that she'd have more time to work? The senseless quarrels, the fights, had they been worthwhile? Tanya looked away as a sense of futility engulfed her.

"Alisha, Dad said we could have anything we wanted of Mama's. Are you taking anything back with you?" she wanted to know.

"Yes, a couple of these feather pillows."

Tanya bent down to examine them. The pink, flowered ticking was soiled and there were brown spots resembling blood stains on them. She could remember as a child, during the long winter months, plucking the down from the bellies of the geese, while they were still alive and quacking their protests as their feathers were pulled out against their will. She'd felt sorry for the poor geese, who were being made to withstand such painful treatment just so they could have fine down pillows to sleep on. But this was the custom in Mama's native Poland, and she'd assured them that the geese simply grew more down to replace that which was plucked out.

"Anna, how about you, what do you want?"

"I don't know if I want anything. .... Maybe this." She held up an aluminum frying pan.

Tanya couldn't believe that she'd want it. Certainly no one could accuse Anna of being materialistic. The outside of the pan, as well as the inside rim, was blackened with a thick crust of baked on grease. Only the bottom showed a circle of silver aluminum. That too, was badly pocked and pitted. "But how will you ever get it clean? Why would you want it?"

"I dunno. I guess it'll be a reminder of home. Mama used to fry potatoes in this pan. You know, I remember it from the time I was born. Cleaned? Maybe I'll have it sand blasted. I'll see." She shrugged and put it aside. "It's a link with the past." She turned to Tanya. "What about you?"

"I found this. It belonged to Mama." She held up a small, white plastic slipper. Inside the shoe, next to a white plastic gardenia, was a cheap bottle of gardenia scented perfume. "And this wool scarf of hers. I found a pair of green gloves to match it. I'll take them."

Allen walked in with Anton and their stepfather. He glanced at his watch. "It's already six. Let's hit the road. I'd like to make it home by midnight."

48

FOR TANYA THE WEEKS WHICH FOLLOWED were fraught with depression. The absolute finality of death, and the absolute separation from Mama, was more than she could bear. She treasured the memory of her last words. Again and again she mulled them over in her mind, at a loss to explain why Mama hadn't said them to her years ago.

One evening, after she'd helped Anna with the supper dishes, she went downstairs to her room. She felt a need to be alone, to sort things out in her mind. October had begun. The day was overcast, cold, raw, with a hint of fall already in the air.

She lay down and turned on a bedside light, then stretched out to full length on the pink, flowered spread. Anna had papered the walls in rose pink wallpaper. There were matching frilly, pink curtains on the window. The room, though pleasant, didn't lighten her sadness. Even the group therapy sessions had failed to stem her grief.

She switched on a small radio on the nightstand. Soft music came floating in. The melody only enhanced her sorrow as a dark wave of depression washed over her. She sagged under its weight. Then she burst into tears, thinking the sadness was too intense, too crippling for her to endure. For a minute she held on, fighting it, then she cried out in a loud voice, "Oh, my God, why was I born? What is the purpose of my life here? Oh, Lord, after I'm dead and gone, what then? Nothing? Is there nothing after that?"

Suddenly, she felt herself dying. She was up at the ceiling, weightless, floating above her bed and looking down on herself. She saw her flesh fall off her bones. She saw her bones become brittle and turn to dust.

Instantly, from the bottom part of her abdomen ... the solar plexus ... a light emerged. It filled her being with a supreme, unmistakable, knowledge. The supreme knowledge spoke to her: "But when you die there is something left. The soul is left. Your purpose in life is to take this light that I give you and touch other people's hearts with it. ... You're to touch their hearts with the light, everywhere you go."

Before her she saw an elevated highway, stretching endlessly. It was well constructed, built high, wide and smooth. There was a great multitude of people all going in the same direction. Tanya found herself standing in a ditch, alone. In her hands, she held her "light," which she knew was her very own soul.

She started walking down a winding, twisting, trail. It was a tiny path with small shrubs and small greenery beside it. As she carried her precious light, she knew that the path she was on was not traveled by many. The vision faded.

Tanya stirred on her bed. Within her, she experienced a feeling of lightness, of warmth, of incredible peace. And wonder of wonders, the depression was gone! She went over every detail of the episode in her mind. She knew that having asked God a direct question, He'd given her a direct answer and a definite purpose for her existence.

49

TANYA TORE OPEN THE ENVELOPE AND QUICKLY SCANNED through the letter her stepfather had written. She was delighted to be remembered, thinking that, though years had passed, her longing to be accepted as a daughter hadn't diminished by even one shred.

She turned to Anna, who was engrossed in making a lemon pie, a family favourite. "You know the house that's being built for Dad in Grand Plains? It's supposed to be ready at the end of October. Uh-h-h, which in fact happens to be this weekend. You know, I'd like to go down and surprise him. He might need help in arranging things ... you know, dishes, furniture. Do you suppose you and Anton might want to come?"

Anna's look was disapproving. "No. I have a child to take care of, so what help would I be?"

Tanya hid her disappointment and began making plans to take the bus.

She arrived in Grand Plains just before noon. There was no one at the depot. She hesitated, then picked up her suitcase and started walking.

Ever since divorcing Lou, she felt a need to be in touch with family. Alisha and Anna had formed their own. And since Mama had died, she'd come to regard her stepfather as "family." Was it the child in her still seeking a father?

Directly ahead unfolded a new development of houses. Tanya paused to scrutinize the address in her hand. A twinge of excitement shot through her when she realized that his was the bungalow directly across the street from where she stood. The bottom half was done in red brick, the top half painted in apple green. What an odd combination of colors! A large picture window faced the street.

Tanya quickly walked to the back and tapped lightly on the screen door. She heard footsteps then her stepfather's face gaped at her in surprise. "Were did you come from?"

"Hi Dad. I came to help you. You wrote that you'd moved. You do need help, don't you?" she asked, wondering if she'd done the right thing.

"Yes, yes, come in. So, you come to help me? ... I didn't expect no one."

She stepped inside. "It looks nice."

His lips protruded in a pout. "I'm glad you here. See the floors? Nobody cleaned 'em. They left it for me." He led her from room to room, showing off with pride the attractive three bedroom design.

"It's a nice plan," she commented, instantly wishing that Alisha or Anna had come with her. There was enough work for the three of them. The vinyl tile floors would require a thorough scrubbing as well as waxing. Every room except the living room was tiled. Dishes, canned goods, photo albums, clothing and bedding, still packed in boxes, sat in the middle of the kitchen floor.

Tanya changed into slacks and blouse then slipped on rubber gloves, deciding to begin without delay and not to waste time in idle talk. She washed the cupboards and put away the cutlery, china and groceries. Then she scrubbed the smudges off the walls left there by the movers.

After washing the vinyl floors, she waxed and buffed every room to a soft sheen. Next the furniture. She pushed and pulled the heavy pieces and placed everything where she thought it looked best. She might have enjoyed it if she hadn't been so tired.

Having found a box loaded with curtains brought over from the old house, she considered putting them up until she saw that they were sun bleached and already crumbling.

Suddenly, her energy ebbed, she eased herself into a kitchen chair, satisfied with the smell of soap and wax. In the living room her stepfather was putting away his collection of records.

"Uh-h-h, Dad, would you come in here for a minute?"

He walked in to look at her blankly.

"Uh-h-h, I just thought you'd like to see what I've done. How does it look?"

He glanced around the room. "It looks pretty good to me. Maybe you can quit for supper?"

"Yes, I'm sorry, you must be hungry. You know, I worked right through lunch without stopping once!" She opened a can of beans and took out some ham, pickles, and bread from the fridge.

Her stepfather talked about his family while they ate. John, his brother, lived in Grand Plains and visited sometimes. Neal, the youngest, was living in Edmonton. "I don't see much of him," he commented.

Tanya was amazed that he'd opened up to her. She could never remember him sharing any thoughts, news, or opinions before. She listened intently, afraid to rise lest her moving break the spell.

They finished off a pot of tea. She got up, reluctantly, and cleared the table with as little clatter as possible. He astonished her further when he picked up a tea-towel to wipe the dishes. For the first time in his life, she felt he was being kind and caring, behaving like a real father would. Her eyes glazed over.

"Tanya, I got to give you credit; you did a lota work today."

It felt wonderful to be praised. "Uh-h-h, I didn't mind it, I'm glad I came."

As soon as the dishes were done, Bill Dansky slipped into his jacket and picked up the car keys. "I need milk. You want to come for a ride?"

"No, Dad, I think I'll stay right here and put my feet up."

"Yeah, you deserve it."

She took one last turn around the spotless kitchen then went into the living room to gaze out of the picture window. The house, built on a hill, gave a wide, panoramic view of the city. She remembered the farm. The animals had always been a source of comfort to her, in some measure replacing the mother and father who had rejected her. She still missed Jip. With a pang of guilt she remembered the kick that she'd dealt him after her stepfather had kicked her. But what was done was done and no lamenting on her part could change things.

The light began to fade and sudden darkness crept into the room. Around her was perfect stillness. She allowed her mind to drift, feeling too tired to even switch on a light.

She felt grateful that she'd had the foresight to put clean sheets on the bed in the middle bedroom where she planned to sleep. The screen door creaked open as Bill Dansky returned. Tanya, captivated by the ever changing sky, could not tear herself away. She rose from the comfort of the couch and walked to the window. "You know, you have a wonderful view from here. I do love it."

Suddenly, she felt his hands at her waist. "Dad, what are you doing? ... What's going on? ... Let me go!"

Her heart leaped as she struggled to free herself from his grip. "Dad, stop it! Let me go! Are you crazy or something?" Her voice rose in alarm when she realized that he was trying to kiss her. She twisted out of his grasp and ran to the kitchen. His footsteps thudded in hot pursuit.

He made a grab for her blouse. She was conscious of a tearing sound as the buttons popped open. Flinging back her arms, she let it slip off and kept going. Must get to the door. Oh God, must get out! His fingers slid over her bare shoulder as the door gave way and she stumbled out. Tanya ran to the garage then frantically tugged at the door to get inside. What if someone should see her dressed only in a bra? Above her, a street light exposed her partly naked form. She crossed her arms over her breasts and looked back to see if he was coming after her. She saw him just inside the screen door. If I have to, she thought, I'll ask a neighbor to take me in.

Her heart began to hammer. Torn with indecision, she called out in a "no nonsense" voice, "Dad, let me come back in. I can't stay out here all night."

"I'm not stopping you. Wy did you run out?"

Tanya began to tremble from shock and cold. Fury seized her, thinking that he had his nerve! "You know why I ran out. Get away from the door. What about your neighbors, what do you think they'll say when they see me out here with almost nothing on?"

A minute later, she caught a glimpse of his face as he went past the kitchen window to disappear from view. Had he given up the chase? Perhaps he'd realized his foolishness and was thoroughly ashamed of himself? Should she return? Step by step, she crept back towards the house. Her shivering increased. Her teeth began to chatter.

Tanya turned the knob and pushed aside the door to the entry, straining for some sound of her stepfather's whereabouts. Then, thinking it was utter nonsense to be cowering outside, she walked in.

The ten o'clock news was blaring from the television in the living room. He was probably stretched out in his lazy-boy and already having second thoughts.

There was a corn broom in the entry which she picked up just in case she had to use it. Slowly, she climbed the two steps into the kitchen. The warm air felt good, but her heart continued to pound. She crept further in, her ears straining for sound.

As soon as she cleared the living room door, she heard his step behind her. She whirled around. "Oh my God!" He was but an arm's reach away. His face told her that he was far from regretting anything!

Quickly, she ran into the middle bedroom and took cover behind the bed. "What do you want?" she cried, swinging the broom in a wide arc just inches away from his head ... wanting to hit him, yet not daring to.

He grinned, "You know wat I want. Just wat you come here to get." His voice became more coaxing. "It's nothing to be ashamed of. You been married. ... I been married. You know wat it's about. I'm not going to hurt you. We both grown up. I'm not you real father. A stepfather is not the same. Now wat you say tonight we sleep together?"

She cringed in revulsion, at the same time furious. "How can you even think of such a horrible thing? What kind of a person do you think I am? That's evil! That's what it is! ... Stand back! I came here to help you, nothing more. My motives were true! ... Sincere! Get that through your head!"

He edged closer. She panicked, this time letting the corn broom swing against his face. "Keep away from me, or I'll hit you harder!"

"Then you gonna get wat you asking for." He laughed and dodged the broom as she made another swipe at him.

"Oh God, I said to keep away from me!"

Suddenly, he flopped across the bed and made a grab for her pant leg. Tanya beat at it with the broom then ran out into the next bedroom, slamming the door with such force that the house shuddered.

"Don't you dare come after me!" she screamed. Fearing that he might try to break in, she began pushing a chest of drawers towards the door. A minute later, she heard his step in the hallway. She watched in horror as the knob began to turn. She started to sob.

"If ... if ... you don't leave me alone, I'm going to call the police and report you. For the last time, get out of here! You know what the penalty for rape is, don't you? You'll go to jail!"

The knob stopped turning. Tanya exhaled her breathe in relief as he shuffled off, knowing that it was the fear of being reported and exposed as a criminal that finally convinced him.

Exhausted to the point of hysteria, she slumped across the bed and lay rigid, terrified that he might still return. Suddenly, she remembered that her suitcase was in the next bedroom and that she had no access to her night clothes. She got up, and went to the closet to put on one of his shirts, then lay down on the bed, tucking the corn broom close to her side.

She lay still, forcing herself to relax, though her heart was still thudding madly inside her chest. After a time, she heard him turn off the television, throwing the house into total silence.

Tanya let out her breath and tried to unwind. Much later, she fell asleep. However, still keeping an uneasy vigil all night, coming to full wakefulness at each sound. Eventually, she slept for several hours. At dawn she awakened, having decided to get her suitcase from the next bedroom.

Carefully, she inched aside the dresser drawer with just enough room to squeeze through. She opened the door a crack and examined the hallway. Her eyelids felt dry and the muscles in her arms ached when she moved. To think that I put myself out for this, this kind of reward, she thought.

His steady snore assured her that he was sleeping. Now, in the next room, she gathered her things and threw everything into the suitcase. Then, with her coat over her shoulder, she went back to the other bedroom.

She pushed the dresser against the door again and changed into the navy blue suit that she'd worn on the bus. It was only four-twenty A.M. and much too early for him to be awake.

I'll come out decently dressed, she thought, as she sank into a chair to wait.

It was almost two hours later before she heard him get up and go about his morning chores. The routine sounds were comforting, somehow restoring order to the madness of the night before. By now, it was already six-thirty. A short time passed, then she heard the clanging of pots and and tap water running into the kettle for coffee. She rose to her feet, wondering if it was safe to come out.

Tanya picked up her suitcase and started towards the hallway. Suddenly, she remembered the corn broom and went back to get it. If he gives me even the slightest reason, I'll use it on him, she assured herself.

He was stirring a pot of oatmeal when she walked in. She looked at him, warily. He appeared dead sombre.

Now he turned towards her. "Good morning."

"Good morning." Slowly, she ventured further in, then put the broom back into the entry, thinking that definitely he was in a different frame of mind. "What's for breakfast?"

"Porridge, I made porridge."

She went to the cupboard and taking care not to get too close to him, she took out two bowls and some cutlery.

He spooned half of the gruel into each bowl and sat down to eat it, his face deep in thought.

She sensed a reserved and dignified attitude with no hint of last night. He had resumed his role of the uncompromising parent, his demeanor telling her that he was still in charge.

Suddenly, overcome with inferiority, she felt like a child that needed to be punished and shrank back into her shell. It took nerve to announce that she was leaving. "Do you think you could drive me to the bus depot?" she asked, not entirely sure of what he'd say.

"Yeah. We'll take the car."

At the bus depot, she tried to read his face for some sign of remorse. He remained impassive, aloof, and avoided direct eye contact.

She held out her hand, "Good-bye, Dad."

He looked up, startled. Taking her hand, his look softened. "Good-bye."

Tanya boarded the bus with leaden feet and made her way to the back, thinking that it would not appear seemly for strangers to see her cry.

The events of the past night made circles in her head as she reviewed them over and over. She felt disoriented. At times, she slept in fits and starts. He'd taken her by surprise; it was the last thing that she'd expected from him. Was it her fault?

It would take some time to adjust to this new knowledge and come to grips with what to do about the relationship. Should she end it? She forced the thought out of her mind. When the pain lessened, she'd deal with it then.

The next day, still very confused, she went to work, her mind whirling as she tried to make some order out of the shocking events which she'd endured. It would mean an entire change in attitude towards him. At the end of the day, she felt more stressed out than ever before as the problem presented itself again and again.

Finally she reached a solution, knowing that for the sake of her sanity she'd have to cut the ties for good.

She entered her apartment and reached into the letterbox for the mail. A smile spread over her face at the sight of a letter marked "special delivery". It was in her stepfather's handwriting.

Her fingers trembling, Tanya tore it open. It read: Dear Tanya, I hope you made it home okay. I'm sorry for the way I acted. It was not a nice thing to do. What for, I don't know. Please forgive a old man. ......
Your Dad.

She smiled to herself. He'd come to his senses! Forgive? Of course, she would forgive! Her problems vanished, her head cleared, as she flew upstairs to call him long distance.

50

TANYA SAT TYPING FURIOUSLY. She felt unsettled to the point of distraction. Her vacation was about to begin, but she couldn't decide where to go.

Outside the office window, the world was etched in thick hoar frost. It was January; generally the city recorded its coldest temperatures at this time of year. She paused halfway through a letter and reached for the telephone remembering that at their last session with Dr. Carlsten, Lea Thompson had mentioned that she was flying to Arizona to visit an aunt. She thought it might help to talk to her. She picked up the phone. ... "Lea, when does your plane leave?"

"I fly to Phoenix in the morning. ... What about you?"

"I, uh-h-h, I'm giving Vancouver some thought, but I can't say for sure. I'd really like to get away from this cold."

"Tanya, if you should change your mind, if things don't work out, I'll give you Aunt Bea's phone number in Phoenix."

"That's awfully nice of you." She laughed. "Who knows, you just might see me there. Actually, I have three weeks of holidays this year. ... Lea, thanks for the offer."

Tanya rushed home after work. Having made up her mind to head for Vancouver, she withdrew $350.00 from the bank to cover bus fare, accommodations, meals, and perhaps do some shopping. Frugality was a way of life with her; she knew all the tricks on how to survive on very little.

The next day she boarded a bus for the coast. She arrived hours later, but the city was far from sunny. Dismayed, Tanya stepped off the bus into a drenching rain. She shrugged, thinking that it couldn't last for more than a day or two. To make things worse she hadn't brought any rainwear, not even an umbrella!

"Taxi! ... The YWCA, please."

Her room at the "Y" was another disappointment; but what could one expect for $8.00 a day? It was small, dreary, and furnished with only the basics: single bed, bare light bulb suspended from a high ceiling, and an upright dresser. A narrow window overlooked an uninspiring parking lot below. In the morning, if the rain stops, I'll book some tours just to get away from this miserable room, she thought.

She awoke early, full of expectations, only to find that it was still raining. Disappointed, Tanya spent the time reading on her bed.

On the third day, instead of diminishing, it began pouring down in sheets. She sprinted next door to the diner for breakfast. By now, her navy blue wool coat was so saturated with dampness that it actually seemed heavier.

Breakfast was eaten in moody contemplation before dashing back to her room. Outside, she noticed a low ceiling of clouds, which made her think that it didn't look too promising for the next day, either. A dreaded thought crept into her mind. What if it rained for the next three weeks? Already three precious days had slipped by.

Frustrated, she mulled over Lea Thompson's offer. So why not try Phoenix? The desert was sure to be dry and warm. Lea would be more than happy to see her. Her aunt's phone number was as good as an invitation. She rose from the rumpled bed and went downstairs to check on plane fare to Phoenix.

She found out the cost was quite minimal. And she'd still have enough left over for a decent hotel room. Tanya booked a late flight and went to repack her bags.

The plane touched down in Phoenix a little after midnight. It had been a smooth trip with almost no turbulence, for which she was grateful. She had a fear of flying. As she stepped onto the tarmac, she was caressed by a soft desert breeze. Suddenly Tanya remembered that there hadn't been time to book hotel reservations. Would she have any trouble finding a room at this late hour?

She cleared U.S. Customs and asked a flight attendant about a hotel. "I'd like something central and not too expensive," she told the girl.

"I think I know just what you want. How about 'The Adams'? Sometimes our crew stays there. But first, phone them."

"Thank you, I will."

The night clerk assured her that they had rooms available. Tanya happily went outside to call a cab. It had been a long day, and she felt spent. Her taxi stopped in front of a stately, impressive looking building. She sat up, wondering if the attendant had really meant this hotel? It looked far too luxurious for what she had in mind.

"This is it, Ma'am, 'The Adams'."

She paid the fare and slowly got out, self conscious about going any further. Marble steps led up to an impressive brass door. Tanya entered the lobby, her feet sinking into a thick, burgundy rug. Even if I can't afford it, she thought, I'll ask about the price. Who knows, they might know of some place that's cheaper. She caught the eye of a tall, thin clerk behind the desk.

"Yes, may I help you?"

Tanya took a deep breath. "Actually, I think we just spoke on the phone about a room." She hurried on. ... "I'm Tanya Hagen, from from Canada, ... on vacation. And, I, uh-h-h, my budget is, uh-h-h, rather limited. ... I was wondering, do you have anything that's not too expensive? In fact, how much is your cheapest room?"

His eyebrows went up. The bellhop standing close by, sidled closer. "How about 526, Joe? Isn't that empty?"

The clerk nodded. "Yeah, it might be." He scanned the register. "Well, Miss Hagen, I believe we can accommodate you. This room is small, but clean. Sorry, no bath. However, you'll find it comfortable." He smiled. "And the rate is $5.00 a night. Occasionally, we rent it to the airlines personnel."

Tanya couldn't believe the price. She gushed out, "Thank you so very much!"

He held out his hand. "My name is Joe Webster. This is Hugh Bronston, he'll take up your luggage." He handed her a gold pen. "Sign here, please. We always get a fair number of Canadians at this time of year. ... If there's anything you need, Miss Hagen, please let us know."

"Thank you," she said, thinking that not only was he downright courteous but he had gone out of his way to be kind to her. Now that was class!

On the fifth floor, the bellboy pointed to the end of the corridor. "If you like swimming, there's a heated pool in there. And, if you want to take a bath, there's a bathtub in room 530. Just ask someone for a key at the desk." He unlocked the door and she went inside.

"Thank you, you've been very kind." She reached into her purse and gave him fifty cents, wondering if that was enough? "Good night, Hugh. It's a pleasure to have met you."

"Yes, thanks." He smiled and left.

She noticed the room was spotlessly clean. The walls were painted in a soft pink. An antique chest of drawers, intricately carved, with ornate brass handles, stood opposite the bed. There was a writing desk to match. The small bathroom contained only a sink and toilet. The rug, a floral in pink and apple green, though slightly worn, was of good quality.

She sat down on the single bed, covered with a rose chenille spread, and slipped off her shoes. Several toss cushions in pink velvet were strewn at the head. Everything was beautifully co-ordinated including a tufted, plush velvet arm chair in apple green by the window. There were elegant, damask drapes sweeping down to the floor.

Tanya caught sight of herself reflected in a white framed, stand-up, full length mirror. Indeed, for $5.00, the room more than exceeded her expectations.

Quickly she washed her face, changed into a night gown, then slipped between snow white sheets, exhausted but content. A far cry from the room at the Y. ... So thankful to be here, Lord. ... Even a bathtub, a few doors from here. ... No need to worry.

She awoke at eleven. She stretched, languishing in the comfort of the bed, then slowly got to her feet. Tanya pulled aside the drapes to encounter a blazing sun. What a relief from the rain! She smiled. Now to dress and go down for breakfast.

Across the street, she found a small cafe, "The Magnolia." It was a quaint diner with non of the flamboyance of an expensive restaurant. She sat down in a booth and ordered lunch. The food was delicious, the meal reasonably priced.

When she finished, she went back to her room to check out the pool. How exciting to have an indoor, heated pool. She noticed that there were several hot shower stalls and thought it fortunate that she'd remembered her bathing suit. Now to give Lea a surprise call.

"Is Lea Thompson there, please?" She tried to keep her voice calm. ... "Lea, this is Tanya," she said, laughing.

"Tanya! ... How are you? Where are you calling from?"

"Lea, I'm in Phoenix! I got here, uh-h-h, this morning, actually. You wouldn't believe it; but it was raining buckets in Vancouver. So-o-o, when it wouldn't let up, I decided I'd had enough and flew here. I'm staying at The Adams Hotel. Surprised?"

"Yes, yes, of course I am." Her tone took on a more formal note. ... "Well, it was nice of you to call, Tanya. We'll have to get together sometime."

Did she imagine it, or was Lea's reception cool? "Yes, Lea, we will." The conversation suddenly went flat, making her wonder if she'd really meant it when she'd invited her to 'come to Pheonix'.

"Nice talking to you Lea. You're right, we'll have to meet soon. Bye for now."

Furious, Tanya hung up. The girl couldn't be that stupid! She must know that I wouldn't know one solitary soul in Phoenix! I came only because of her invitation. Why didn't she suggest a definite place and date to meet? She didn't even ask me what room I'm in.

Suddenly, weariness swept over her. Tanya reached into the nightstand and brought out a steamy, adventure novel. The velvet cushions looked inviting; she lay back and began to devour the pages.

The next three days she spent secluded in her room, reading and sleeping. She reveled in its coziness, grateful to be in such appealing, pleasant surroundings. She shrugged off the fact that Lea didn't try to reach her.

Tanya, with ample time on her hands, made friends with the hotel staff. They were more than willing to talk to her, making her stay all the more enjoyable.

On the fourth day, well into the afternoon, she tore herself away from her book long enough to change into a white, lycra, two- piece bikini, which showed off her slender form to perfection! She reached for a thick, white towel and sauntered down to the pool, wondering who her neighbours might be? Other than some teen-aged children that she'd heard splashing in the pool one night, there didn't seem to be one solitary person around.

She'd almost reached the end of the corridor when she heard the distinct sound of a door closing. Tanya paused, turned, and examined the hallway behind her, expecting to see someone. However, there was no one in sight. The back of her neck stiffened. For some reason, she had the strangest feeling that unseen eyes were watching her.

She dived into the pool, thinking that it was absurd to think that someone would be watching her. Once in the warm water, she swam until fully exhausted before pulling herself up on deck. Then she showered and wound a towel, turban style, around her wet hair before starting back. As she was about to turn the key, once more she was startled by the soft click of a door. Alarm shot through her. With pounding heart, Tanya turned to scrutinize the hallway only to find it empty. This time the eerie feeling stayed, and thinking that things were not quite what they appeared, she went inside and locked the door securely.

As soon as she'd changed her clothes, she fell back onto the bed into the ready comfort of the pink cushions and her book. Almost instantly, she was asleep. The paperback slid off her chest with hardly more than one paragraph read.

A short time later, she awoke, knowing that with nothing to do, boredom had already set in. The room might be comfortable and lovely to look at, but it was time to see something of the outside world.

She touched up her make-up and went downstairs. The bellboy was in the lobby. She caught his attention. "Hugh? Tell me what kind of activities do you have for a tourist? ... For instance, what do you do?"

"Me? Well, on my days off, I go horseback riding to a dude ranch. ... "The Horseshoe Ranch," actually." As soon as he noticed her interest, he went into greater detail.

Tanya was completely sold on the idea. She awoke early the next morning and took a bus out of town. Since she'd never before sat on a horse, she knew that she'd have to sign up for riding lessons. The trainer assigned a horse called "Stardust" to her, a gentle, docile animal. She happily took to him.

From the start she hung on to the bridle, as well as his mane, expecting at any moment to be bucked off or thrown off.

However on the second day, she became bolder and urged Stardust to a confident trot. ... The third day to a gallop. Eventually, she streaked over the range, exhilarated by the rush of wind in her face and her hair streaming back.

Stardust seemed to sense just how fast he should run. She had no trouble controlling him. For the next five days, Tanya went to the ranch every day. Though the riding made her feel happy, free, she still felt that something was amiss. She knew that tucked away, waiting in the wings of her thoughts, burned the intense hope of meeting that certain person.

On the fifth day, the lesson over, she returned Stardust to the stables for the last time. They'd been together for only a short while, but she already loved him. What a pity to be saying "goodbye" so soon. She stroked his neck, thinking that it would be wonderful, although impractical, if he were hers.

At four, she was back at the hotel and went up to shower in one of the stalls by the pool. When she finished she changed into a turquoise, cotton shift, with matching turquoise earrings, then ventured across the street to the cool comfort of The Magnolia. She was thoroughly parched and longing for a drink.

Inside it was the slack time of day and there were very few customers. She smiled at the bartender and slid into a seat by the counter. "A glass of ginger ale, please."

He put down a tall, frosted glass in front of her. Behind her the door opened. She raised her eyes and glanced into the mirror. The man who entered looked about thirty. He was of medium height with pale complexion and dark hair smoothed back. She noticed that he was clean shaven and dressed casually in a short sleeved, white shirt and teal blue dress pants. "Suave," she thought would best describe him.

He glanced around the room and came to sit next to her.

"Sir, what'll it be?"

"Coffee."

Tanya looked straight ahead, keeping her eyes on her drink, though she sensed him looking at her.

"Hi. Hot, isn't it?"

"Hm-m-m, yes." She wasn't surprised when he spoke to her, her intuition told her that he would. She glanced at him sideways. He smiled, the smile giving his face a boyish look. She sought for a first impression. She put great stock into first impressions. Handsome, but not my type.

"Are you here alone?" he asked.

"Yes."

"Vacation or something?"

"Yes, vacation. Why do you ask? Does it show?"

His blue eyes narrowed. "You're not from Arizona, are you?"

"No. How do you know that?"

"Uh-h-h, you don't speak the same as us. It's your accent. ... Don't get me wrong, it's all right. It's just ... unusual, that's all. You speak distinctly. You don't drawl out your words like we do." He took a sip of coffee. "My name is Roy Billingston." He held out his hand. "I'm pleased to make your acquaintance!"

Remembering her promise to Dr. Carlsten about not picking up strangers, she hesitated for a moment, yet how could she avoid it? ... "How do you do, I'm Tanya Hagen."

"Tanya, so where exactly do you come from, if you don't mind my asking?"

"Uh-h-h, Canada. Actually, Edmonton. I'm sure you've never even heard of it."

He laughed. "You're right, I haven't. But, welcome to Phoenix!"

"Thanks. So far, I just love everyone I've met here. Everybody's so friendly," she said, thinking of the staff. "And I think your weather is simply so wonderful." His hands, holding the cup, were beautifully manicured.

"Yeah, I know what you mean. I live on a ranch with my grandmother near Tucson. I'm here with a friend of mine. We're staying in a motel a few miles out. What about you?"

"Me? I'm staying across the street at The Adams."

"Yeah? Looks like a nice place!"

Their conversation picked up momentum. She missed having someone to talk to and opened up readily to his questions. At the same time, some things she left unsaid.

An hour later, they were still talking. Roy glanced at his watch. "Tanya, how would you like to have dinner with me?"

She hesitated. "Uh-h-h, I'm not really sure that I should."

He looked directly at her. "Tanya, please, let me buy you dinner."

Thinking that it was charming of him to have spent so much time with her, she didn't have the heart to say "no". ... "Well, if you insist."

He rose to his feet. "Let's move to a booth."

She nodded, and slid into a padded seat, thinking it would be easier to talk facing each other.

He handed her a menu. "Go ahead, order anything you like," he urged.

"Thank you." Tanya scanned it, looking for the cheapest item. This early on, she didn't want to be indebted to him. "I'll have the hamburger special. Uh-h-h, it comes with fries and a drink." The price, she noticed, was only $2.50.

Roy motioned to the waiter. "The lady wants the 'burger special', and, I'll have the steak and fries."

The conversation veered from one subject to another. Their order arrived. She ate the hamburger with relish. Roy seemed very well informed on almost any subject.

Much later they sat sipping the last of their coffee. Outside, the street lights had been turned on for some time. Tanya checked her watch. "Oh, already ten! Sorry Roy, I must be getting back. It's been nice talking to you. Interesting, too, I must say."

He smiled. "Please, may I walk you to the hotel?"

"If you wish. But it won't be necessary. It's only across the street. No need to go out of your way."

"Don't mind in the least."

Roy paid the bill and held the door open for her. "Tanya, I'd like to see you again. How about tomorrow night? Uh-h-h, there's a good picture playing at The Grande. We'll have drinks first, dinner, then the movie. How about it?"

She hesitated, feeling that the evening was going far too fast for her. "Roy, I'm not sure. Call me tomorrow, I'll let you know then."

He frowned. "It would mean a lot to me if you would say "yes". You see, I don't know anyone in this town, either. How about it?"

He'd make a very handsome escort, she thought, until someone better came along. "Well, if you put it that way, I guess I'll say "yes"."

Outside there was a gentle breeze blowing. Surprising that after each hot day, the evenings were so refreshingly cool! The almost perfect weather never ceased to amaze her; she wondered if the locals felt the same about it? Roy took her hand. She was struck by the silky softness of his skin; it rivaled her own. Was he some gentleman rancher with servants to do all the work? It was a distinct possibility. With Tuscon being next door to the Mexican border, he'd have easy access to cheap labor.

They reached her door. I won't ask him in, she thought, feeling uneasy about the way they'd met. Yet it seemed so natural. What could be wrong with it? "Roy, I've had a delightful evening. Thank you very much, for dinner ... and good night!"

"It was a fine evening for me too, Tanya. I can't remember having such a good time in ages. Only sorry thing is that it has to end so soon. See you about seven-thirty tomorrow night?"

She nodded. Then, sensing that he was about to kiss her, she turned her head slightly to one side. The kiss grazed her cheek, landing close to her ear. It's too soon for kissing, she thought. Their brief encounter didn't warrant such intimacy. "See you tomorrow night, Roy."

A look of annoyance flashed over his face. He quickly turned on his heel and left her. Tanya waited until he'd walked away before going in.

She kicked off her sandals, washed her face, and prepared for bed, thinking that though he was very handsome and appeared, to the outward eye, to be attentive, she found him strangely detached. There were times during their conversation when his mind seemed to wander. It was almost as if his heart wasn't in it.

The next day, anticipating her date with Roy, she began washing her hair at three in the afternoon. Usually it took a long time to dry. She changed into her bathing suit, lathered on shampoo, then ran down the hall to a shower stall to rinse it off. When she felt it squeaky clean, she returned with her head wrapped in a towel prepared to air dry it. She made sure that the door was locked before taking off her bathing suit and putting on a slip, because she'd forgotten to bring a bath robe. Tanya was busy towelling off when the telephone rang. She reached for the receiver with annoyance. ... "Hello?"

"Tanya? This is Roy. I'm in the lobby. Mind if I come up to see you?"

Dismay shot through her. "Roy? Uh-h-h, but you're not supposed to be here until seven-thirty! Besides, I'm not ready!"

"But, I must see you right now! I have to talk to you about something. ... Uh-h-h, it's very urgent!"

"Sorry Roy, you can't come up. I mean I'm not ready. In fact, I've just washed my hair and it's still dripping wet. Sorry. ... So-o-o, if you don't mind, I'll see you at 7:30, just as we planned, okay?"

"But ... but, Tanya, this won't take long, I promise. ... I need only a few minutes to explain something."

Her anger mounted. Entertaining him in her slip would be unthinkable! "I'm sorry, Roy, but that's impossible! Not only is my hair wet, but I'm not dressed, either. I've gotta run. Bye!" She hung up, wondering what on earth could be so critical that it couldn't wait for a couple of hours?

Seconds later she jumped as a fist hammered on her door. Her heart began a rapid pounding, wondering whether it was Roy? How could it be him so soon when he'd just phoned her from the lobby? It would take him longer than a few seconds to come up. ... "Yes, who is it?"

"It's me, Roy. Tanya, open the door and let me in!"

"Well of all the ... !" He had his gall! "No, Roy, I'm not going to open it because I can't. I mean I won't. I'm not letting you in and that's final!"

"But there's something I have to talk to you about real bad. I need only five minutes!"

"No, Roy! Please, leave! I'll see you later," she said emphatically, making her wish that she hadn't made the date.

"But, I must see you."

"Whatever for?" She sighed. "Okay, I'll tell you what I'll do. ... I'll meet you downstairs in the lobby in half an hour. How's that?"

"Okay, half an hour."

As his footsteps grew fainter, she breathed a sigh of relief.

However, she speeded up dressing, losing no time in putting on makeup, tying back her still wet hair, then slipping into a crisp Hawaiian print.

The half hour was nearly up. She found her pearl beaded evening bag into which she stuffed lipstick, compact, and comb. She paused. Should she take all her money with her? She opened her leather purse, removed all the bills and put them into the evening bag. But what if she should lose it? She took the roll out again and counted out $8.00 then put the rest under the mattress. For an emergency, it'll be enough, she thought. Why did Roy sound so desperate?

He was waiting for her when the elevator door opened on the main floor. He looked worried. "Hi."

Her anger dissipated, sensing an urgency in his manner. "Roy, what's wrong?"

"I want to ask you something. You might be able to help me. Let's go to The Magnolia for coffee."

"Yes, of course."

He chose a booth by the window and they sat down. Roy signaled the waiter. "Jack, a couple of coffees, please."

It took a minute to fill the order, with Tanya wondering in suspense about his problem. She noticed that occasionally, he looked nervously toward the street than forced his eyes back to her.

"I'll tell you what's happened."

"I'd like to hear it."

"Remember I told you I lived with my grandmother?"

"Yes, I do remember that you said that."

"Well she got real sick. ... It was sudden like. They've taken her by ambulance to a hospital. I've got to find a way to get back to Tuscon tonight. The doctor says it's mighty serious with her. Uh-h-h, and you know what else?"

"No."

Again, his eyes wandered out the window and directly behind her. "I don't know how to explain this ... but I overspent. Uh-h-h ... it turns out that I'm short of cash." He covered her hand with his. "I don't like to ask, and under different circumstances I wouldn't ... but I need to catch a plane to Tucson, real quick. There's a flight out of here at seven-thirty tonight. I'd give anything to be there with her. She needs me. She's all the family I've got in the world. ... Tanya, you wouldn't have any extra money that you could lend me, would you?"

"Roy, I'm so sorry to hear about your poor grandmother! I hope she'll be all right! I can see that you're very concerned about her."

He nodded, emphatically. "You bet."

Tanya, being the decent Christian at heart and wanting to do the decent thing, felt that this was her chance to do a good deed. Part of her nature had always leaned toward helping others. She opened her purse. "Uh-h-h, it so happens that I only have $8.00 with me. How much can I spare? ... Lets see. ... Since I have to get back to Canada ... about $8.00. I'm not rich. Just a poor working girl ... that's all I am."

He appeared crestfallen. "You wouldn't have more, would you?"

She noticed him looking out the window again. Curious, Tanya followed his gaze and looked over her shoulder. She saw a long, sleek, shiny, pink Cadillac parked by the curb. There was a short, very fat, bald headed Mexican sitting behind the wheel. "Uh-h-h, excuse me, I couldn't help but notice ... uh-h-h, do you know the man in that car?"

He nodded. "Yeah, he's a friend of mine. He's waiting to drive me to the airport."

"Oh!" His friend must have all the time in the world, she thought with nothing better to do than sit in his car and wait for him. Roy should have asked him to come into the cafe. She wondered why he hadn't? She reached into her handbag and took out the $8.00. "Roy, here's the money. Sorry it can't be more."

"Thanks."

"Oh, wait!" I'll give you my name and address. I'm sure you'll want to send it back to me when you get the chance." She picked up a napkin and wrote her Edmonton address on it. Then she emptied her change purse and paid for their coffee. In that instance, he reminded her of Lou.

"Thanks, you don't know how much I appreciate this."

"That's okay." She stood up. "Uh-h-h, I do hope your grandmother recovers soon. Good luck to you, and have a safe flight home." She held out her hand. "Good bye, Roy. It was nice knowing you."

"Yeah, same here. Good bye. And thanks."

They parted, each going their separate ways. She looked over her shoulder to see Roy getting into his friend's pink Cadillac. Couldn't he have borrowed the money from him? Or was he broke as well? A car like that took money to maintain. She sighed. Some people were poor money managers.

Nevertheless, she walked into the lobby feeling jubilant. Some of the staff were gathered at the reception desk talking to Joe Webster. She noticed Lin Holmes, the hotel maid, and Dick Hanson, the accountant. She smiled at them.

Dick Hanson nodded to her. "So, what've you been up to?"

"Dick, you'll never guess! Actually, just now, I did my good deed for the day."

The accountant swiveled his head toward her. "And what may that be? Care to tell us about it?"

"As a matter of fact, first let me tell you about this guy I met at The Magnolia Cafe. ... I hate to admit it, but we only met yesterday, and, we got to talking. He bought me dinner. Then he asked me to go to a movie with him ... that was supposed to be tonight. He said he was a rancher and lived with his grandmother near Tucson. Uh-h-h, just a while ago he found out that she was sick, so he wanted to fly back to Tuscon on the seven-thirty flight to be with her. Well, it turns out that on top of everything else, he's broke. So he asked me if I could help him out. ... I gave him $8.00. It was all I had on me. Actually, to tell you the truth, it's all I could really afford to give him."

Dick Hanson frowned. "You shouldn't have done that."

"Why not?"

"For the simple reason that he may have been trying to con you."

Joe nodded. "Yeah, he's right, you know. That was a mistake. There's lots of guys out here looking for a handout. You never know, he might be one of them. I know, because we've had some of them staying in this very hotel. Remember, this city is a tourist haven and most tourists, when they travel, bring plenty of cash with them. Whenever one of these con artists come into town, they pick on someone new to the area. You know, someone lonely. Then they give them a sob story about how they're short of cash ... happens all the time."

Her smile faded, wondering if he was right? "Oh, do you really think so? Well, he could have fooled me. However, it wasn't that much money. And who knows, maybe he was in need ... so why not?" She remembered the Cadillac, thinking that he didn't appear to be all that needy!

Lin Holmes lowered her voice, "Just the same, I'd be more careful if I were you, Tanya."

She nodded. "Yes, I can see that. But, he's gone. So, we won't worry about it. I think I'll go up to my room for a while. See you, later."

She picked up her novel and settled back, wondering if she'd been conned? At exactly seven-thirty, she left her room and took the elevator downstairs. It was time for dinner. She smiled at Joe Webster behind the desk. "I'm off to The Magnolia, they've got Louisiana shrimp on the menu."

"Sounds delicious!"

Outside the street was crowded with people; feeling a sense of buoyancy, she breathed deeply of the pleasant night air. Suddenly, she stopped dead in her tracks! Roy Billingston was coming directly towards her! Another second and they were face to face. She looked at him in disbelief. "But ... but ... aren't you supposed to be on your way to Tucson?"

His pale face paled a touch more. The muscles in his lower jaw sagged. He looked uncomfortable. His eyes swerved in one direction then another before coming to rest at his feet. "Tanya, I can explain all this ... if you'll let me."

Instantly, she recognized the look. Joe Webster was right! He had conned her! And she, like a dummy, had fallen for it! Looking at him, she sensed that he was lying to her. No doubt, he'd figured her as easy pickings! Her dislike for him soared.

"Explain? What's to explain? You were lying to me, weren't you? You were taking advantage of me ... weren't you? Well, tell you what! I want my money back! Do you hear me? I said I want my money back! You can hand it over to me, right now!" Furious, she held out her hand.

"Okay, okay, quiet down. I'll give you your money back. But stop shouting. ... Aw ... come on, Tanya, give me a break, will you? ... I told you I can explain it. It's not the way it looks."

He motioned across the street. "Come with me to that car. We'll talk in there."

"I'm not sure that I ought to." ... Her voice trailed off. The pink Cadillac was parked at the curb, and barely clearing the steering wheel, she saw the swarthy face of the Mexican.

The light switched to green. Roy started across the street. "Come on!"

She held back. By now, he'd nearly reached the other side. In view of everything that had happened, she wasn't sure of what she should do. Slowly she started after him, ignoring her instincts which recoiled at having any more dealings with such a person. The Cadillac beckoned like a neon light. Suddenly, looking at it, Tanya sensed danger. At the same time, barring her advance, she felt a strange force of an ethereal nature stopping her. She remained still, held firmly back by an unseen hand, with half of her wanting to go, while the other half warned her against it. While she debated, the light changed to red. Tanya, much relieved, stepped back to the sidewalk.

A rush of wind attracted her attention as a police cruiser pulled up in front of her and stopped flush with the curb where she stood. There were two men inside. Again, her anger took over.

Catching the eye of the trooper at the wheel, she made a motion that she wished to speak to him. His partner rolled down the window. She put her face close to his then pointed to the car. "Do you see that pink Cadillac over there?"

"Yes ma'am, shore do." he drawled.

"I'm from Canada, and, you know, one of those men in that car, he just conned me out of some money. And I don't know what it is, but there's something dreadfully wrong with that car. And those men in there ... officer, if I were you, I'd check them out."

The light switched to green again. Tanya straightened up. She'd done her duty! She felt somewhat better as she went back to the hotel, too upset to think of food at the moment. She'd reported a crime and if the police were smart, they'd take her advice and do some investigating.

Back at the hotel she marched to the desk. "Joe, I came to tell you that you were right. You won't believe this, but ... that guy I was telling you about? I just met him in the street. He didn't fly to Tuscon. He told me about his grandmother so I'd feel sorry for him. The nerve of him!"

Joe shook his head. "Well, I hate to say 'I told you so', but like I said, it happens all the time."

Dick Hanson looked up from his ledger. "I'm curious Tanya, what did he say to you? What kind of excuse did he give you?"

"None! He had no excuse. He told me he could explain it. But, by then, I was so mad that I never gave him a chance. You know, for some reason he kept saying that he wanted me to get into his friend's car. Whatever for, I don't know. He wouldn't tell me. His friend owns this impressive looking pink Cadillac, of all things! Imagine owning a Cadillac and not having any money! Well ... I just happened to see a police car, so I told them to check those guys out. I hope they do."

Hugh Bronston suddenly came to life. "Tanya, what did this guy look like? Was he kind of pale, tall, with dark brown hair combed back? ... And his friend, is he Mexican ... short and fat, ... am I right?"

"Yes, that's Roy. How do you know him?"

"How? My God, they're both staying right here at this hotel. ... As a matter of fact, they're directly across the hall from you. Wanna know their room number? ... They're in room 527!"

Joe nodded. "Hugh's right. They're on the fifth floor same as you."

Tanya's eyes widened. "What? Then why would he tell me that they were staying in a motel?"

Joe shook his head." Your guess is as good as mine. Who knows what they're up to."

Tanya's face suddenly drained of color. "Wait a minute! I must tell you something. It was so strange, because several times I had the feeling that I was being watched when I went to use the pool. And you know, I never did see anybody around there. But I'd hear a sound like a door closing. Every time I looked to see who it was, there was nobody there. ... It scared me! It must have been them! But why? What would they want with me?" This new revelation injected fear into her. Tanya's hands flew to her face. "What am I going to do?"

Joe looked at her, sharply. "You know, if they're spying on you, you just might be in some kind of danger. Tell you what we'll do ... we'll switch your room. Hugh, go up with her and move her to room 811. Just a precaution. ... I wouldn't want them breaking in during the night. No telling what could happen. And I'll speak to the house detective about keeping an eye out for them." He noticed Tanya's horrified look. "It's nothing to worry about, you'll be all right."

Suddenly, Carol Denning, the operator at the switchboard, signaled to her. "Tanya, there's a call for you. I think it's Roy. He wants to speak to you. If you ask me, he sounds angry."

She froze. "What should I do? I don't want to talk to him!"

"Answer it," Joe urged her. "Here, take it on the house phone."

Tanya, her hands trembling, reached for the receiver. "Hello?"

"Say, you really are angry, aren't you? You mean business! You want your damn money back, don't you? Look, you want it back that bad, I'll give it back to you. The entire bankroll, $8.00."

Roy's voice, almost a whisper, sounded strangely hoarse. His words were charged with suppressed anger. Suddenly, she wished that everything could be forgotten, that she'd never set eyes on him. No longer caring whether he returned the money or not, her fear of him had become the real threat, and what she was feeling at the moment was more than she could handle. However, in the back of her mind, something told her that there was no turning back. That she'd have to go through with it. Feigning a bravado that didn't exist, she rushed on to add, "Yes ... yes, I'm angry. You lied to me! Why did you lie to me?"

"Tell you what. I'll give it all back to you. Every bloody cent! Meet me tonight at The Magnolia!"

She hesitated. ... "No, you come in here ... to the hotel. I'll be in the coffee shop at the counter." He could have revenge on his mind, she thought. No doubt he'd seen her talking to the police. Here, at least she'd be surrounded by friends who could protect her.

"Okay, name the time!"

"How about nine?"

"Yeah." He hung up.

Tanya put down the phone with trembling hands. "Well, I'm meeting him in here, in the coffee shop, at nine. He says he's going to return my money. Look, I'm scared of this guy. You're going to have to help me. Oh my, what should I do? I can't believe this is happening!"

Joe Webster put a restraining hand on her shoulder. "Don't worry ... meet him like he says he wants you to. He can't do much with everybody looking on. All right, first things first. Hugh, go up and get going on the switch to 811. Tanya, if it'll make you feel any better, I'm going to tell Ralph Owens, our security man, to watch your room all night ... as well as theirs. Tanya, listen to me, if you hear so much as a twig snap, we'll rig your phone so all you'll have to do is pick it up, and we'll know it's you. You won't have to say a word! Hugh, quick, before they get back! Get her stuff out of there as fast as you can."

"Thank you," she said, "thank you so much for helping me."

Roy's spying on her had unnerved her.

With the bellboy's help, it took only fifteen minutes to repack her clothes and move to the eighth floor. Her heart was in her throat as each drawer was emptied. She put away her things in the new room and lay down to wait for her rendezvous with Roy.

As the hour approached, she wanted to present a casual, innocent attitude, as if she knew nothing about him. She changed into a white sundress and white high heeled sandals. At 8:45, feeling tense and fearful, she made her way into the coffee shop and sat down at the counter.

She ordered a coke and glanced anxiously around the room for Roy. The booth opposite her was filled with four state troopers. Tanya, without further ado, walked to their table and lowered her voice. "Excuse me, please. My name is Tanya Hagen. I'm from Canada. I'm on my vacation and I'm staying at this hotel. ... I'll make this quick. Please, you must believe me. .... Tonight I'm supposed to meet a man in here, at nine o'clock, at this counter. He, uh-h-h, conned me out of some money. Anyway, he's coming here to return it to me ... or so he says. But I don't trust him! This man, if you ask me, has been acting very suspiciously and I'm really afraid of him! You see, I'm afraid he's going to try to do something like kidnap me. Please, could you keep your eye on him when he gets here?" Would they think her request a strange one? She didn't care; it was better to alert the police than to take foolish chances.

All four smiled at her, then one of them drawled out, "If that's the way you feel ma'am, we shore will."

"Thank you. I'd feel better if you did ... watch me, that is."

She felt relieved. She returned to her stool and picked up her glass. The minutes stretched into an hour with no sign of Roy. At ten, she turned toward the troopers. "Sorry, uh-h-h, as you can see, he didn't come. ... But thank you for staying here. He really did say he was coming. Thanks, anyway."

"Pleasure, ma'am. Now, you'all have a good night."

Tanya got off on the eighth floor and checked the hallway before going to her room. Trembling, she undressed in the dark then groped her way towards the bed, straining for unusual sounds. She lay down, every nerve taut with anxiety. Each small noise brought forth a fresh wave of terror as she imagined that it was one of them and that somehow they'd gotten access to her new room number.

Outside she could hear a gale blowing. The wind swept over the hotel sending the windows into shudders with each passing gust. Large hordes of clouds in strange looking shapes sailed past the moon, throwing grotesque shadows across the floor. She observed the scene from her bed with palpitating heart, while lying pressed wringing wet into the sheets. Once a scratching sound against the window brought on a wave of alarm. She stiffened; her hand strayed to the phone. She let a minute or two pass before she withdrew it when she realized that it was only a branch from a tree rubbing against the corner of the building.

Unable to sleep, she lay perspiring while waiting for dawn to break, knowing that her life could depend on her being in a wakeful state. At four o'clock, the weariness won out and she gave in to sleep for an hour.

Promptly at five, she started up again. Roy, the money, the pink Cadillac, everything came back at once. The tension had become unbearable. Lying helpless, a prisoner to her rampant thoughts, she tried to decide what to do. She knew that frightened or not, for her mental well being, it was best to behave as normally as possible.

On impulse, Tanya threw back the sheets and reeled to her feet. She would not let herself become a slave to fear! Why not put on a bathing suit and go to the pool for a swim? An unlikely place for Roy to be looking for her at five in the morning! First a call to the switch board to let them know. "Carol, this is Tanya."

"Tanya! Is everything all right?"

"Yes, I'm fine, thank you. But I had a terrible night."

"I'm sorry to hear that! Did anyone bother you?"

"No! No, not a soul! Carol, I'm exhausted. I'm going down for a swim. I think at this hour it should be safe."

"All right Tanya; I'll tell Ralph."

"Thanks." She changed, picked up a towel and took the elevator to the fifth floor, treading softly past room 527.

The warm water in the pool soothed her ragged nerves. She swam, purposefully tiring herself, working out the exhaustion, while thinking about her predicament. An hour later, too tired to do another stroke, she decided that she couldn't and wouldn't stay at the hotel during the day. It was too dangerous. She might be a target for whatever it was that Roy had schemed. The thought that they might want to kill her crept into her mind, bringing on another wave of dread. Well, I just won't be here, she assured herself. How did I ever get mixed up with the likes of Roy Billingston? Suddenly it struck her that it was he who had singled her out.

Tanya put the questions on hold. Where did one go to get lost for a day? A conversation she'd had with Lin Holmes gave her an idea. The maid had described "The Desert View Shopping Centre" that had recently opened up in a different part of the city. 'It takes about an hour and a half to get there by bus,' she'd said. It wasn't likely that anyone would think of looking for her there. She hurried back to her room to dress.

She sped through the lobby, not stopping to speak to anyone. Once outside, she lowered her head and turned up her collar. Looking for Roy at every turn, Tanya squeezed into the center of a group of people at the bus stop.

A lady next to her commented that the bus was about to board. It was an express, going directly to "The Desert View." My chances of meeting Roy there are slim, she thought. He wasn't the type to be spending his time at shopping malls. Nor would he be taking a bus when one considered the luxury of the pink Cadillac. However, she found a seat at the back to observe the people who boarded, just in case.

Once inside the mall, she searched for a secluded restaurant, then sat down in a darkened corner. Though she wasn't at all hungry, Tanya planned to spend a long time eating. She ordered breakfast feeling, for the time being, that she was reasonably safe. Having eaten and after drinking three cups of coffee, she reluctantly joined the crowd of Saturday shoppers.

Even while browsing through racks of clothing, she kept alert, scanning the faces around her for Roy or his partner, with shopping the farthest thing from her mind. The vigilance was exhausting. All day she kept to the shadows until the mall was about to close. Then quickly she boarded a bus back to the hotel.

As soon as the vehicle was in motion, she leaned back to meditate upon her predicament. Being terrified and in a constant state of anxiety was too much, too harrowing, she thought. I can't keep this up. By the time they reached the hotel, she'd decided to pack her things and quietly leave for Canada the next day.

As she walked into the lobby, the clock registered nine P.M.. At the same time, she noticed at least fifteen staff members crowding around the reception desk. Some she recognized, some she didn't. She thought it strange that they should all be there at once.

Hugh Bronston and Lin Holmes, who were closest to her, motioned to her. Heads turned as she walked in. She wondered whether it was her imagination or were they all smiling at her? Puzzled, Tanya looked toward Joe Webster. "Joe, what's going on?"

Joe immediately walked around the desk and stopped in front of her. He put his hand on her shoulder. "Tanya, am I glad to see you! Where have you been? We've been looking for you everywhere. You had me worried. Do you have any idea what happened while you were gone?"

She shook her head. "No, I don't. ... Joe, I went to a shopping center early this morning to get away from Roy. I didn't want him to find me. Just this minute, I got off the bus."

"Tanya, you know Roy and his Mexican friend? By the way, his real name is Roy Blakey. Well, early this morning, Ralph, you know, our security guard, he, uh-h-h, Ralph caught them trying to sneak out of the hotel with a television set. They were on the mezzanine floor. He noticed them carrying it out and called the police. They were both arrested. I guess they were so broke, so desperate for money, that they were planning to hawk the T.V."

"No!"

"Yes, but you haven't heard the worst. Apart from that, they're wanted for a number of crimes ... state-wide, no less. And, uh-h-h, we, I don't know who it was, but somebody tipped the police off that they were here in Phoenix and staying in this hotel."

Tanya's hand flew to her face. "Really? Joe, that could have been me. Yesterday I talked to a couple of officers in a cruiser. I told them to check out the Cadillac and them as well."

The staff pressed closer to hear what Tanya had to say.

Joe shook his head in disbelief. "That's not all, there's more. You'll want to hear this. ... Both are escaped convicts from the State Penitentiary. They're wanted for robbery with violence, theft, kidnapping, extortion, and transporting young women into Mexico for the purposes of prostitution! In fact, they're wanted in other states besides Arizona!"

"What!" Tanya felt herself go weak. The pieces of the puzzle fell into place. "Oh Joe, do you see what they wanted from me? Remember Roy? I told you how he kept asking me to get into the Cadillac. He said he wanted to talk to me in ... in their car. Joe, I could easily have been kidnapped and taken to Mexico if I'd listened to him." She shivered. "Oh, Joe, I almost did, you know. But something ... something held me back. And the fact that I'm an unknown, and alone ... that was even better for them."

"Really? Tanya, they would have driven you across the state line and sold you to a brothel. You know, you were lucky, because once inside that border," he shook his head, "no one would ever have found you. And you could never escape. You would have been drugged and ... and they have other means of keeping you. We've heard rumors of this kind of thing happening, but it's never hit so close to home."

"Oh, Joe, I'm so glad I had the sense not to go with them."

She paused contemplating having to perform horrible, degrading acts, having to live a life of hell! The picture of herself about to cross the street flashed through her mind. She remembered the restraining force that had kept her from following Roy. Tanya knew that it was more than luck that had held her back. Her fear dissolved into thin air. The nightmare was over. Silently, she thanked God!

Hugh Bronston came up to her and held out his hand.

"Congratulations, Tanya. We all figured you helped with their arrest."

"Thank you!"

Lin Holmes turned to hug her. There were others who waited their turn just to shake her hand. She laughed, feeling giddy. "Thank you, everybody. This is all too wonderful. I really don't deserve such honour." She turned to Joe. "You won't believe this, but I was planning to go home tomorrow! I couldn't take it anymore. Joe, just think, tonight I won't have to worry about anyone breaking into my room." She suddenly sobered. "Joe, I'm still in shock ... but very relieved!"

Joe nodded. "You know why he didn't show up last night, don't you?"

"Why?"

"Because he saw you with the state troopers in here. He couldn't take a chance on being recognized."

"Oh! ... Or maybe he thought that I'd already turned him in, and they were waiting for him." She laughed. "Imagine all this happening over $8.00!" Suddenly, she clapped a hand over her mouth. "Oh Joe! ... I just remembered something!"

"What?"

"I gave him my home address so he could return the money."

He laughed. "Well, he certainly won't be able to do that from jail, will he?"

"I guess not. Joe, I'm so tired. I think I'll go up, take a long, hot bath. ... And, you may be sure, tonight I'll sleep like a baby." And one more thing, I'm going to enjoy the rest of my vacation! Good night, Joe. Good night, everybody."

51

THE GROUP IN DR. CARLSTEN'S OFFICE SAT IN DEAD SILENCE as Tanya told them of her narrow escape in Phoenix. "... You know, I was really lucky that they were both captured," she wound up.

Pierre Sutton was first to speak. "Tanya, this story, it sounds like something from a gangster movie."

She nodded. Pierre had on a beautifully tailored grey suit. Judging from his dress, he was playing it straight.

Though Lea Thompson smiled at her when she first came in, she made no comment about anything else. Tanya held her breath as she turned to Dr. Carlsten. "Well?"

He looked at her, exasperated. "Tanya, you've done it again! You remind me of a skater on a lake. I see you skating ... and as you skate, you get closer and closer to that dark spot in the middle that hasn't quite frozen over. Finally, you fall into the water, slip under the ice, never to be seen again. Now stop and think, is this what you want to have happen to you?"

She shook her head. "No!"

"Can't you see, because you've always been a victim it's like replaying a broken record? The same scene repeats itself and repeats itself, whether you admit it or not, you're deliberately punishing yourself. All these men that you're attracted to have one thing in common ... they all end up abusing you. The abuse, it goes right back to your childhood. In fact, it started with your stepfather." He shook his head. "If you don't stop this destructive behaviour, you're as good as dead."

She lowered her head and burst into sobs. "Oh, Dr. Carlsten, so far, all the men that I've met have been horrible and getting worse. ... I ... I, want to share my life with someone. ... I want to ... to ... love someone. I want someone to love me. I'm no different from anyone else. Is that so impossible?"

"No, it's not. But if you want to survive, you'll have to learn to recognize this type of personality beforehand and avoid becoming entangled with such a person, or you'll end up with someone who'll destroy you!"

"I know, Dr. Carlsten, I know!"

52

HER DESK WAS PLACED SQUARELY IN FRONT of a long counter close to the door. The office was brightly lit and large enough to accommodate the fourteen tax assessors that she would be working for. Had it been the right move? she wondered.

For a change of pace, she'd transferred out of the steno pool and applied for a job with the Department of National Revenue. Mr. Dunlop, from personnel, had approved the position after checking through Tanya's work record. There had been a small raise in salary.

Now Tanya listened patiently as Meg Hill and Sandra Yule briefed her on her duties. Like the others in the room, both women were tax assessors and her superiors.

"... and if someone happens to walk in, it's your job to ask them what they want. Uh-h-h ... and the phone, you have to answer the phone. You'll be taking shorthand from Jake Werner, he's head of the department. Some of the other assessors might need you for that as well. ... You'll have to type legal forms, releases, that sort of thing. Once you do one or two, you'll get the hang of it very quickly." Meg Hill indicated a wire basket beside her desk.

"All the assessors put their work into this basket, it's up to you to check each file to see what they want done."

Dismayed, Tanya looked at the basket. The files were stacked two feet high. Would she be able to handle it? It looked impossible!

"Tanya, do you know how to operate a dictaphone?"

"No."

"Well, let me show you how it works. All the assessors like to use them. It saves time." Meg pointed to a rectangular metal box on the desk and picked up a small plug. "First, you slip a tape into this slot and put this plug into your ear. There's a pedal on the floor that turns it on or off. It's really quite simple. And one more thing, if you have any questions don't be afraid to ask either Sandra or myself."

"Thank you. I'll appreciate all the help I can get. Sorry, I feel so nervous! What's Mr. Werner like? I mean, is he nice to work for?"

"Jake? Yes, he's very nice. You're lucky to have him. Don't worry, I'm sure you'll like him."

"Thanks. I hope so."

They returned to their places, leaving Tanya to fend for herself. She picked a file out of the basket and opened it. It was a release form, having to do with estate tax. Sighing, she got up and made her way toward Meg Hill.

All morning, she worked steadily on the files. Her progress was slow. Occasionally, one of the assessors added a new file to the basket. Tanya had a moment of panic when she realized that she was the only steno doing all the typing for everyone in the entire room!

The mail arrived a little after ten. Jake Werner signaled for her to come into his office. Rising shakily to her feet, she followed him inside.

He smiled as she entered. "Tanya Hagen? I'm glad you're here. We're quite desperate for a good secretary. Uh-h-h, I want these letters to go out this afternoon."

"Yes, of course, I'll see to it." She smiled, her heart pounding madly. Taking shorthand always made her feel tense, uneasy. It took concentration. She was afraid of making a mistake and missing something. Hopefully, the dictation wouldn't take too long.

Jake Werner was tall with a shock of black hair and very bushy eyebrows that actually curled up at the ends. The backs of his hands were covered with a black, curly fuzz, making him look very masculine. She tried to read into his face, wondering whether he was kind. He struck her as being a man of integrity.

The three letters he dictated were fairly brief. Tanya returned to her desk and typed them off as quickly as possible, then went back to the files.

By closing time, the work had entirely sapped all her energy. She felt like a bear fit to climb a tree. Once home, she folded up on the couch for a few minutes. A hurried supper followed ... then a hot bath. She was in bed by eight.

Tanya, after several weeks, established a rigid routine to combat the immense work load. Her goal was to keep abreast of the files, letters, forms. Sometimes she worked through her coffee breaks. Sometimes she stayed and typed after office hours. There was no question of pay for overtime. She just assumed that it was part of the job. It was steady work; the wire basket was rarely empty. Still, she felt it was her duty to see that it was done. Eventually, she managed to catch up and keep up with the flow.

The dictaphone she compared to a ball and chain, when she considered how she was bound to it both physically and mentally. But once having committed herself, and having accepted the challenge, she knew she would master it. Being a perfectionist, she not only did the work but did a superior job.

After a time, she noticed that almost everybody in the department had time to joke, laugh, and lead a fairly active social life amongst themselves. There were some who brought novels to read. She looked with envy at a couple of women who were knitting and crocheting.

However, Tanya blocked out the unfairness and went on with the stacks of typing. She learned to be accurate, disciplined, and invisible.

Meanwhile, in her private life, she continued to search for Mr. Right. Whenever it was time for a vacation, she traveled to Florida, Mexico, or Hawaii, with the hope of meeting someone. It was disappointing to find out that most of the men she encountered abroad she couldn't trust. The relationship always petered out once the holiday ended.

In a fit of restlessness, she left Anna's safe basement haven and settled in a one bedroom apartment, thinking that what she needed was independence. There were many moves after that in search for a better and more perfect place to live. Often, it was because the rent was too high. Sometimes she picked up a roommate along the way to share expenses. This was done by word of mouth, through a friend, or the local paper.

Some had boyfriends and got married. In fact, Tanya was bridesmaid six different times and had six different gowns hanging in her closet to prove it. The sight of them irked her, reminding her that she was still single and getting on. A wedding always meant another move.

The moves were painful, making her feel as if she was being ripped out to be transplanted into new surroundings. Exasperated, she wondered if it was possible to find a permanent location, a final place to settle down, a place to call her own. ... But with whom?

Among her many roommates, she encountered many varied personalities. Accordingly, she had to adjust to each person differently. She was so willing to be compatible that her real character took a step backward in an effort to be accepted, to be loved. Why couldn't her life be like Alisha's or Anna's? They had perfect husbands and perfect children. She longed to live in her own house with her very own perfect husband!

One day, walking home through the snow, she felt the sting of tears, remembering that Skydrid, the girl she was living with currently, hadn't spoken to her for several days. Skydrid was in one of her black moods. Last night she'd come home filled with anger and had totally withdrawn from Tanya. The girl lacked nothing as far as Tanya could see. She was slim, glamorous, drove a Carmen Gia, and ate health foods. Not only was she moody, but she had a very distinct, physical way of projecting her temper: a hard bounce into bed when she came in after a late date, rousing Tanya, who peered at her in concern: the slam of doors and cupboard shelves, causing the china to rattle. Every time Tanya attempted to pry some of the rage out of her, she rebuffed her.

Later in the week, with Skydrid away at work, Tanya called the movers and fled to a different apartment. The very next day she received a call from her.

"Tanya, why did you go? ... Why?"

"I'm sorry, Skydrid, I just felt that you didn't want me around anymore!"

"But that's not true. Couldn't you tell it was just "my way"?"

"Sorry Skydrid, but I can't live like that."

There were days when Tanya came directly home from work and, though dead tired, dolled herself up and went to the Silver Ballroom to sit through the entire evening without one solitary man asking her to dance. Riding home on the bus later, she felt more depressed than she'd been before she left.

Now, since leaving Anna's, she no longer shared any confidences with either her or Alisha. She felt that she owed them nothing, nor did she give them any hint of what was happening in her life at any given moment. Of course, she still came to visit at Christmas, Easter, or the children's birthdays. However, because they could be so critical, she was wary of them.

53

TANYA REMAINED IN THE DEPARTMENT OF NATIONAL REVENUE for seven years. Each day was busy, each day rushed, and the days never long enough.

After a time, she viewed the fourteen tax assessors as her extended family. At work, she handled their business files with expertise and knew something about each person's private life. Meg Hill and Sandra Yule, through their support and encouragement, were a valuable source of daily succor in her struggle to deal with the mountains of work.

Richard Cameron, a tax assessor, whose desk was close to hers, often asked her to get his brother-in-law, Brampton Major, on the phone at Sunland Finance, the company where Anna worked.

Since Anna manned the switchboard, they often chatted. Anna usually brought her up to date on her family life, and Tanya regarded the talks as good as a visit.

Amy Wheaton occupied a space behind Richard's. She always threw her file into the basket as if it was a piece of garbage, nearly toppling it over.

Tanya, annoyed, sensed a great deal of antagonism behind the act. But other than giving her a sharp look, she kept her thoughts to herself.

54

ONE MORNING, JAKE WERNER OPENED THE DOOR SLIGHTLY and, raising his bushy eyebrows, signaled her into his office. This was the second time that she'd been asked to come in that morning. Tanya picked up her note pad, thinking that though she'd been doing it for a long time, it still bothered her to take shorthand. As usual she became flustered, as though it was her very first time.

She had been right about Jake. He was a man of conscience and integrity. Once he mentioned a wife who had arthritis, making Tanya feel that the illness was quite serious because he'd discussed it with her. He mentioned two adopted children.

Now she sat with her pencil poised, hoping that he wouldn't notice the jitters.

Jake leaned back in his chair, looking pensive. "I want this letter to go to a Mr. Thornton at head office."

She scribbled some words at the top of the pad and fidgeted.

He sighed. "Tanya, if you're going to be that nervous, why don't you take barbiturates?"

A shock went through her. Was it that obvious, or was he making fun of her? "Barbiturates? What's that?"

"Haven't you ever heard of pills to make you more relaxed?"

How dare he! She looked at him evenly. "No, Mr. Werner, I don't think so. Actually, I don't want to take any kind of pills. In fact, I think I'd rather shake, rattle, and roll than take pills."

He flushed, looking guilty. "Sorry! Let's get on with the letter."

"Yes." She finished taking the shorthand in a calmer frame of mind and returned to her desk.

Strangely, after that incident Jake showed her more consideration and respect. It seemed that despite the nerves, he'd seen a glimpse of her strength. It established a bond between them and aided her in becoming more disposed to do the work.

She came into the office with a spring to her step. Summer was at its peak. Everywhere she looked there were masses of colourful, vibrant flowers. The trees and lawns were dressed up in sumptuous greens. It lifted her spirits.

As soon as she walked in, Sandra Yule came hurrying towards her. "Tanya, have you heard about Richard Cameron?"

"Richard? No. What about him."

"He's had a heart attack. His wife phoned to say that he's in the hospital."

"Really? But he just turned fifty! Still young ... I'm sorry to hear that. Poor Richard! Is it serious, do you know?"

"I don't know. Jake said his wife phoned to say that he was resting comfortably. Apparently last night he keeled over in front of the T.V., after complaining about having chest pains."

"Thanks for telling me." Tanya sat down at her desk. She picked up the mail and hurried into Jake's office.

"Mr. Werner, do you know if Richard is all right?"

"Yes. Uh-h-h, I think so. I think he is." He frowned, his heavy brows nearly eclipsing his eyes. A hair actually remained stuck to his lashes when at last he looked up at her.

Without a second's hesitation, Tanya stood up, reached out, and gently swept it back into place. "Sorry! I thought it might be bothering you." Surprised at her daring, she wondered if it had been the right thing to do? But why not?

Jake Werner's face turned pink. He stared at her, then drawled out, "You know, you're very pretty ... very attractive ... and uh-h-h, a very desirable young woman!" Having said that, he looked down at the letters on his desk. "Shall we get on to the business at hand?"

She blushed. "Thank you. By all means, Mr. Werner!"

As soon as they went through the mail, she streaked back to her desk and pulled out a dictionary to look up the word "desirable." Nobody had ever called her that before. The meaning read: agreeable, pleasing, worth having! She thought about it a moment. Somehow, his compliment fed her. She remembered that he'd said it in a fatherly, protective way, making her feel that she was very important.

Richard Cameron, on the advice of his doctor, retired from his duties as tax assessor as soon as he recovered. However, he still made weekly visits to the office to keep in touch with his colleagues. Most Wednesdays they could expect him at lunchtime.

Tanya greeted him warmly the first time he showed up. He acknowledged her with a stiff nod and headed straight toward his buddies. Of course, he still regarded her as nothing more than a lowly steno. But from the corner of her eye, she saw Meg Hill give him a hug. Tanya, though envious, reminded herself that Meg had that right. They were co-workers, both on the same level.

The next Wednesday he came into the office carrying a paper bag. She flashed him a smile. "Hi. Nice to see you, Mr. Cameron."

"Hi. Is Jake in his office?"

"Yes, I think he is."

It was her lunch hour and Tanya picked this time to type a letter to her stepfather. The city had just re-elected a very controversial mayor for a second term. During the election, there had been a fracas about Mayor Greko having tampered with public funds. Everybody in the office had voted against him, except Tanya.

She had cast her ballot in his favour, because she felt that there was nobody better to do the job. He'd won even after taking a lot of mud-slinging from the other candidates. She thought her stepfather would be interested in the affair because of the ethnic connection.

To her left, through the corner of her eye, she saw Richard dipping into the paper bag that he'd brought. She watched him place a chocolate bar on each desk. However, he went past hers as if she didn't exist.

Tanya froze. She sat horrified. Why would he account for everyone but her? Hearing exclamations of "thank yous", she kept her eyes riveted to her letter. Then, when she couldn't stand it any longer, she quickly rose to her feet and made her way to the bathroom, remembering all the times that she'd stayed late to type his work.

She waited for a time to compose herself before going back into the room. Suddenly she stopped, surprised to see him sitting at her desk, fully absorbed in reading her letter, his head bobbing back and forth in quick, jerky movements.

Her fury boiled over. She burst into tears. "What are you doing? How dare you? ... You come in here, and you ... you ... think me too insignificant to even buy me a chocolate bar! And now you sit there and think you can read my personal mail as if I was nothing? Well you certainly have your nerve, don't you?"

Richard's mouth dropped open. She'd taken him completely by surprise! Shamefacedly, he got to his feet and hurried out of the room.

Tanya slumped into her seat as heads turned in her direction. She couldn't believe that the words had come out of her mouth. She heard a crash as Amy Wheaton delivered a file into the wire basket.

Without thinking, Tanya shouted out, "Amy, would you please stop doing that? This is not a waste paper basket!"

She watched as Amy's face turned beet red before she burst out laughing. "Okay, Tanya, sorry!" Picking up her file, she laid it down ... gently.

"Thank you." Tanya rose to her feet, and walked blindly towards Meg Hill and Sandra Yule.

"Meg ... Sandra ... I've got to talk to you. You know Richard, well, he brought everybody in this office a chocolate bar except me. Can you imagine him doing such a cruel thing? You have no idea how it made me feel." Her tears started again.

She felt both girls hug her at the same time. At that moment, it dawned on Tanya that because of the group sessions, and Dr. Carlsten's counselling, this was the first time in her life that she was able to verbally express her emotions in front of other people. The thought was comforting.

The next day it rained, and she had to fight a strong wind on her way to work. However since her apartment was centrally located it made good sense to walk.

She reached the office, hung up her coat, and started towards her desk. She stopped, seeing a gift wrapped package sitting on top of her typewriter. She tore the paper off to reveal a box of chocolates. Tears sprang to her eyes. It was from Meg and Sandra.

Noticing their smiling faces from across the room, she could only nod her "thank you" to them.

All week long Tanya grieved, nursing her rejection. Finally, after thinking it over, she decided not to let it get her down. The following Wednesday, as soon as Richard walked in, she felt her hackles rise and purposefully turned her head away from him. She thought it better to begin working. When she looked up she noticed that Richard had quietly placed a chocolate bar on her desk. A small shock of surprise went through her. A smile creased her face. "Thank you, Mr. Cameron."

He smiled back. "You're welcome, Tanya."

After that incident, she noticed that the staff treated her with more dignity.

55

EVENTUALLY TANYA FOUND SOMEONE that she thought would be perfect for her. Though at this point some of the naivete had left her and she was more aware of the hardness of people's hearts.

She met Harold Vandermeer at a dance at the Thirty-Forty Club. He was very good looking with wavy, raven-coloured hair and sparkling blue eyes that twinkled at her from behind horn rimmed glasses. Tanya noticed that he was a sharp dresser. Harold danced like a dream. She went through a series of intricate steps with him with no difficulty, his hand at her waist, giving her all the right signals.

He seemed as enthralled with her as she was with him. Before the evening was out, he had her phone number in his pocket, which she'd hastily written on a napkin, for she'd come to the dance with someone else. While dancing with him, she found out that he was the principal of Thomas Lawrence School.

Harold didn't waste any time getting in touch with her. The next day he phoned to make a date to take her to dinner on the weekend.

The following Saturday, Tanya opened the door to find him formally dressed in a dark suit and black bow tie. A genuine diamond glittered from the center of gold cuff links.

"Tanya!" He took both her wrists in his hands. "This is such a pleasure. I'm thoroughly delighted. How are you? Are you ready, my dear? Tonight, I'm going to treat you to a wonderful meal. I hope you're hungry?"

"I'm starved, Harold!"

"Good! Let's hurry. I have a surprise for you. I've made reservations at Duval's. Have you been to Duval's?"

"No-o-o, Harold, I haven't. ... But I've heard of it. I hear it's expensive."

"It is. Yes, my darling, you are right. Is this your coat? You'll need it. The forecast is for frost tonight." He helped her on with her coat and guided her out. Tanya slid into the front seat of a shiny, black Lincoln. Inside, it was all leather and luxury. "Harold, your car, it's a ... a ... block long," she exclaimed, delighted. The car made him seem even more like the perfect catch.

He looks like the type of man that people respect, she thought. There was success and quality written all over him. A valet parked their car when they arrived. Duval's was a classy, French restaurant.

The maitre d', who seemed to know Harold, showed them to a table covered with spotless, white linen. A candle, nestled in a heavy brass holder, exuded a soft flicker of light. The chairs, she noticed, were actually comfortable, padded arm chairs.

Harold ordered a filet of beef with king crab. A butter sauce and some choice vegetables came with it. As she was about to take the first bite, she noticed him sitting back watching her.

"Harold, this is absolutely delicious. And this steak, it's so tender! Why don't you taste it? I wonder how they cook it to make it this tender?"

"Why don't we ask the chef?"

"Oh no, I was only joking!"

"Here, have some of my mushrooms."

"But don't you want them?"

Smiling, he transferred a spoonful to her plate. "I still have plenty. There. ... Now eat!"

"But Harold, why aren't you eating?"

He laughed, contemplating the wine in his glass. "Because, looking at you eat is a meal in itself. Sweetie, you look so charming, so innocent, I can't get enough of you."

She blushed. "Harold, stop that!"

The evening unfolded; he kept her laughing with amusing anecdotes, stories, jokes. He had a wonderful rollicking sense of humour. Mellowed by Harold's attention, the good food, the wine, contentment swept over her. It was good to laugh. Life should be full of laughter.

They finished the entree. A nod from him, and the waiter came running. "Louis, would you bring us some Irish coffee, and we'll have a piece of the chocolate, pecan cheesecake. Just one, please ... we'll share."

The waiter nodded and disappeared. He returned with the coffee, cheesecake and two forks.

Harold cut off a forkful of cheesecake and leaned towards her. "Here, have a bite, you'll love it. My sweet, I like a woman who enjoys her food. In fact, I myself am a good cook. ... I love to cook."

"Thank you, Harold. Hm-m-m, you're right. It is delicious."

Other than a taste for himself, he fed the entire cake, one fork at a time, to Tanya.

His attention was overwhelming! Had anyone ever treated her with such kindness, such tenderness? She couldn't remember ...ever.

Harold put down the fork and picked up his wine. "Tanya, do you notice me the way I look now?"

She nodded, "Yes Harold."

"So tell me honestly ... do I look like the type of guy who would drive a truck for a living?"

"No, Harold, far from it. You look like an executive or ... or school principal," she answered, laughing.

"Well, sweetie, I have news for you. I used to be a truck driver."

She looked surprised.

"Yes, me, a truck driver. After that, I was a mechanic. For a while, I even worked in a garage. I was good at it, too. But I wasn't satisfied with that kind of a life. You know, my hands were always in grease, always smelling of solvent, dirty. ... So, I went back to school, upgraded myself, and when I graduated, I got a job teaching shop at NAIT. Now, you'd think that I'd be satisfied with that, wouldn't you?"

"Well, I'd think you would be, Harold."

"Well, not me. It still wasn't good enough for me. So I enrolled in University, and I got a degree in education. That's how I became a principal. I figured if other guys could do it, I could do it, too!" He nodded. "I graduated with top marks. Look at me now, Tanya. I drive a nice car, I wear nice clothes. I'm having the time of my life. Anybody with half a brain can do it, provided they're determined enough. ... Tanya, life is good." Smiling, he raised his glass. "Let's drink to life!"

"To life ... and to you, too, Harold. ... To your success! Let's drink to that, your success! You've pulled yourself up, literally, by your bootstraps. You deserve to be toasted. ... Harold, I congratulate you! You did yourself proud."

He smiled. "Thank you."

They left Duval's at one in the morning. She noticed a full harvest moon in the sky. It enhanced the feeling of romance.

Harold's arm encircled her waist as he walked her to her door.

Would he want to see me again? she wondered. With his manners and style, he could have almost any girl he liked.

"Tanya, could we do this again next week?"

"Yes, thank you, I'd love to. Tonight, well ... I don't have to tell you, I loved every minute of it."

He sighed. "Tanya, I find you so ... so ... innocent, so sweet, so gentle. ... I'm the kind of man who treasures those qualities in a woman. Not all men do, you know! Good night, my sweet."

His kiss was unhurried, like their dinner, though she pulled away when his hands began to wander. "Sorry Harold, but we've only had the one date."

He looked surprised, then laughed. "All right, Tanya, I'll call you."

She went in with a part of her wanting to be with him, wanting him to remember her, thinking that she was already falling in love with him. Surely this time it would last. He had all the makings of a wonderful husband; he was handsome, kind-spirited, well off, intelligent, and he was going places.

For the next six months, they saw each other not half enough for Tanya's liking. She became more trusting. She even bragged about Harold to Sandra and Meg at the office.

Harold was exciting company to be with. Never once was he rude or mean to her. She never caught him in a lie! And he kept coming to see her even after she made clear to him her views on sex before marriage.

"But you've been married before, I don't see why you deny yourself," he'd argued, laughing.

"Even if I've been married before, that doesn't make it right, does it?"

"If that's your choice, sweetie."

But his demands didn't relax. Each time he came, he excited her, and each time she put him off. It was a continual game between them. It added spark to the relationship, as well as keeping her on her toes. She found she was constantly searching beyond herself to see whether there was something she could do to make him commit himself.

Though the subject hadn't been discussed, she took for granted that he was being as true to her as she was to him.

One evening, he came to take her to a movie. She opened the door to let him in, her face aglow with expectation. An evening with Harold was an evening to look forward to.

He paused in the doorway. "Tanya, you look terrific in violet, did you know that? That color suits you."

"Thank you, Harold." That was another thing that she liked about him: Harold noticed everything about her and never once missed a chance to compliment her, taking notice of even the slightest changes ... right down to a change of tint in her hair!

A feeling of tenderness swept over her. How different he was from the other men that she'd known. A solid image of dependability, and honour!

Spiritually, she felt connected to him. The thought of marriage crossed her mind. Taking into account his attention and concern, he might be proposing to her very soon, she thought ... or at least in the near future.

As usual, he helped her into the car before getting in himself. She wondered if it would continue after they were married? They started to move.

He leaned back, throwing her an inquisitive look. "Tanya, you know, you look quite gorgeous tonight. ... I mean beautiful. How come, after your divorce, you never married?"

"Thank you for the compliment, Harold. ... I don't know. I guess because the right man didn't come along. And after Lou, I was on my guard. I didn't trust anybody!" She looked at him, meaningfully. "Until now, that is."

"I see."

Her heart quickened, knowing that he'd left himself wide open for what she was about to ask him. "Well, and what about you, Harold. You're handsome, ambitious, have you ever thought about getting married?"

He laughed. "Oh, sure! Maybe someday, I'll get myself a young seventeen year old ... settle down ... have a couple of kids. ... I like kids.

I think when I'm about fifty, though. Not right away. Uh-h-h, you may be sure of that! Uh-h-h, I figure I'm still too young. ... And single, I'm having such a good time!"

"Oh!" She felt a pall descend on her, when she realized that his future didn't include her. Was she nothing more than a passing fancy to him? She struggled with the implication of this open admission ... only to block it out immediately after. I'll make it all right, she thought. I'll make him love me. Once he really knows me, he'll know that I'm true and right for him. He'll forget all about finding some empty-headed seventeen year old!

He looked at her. "Ah-h-agh, women! Can one really trust them?"

There was a hard edge of cynicism behind the words, making her wonder if those were his "true" feelings? She probed deeper. "Why, of course, you can, Harold. ... What exactly do you mean, 'can one really trust them'? ... Don't you trust me?"

"You? I don't know. Perhaps. But speaking from experience, there isn't one solitary female I know that I'd trust. I'll tell you why. ... It's because they're all alike. ... Usually turned on by a man with money. All you have to do is wine 'em and dine 'em, and they're all over you. That's why I don't trust anyone."

He's dead serious, she thought. No doubt, this was the "true" Harold speaking. It disturbed her to think that they were so far apart in their concept of each other. But why the bitterness? Perhaps a lost love ... or a rejection? She didn't want to hear anymore. Somehow, she'd make it up to him, and he'd end up crazy in love with her. ... Nor would he want anyone else when he saw what she had to offer. ... And when the time was right, he would propose, of that she was certain.

She kept Harold a secret from Alisha and Anna. Though she had every intention of introducing him just as soon as they became engaged. "Alisha, this is my fiance, Harold," she'd say with pride.

56

Her work was stacked up a mile high the morning that Dot Woods walked into the office as Richard Cameron's replacement.

Tanya stopped working and stared as the statuesque blonde strolled in. She was sheathed in a tight fitting, black suit. Tall, striking, she had a big frame and large bouncing breasts. She made quite an impression. Was there a bra under that blouse? Later, Meg told her that Dot was married and the mother of two teen-aged children.

Dot settled in quickly and took over Richard's desk and his files. After several days, Tanya noticed that the quiet, staid atmosphere in the office had changed due to her presence. She was everywhere, teasing, joking, and making a supreme effort to worm her way into everybody's heart by every method possible.

She was especially charming to Jake. Though as soon as she realized that her smiles and wit were wasted on him, she left him alone.

A week went by before she zeroed in on Tanya. Tanya had just come out of Jake's office when Dot approached her, carrying a file.

"Tell me, if you're Mrs. Hagen, why aren't you wearing your rings? Are you divorced or something?"

Tanya looked blank. Dot had a habit of speaking a mile a minute and the question didn't register immediately. At that moment she took an instant dislike to her, sensing that Dot was aggressive to the point of being obnoxious. "Yes, as a matter of fact, I am. ... That file, is it for me? I'll do it next, if you like."

"Have you found yourself another guy, yet?"

"Excuse me, I really don't have time to talk, as you can see."

Dot flushed, handed her the file, and walked away. Tanya had a strange feeling that she was jealous of her. Was it because she had the privilege of walking in and out of Jake's office? Or was she just being plain mean because she'd spotted her as the weakest person in the room?

She noticed that Dot had misspelled two words in the release form that she'd filled out. Tanya typed up the sheet, corrected the mistakes, and laid the file on her desk without pointing them out to her.

Dot was back a short time later, this time with a letter she wanted typed. "Tanya, tell me, don't you do anything other than work?"

"No."

The woman turned to everyone in the room and raised her voice.

"Would you look at her, everybody! She sits at her typewriter all day long ... busy as a beaver ... typing! So, while the rest of us are having fun, Tanya works. That's because she wants to be the best and most needed person in this office! Tanya, whatever would we do without you?" she asked sarcastically.

Everybody kept busy and no one seemed to notice. Tanya allowed the insult to ride. She had a deadline to finish a letter that Jake had just dictated to her. I have no time to scrap with her this late in the day, she thought.

She decided, while walking home after work, that no matter what happened, she would ignore her. No telling what a fighting match with someone like Dot would lead to.

57

T ANYA THREW OFF HER LIGHTWEIGHT SPRING COAT and draped it over a chair in Dr. Carlsten's reception room before joining the rest of the group in his private office. She felt smug, content. Harold had picked her up last Friday, and they'd gone out for a romantic, candlelight dinner. She often talked about him to the group, though actually never calling him by name. For once in her life she felt loved, wanted, and that no one need pity her. Since meeting him, her ego had definitely been elevated.

"Hi." She smiled at Dr. Carlsten. They were all there. Tanya plopped down beside Laurie Schmidt. The comely blonde apparently had the floor.

"Go on Laurie, tell us what this man is like," Dr. Carlsten prompted.

Tanya yawned, thinking that she'd rather dwell on Harold, while the poor girl continued to expound about one boyfriend and another, filling the group in on all the lewd details. Every week it was a different man but the same story. Laurie goes on date, Laurie falls into bed. Laurie is depressed. Didn't she realize that these casual relationships led to a deterioration of her inner self when later she had to deal with the guilt?

Now she sat with her head hung low, speaking in a monotone, her long, blonde hair a silken curtain concealing her face. "I want to tell you about last weekend. ... I was, uh-h-h, feeling really low. And I mean low. So I went to see this guy. Don't ask me why. Remember, I mentioned him to you before. Actually, we're really good friends and nothing more. One reason I like Harold so much is because I can always count on him to listen to me. And yesterday, with the depression and all, I was desperate. I felt I had to do something, so I went to see him. Well, just as soon as I got there, and as soon as he saw me so depressed, he offered to make supper for me. I must tell you, Harold's a very good cook. Later he insisted on making tea, and just before we went to bed he brought in a tray and served it to me in bed. Imagine that! Then he asked if I'd like to stay a couple of days instead of just overnight, because I was so depressed. So I decided that since I wasn't feeling so hot that ... well ... I would. So I did."

"Actually, I ended up staying at his place for the weekend. You know, when I first got there it wasn't with the intention of staying all night, since I hadn't brought any clothes with me. But it didn't seem to matter to him, because he assured me that it was okay and he gave me one of his shirts to wear. Harold is sensitive and lots of fun. But after thinking about it, I don't think that I'm ready for a serious kind of relationship with him or anybody. You know, I got the impression that he's ready to get serious with me, just like all the other guys I know. I really don't know what I'm going to tell him. I know he likes me a lot, and I don't like to hurt his feelings ... but I don't have the same feelings for him that he has for me. Then sometimes I think that it's all sex with him, and he doesn't really care about me the way I think he does. Now don't get me wrong ... I like him a lot ... but not enough to make any kind of commitment to him at this time. However, I just hate to be the one to break it off. ... Though, actually, if I could, I'd really like to get out of the affair. But I don't know how without hurting him." .... She droned on.

Tanya straightened up at the mention of "Harold". Harold, being a common name, it couldn't be her "Harold", she assured herself. "Excuse me, Laurie, sorry to interrupt, but what is his last name?" She wouldn't be able to sleep if she didn't clear it with herself.

"His last name? Let's see, uh-h-h ... oh, yes ... he said it was Vandermeer. .... Yes, Harold Vandermeer. Like I said, he's a real nice guy, and you couldn't ask for one better, but I'm not sure I like him well enough to get in any deeper."

Tanya gripped the arms of the chair, fighting for control. Her head started to sway; she felt nauseous. Harold and Laurie? How could she accept his sleeping with this young girl, while pretending that she was so special to him? She steadied herself. Nothing would be gained by telling the group ... especially Laurie. The poor girl had enough problems without adding to her misery.

She endured the session to the end then went home in shock to analyze and reflect further. The thought of losing him made it all the harder. In her present state, she found it devastating. Her fury turned on Laurie. What decent girl would go to bed with someone on such a casual basis?

That night, Tanya beat her pillow in frustration. Doubts began to surface about Harold, and her worry intensified. How could she resolve it? He wasn't trustworthy! She couldn't bear to face his unfaithfulness! Yet, she stilled the small voice that insisted that she let him go.

Finally she settled everything by telling herself that once they were married that he would change. She would make him forget Laurie. In fact, he'd be so content with her that he would forget about all the other Lauries in the world. The night whiled away. Little by little, she forgave him, excused him, and smoothed things over to her liking. As she was about to fall asleep, it was to remember that Harold was to take her dancing to the Club Mirimba on the weekend.

The rest of the week, she agonized about what to wear. It would have to be something special if she was to enchant him. Her final choice narrowed down to a white satin blouse, a black velvet skirt, and a classic string of pearls.

She had her hair done at a beauty salon early Saturday morning, then hurried home to finish dressing. Her make-up had to be just right. ... Harold would surely comment that she'd changed her hairstyle.

At five o'clock she heard his ring and rushed to let him in, having decided at the last minute not to mention his indiscretion, picturing in her mind his telling her himself when he proposed and professed his love for her, then asked her for forgiveness. Whatever happened, she assured herself that the outcome would have a happy ending!

"Hi." He smiled, and bent down to kiss her, looking impeccably groomed in a summer weight, grey suit. "Are you ready? I have some people waiting in the car. We should hurry."

"Oh! ... Yes, I am." Disappointment flowed through her. Tonight, of all nights, she had a need to have him all to herself.

He helped her on with her coat. They walked to the car. He opened the door on the passenger side and waited for her to get in. Tanya's mouth dropped open in surprise. In the very spot that she usually occupied, directly next to Harold, sat a vivacious-looking blonde. Tanya was conscious of a painted red mouth, long red nails, spiked red shoes, and a slinky red dress a size too tight. A high slit exposed a thigh. The back seat was packed tight with people. She told herself to be calm and forced a smile for everyone.

"Tanya, I want you to meet Gerta Stein," Harold motioned to the blonde. "Gerta is a neighbour. She lives in the apartment next to mine. Mornings, sometimes, we have coffee together."

"I see. Hi." Tanya remembered her name from past conversations with Harold for he often mentioned that he had a neighbour who liked popping in on him. But he'd never let on what she looked like.

Tanya, seething with indignation, edged in next to her after she realized that Gerta had no intention of giving up her seat. It was a pity the poor girl didn't know that Harold, after all, was her date and that she should rightly be sitting next to him. At the same time, she hated to spoil the evening for herself by being angry from the very start.

Harold's laugh rang out as he started the motor. "Is everybody happy?" A "yes" chorused from behind. He nodded, accelerating to the proper speed.

Tanya sat erect and glum. It hurt to know that he seemed unconcerned about her unhappy frame of mind.

"Tanya, let me introduce you to the back row. ... On your far right is Hans Vogel. I'd like to point out that he's a very handsome guy, though you might have noticed that by yourself. Hans is a very good friend of mine. And sitting on his knees, Noreen Wagner, his date. ... Uh-h-h, next to Hans, Mike and Mary Franz, and Lil and Jack Munrow." He laughed. "I never knew that six people could actually fit into the back of my car."

Still irate with Gerta, Tanya threw Hans a cursory look over her shoulder. He was grey-haired, distinguished-looking, and looked about fifty. Noreen, also in her middle years, was an attractive redhead. She and Hans were locked in an embrace. Tanya nodded to the other couples. That left Gerta who apparently had come by herself.

Tanya kept silent until they reached the club where a reserved table waited for them.

"Waiter, bring us a bottle of your best house wine." Harold turned to the others. "Folks, this one's on me, so tell the waiter what you'd like to drink. Hans, whatever is your pleasure ... remember I'm treating."

Hans put up his hand. "Harold ... Harold, don't vurry about me."

"Good! Then, you'll excuse me if I ask Tanya to dance?" Harold bowed before her. "Tanya, my sweet?"

It was a fast two- step. Tanya, burdened with anger, couldn't find the words to express to him her true feelings about Gerta ... the others ... all intruders, as far as she was concerned.

While dancing, Harold portrayed a bright, casual air. Smiling, congenial, he made small talk about what a fine person Hans was and that he was honoured to have him in the group. Tanya nodded stiffly, in half-hearted agreement. The music stopped. He led her back to her seat. As soon as she sat down, he went to Gerta and placed a hand on her shoulder for the next number.

Tanya looked up to see Hans in front of her. "May I hef thee honour?"

Though unwilling, she answered, "Yes." With Harold fawning over him, she surmised that he must be moneyed. She noticed that on his left hand, he wore an expensive gold and diamond wedding ring. Much like Harold, the cut and style of his clothes looked expensive.

"My dear, I fint myself attracted to you," he remarked, pressing her closer.

"Are you married, Hans?"

"No."

"Separated?"

"Yes."

"Where's your wife?"

"She's heffing herself a goot time in Chermany weeth my chiltren."

"Oh! What's she doing there?"

"She's on a holeeday."

What a worm, she thought, to be stepping out on her when she was merely visiting relatives. "Then you're not separated, after all, are you? Pardon me for asking, but why are you dating that woman ... Noreen, if you have a wife and children?"

He laughed. "My vife vill be avay for six muntz. A man has a right to henjoy, himself. Don't you theenk so, my darlink?"

"Not if he intends to go back to her when she returns."

"My dear, you dence like a dream."

"Don't change the subject."

He ignored her. "Wood you conesider hefing dinner weeth me, sometime?"

"No, Hans, I would not because you're married."

"Oh, come, come, det's no reason."

"Well, I don't know about you. but for me ... you're like on the other side of the world. You're completely ineligible. You see, I don't go out with married men."

"But my dear, I don't know vat my vife is doing in Chermany. Eet's no harm for me to hef thees kint of fun."

"Oh, yes it is. You may not think so, but if it involves other women, there is harm in it." She thought of Lou and his women. The dance ended. He led her back.

Her eyes wandered over the room, looking for Harold. He was returning with Gerta. Gallantly, he pulled out her chair before sitting down himself. Tonight it seemed all his attention was directed at Gerta. Were they more than just neighbours?

Harold leaned back in his chair. "Hans, I saw you and Tanya dancing, you sly dog. Are you two enjoying yourselves? Huh? Don't be ashamed to admit it, if you are." He looked at Tanya and winked.

"Most certainly, ve are, tenk you, Harold. And you vur right. She's a wery goot dencer. I shall claim her for de next dence, as vell."

The other two couples joined them with drinks in their hands. Harold, playing the charming host, told several off-color jokes. Everybody laughed as Tanya sat mute, engrossed in a silent war within herself, barely able to concentrate on what was said.

Harold whispered something into Hans' ear. Then rising he held out his hand to Gerta again, reminding Tanya of the first time they'd met and how he had done the same thing to her. She felt a stab of jealousy. Was it her imagination or was Harold deliberately trying to palm her off on Hans?

"My dear, do you vish to dence? Please do me thee honour!"

"I guess so." Because of Harold, she felt pressured into accepting. She looked at Noreen, dressed in a tight-fitting, blue satin, strapless gown. She appeared totally unconcerned that her date was making a play for Tanya and lounged back in her chair, contentedly sipping on a drink.

Tanya put some space between herself and Hans. She found him tedious. Anger tore through her. But it was either dance or sit pouting at the table.

One dance followed the next with Hans claiming her each time. It was obvious that he was deliberately monopolizing her time. And with Harold, she'd had but three dances.

Tanya decided that as soon as he brought her home, she'd have a "heart-to-heart" with her so called "steady."

The lights dimmed for a slow waltz, her heart cried out that she should be dancing this dance with Harold.

She could feel Hans' hot breath on her neck. She pushed him away, wondering why she should be fighting off this boorish man? Her eyes searched for Harold. ... He was dancing with Gerta, his handsome face bent close to her ear, her blonde head nestled on his shoulder. At the sight of them, Tanya's jealousy shot up to epidemic levels. How ironic! He was having a wonderful time ... while she was in misery. She looked away and thought of Lou.

Why did Harold bring her? she wondered. The waltz went on, endless. Hurt welled up in her throat, as she realized that once more she'd given her heart to someone who thought nothing of trampling on it. "No, please back off, I can't breathe." She shoved Hans back; tears gathering in her eyes. Suddenly, she couldn't wait until they got home, she'd have it out with Harold right here and now!

The music stopped. "Tenk you, my dear."

Tanya said nothing, feeling her body start to tremble from the brutal evening. Keeping her eyes trained on Harold and blocking out all extraneous matter, she marched quickly to where he stood with Gerta.

"Harold, please, I'd like to speak to you."

Gerta raised well-plucked eyebrows at her, as Tanya took hold of Harold's arm and led him out of earshot. She drew in her mounting fury. "Harold, I want to know what's going on between you and Gerta? And I want the truth!"

The smile melted away; guilt swept over his face.

"There's something not right here, I think you know what I'm talking about."

At that moment, the orchestra interrupted with a lively number. The smile returned. Leaning over, he put both arms around her and gave her a hug, making her suspect that he was only trying to lighten her mood.

"Let's dance, okay?"

Even dancing, her anger remained intact. As far as she was concerned, the hug hadn't resolved anything.

"Harold, why is that girl here? How come you brought both of us? I've never been on a date with three people! Harold, you let me down! You made me believe that that there was no one else ... that I was special to you. Are you leading me on?"

"Come on, Tanya, don't be angry! We're all having such fun together. We're a great group. Enjoy yourself! We're here for that reason, aren't we? Gerta's just a friend; can't you see that?" His smile began to wane.

"Then tell me, why do I get the feeling that you want me to be with Hans? He didn't ask me out, you did! Why are you pushing him at me? He's married. I don't go out with married men. He makes me sick!"

"Tanya ... Tanya, he's nice, isn't he? He's my friend! Be nice to him. We're ... we're ... just like one, big happy family, you might say. Everybody's having a really great time; I don't see what the problem is. Gerta's my neighbour, I have to dance with her. Tanya ... listen to me. You and I ... we're not committed to each other in any way! So why not? You're free ... I'm free. Now, let's enjoy the evening, okay? When the time is right, we'll consider getting serious."

A shock rippled through her. "Well, that may be enough for you, Harold ... but it's not enough for me! Furthermore, you gave me the idea that you cared about me. Well ... I see that I was mistaken. Harold, I hate to be a spoil sport and wreck your good time, but could you take me home ... now?" At this point, staying any longer, only to prolong her agony, was unthinkable.

"Tanya, can't you wait a bit? And you're wrong about Gerta. She means nothing to me. It's you I'm interested in. But we still have plenty of time, don't we? Why rush it? Uh-h-h ... we're all going out for pizza after the dance. Why not stay and come along? ... Please? ... It's only eleven." He flashed her a disarming smile.

Tanya, her body shaking, recognized the patronizing undertone. Harold, unwilling to let the evening be spoiled, was thinking of himself and his friends. ... Also, he hated scenes. Still, the remote chance that, perhaps he was, as he said, "still interested in her," tugged at her. Her jealousy could blow the whole thing. Sadly, something told her it was all over between them and no amount of sweet talk or vague promises would change things.

She sighed. If nothing else, by being open she'd made him face the truth. If he didn't want to act on it, she couldn't force him to. She bowed to the inevitable. "Okay, Harold, I'll wait."

He brightened, giving her a squeeze. "Now that's my Tanya. Let's go back to the table."

Suddenly Harold changed. He became more attentive toward her, a model of good manners. His spirits uplifted, he told one ribald joke after another. Everyone except Tanya rolled with laughter, as the sick feeling at the pit of her stomach persisted.

"Okay, shall we go to Rudy's for pizza? ... Yes? Then what are we waiting for? ... Let's go! ... Tanya, wait right here, I'll get your coat."

Harold herded them out of the building and into the car, with Tanya wondering how she would hold together? This time he insisted that she sit next to him.

As usual, Harold had reserved a table. The pizza arrived, hot and melting. Harold portioned off a generous slice, dripping strings of cheese and sausage, and held it out to Tanya. "Sweetie, open your mouth. I want you to have the first bite."

"But I really don't want any."

"Oh, come now! Try a little! I picked pepperoni and mushroom only because I thought you'd like it. Here, take a bite. Rudy makes the best in town."

Her stomach churned. To oblige him she bit off a small piece, thinking that she'd never known him to be more attentive than at this moment. She wished only to go home. It was difficult to maintain her composure for the sake of propriety. They left the restaurant only after the last piece was eaten.

On the way home, she saved up more burning questions for Harold. The black Lincoln turned into her street and stopped. Harold left the car running. "This is it. We're home," he said, with make believe cheerfulness.

Damn him! she thought. He has his audacity dropping me off first! Shows how much he really cares!

"Night, Tanya," Gerta drawled.

Hans got out and planted a kiss on her hand. "Goot night my leetle dencer. I call you sometime?"

She ignored him. "Night, everybody." Harold came to the passenger side to open the door for her. He seemed most jubilant. Taking her hand, he walked her to the apartment.

She turned, "Harold I ..."

His lips crushed hers in a loud, smack. "Good night! I'll call you. Sorry I can't stay, but," his laugh sounded nervous, "I have guests waiting in the car. You understand. ... "

"Good night, Harold." Tanya understood. It was over. His footsteps echoed down the cement path. She went inside, feeling wrung-out in the pit of her stomach, thinking how the relationship had definitely opened her eyes even more. Regardless of how good- looking, brilliant, or eligible he was, she could never accept his infidelity. It would stand in the way, and she would be left wondering whether she was good enough. She'd have to let him go, no matter how good a catch he was.

As she shut the door behind her, she wondered how she was to console herself?

58

IN LATE FEBRUARY, SIX MONTHS AFTER DOT STARTED WORK, Jake Werner asked for a transfer to Victoria, B.C.. The news came as a shock to Tanya.

"It's my wife," he told her. "I'm doing it for her. Her arthritis is so severe the doctor recommended a change of climate as the only alternative. It's that or a wheelchair."

Tanya swallowed hard. "Mr. Werner, I'm sorry to see you go."

His eyebrows came together. "M-m-m-m, yes, I hate to leave, too."

She cried to herself walking home that evening. Jake, she thought, was the one reason she could take Dot. She'd learned to depend on his praise and his appreciation of her. Between them existed an unspoken, mutual understanding of trust and admiration.

It made her stronger, braver, more tolerant. She would miss him.

59

AFTER JAKE, MITCH BURROWS CAME to manage the department. He was tall, red-haired, he'd been a pilot in the Second World War. Mitch was married and had several children.

As soon as he took over the office Dot Woods began a flirting game with him quite openly. Tanya wondered what kind of marriage the woman had to be so flirtatious with a stranger, especially since they were both married. Once, Tanya, having wandered into his office for a signature on a letter, caught her close at his side pressing shoulders with him.

Dot beamed at Tanya. "She's the one I was telling you about, Mitch. You know, the miracle worker!" She let her hand rest on his as she spoke.

"Is that so?" Tanya's new boss, his face all smiles, signed the letter, obviously enjoying the attention that Dot was showering on him.

"Thank you, Mr. Burrows." Tanya returned to her desk, wondering just how far the flirtation would go? At this point it looked as though they were getting in with both feet.

Later that summer Mitch Burrows invited the staff to his house for a barbecue. For some reason Dot came alone, though the invitation included her husband. The sky was black the entire time. It started to pour rain. Somehow Mitch and his wife, Ellen, managed to cook the steaks on the outside grill with an umbrella perched over them.

When they thought no one was watching, Tanya noticed hushed talks between Dot and Mitch. After eating their fill of steaks, baked potatoes and salad, he generously offered to drive Dot home. A meaningful exchange of looks and she readily consented ... perhaps too readily for the gesture to appear innocent.

On Monday, back at work, Mitch opened the door to his office and barked for Tanya to come in.

"Yes Mr. Burrows, you wanted to see me?" She noticed he had her personal file open in front of him.

"Tanya, I'm evaluating your work here. ... I've been hearing something about you. Most of the staff seem to think that you're some kind of a superwoman. However, I see that you're normal, like the rest of us ... a steno and, as far as I'm concerned, nothing out of the ordinary. ... You're certainly no superwoman!"

She stared at him. Why was he tearing her apart? Her group therapy sessions had taught her that someone like Dot might be jealous of her abilities.

"Why don't you get a job with an airline? ... A pretty, strawberry blonde like yourself would have loads of fun. You'd have boyfriends galore! You'd make a fine airline stewardess."

Anger jabbed at her. "Mr. Burrows, I hate flying! But whoever gave you the idea that I was a superwoman? I never claimed to be a superwoman! Where did you hear that?" This was the final straw! She would transfer out! To be put down because she was good at her job was an insult! He'd soon find out just how much work she really did! It had to be Dot, for how would he know anything if it wasn't her filling his ears with gossip?

"Was there anything else, Mr. Burrows?"

"Uh-h-h, well, not really." Looking sheepish, he seemed at a loss for words and waved her out.

As she walked back to her desk, she told herself that she'd move heaven and earth to leave.

It seemed odd that shortly after the barbecue a promotion and raise came through for Dot and, thankfully, she moved to a different office.

Tanya began to apply for everything that came along. However as fate would have it, it wasn't until three years later that she was able to transfer out. During that time, Mitch Burrows found out first-hand, what Tanya's work load was like.

She returned from a vacation to find him waiting eagerly to talk to her. "Tanya, I'd like to see you in my office."

"Yes, Mr. Burrows. Shall I bring in my notebook?"

"No. That won't be necessary."

She walked in and sat down.

"Tanya, I'm very glad you're back! I think I made a mistake in judging you when I first came. I realize now the supreme effort that you put into your job. While you were away the entire steno pool has been doing the brunt of the files. And I must say, the quality that you gave everything just isn't there."

A small thrill went through her. "Thank you, Mr. Burrows." She always personally checked the files and letters for mistakes that came back from the steno pool. If there were too many errors, she retyped the work herself.

"Mr. Burrows, if you don't mind, I think I'd better get started. Uh-h-h, I'm training the new girl that's replacing me. I'm transferring to the Citizenship branch at the end of the month. They had an opening so I applied."

He nodded. "Yes, I'm aware of that. Sure you won't change your mind and stay?"

"No. Sorry, Mr. Burrows, it's time I was moving on."

She walked back to her desk feeling smug, satisfied. The work basket, she noticed, was stacked to overflowing.

On her last day at work, Meg and Sandra met her at the door with a corsage of red roses and a large bouquet of flowers, which Meg presented to her with a hug. "Tanya, this is from the staff. It's our way of saying "thank you."

Tanya, accepting the gift, was suddenly overcome with tears.

Meg continued. "The entire department has a luncheon planned for you at the Holiday Inn at noon."

One hundred and eight people showed up at the restaurant. Several tables had to be placed together. Somehow the hotel staff managed to have everybody sit as a group.

As guest of honour, Tanya sat at the very head. The tax assessors, her extended family as she liked to think of them, stood up to offer her their accolades, their thanks. It thrilled her; it saddened her.

Mitch Burrows rose to speak. "Tanya, let me say, I actually found out that you really and truly are the super worker I was told about when I first came. Your exceptional skills, your exceptional dedication has been a definite asset to this office. No matter who I've asked about you, they, everyone, told me how dependable and how loyal you are and that you could always be counted on to get the job done, even if it meant staying late." He raised his glass. "With heartfelt thanks, let's drink to you ... Tanya. I know everyone, we ... all wish you the very best in your new position."

Tanya drank in the moment as they rose together to toast her. She felt a tear trickle down her cheek. It was a moment that she'd always treasure.

"I hear that you like to travel. Well, what we have here for you is a slide projector. From the staff and myself, please accept it with our deepest appreciation."

She felt herself getting up. "Thank you, Mr. Burrows, and everybody, thank you. I'm very happy to see you. You've gone to a lot of trouble on my account. Doing the work ... has been my pleasure. Thank you for the gift. And, thank you for coming to my farewell dinner. I'll miss you." Her tears cut off further words.

Tanya moved her things to the Citizenship branch the next morning. Since the office was run by only two people, her work load would be much lighter.

Several months later she went to see Meg and Sandra. "So, tell me, the new girl, the one I trained, how's she doing?"

"Oh, Tanya, haven't you heard?"

"Heard what?"

"She quit after two months. She couldn't take it. And Mitch Burrows, he was forced to hire two extra girls, full-time, to replace you. And even with the two of them working full-time, they still can't keep up. So, every day we have to pass whatever's left over to the steno pool! What do you think of that?"

"Oh, Meg, you know no one helped me. I did it all myself."

"I know, everybody used to talk about you and we'd all wonder how you did it. In fact, when Dot came, she was so jealous of you that she nicknamed you "superwoman"!"

60

"IT'S REALLY STRANGE. YOU KNOW, I still keep thinking that Harold will come back to me. Even after everything he put me through. So what do I do now? ... Give up?" Her voice sounded flat.

Caroline Hall looked at her with determination. "Don't give up, Tanya! But if Harold happens to call, remember you're better off without him."

"Maybe so, but it puts me right back to square one again with nobody!"

"Yes." Dr. Carlsten removed his pipe. "To have nobody is better then to have someone who's going to abuse you!"

Tanya left after the discussion ... clinging to the remote possibility that Harold might surprise her and phone to straighten out the mess, her mind still unable to fathom that it was over and done with between them.

The following Saturday, in an effort to put Harold behind, she went back to the Silver Ballroom. The evening ended a total write off; no one seemed interested or interesting, and she went home alone and dejected. Yet she couldn't give up. Being alone was too final. Didn't people, animals, insects, all come in pairs?

Tanya awoke on Sunday, depressed, with Harold still very much on her mind. Sometimes it helped to talk it out. ... She decided to visit Alisha.

Alisha was loading a roast into the oven when she walked in. Tanya pulled a stool up to the kitchen counter, thinking that she looked remarkably well for having borne three children.

"Will you stay for supper?".

"Yes, I'd like to see Allen and the children. Uh-h-h, where are they?"

"They went to visit his mother." The oven door screeched as she closed it.

"You know Alisha, I still haven't met him ... you know who I'm talking about. The stories I could tell you about some of my so- called "romances" and how they turned out ... it would make your hair stand on end if you knew. I don't know what it is about me, but men just don't like me. Maybe I'll end up an old maid." Her confidence shattered, she was on the edge of tears. ... "After all the searching I've done you'd think I'd have found someone by now, wouldn't you? I'm going to be thirty-six this year and I'm still single. Now be honest, do you think there's still hope for me, or am I too old?"

"What a question! Of course there's still hope for you. Why do you ask? And you're not old at thirty-six!"

"I'm so tired of it all, the hoping ... just everything."

"Oh Tanya! When you were married to Lou, I was so afraid for you. I knew you were in trouble, but there was really nothing anyone could do to help until you left him. I even thought he might kill you, especially after you told me that he had a gun. People don't usually own guns unless they intend to use them. Now as far as I'm concerned, if there's no one better out there, I'd rather see you by yourself, alone, single, than married to some scum!"

Tears welled in her eyes. "It's all very noble for you to say that, because you've already got a husband. ... But me ... what's going to become of me?"

"Stop it! Nothing's going to become of you! Of course, you'll find someone. You need more time, that's all." Alisha began chopping a head of lettuce. "I had a letter from Dad this morning. He seems to be doing okay in his new place. Does he still write to you?"

"Yes, and I write to him. You know me, I'm not one to hold grudges."

Thoughts of her stepfather crowded into her mind. She'd given Alisha but a brief sketch of what had occurred when she'd gone to help him with his house with none of the horrific details. The attempted rape had been soul-shattering. Later in the week there had been a discussion within the group about the incident. Dr. Carlsten had asked, "Do you think it happened because your Dad was lonely and still grieving, or perhaps that he might have gone a little wild?"

She'd thought a moment. "Uh-h-h, I think that his ego had been blown out of proportion because of all the crazy widows chasing after him. ... All that attention he was getting, it must have gone to his head. Most of the women in the district figured he was a good catch."

Dr. Carlsten had smiled slightly and agreed.

Whatever the reason, the instant she'd read the letter from him asking for forgiveness, she'd forgiven him.

Allen arrived with the children. There were hugs and kisses warding off the depression that she was battling. When she left she felt no better and no worse for having told Alisha.

61

FOR THE NEXT TWO MONTHS SHE FORCED HERSELF to go to the Silver Ballroom every Saturday, once more to become a familiar face in the crowd of single women.

It was Anna who broke the pattern in mid-November by inviting her to a twenty-fifth wedding anniversary celebration for Anton's cousin.

"There's a guy coming that you might know. Do you remember a Walter Kushinsky? We met him at a wedding about two years ago. He works for Ford Motors. He's an appraiser. ... He's single and divorced."

Tanya could vaguely remember someone tall with light brown hair and a clean shaven look. No doubt Anna had plans to pair her up with him. She consented to go if only to humour her.

Though most of the month had been unseasonably warm, a heavy snowfall came down on the day of the party. It continued to snow all day and well into the evening. By the time Anton came for her, the roads were treacherous. They arrived at the Dalton Community Hall to find the drifts almost knee high. Tanya carefully picked her way through the snow towards the building.

She stepped inside and noticed Alisha waving her over. Alisha pulled out a chair for her. "I like your dress," she commented.

"Thanks." The dress, a wine coloured print, enriched her coloring.

The band struck up a polka Allen reached for Alisha's hand. "Come on, this is our dance."

Tanya dropped into a chair and tapped to the music until she felt someone touch her shoulder. She looked up to see Anna with Walter Kushinsky. Her face flushed. "Hi!" From where she sat she liked the slope of his forehead and the angle of his cheek and jaw.

He smiled at her. "Hi! ... Tanya, remember me?"

She nodded, noticing his pale jade-green eyes.

"Would you like to dance?" he asked.

"Yes. And yes, I do remember you."

His step was smooth and light; she could follow him perfectly.

"You're a good dancer," he remarked.

"Thank you!" When the music stopped, Alisha and Allen were directly ahead of them. "Alisha, wait, I want you to meet someone. ... Alisha, Walter Kushinsky. ... Walter, my sister, Alisha, and her husband, Allen Semco." For some reason she thought they should meet. The two men shook hands.

For the rest of the evening Walter danced nearly every dance with her. He struck her as being genuine and totally himself. Her spirits lifted as Harold departed from her thoughts and Walter took over.

Just before midnight they lined up for a lavish buffet, filling their plates with a tantalizing turkey dinner. They were almost back at their table when Tanya noticed a young girl talking to Anna. She stopped short and touched Walter's sleeve. "Uh-h-h, that's Jessie Marenco with Anna. Do you know her?"

He nodded "yes."

Jessie was training to be a nurse. She was living with Anna and at present renting Tanya's room in the basement. Anna had taken her in because she was a distant cousin of Anton's. Jessie was strikingly beautiful. Tanya smiled at her, wondering whether Walter would be taken in by her beauty? "Love your dress Jessie. It's gorgeous. Uh-h-h, Jessie, this is Walter Kushinsky."

Jessie flashed pearly white teeth at him. "Yes, we know each other, don't we Walter? How are you?"

He nodded. "Fine, thanks, Jessie."

By far, she was the most beautiful woman in the room. Only nineteen, Anna had said. Small, black ringlets framed a perfectly oval face. Her almond-shaped eyes were a deep blue. Her skin, perfect. There was a hint of blush on her cheeks. Her dress, in off white lace, had a Spanish look to it. The skirt, with horizontal tiers of gathers, clung seductively to her figure. It was cut fashionably short.

Anna pointed to a chair opposite her. "I hope you don't mind if Jessie sits here," she said to Tanya. "She came alone. Walter, take that chair next to hers."

"Thanks." Walter pulled out Tanya's chair first, before he sat down on the other side of Jessie.

Tanya was determined to take whatever happened in stride, reasoning within herself that since she hardly knew him, and if it turned out that he couldn't resist the girl, it was better that she find out right away. I'd have lost nothing, she thought. She listened with interest to the interaction between them.

"Walter, like my rose?" Jessie pointed to a red rose pinned auspiciously to her hair, batting long, black lashes at him.

"Yes, it looks nice, Jessie."

"Well, somehow it survived the snow and everything. You know, I was sure it would freeze."

His eyes flicked over her with merely casual interest. "Seems to me that roses can withstand a pretty cold temperature."

Jessie's perfectly manicured nails, tinted the same red as the rose, touched the flower briefly, coming to rest on his arm.

"Walter, you might be right. But, listen to this. I didn't even bring a pair of boots with me. So can you imagine little ol' me, slipping and sliding all over the place in my spike heels! And every time I took a step, I nearly fell." Her large eyes held his.

She may be young but she's a pro, Tanya thought, sensing that she was doing everything she could to attract him.

Half smiling, Walter nodded absently. Suddenly, he leaned past Jessie to catch Tanya's eye. "Everything all right? Can I get you a coffee?"

"Why yes, thank you, Walter, coffee would be fine," she answered, surprised that he could even think of tearing himself away from such a beauty.

Jessie touched his arm. "Uh-h-h, Walter, me too. I'd like some. Black, please, if you don't mind."

"Okay, Jessie, be right back."

They sat through speeches and anecdotes for the couple whose anniversary was being honoured. Soon after, the orchestra struck up "The Anniversary Waltz."

Walter pushed back his chair, walked around Jessie, who gave him an expectant look, and came to stand behind Tanya. "Dance?"

Tanya nodded, relieved that despite all of Jessie's efforts to captivate him, Walter seemed immune to her. She fell into step with him.

"Tanya, I think you should know that I'm divorced."

"So am I, Walter!"

"I've been divorced for ten years and it was my wife who gave me reasonable grounds."

Their eyes met. "Really? Then we have something in common because it was my husband who gave me reasonable grounds. And it's been ten years for me, too! ... Walter, uh-h-h, are you going steady with anyone?"

"No, I'm free. How about you?"

"No, no one. Actually, I just broke up with someone."

"Well, I do know some guys that I meet up with once a week. Fridays we meet in a bar to drink beer. ... Tanya, if you're ready to go, I'd like to drive you home."

She laughed. "I'm sure Anna and Anton will be very happy to hear that. I came with them. ... Let me get my coat."

"Wait, I'll get it."

In the car they discussed their past lives. When they reached her apartment, Walter said "good night" to her in the hallway. Leaning over, he kissed her lightly on the cheek. Tanya thought about asking him in for coffee. However, since the hour was late, she changed her mind.

"Can I see you again?" he asked.

Although unsure, she nodded. "I think so."

"How about tomorrow, can I call you? ... Yes? ... Good night, Tanya."

"Good night, Walter." She opened the door and went inside, thinking that she liked him. He made her feel comfortable, secure.

There was a different quality to him from the other men that she'd known. He was considerate, chivalrous, natural, yet shy. Why do I feel as if I've known him for years, she wondered. Though he was a far cry from Lou, could she trust him? Or like the others, would he show his true colours and let her down the minute she showed some obvious interest in him?

Sunday afternoon Walter phoned her. She suggested that they go swimming. "You'll love it," she exclaimed. The pool happens to be directly across the street from my apartment." Years ago she'd taken lessons. Now she wanted a chance to show off her ability as a swimmer.

He agreed. "I'll see you in half an hour."

They walked across the street to a pool at Victoria College. Once inside the building she changed into an attractively cut, turquoise, one-piece bathing suit and went to find Walter.

His admiring glance swept over her.

She smiled at him and cut the water with a clean dive. Walter sat down at the edge of the pool with only his feet immersed. Tanya came up for air and beckoned to him. There was a noticeable roll of fat above his blue trunks, making her think that he could do with some exercise.

"You swim like a dolphin."

"Thanks. Walter, don't just sit there, come on in."

He let out a laugh.

"What's so funny?"

"It's me. I can't swim a stroke."

"Oh, Walter, really? ... Come on, I'll teach you."

"No you won't. I'm not a fish, I don't care if I swim or not."

"Aw-w-w, don't say that." Tanya took his hands and pulled him in beside her. "I'll show you how to float. Just lie on your back and relax. That's all there's to it." By the time the hour went by, he was treading water and liking it.

They went back to her apartment to sit on the floor and talk. His parents were still living and he had a sister. Tanya brought out cheese, crackers and coffee for a snack. Walter left at ten assuring her that he'd call. She shut the door behind him, satisfied that the afternoon had gone very well.

62

FOR SEVERAL WEEKS WALTER PHONED HER nearly every day. Tanya always managed to arrange something different: a travelogue, a trip to the museum, or a cup of coffee at a favourite restaurant. She enjoyed his company. He made her feel alive, worthwhile. Then there were moments when he brought her home and she ended up in his arms, savouring his kisses. Yet fearful of becoming enmeshed and hurt again, she didn't harbour any hope or imagine that the relationship would go any further than it already had, and even convinced herself into thinking that he was just a good friend, nothing more. ... Friendship, she could handle. At the same time, she was determined to keep things on a platonic level until she could gauge which direction they were headed. Another thought entered her mind, if someone came along that she liked better, she wouldn't hesitate to break if off.

In fact, she'd only recently met Peter Laufman and had been giving him a lot of thought. Peter was German and a bookbinder by trade. One afternoon he'd come into her department to deliver a book to her boss. After he'd introduced himself, Tanya had shown him into Mr. Sanderson's office. Peter had curly red hair, freckles, blue eyes, and a thin face with a strong nose. He wasn't much taller than she was. She could tell from his admiring glances that he was attracted to her. In order to focus attention away from herself, she'd asked him about the book he'd brought. He'd explained about the special leather binding that Mr. Sanderson had requested. He didn't stop there but persisted in finding out who she was. By the time he left they had established the beginnings of a friendship.

The next day he called her at work and asked her to go dancing with him. It happened to be a Friday. She knew that Walter would be meeting his friends. She'd said "yes." There had been several casual dates with him after that.

He had a warmth and sincerity that echoed something within her own character; she felt drawn to him. However, though she knew that he had a lot of feelings for her, she couldn't, for some unexplained reason, reciprocate. Perhaps in the back of her mind, she couldn't let go of the picture of Harold, who was part German, and his shabby treatment of her. Still, she liked Peter and considered him sensitive, charming, and highly intelligent. It was a pleasure to converse with someone of his calibre.

Tanya felt it was perfectly all right to date him, because she wasn't committed to Walter. If the relationship between her and Walter didn't pan out, she could use Peter as a cushion.

One evening she dressed in a pale mauve creation. The top of the dress was made of delicate lace, the skirt, sheer and floating. She was thrilled that Walter had made a date to take her dancing to the club Mirimba. She was putting on a dab more colour to her cheeks when the doorbell rang.

Smiling, she went to answer it. Walter's eyes widened as he took in the dress.

"Uh-h-h, is it all right?" she asked.

"You, you look like something out of a magazine. Come here!"

He pulled her close and found her mouth, as her heart leapt inside her. They stood together, with neither wanting to be the first to break away. She clung to him, wanting the moment to go on, to savor it, to remember it. From behind, she heard the phone ring. "I should answer that," she said, apologetically. They separated.

"Hello?"

"Tanya, this is Peter Laufman."

Now flustered, she lowered her voice. "Oh, Peter! How are you?"

"Tanya, would you like to come to dinner with me tomorrow night? I had in mind the top of "The Caravan"."

"Uh-h-h, I'm not too sure. Give me a minute." At the moment, she couldn't think of any reason to say "no" but neither could she say "yes." Not with Walter there. "Peter, could you call me back in about fifteen minutes? I'll let you know then." She hung up and faced Walter. She noticed his face had turned a light pink.

"Who was that?" he asked, angrily.

She hesitated before answering. "Uh-h-h, actually, a friend of mine, Peter Laufman. He wants to take me out to dinner tomorrow night." I have nothing to hide, she thought. We're only casually involved.

His voice rang with jealousy. "Well, you better tell him that you're going out with me."

"What are you getting so angry about, we're not going steady or anything."

He looked at her, dead serious. "Well then, you gotta make up your mind, it's either him or me. ... You can't play the field, Tanya."

Her thoughts went racing madly as she tried to sort out her feelings. She had more in common with Walter than she had with Peter. He was her kind. They had the same ethnic background. It made a difference in the long run. Harold, like Peter, was highly intelligent, and she'd thought that she knew him. What did she really know about Peter?

The phone rang again. Tanya, her heart pounding from indecision, picked up the receiver. "Hello?"

"Tanya, what about tomorrow night? Are you free?"

"Uh-h-h, Peter, I'm sorry, actually, I've met someone else and ... I'm dating him."

She heard a flat silence at the other end ... then his voice, disappointed, "Sorry to hear that. Well good luck to you!" She turned to find Walter right behind her. He reached out and put a possessive arm around her waist.

"Thanks. You're my girl. I'm not letting you go."

The incident established an unspoken bond between them. She found Walter was never mean or critical. If he detected a problem between them, he'd point it out to her in a very kind and diplomatic way. Neither did he try to shut her up if she happened to express some hidden concern about him. Their relationship progressed on an even keel. She found him comfortable as well as exciting to be with. His openness appealed to her.

At Easter they went to the Polish Catholic Cathedral to celebrate midnight mass. Halfway through the service, she looked down to find Walter on his knees, his head bowed, his hands folded in prayer. She was moved to tears.

One evening in late March, they went for a walk through a park close to her apartment. The air was scented heavily with the signs of an early spring. Suddenly she realized that she felt closer to him than she'd ever been to anyone else. To her delight, he was always open and honest with her. This redeeming trait increased not only her love but her admiration and respect for him. As time passed, Tanya became more open, more giving, more trusting toward him.

Walter called on her faithfully every Wednesday and Saturday.

It never ceased to amaze her that unlike other men she'd dated in the past, he never expected any undue payment from her. The heavy hand of experience had taught her that should she order more than a hamburger, the men who footed the bill expected more then a peck on the cheek in return. Ultimately, at the end of an evening, she'd found herself engaged in a wrestling match when she'd emphasized "no" to them. It was disheartening.

From Walter she felt no such pressure. If he thought she was cold, he didn't hesitate to put his jacket around her shoulders. He knew that she liked cream and sugar in her coffee. How very gallant that he tried to put her first in everything. Gradually he began to take over her waking thoughts.

The only fly in the ointment was the time he reserved to drink beer with the boys. Every Friday, as if on cue, Tanya began to develop migraines. Sometimes they carried over into Saturday when he came to take her out. If she was too sick to leave the apartment he'd turn on the television content to sit and watch some show until it was time for him to leave. In the meantime, she kept the true cause of the headaches to herself.

It resolved nothing. Tanya, frustrated, confessed her problem to the group. "Do you think I should keep on seeing him, Dr. Carlsten?" she asked.

"Not if his drinking is going to upset you to that degree. If you're getting sick about it, you shouldn't see him. If I were you, I'd think twice before going any further," he cautioned.

She nodded, feeling miserable. "You're right." She sighed, neither willing to listen, nor be overly influenced by any advice if it happened to be contrary to whatever conclusion that she herself had arrived at. Though she didn't approve of Walter's drinking buddies and his spending time with them, she couldn't expect him to change overnight, reminding herself that he'd formed his habits long before he'd met her.

Five months later they were still dating despite the problem that existed between them. For Tanya, as time glazed over some of her concerns, she became more accepting of the situation, and began to relax and feel confident that regardless of all, the relationship would last because her love for him would overcome the problems. However, to date, love hadn't even been discussed. But it'll come to that, she thought. I can feel it.

One evening she was about to shampoo her hair when the phone rang. She reached for the receiver. It was Walter. He sounded anxious.

"Tanya? I was wondering if I could come and see you right away. ... I mean right now."

"Why yes, come whenever you like."

"Uh-h-h, but is now a good time for you? ... I mean if you're busy or something I won't come."

"Walter, definitely, now would be fine. And Walter don't be so formal. I was getting ready to wash my hair but it can wait. See you soon." She went into the bedroom and changed into a plaid skirt and white sweater. Fifteen minutes later, he was at her door. She ran to let him in, eager, expectant. Walter looked strangely serious and tense. "Hi. Is something wrong?" she asked.

He nodded, brushed past her and sat down at the table while searching for something to focus on outside the window. Tanya felt a sinking feeling within her.

"Tanya, I've gotta get this off my chest. Uh-h-h, I don't know how to say it. ... Uh-h-h, for some time now, I've been thinking about it. It's about you and me. Uh-h-h ... Tanya ... the way things are going I don't think we should see each other any more."

"What?" Her strength ebbed. She gripped the back of a chair for support, wondering if she was strong enough to withstand yet another rejection so soon. "Walter, what's wrong? Have I done something to make you feel this way?"

"Well, no, not exactly. Uh-h-h, it's not that. ... Actually, there's nothing really wrong. ... It's me, I think we're getting too serious, too quick. Uh-h-h, it's just that I feel I'm not ready to settle down to anything permanent. Tanya, it wouldn't be fair of me if I let you think anything different. I wouldn't do that to you. I like you but I like my friends too. ... I like my freedom. Uh-h-h, that is, I want to be free." He looked at her in agony then quietly added, "The truth is, I came to say good-bye."

Tanya hung on to the chair as she felt her very life draining away. With concerted effort she forced herself to go on. "I see. So you came ... to say ... good bye? ... Well, in that case, this is good-bye, isn't it, Walter?" She let go of the chair and held out her hand.

He seemed overcome with surprise and jumped to his feet. They shook hands as strangers meeting for the first time. He looked dumbfounded. Did he expect reproach, tears? Certainly not! She wouldn't satisfy him with such a show and kept a tight reign on her feelings. "Good luck, Walter! I guess we won't be seeing each other." Withdrawing her hand, with a make believe smile glued to her face, she quickly walked him out.

The door closed behind him. Tanya stood still as the meaning of his words sank in. No one wanted her! Not Harold! Not Walter! Not anyone! And she'd just lost Peter! Shock waves coursed through her body. She felt herself disintegrate; slowly she sank to her knees as heaving sobs wrenched free. From her knees she dropped to the floor and lay fully prostrate, her tears flowing unchecked. "Oh Lord, I love Walter, why can't he love me? Am I to end my life alone? What am I supposed to do? I can't live by myself. Lord, I need him! Oh Lord, I do need him! ... I can't go on! ... Just won't!"

Two hours later she was still sobbing while beating her fists against the floor. Finally, utterly wearied, she raised her head and struggled to her feet. The room had grown dark. She switched on a light and groped her way to the bathroom to splash cool water over her face and swollen eyes. Then she put on her pyjamas and went to bed. She knew that she must rest, must sleep. She must not give in to the misery that she felt inside. Tomorrow was another work day. Have to be fit to face it.

The next night Tanya dressed very carefully in a new dress and went back to the Silver Ballroom.

Two weeks went by as she reflected bitterly that Walter hadn't come by or phoned to see how she was ... not that she had any such expectations from him. It would have been nice, though.

Sitting across the table from her was Tom Athill, her new escort. She took a sip of her coffee, thinking that it definitely tasted bitter. He was middle-aged, well-dressed, well-mannered, and he'd suggested that they stop for coffee before he drove her home. They'd just met at the Silver Ballroom. Inside, she felt the pain about having to start over.

"Tom, tell me, why do you go to the Silver Ballroom?" She wanted to know, thinking that since she'd found him attractive, other women would too. It was a sure bet that he wouldn't have to pick anyone up.

He grinned. "Uh-h-h, I guess being a business man, I don't have much time to socialize. ... One gets tired of working. I like dancing. ... It's relaxing. ... Uh-h-h, I don't go there that much. What about you?"

"I enjoy dancing, I guess." She looked at her watch. "I'm sorry to rush you, but it's after one. I think I'd better be getting home. My roommate, she'll wonder what's happened to me."

"By all means." He paid the cheque and they left.

Though he seemed anxious to please, she knew that she was far from ready for further involvement. Perhaps in time. With each passing day, Walter was becoming more obscure, especially since she no longer allowed herself to hope or think of him.

After the break-up, Susan Forbes, a girl from work, had moved in with her. Susan was quiet, tall, regal looking and blonde. She was very efficient and kept the apartment in immaculate order. At Tanya's suggestion, she'd moved in on a trial basis only. She was congenial, and they got along very well.   Tom stopped his late model sedan in front of her apartment and went to the passenger side to help her out.

"Good night, Tom. Thanks for the coffee and thanks for driving me home."

"Good night. ... Tanya, can I call you sometime?"

She nodded in the affirmative. He smiled, squeezed her hand, then turned and walked away. He wasn't that bad, she thought. She might ... yes, she just might consider going out with him ... should he call.

Susan was waiting for her and burst out when she opened the door, "Tanya, am I glad you're home! Some guy's been phoning and asking for you about every half hour. The last time he called, it was twelve-thirty. He sounded really desperate. He said he had to talk to you."

Her heart gave a leap. "Did he give his name?"

"Yes, he said it was "Walter."

She felt a slight shock go through her. "Walter? I wonder what he wants?" She checked her watch. "Too late now, I'll have to call him tomorrow."

Just then the phone rang.

Susan smiled. "I bet that's him. You answer it."

Her hand trembled as she reached for the receiver. "Hello?"

"Tanya? This is Walter."

"Yes? How are you?"

"Fine! Fine! Am I glad you're home! Can I come over? I have to see you ... now! ... I mean tonight!"

With a pang, she remembered the last time he'd said those same words to her. ... "At this hour? ... But why?"

"Well, it's like this. There's only one thing I can say, you, ... you, Jezabel you!" He laughed. "Tanya, you got stuck in my head. ... I swear, I couldn't get you out! I tried, Lord, believe me how I tried! But you wouldn't budge. I finally had to admit that you were there to stay. Tanya, can I come over? We have to talk."

Her mood changed. She felt buoyant. "Yes, we can talk. But I'm warning you, I've got plenty to say to you! So be prepared to listen, okay? ... I'll see you in a little while."

She hung up, feeling giddy as she turned to Susan. "That was him! Walter! He wants to see me! Oh Susan, what'll I wear? My light blue rayon dress? Do you think it looks nice on me? Yes? I'll wear it." She began a frantic search for the dress. She found it and slipped it on. "Now the make-up. ... oh Lord, I look like a rag, don't I? Where's my eye shadow? I just know he'll come and I won't be half ready!"

Susan, with a surprised look on her face, observed Tanya from the bedroom door as she rushed around getting dressed.

Fifteen minutes later they heard his knock.

"Well he didn't waste any time in getting here," she remarked.

Tanya, speechless, only nodded. With thundering heart she tried to appear calm as she opened the door to let him in. "Walter, how nice to see you. Tell me, how've you been?"

"Tanya, never mind that now. ... Come here! He stretched his arms out to her. "Tanya, please, please, forgive me for being such a damn fool!" He put his arms around her and pulled her towards himself. Holding her close, he kissed her neck, her ears, her face.

She noticed his eyes glazed with tears and her heart melted. "Oh, Walter, I'm sorry, too. "Her breath caught in her throat. She couldn't and didn't resist. A rush of warmth spread through her body. Suddenly, everything seemed so wonderful, so right. "Walter, you're forgiven."

"Can we go somewhere and talk? You know the little place that served the cappuccino? I think it's open all night. Let's go there."

She walked out with Walter's arm around her shoulders.

"I don't know what it was but, for some reason, I just couldn't stop thinking about you. You kept coming back to me. Then I thought that maybe I was too late ... that maybe you'd found someone else. ... You know, I nearly went crazy with worry. I'm glad I wasn't too late." He looked dead sombre as he turned to her. "Tanya, am I too late?"

"No. Walter, I wasn't about to let myself get involved with anyone else that quick ... not after what happened between us. Actually, it's happened to me too many times. After you I couldn't trust anyone."

"Tanya, I'm sorry. I'm really sorry. How I missed you! I even decided that I'd give up my Fridays with the boys! If I have you, who needs them? You know, they pressured me into breaking off with you. ... And I was such a damn fool to listen to them."

Hearing his words, her joy rebounded. "Oh, Walter, what a relief! You remember my headaches? They were all about you and your drinking with the boys!" She sighed. "I missed you, too. And when you first left, I thought I would die. ..."

They were still talking when the sun came up.

63

WALTER AND TANYA ANNOUNCED THEIR ENGAGEMENT at the end of the month. Having decided to wait a year before taking the final step, a wedding date was set for late October.

Tanya knew that it would be a period for testing each other, making her wonder if she would still feel the same after the year was up.

The months passed swiftly. They had some bitter arguments as well as differences that they had to face. But after the year had passed they acknowledged that their feelings hadn't changed.

A week before her marriage Tanya announced her intentions to the group. "Dr. Carlsten, I must say that compared to Lou, Walter is a complete antithesis. In fact, I can't compare him to anyone I know. He has good morals, he's open, he's willing to listen to anything I have to say. I know very definitely that I won't regret marrying him. I just know it."

Dr. Carlsten nodded his approval. "You're sounding much different than you did when you first met him. And your optimism is refreshing. I feel you've come a long way since you joined us. In your heart, you never did give yourself entirely to Lou. I suppose in that respect you're almost like a virgin. I'm pleased to offer you my sincere congratulations." He rose with outstretched hand and came towards her. "I hope you and Walter will be very happy."

Tanya stood up to shake his hand. "Thank you Dr. Carlsten. You've been like the father that I've never had. But ... but, have always longed for. Your wisdom, your advice ... I can't thank you enough." Her tears choked off the rest and began cascading down her cheeks. She couldn't stop the flow, thinking about what might have happened if he hadn't been there to help her.

Gently, she felt his arms go around her. Her head came to rest on his shoulder.

"Tanya, Tanya, don't cry. You're going to be fine, just fine. You've changed so much. I've watched you grow in spirit. And if you need my help again, you know where to find me."

Tanya stood crying, unrestrained. Dr. Carlsten patiently held her, while she fought to stem the flow of emotion. Lea Thompson came to her rescue with a kleenex, while Caroline Halls' arms enclosed her in a hug. One by one, her extended family embraced her to say "good bye" and wish her luck.

In her heart, she knew that if things went well she would not be coming back. She left the group with mixed emotions, both sad and happy.

64

A LISHA SEWED HER WEDDING DRESS FOR HER ... a wispy sheer, gown in pale peach. There were soft gathers at the waist. The the skirt fell to mid-calf. She wore a string of pearls and a white flower in her hair.

Walter and Tanya exchanged their vows at the end of the third week in October before a Justice of the Peace at city hall. Tanya appeared transformed by an inner, spiritual change that had taken place within her.

Her wedding night was everything that she had dreamed it would be. She was eager to share and to give of herself to someone who really and truly loved her. Walter, who was tender, thoughtful, shy, fulfilled her every expectation.

When she awoke the next morning she raised her head to examine his smoothly tanned skin. Delighted at the sight of him she touched his cheek.

He opened his eyes and reached out to pull her close. "Come here, let me look at you in the light. ... Tanya, my Tanya! I'm so glad it's you in bed with me." As his arms went around her, her soul rejoiced.

And Tanya, who had never known happiness, felt confident that at long last some real joy had come into her life.

65

"A NNA, HAVEN'T YOU NOTICED THAT TANYA'S CHANGED? She looks different, somehow," Alisha commented.

"Yeah, I think I know what you mean."

"I don't know if you could tell but even her voice doesn't sound the same. You know, sometimes she even quotes the Bible to me. I can't stand it! What about you?"

Anna nodded emphatically. "Me neither. I wonder why she does that?" Tanya quoting the Bible? This was a new Tanya. No one in the family had ever quoted Scripture. Now occasionally, in the middle of a conversation, she threw in a "Praise the Lord."

Both sisters, unsure of how to handle it, generally frowned, looked puzzled, and nearly always admonished her, wishing to bring her back to her senses and the real world, believing it was for her own good. At other times they ignored her religious outbursts, hoping that she would stop.

66

TANYA, DEEP IN THOUGHT, BROUGHT UP A SUBJECT that she wasn't sure how to approach. "Walter, we've been married a month now. I think it's time you met my stepfather. In fact, we'll go see him next week. ... November 11th, it's a holiday and happens to be my birthday. We'll go then."

Walter, sitting across from her at the kitchen table, nodded reluctantly. "If I gotta, I gotta, but I'm not crazy about it."

"Oh, he's not so bad; besides, I want to show you off," she said with pride. "Uh-h-h, should I phone now to tell him that we're coming?"

"Yeah, go ahead."

The temperature hovered near zero when they left. A light snow had fallen over the landscape. By the time they pulled into the driveway Tanya could tell by the set look of Walter's mouth that he was nervous. "Uh-h-h, it's already ten; I wonder if he's still up?" she mused.

"He better be."

Her stepfather opened the door to their ring. Surprised at the sight of Walter, Bill Dansky stepped back. "Tanya, who you got here?"

Tanya smiled broadly. "Dad, I told you on the phone that I was bringing my husband to meet you. Dad, this is Walter Kushinsky, my husband. I'm married to him."

He managed a watery smile, as he shook his hand. "So you Tanya's new husband?"

"Yes, sir. How are you?"

Bill Dansky appraised him critically. "Uh-h-h, pretty good. Tanya, you got yourself a good-looking guy."

She smiled. "Thanks, Dad. I think so, too." The tension broken, she felt relieved and went to her room to unpack their suitcase. Walter stayed behind with her stepfather. A short time later he walked into the bedroom.

"Uh-h-h, so what do you think of him?"

He shrugged. "I can't say for sure, because I just met him. I guess he's all right."

She laid his pajamas on the bed. "Tomorrow you'll get to know him better. He's okay, really." The next morning, She started cleaning the bungalow right after breakfast, thinking that he'd let things pile up. "Walter, did Dad tell you that he needed some work done on his car? Could you please check it out for him?" Walter was quite adept at fixing cars.

"Yeah, I'll take a look at it." He turned to Bill Dansky. "Can I have the keys?"

Bill reached into his pocket. "It could be the spark plugs."

"I'll let you know."

He frowned. "Tanya, your husband, does he have a good education?"

"As a matter of fact, he finished Grade eight. ... Why?"

"That's no education. Why you marry him if he not educated?"

"Dad, don't say that, I love Walter!"

"Love don't buy you food."

She began emptying some cupboards to be cleaned. "Dad, it's too late! Stop upsetting me with this kind of talk. Besides, he has a good job! We're not starving," she added, wondering what business it was of his.

The door opened and Walter came back. "Your car is as good as new. It was the spark plugs. I got some from the Esso station."

Bill nodded coldly. "Thanks."

She felt that Walter was due more than just a mean look from him. "Dad, isn't it nice that Walter fixed your car so quickly? And he saved you some money, didn't he?"

"Yeah, he sure did. Walter, you remember to lock the side door in the garage when you left?"

"No, sorry. I'll go back and lock it."

"No, I go. I always keep that door locked. You can't tell when someone could break in."

Tanya, who could see that her stepfather was doing his best to put Walter down, wondered if, in some demented way, he was jealous of him.

He continued to harangue Walter the two days that they were there with his "know-it-all attitude." It soon became apparent that Walter endured him only because of her. By the time they were ready to leave, the situation had become quite intolerable between the two men.

She was relieved that the stay was over. It upset her to talk about it, but she thought the visit should be aired out. "Walter, I know he wasn't as nice as he could have been. I'm sorry, it's just his nature."

Walter looked grim. "Tanya, I've gotta tell you something. I'm sure glad he's not my Dad, because he doesn't act anything like a Dad. Furthermore, if he was my Dad I'd sure tell him where to go. Uh-h-h, you can bet I wouldn't put up with him. Tanya, you take a lotta crap from him."

"Yes, I know what you mean." Even while agreeing with him, she was already planning to, somehow, make peace between them.

In February, they went back to Grand Plains to celebrate his birthday. Tanya brought along a cake for the occasion. And Walter generously took him out to dinner to a Chinese restaurant. Bill Dansky appeared to be more tolerant and jovial than usual.

The next morning she began her usual routine of cooking and cleaning. Midway to lunch, she motioned Walter aside. "I was thinking that maybe you should go to the Safeway and get a few groceries. It might be a good idea if I cooked something that he could eat when we're gone. You know, something like a roast, or chili, or some stew. I could put it into jars or into the freezer and he could eat it later. What do you think?"

"Huh! Sounds like a heck of a lot of work to me."

She stood her ground. "I know, but I think I'll do it anyway."

She turned to her stepfather as soon as Walter went for the groceries, explaining what she had in mind.

"Tanya, you shouldn't bother that much with me."

"Dad, it's no bother. I don't mind."

He shrugged his shoulders and left the room.

As soon as Walter returned, Tanya called up from the basement where she was doing the laundry. "Walter, could you come down here a minute please?"

He thumped the groceries down on the counter and came halfway down the stairwell. "Yeah?"

"Walter, have you seen Dad's garage? It's a total mess. I was wondering, could you please clean it for him? ... And Walter ... uh-h-h, don't go yet. ... I, ah-h-h-h, you know his bedroom door? It looks really awful. Dad just told me that it's never been varnished. ... He said it was the workmen, they forgot to do it. D'you think we'll have time to do it this trip?"

He shook his head. "You know Tanya, I don't like coming here just to work. I work hard at my job, and a holiday should be a holiday. Now why can't we just come to relax and do nothing, sometime?"

"Yes, well, maybe next time. Besides, you know as well as I do that he can't possibly do all these things by himself. ... I think there's brushes and varnish in here ... somewhere. Why don't you check? If not, just slip over to the hardware and buy some. You know your way to town."

"And at my expense, I suppose?"

She turned a deaf ear to him. It was as if they had a month to spend instead of a couple of days. She scrubbed, cleaned and cooked her way through the house, returning home exhausted.

At Easter Bill Dansky invited all three families to spend the holiday with him. Alisha and Anna accepted readily.

They arrived on Good Friday. The children, having been confined for several hours during the trip, went screaming and chasing each other through the house.

Dan leaped into the recliner, setting the vibrator into motion. It started a thudding noise, alerting his grandfather, who came marching in. He glowered at Dan. "Stop that! You gonna break it. Get off! I said get off ... right now."

Alisha went in to see what the shouting was about. "Okay Dan, that's enough, go play somewhere else."

Dan's smile faded; he slid down and walked quietly away. Though only six, he was very perceptive for his age. To Alisha, one thing stood out very clear: her stepfather was as sharp with the little ones as he'd been with them.

Alisha and Anna began planning a Sunday dinner while Allen and Bill played records in the living room. Allen was trying to coax him into playing his violin.

Bill held back. "I don't think I'm that good." But he squeaked out some of the tunes that Allen suggested.

The next morning everybody except Tanya and Walter went to the Safeway for the turkey.

Bill Dansky began filling a cart with groceries. "Let's see, we need a turkey, ham, and uh-h-h, let's try this coffee, some cream. I'm outa cream. Here's some pickled pigs feet. Oh, I tell you, there's nothing as good as them. Uh-h-h ... cranberries, butter, bacon, eggs, bread, salad stuff. Seems to me, I don't have no more potatoes." He threw in a bag of potatoes. He piled the cart to overflowing and started towards the checkout.

Alisha turned to Anna. "I don't believe this. I've never seen him buy so much. Mind you, when he comes to our house Allen doesn't spare any expense on his account either."

Anna shrugged. "Maybe it's his way of reciprocating."

They reached the till and fell into line. Bill suddenly turned and muttered to no one in particular, "Where's the Mars Bars? You know, I forgot to get Mars Bars. It's such a good chocolate."

Alisha looked at him in alarm as he turned and sped past her.

"But, it's our turn at the till ... where are you going?"

The cashier began ringing in the groceries as Allen unloaded the cart. Alisha, craning her neck, looked to see where he'd gone. "These groceries are his, where is he?" she muttered. The clerk quickly bagged the groceries and handed the bill to Allen. "That'll be $65.86."

Alisha gasped as Allen pulled out his wallet. She put out a restraining hand. "Wait, he'll be back to pay for this, I'm sure."

"Geez," he whispered angrily, "what a naive thing you are! Can't you see he has no intention of paying for anything? That's why he left!"

"But he only went to get some chocolate. He's coming back, I know it."

"Don't count on it. I know damn well why he went!"

"Oh look, there he is by the candies."

They saw him linger, trying to decide what kind to buy, while killing time.

"Your total is $65.86, sir," the clerk repeated.

Allen sighed and handed her the money. He was scooping up his change when Bill returned.

"Uh-h-h, I just had to find this chocolate. It's the best, I tell you." He put down two bars on the counter and a dollar to pay for them as Allen began wheeling the groceries outside to the car.

He made no offer to reimburse Allen.

As soon as they walked into the house, Alisha whispered the incident to Tanya. "It really shocked me. I can't tell you how angry I feel right now."

Tanya nodded. It was no secret that her stepfather was well- off and gratified himself with the best of everything. He owned several brand name wrist watches. His closet bulged with fine clothes, his shoes were made of the finest leather ... and when he traveled, it was first class. He never gave a thought to the cost.

The next day the three sisters cooked the turkey dinner with all the trimmings; but nobody had the nerve to bring up the fact that he owed Allen money for the groceries.

67

IN NOVEMBER TANYA WENT CHRISTMAS SHOPPING to beat the pre-Christmas rush, telling Walter that since the crowds were small and the weather still holding, it made good sense. Her stepfather's name was first on the list.

"Walter, let's get him a sweater. The last time we were home, I noticed that his looked quite worn. ... What about this one?"

Walter fingered the fine wool. "Mm-m-m, nice material." He peered at the price tag. "Tanya, $80.00?" Tanya had no sense of restraint when it came to her stepfather.

"Yes, Walter, this one's cashmere, you know."

"Yeah, but does it have to be so expensive?"

She hesitated, as guilt engulfed her.

Walter relented. "Oh, go ahead and buy it, I was only kidding."

She smiled. "I'm sure he'll love it. I've got your Mom down next."

She mailed the sweater ten days before Christmas and called him long distance on Christmas morning. "Merry Christmas, Dad! Did you open your gift?"

"Yes, yes, I did, thanks. The sweater, it fits real good. Exactly my size."

"Dad, I'm glad it fits you. Here's Walter, he wants to say something. Oh, and thanks for the maraschino cherries. I've got them half eaten." She hadn't eaten them, fearing that her face would break out. They were a standard gift that he sent to each family at Christmas.

Now Tanya held the phone out to Walter. She noticed that he was shaking his head and waving her away. "No, no, I don't want to talk to him."

Tanya, deaf to his pleas, thrust the receiver into his hand. "Walter, he only wants to wish you a Merry Christmas!"

He gave her an exasperated look. "Uh-h-h, Dad? ... uh-h-h, glad you liked it. ... Tanya and I, we both wish you the same." He put down the phone and turned to her angrily. "Tanya, don't ever do that to me again. I never know what to say to him."

"Oh, Walter, what's wrong with just "Merry Christmas"?"

"It's not that! It's, it's him. I can't stand him!"

She sighed, comparing them to oil and water.

Tanya gave Father's Day a lot of thought before telling Walter what she had in mind for a gift. "You'll never guess what it is, Walter!"

He looked at her suspiciously. "A new car?"

"No, silly! A transistor radio! He can play it before he goes to bed or first thing in the morning. The Bay has a sale on now. Brand name, too. ... I don't want it breaking down or anything."

Tanya gave only the best to her stepfather. She was more than a daughter to him, she was a caring daughter.

However as time passed "Dad" became more demanding. Spoiled by her attention, he frustrated Walter to new heights.

68

IN JUNE WALTER'S THREE WEEK VACATION CAME UP, and they began planning a trip to the mountains. Tanya brought up the subject one evening, wondering and dreading to tell him that she'd made a slight change to their plans. "Walter, I hope you don't mind, but I wrote and told Dad that we'll be spending the first week of our holidays with him. However, if you do mind, I want you to know that I'm prepared to say that we're not coming. Is that okay with you?"

His smile faded as exasperation set in. "Damn it, Tanya! ... Well, uh-h-h-h, I guess it's all right. But just one week. I can only take him in small doses. Then I don't care what you say, because we're off to Banff."

She nodded, grateful that he didn't question her undue concern for someone who, in truth, resented the very sight of her and Walter both. How could she explain to him that she was driven by a powerful force and some deep-rooted need within her to help him?

Having experienced loneliness, she knew he must be lonely, and to this very day there was still a part of her that cried out to be accepted by him. If only she could make him see that no one really cared whether he lived or died except her. At the same time she was grateful that Walter was being very tolerant of her eccentricities. Had he refused to go to Grand Plains, she really couldn't have blamed him.

As it turned out, when they showed up at her stepfather's house he was very receptive to both of them.

Tanya began spring cleaning early the next morning while Walter started painting his bedroom. At noon Walter, with paint roller in hand, walked into the kitchen to find her scrubbing the floor.

She looked up. "How's the painting coming? You know the entire house has had only one coat of paint from the time he bought it. I think

Dad should have complained to the contractor about it."

"Yeah. I've just finished doing the bedroom. Looks okay now." He went to the sink and began washing out the brushes.

Bill Dansky came into the room smiling. "Walter the paint job looks real good." He brought out his wallet and took out a twenty. "Here, here's something for your trouble."

Walter flushed. "No ... no thanks. You keep it."

"Walter, don't be shy, take it!"

Walter angrily sidestepped around him and went outside.

Tanya's heart sank. All she needed was an all-out war between the two of them. "Dad, Walter doesn't like being treated like a child. Don't do that."

"I don't like to owe nobody nothing."

"Well, just the same, I'd put away the wallet before he gets back." She finished the floor and picked up her pail. "I'm done here. I think while there's time I'll go clean out the back bedroom."

He threw her a disdainful look and went to sit in his recliner.

Tanya went to the closet and began taking out his clothes. It was packed tight with suits.

Suddenly his voice startled her from the doorway. "You leave that closet alone. There's nothing in here for you to clean."

She looked up in alarm. "Listen, Dad, I want to send some of these things to the cleaners. They smell really strong of body odor, you know."

"I don't care. I said to leave it alone. If it smells, it smells, leave it!" He pointed to the door. "Get out!"

Her heart sank. Though she wanted desperately to finish, she began putting everything back. No telling what he'd do if she persisted. An acrid odor of perspiration came from the closet. Some things she'd planned to give away to the Goodwill. However in his present mood it would be disastrous to even suggest it. She let it go. After a hasty good-bye, she and Walter packed up and left for Banff.

Later, reflecting on the visit, she felt her stepfather's hardness hadn't changed. But no matter how she tried to win him over, it wrung her heart to know that his meanness continued to abide despite her dauntless efforts to make him see that she only wanted the best for him.

69

"TANYA, DID YOU KNOW THAT DAD'S SELLING THE APARTMENTS? He's put them on the market," Alisha told her.

"No, I didn't. ... In fact, that surprises me, because I thought he said it gave him something to do. ... Hm-m-m, though once he did tell me that he was getting too old to shovel the snow and cut the grass, because his knees were bothering him."

"Well I shouldn't wonder, he's nearly seventy. But you couldn't tell by looking at him."

"Maybe Walter and I will drive down and check on him."

"How often do you go there?"

"Oh, uh-h-h, about once a month. Somebody has to look out for him. ... Besides, you and Anna don't go."

"It's different if you have children. With school and everything, I can't just leave any time I want to."

"I suppose not."

Sometime later Tanya received a letter from her stepfather confirming that he'd sold the apartments. She convinced Walter that they should visit him.

She was appalled by the change in his appearance and stood back to exclaim, "Dad, you're getting fat!"

"Am I? Maybe a little." He looked down at his paunch.

"No, I mean a lot. I knew this would happen." She walked to the the refrigerator and opened it.

"I eat good," he told her.

She nodded. "Yeah, I bet you do. What's this pie doing in here? And lemon tarts. ... Why are you eating sweets? ... I think I'll go downstairs and check the freezer."

She was back in a few minutes shaking her head. "Dad, how long has that food been in there? The freezer, it's full of stuff that's freezer burned. It's spoiled. I'll have to throw it out!" She looked at him closely. "You know, you're looking kind of pale. Do you get any exercise? I hope you don't sit around eating all day!"

"Well, I go to the Post Office ... to the bank. I walk alla time. I don't use my car much."

"I'm glad to hear it. How do you feel?"

Walter, who had been listening in the kitchen, now came into the room frowning. "That's enough, Tanya. Your Dad has a right to eat anything he likes."

Tanya gave him a piercing look, while her stepfather went on.

"Well, about a week ago I tell you what happened. I been sitting here in my chair and listening to the stereo. I can't remember much, but you know ... when I woke up, I was on the floor! I think I fainted."

"You think you fainted? ... Walter did you hear that? ... Dad thinks he fainted."

"Did you see a doctor?" Walter asked.

"No, I didn't bother."

"You should. Could be something serious!"

"Maybe you right. Maybe I should ... I don't know."

Tanya stood up ... "That does it! While we're here, we'll see a doctor and get you checked out."

The next afternoon, Dr. Douglas, after examining Bill Dansky, gave his prognosis. "Mrs. Kushinsky, it looks like Bill has had a blackout ... perhaps even more than one." He turned to look at him. "A-h-h-h, Bill it's possible that you may have had others that you don't remember. The electrocardiogram shows some slight muscle damage to your heart. I'd say that you've also had a mild heart attack. ... Though not too serious and nothing to worry about. ... I'll give you a prescription for angina, just in case. Ah-h-h, your cholesterol, it's unusually high. I'll have to put you on a diet."

Tanya remembered the pastries. "I'm not surprised."

"Come and see me in about a month. Oh, by the way, have the dentist look at your teeth; you could use some dental work." He took out a pad and wrote out a prescription.

Tanya got to her feet. "I'll see what I can do about the dentist ... and his diet."

They returned to the house in silence. She wondered if he was using the pastries as a consolation for his loneliness, or maybe frustration? "Well, Dad, you heard what the doctor said about your diet."

"What did he say?" he asked, lowering himself into the recliner's cushions and stretching out his legs.

"What he said means, you'll have to cut out the sausage, egg yolks, cream, butter, and ... no pies, or cakes, or anything fried. Because if you keep eating the way you are now, you may get a stroke or have another heart attack. I'll make a list of the foods you can eat and of the foods you can't eat."

He grinned at her from the comfort of the chair.

"It's no joke. This is serious. Did you hear what I said?"

"Yes, I hear you."

"And one more thing. I'm making your appointment with a dentist today. No point in waiting. Let's see your teeth."

There were empty spaces where he'd lost teeth. Discoloured and half rotten molars made her grimace. "The doctor was right. No wonder he mentioned it."

He closed his mouth. "My teeth? My teeth are okay."

"Well, maybe they are to you, but we'll see what the dentist says about it. You know, your teeth can affect your general health. They can actually poison your system and make you sick if you don't look after them. I don't know how I'm going to do it, but I'll try and get you in before we leave."

She made the call to the dentist, explaining to the receptionist that it was an absolute emergency. Luckily, there had been a cancellation. He was booked for eight A.M., the following day.

The next morning Tanya rushed both men through breakfast and herded them out the door by seven-thirty. She knew that if left to himself her stepfather wouldn't have his teeth fixed. She was nervous about letting him go with Walter. Nevertheless she decided to stay home and let the two of them go alone.

70

WALTER GLANCED AT THE OLD MAN SITTING BESIDE HIM, proud and arrogant as a peacock. He pulled into the shopping centre and shut off the motor. "You live close to everything. It took us five minutes to get here."

"Yeah, makes it handy." The old man climbed out and they went into the Grand Plains mall. Dr. Beck's office was the last in a long row of offices. Walter checked the dentist's name on the door and reached for the knob. "This must be the place."

The old man put his hand on top of Walter's. "Wait!"

"Yes?"

Bill Dansky backed away from the door. "Now you wait just a gol darn minute here. Not so fast. I'm not going in there. There's nothing wrong with my teeth. My teeth don't give me no trouble! That doctor is nuts." The look on his face defied Walter to contradict him.

Walter let go of the handle. Damn him! "But what about your appointment? What are you going to do about that? Since we're already here, don't you think you should ... if you ask me, you oughta get em fixed. It's not gonna hurt. The dentist just puts a little freezing on it and you don't feel a thing. You ..." his voice trailed off. The old man was already walking away. "Okay, have it your way. I don't know why I'm even wasting my time. Hell, I got better things to do." Angry now, Walter strode after him to the parked car.

71

TANYA LOOKED UP, SURPRISED to see them coming back so soon. "Walter, what happened? I didn't even have time to do the dishes."

Walter looked grim. "I drove him there but he wouldn't go in. What do you want from me? He's no kid!"

"But why not?"

"Ask him!" Walter opened the fridge and took out a beer.

Her stepfather smiled at her sheepishly on his way to the recliner.

Exasperated, Tanya looked from one to the other, feeling that she should have gone with them. Suddenly anger and the determination to get to the bottom of the matter seized her. She strode into the living room to confront her stepfather. "Well, why didn't you go? ... Tell me? ... Why wouldn't you even go in? Your teeth are rotten. And after all the trouble I went to getting you that appointment! ... I've just about had it with you!"

She suppressed her rage as he pressed a lever and set the vibrator into motion.

"Don't treat me like a baby. I already told you, my teeth are okay! They don't bother me, so why you worry about it?"

Tanya sagged. "Have it your way. ... I'll go cancel. Now because of you, I'll end up looking like a fool." She picked up the phone to dial the dentist's office. ... "I'm sorry, he just didn't feel up to it. ... We couldn't get him to go. Sorry. Maybe next time. ... Thank you."

They went back to the city after lunch. Tanya sat staring out of the car window, her head turned away from Walter. For the past ten miles they hadn't spoken a word to each other.

Overhead, the sky was painted a bright, clear blue, sharply bringing into focus the winding road and the snow covered spruces on each side.

Her stepfather's parting words still rang in her ears. "Don't worry about me. Mind your own business. I don't need nobody to take care of me. ... And don't bother with the house. For me, it's clean enough."

He made her feel that her help was no more than a hindrance. She could take the ridicule ... but what about Walter? Would he understand?

They went around a curve and Walter broke the silence. "I'd call this a working weekend, wouldn't you, Tanya? ... And your Dad, he was really mean to us on this trip."

In vain she fought back the tears.

"Tanya! ... Tanya! ... Are you crying? Tanya ... look at me!"

She turned her head and began to sob.

"Tanya, it's okay! He's not worth crying over. It's ... it's, all right. Honest honey, it really is! Tanya, listen to me. He's not worth ... not so much as one single tear drop. Do you hear me? Please, stop! ... He makes me so mad I could shake him!"

"You know Walter, it's because I really care about what happens to him. I really do care!"

"Yeah, I know. Damn thing is you'll never convince him of it. I guarantee it. He's totally blind that way."

72

WITH HIS MEDICATION ADJUSTED and the apartments sold, Bill Dansky, still in reasonably good health, took to travelling. For the next nine years he enjoyed trips abroad to Europe, Russia, Mexico, and Eastern Canada. Occasionally Tanya received a post card telling her about the wonderful time he was having. He's fine, she thought. I don't have to worry, he's all right. Occasionally, she and Walter still went home to keep up with the housework and the maintenance, though now she wasn't as intense about it.

He turned 79 on February 18th, 1984. Tanya, in honour of the occasion, sent him an expensive dressing gown. From Anna, he received a card marked "special delivery". And Alisha sent him a box of chocolates.

Tanya expected at least a phone call to thank her. But after a few days had passed and she heard nothing she decided to call him instead.

She stood wondering whether she should call him. Walter sat just a few feet away watching television in their new home. Several years earlier they'd built a spacious, attractive, three bedroom bungalow. The ceiling was lofted, cathedral style. There was a fireplace and a large kitchen. It was cosy and easy to maintain. It more than fulfilled Tanya's dream of a house.

She glanced at Walter, feeling somewhat inhibited. She'd spoken with her Dad only a few days earlier. Yet here she was bothered with an urgency to talk to him again. ... Would Walter object to yet another long distance call so soon? ... "Uh-h-h, I'd like to phone Dad and ask him if he received the dressing gown."

"I thought you phoned him yesterday."

"I did, but I didn't ask him if he got it. You know, just now I had the feeling that I should call him again. ... I can't explain why."

"Go ahead. You don't need my permission."

"Thanks." She dialed his number. ... "Dad? It's me, Tanya. Are you all right?"

"Yeah, fine. I think you should know something. I'm selling the house, and I'm moving into a lodge."

"You're what?"

"I'm selling it, the house. I'm getting too old to take care of it."

"But Dad! It's good to be active ... Why are you moving? Besides, most of the time Walter and I are down there looking after it for you anyway."

"Don't you know why?" he asked.

She caught a hint of cynicism in his voice. "No, why?"

"I'm going to die. That's why. They gonna bring me out in a coffin."

She felt a shock go through her, realizing that he was telling the truth. "But why should you think like that? Are you sick or something?"

"I'm old. Nobody wants a old man around. My circulation is poor ... sometime I get dizzy."

"Okay, enough of that kind of talk. Some of those lodges are run like a hotel. They take good care of you ... and I hear they serve wonderful meals. ... Uh-h-h, what about the house and all the furniture?"

"Auction sale. ... I'll sell the house and have a big auction sale, that's what."

"If you're serious about selling I'll call Alisha and Anna and tell them. Maybe, we'll all come home and help you to get things packed. I'll let you know tomorrow. ... Uh-h-h, could you call me tomorrow?"

"Why should I call you? I know all you guys are waiting for is my money. Well, you have it soon enough."

Tanya bristled. "Dad! We don't want your money. Tell me, have I ever asked you for money? You make me very upset." She sighed. "Good bye, Dad." Unwilling to be disrespectful she listened for his "good-bye" before hanging up.

"Walter, Dad just told me that he's moving into a senior's lodge. He says he's going there to die!"

Walter looked up at her. "What's he worried about? He's still in good health, isn't he? Lots of people live in senior's homes. I think he's overreacting, like he does about everything. Now don't you go worrying about it."

"I won't worry, but he's angry about something."

"Tanya, when you're 79 you might want to move into a senior's home as well. I'm not surprised. My opinion, I think it's for the best."

"But doesn't it seem strange to you that he's giving up so easily?"

"If that's his choice what can we do about it?"

"Yeah, I guess you're right."

"Did he get the housecoat?"

"Oh, Walter, I forgot to ask."

"Tanya!"

"Sorry." She fled from the room to draw a hot bath. By ten she'd curled her hair and was in bed. Walter came in after the news and turned out the light on the night stand. His lips brushed against her cheek. She nestled close to him, seeking comfort that he was not able to provide. In no time, he was asleep while she lay wide awake ... a prisoner of her thoughts.

The night wore on, bringing with it all manner of fiendish images, threatening and sinister. Replaying over and over was the thought that her stepfather was going into a nursing home to die, and there wasn't a thing she could do about it.

Perhaps he was depressed and needed medication to overcome

it? She turned on her side and closed her eyes. Her pulse picked up speed. She lay rigid and soon became covered with perspiration, while listening to the worrisome hammering of her heart pounding against her ribs.

At dawn she found herself as wakeful as when she first lay down.

She started when the alarm sounded at 5:45 A.M., threw back the covers, and tottered to her feet, feeling exhausted. A wave of nausea swept through her. Almost before she reached the toilet, the vomiting began with such violence that it put fear into her.

Behind her she heard Walter's anxious step. Tanya pulled herself up to a standing position. "Walter, uh-h-h, I don't think I'll go to work today. I just can't. I have such a migraine. Maybe if I stayed in bed? ... Oh, my head! What do you think?" She hated missing work. Even if she was sick, she often showed up. But today was different.

Walter's forehead creased into lines. "Yes, you should stay home. Do you want something to eat?"

"No thanks. The way I feel, I don't think I can eat anything. ... Oh Walter, I feel so dizzy and so nauseous."

"Get into bed and rest. I'll make my own breakfast. I'll try and call you from work." He helped her back into bed and tucked the covers around her. "Be home as soon as I can."

However, as he was leaving the house, he heard the sound of flushing water and Tanya's audible heaves.

Alisha called later in the day; Tanya explained about the strange "flu" she had.

"Be sure to drink something like tea or juice. You could get very dehydrated throwing up like that," Alisha warned.

"But I can't seem to stop, that's the problem. It almost feels as if I have the hiccups in my stomach."

"If you lie still you might be able to keep something down."

Alisha hung up when she had to run to throw up in the middle of their conversation.

By mid-afternoon, the spasmodic heaves still hadn't abated. Tanya lay as though paralyzed, too frightened to move, praying that the vomiting would stop. Suddenly the phone rang.

"Is this Mrs. Kushinsky?"

"Yes."

"This is Sister Julia from the Holy Rosary Church. Do you think you can help us with the bake sale this coming Saturday? We need volunteers."

Tanya paused, trying to place her. "I think you must have the wrong Mrs. Kushinsky. You may want my mother-in-law. She goes to that church."

"Oh, sorry, you're probably right. Would you have her number, please?"

Tanya gave the phone number to the nun. ... "U-h-h-h, just a minute Sister Julia, please don't hang up yet. I need to talk to someone. Maybe you can help me. I must tell you that at this very moment, I'm very sick. And though I've stayed in bed all morning, I'm not getting any better. It's because I've been vomiting all day and I have this very bad headache. I can't even keep water down. Sister Julia, what should I do?"

"My dear, you must go to emergency immediately. They'll give you a shot to calm your nausea. It sounds as if your stomach has become oversensitized by something. ... With all that throwing up, by now I'm sure you're in need of fluids. Can someone drive you to the hospital? You mustn't drive yourself, you could pass out."

"Yes, my husband. He'll take me as soon as he gets home. Sister Julia, thank you. I'll do just as you say, I'll go to emergency."

"My dear, I hope you're better very soon. I'll say a Hail Mary for you."

"Thank you, Sister. Thank you very much!"

She wasn't sure what had prompted her to tell the nun about the illness ... except that being a nun, Tanya felt she would know what to do. Furthermore, she thought that while she still had the presence of mind, she had to do something and the nun had helped her make the decision.

Tanya sat up very carefully. Instantly, her head started to turn. She fought to remain conscious. Then holding on to the wall with one hand, she began to dress with the other. She barely finished when she heard the rumble of the garage door opening. "Oh Lord, let it be Walter!" she cried aloud.

As if in answer to her prayer, the door opened and Walter walked in.

He stopped short at the sight of her white face and sunken eyes. ... "Tanya!"

"Walter, could you drive me to the hospital? I'm still throwing up. And I've still got that awful headache." Her voice was a mere whisper. ... "Walter, I have to go now!"

"Yes. You ready?"

"Yes. Here, help me walk. ... I feel dizzy."

With Walter's arm guiding her, she slowly walked to the car, thinking that he couldn't have timed it better.

There were no vacant seats in the emergency room, and she was forced to wait outside in the corridor while leaning against the wall for support. After an arduous ten minutes, a young Chinese doctor examined her.

"Mrs. Kushinsky, I'm Dr. Pon. You have severe nausea? Tell me how you feel."

Tanya began to shake and was forced to hold on to her stomach as she spoke. "I, I started throwing up early this morning ... and can't seem to stop. And, I, I have this awful migraine. It won't ... go ... away." Suddenly she gagged as a spasm seized her.

"Let's have a look at your tongue; open your mouth, please. Oh my God!" Dr. Pon straightened up and walked swiftly to the hospital phone. He gave some orders into the receiver then returned to where she stood. "You need fluids ... and quickly."

A minute passed before a nurse appeared wheeling in an intravenous. She helped Tanya undress. As she climbed into bed, she was thankful that she didn't have to stand any longer.

The nurse pulled down the covers and injected her with a shot. "There, that should make you feel better. Here's something for your headache. And the intravenous, it'll replenish your fluids."

The effect was instantaneous. She slipped away, unresisting, into the indulgent arms of sleep. Several hours later she awoke. Her watch read one-thirty A.M.. Blissfully, the spasms had stopped, the headache was gone.

She noticed Walter asleep in a chair by the window, his body hunched over and uncomfortable. Poor Walter, what would she have done without him?

He shifted slightly and opened his eyes.

She smiled at him. "Walter, I'm better. My headache's gone. And I don't feel like throwing up any more. Walter, isn't that wonderful?"

He yawned and rubbed his eyes. "Are you sure? Dr. Pon said you could go home as soon as you woke up ... provided you were feeling okay. He said you were low on potassium. You know what else he told me?"

"What?"

"He said that you could have gone into shock and died on me if I hadn't brought you in when I did. They did some other tests, but they were normal."

"I still feel weak. I wonder if I can get up." She raised herself slowly, then lowered her feet to the floor. "My stomach muscles feel very sore. I think I'm okay. I feel like I've lost some weight. Walter, look, I'm standing. Walter, I'm all right! Oh, Walter, I'm so happy, ... I'm all right!" she exclaimed, smiling.

Once home and in her bedroom Tanya undressed and slipped under the covers, her body craving more rest. She yawned. "Night Walter. Love you, Walter. ... Just love you ... thanks."

"Love you too and thanks for nothing."

There was no sign of him when she awoke. She stretched, feeling deliciously rested. Oh Lord, how wonderful to wake up well! The clock read two-thirty P.M.. Tanya gave it a second look. She'd slept for a full twelve hours. My job, she thought. What did Walter tell them?

Slowly the events leading to her illness came unbidden. Odd that the nun had called at just the right time, and Walter had come home at the exact moment that she'd finished dressing. And when I needed You most, Lord, You were there, she thought. Lord, You're wonderful, how very wonderful You are! Thank You!

And Walter, was she being fair to Walter with her continuous obsession to indulge a stepfather who fought her on every issue? It was something that she could hardly understand herself. Last night's experience had been terrifying. She slumped back against the pillows, having decided to sort it out later. The day was half gone; she was still tired. Why not stay in bed and sleep?

73

D R. DOUGLAS PRESSED THE STETHOSCOPE to Bill Dansky's chest. "I believe it's stress-related due to the move. It's not much to worry about. A minor stroke. You can see it hasn't paralysed him or affected him in any way. How do you feel?" he asked Bill.

Bill buttoned up his shirt." I feel all right. Maybe a little dizzy if I move too fast."

He'd told them that he hadn't been conscious of any pain. Only of blackness sweeping over him before going under. When he came to, he'd called for matron in a panic. ... She, in turn, had called the doctor. It was only by sheer coincidence that Tanya and Walter had shown up at the lodge on that very same day.

The doctor snapped his bag shut and took out his pad. "The blackout was a prelude to the stroke. Bill, take these pills, and you'll be as good as new in about a month."

"Dr. Douglas, next month he's going to Mexico. Will he be well enough to travel by then?" Tanya asked.

"Barring unforeseen circumstances, I don't see why not!"

A month later, while on his way to Mexico, Bill stopped to see Alisha and Allen for a visit.

Though Tanya would have liked it if he'd stayed with her, he'd complained that her house was too cold for him. "The last time I stayed there I caught cold in my kidney."

Poor Tanya! He never knew how he hurt her with his outright rejection of her hospitality.

He eliminated Anna's place as well. "Her kids make too much noise," he'd said about Anna.

Anna accepted this, and she never pressed him to stay after that. She still had her two teen-aged sons living with her. Laura was married and had two children, whom she often brought over for Anna to babysit.

The grandchildren, a boy and a girl, were always at Anna's, squealing, scrapping, and carrying on as children were wont to do.

Alisha always informed both sisters whenever their stepfather was in town. They congregated at her house to talk and laugh with him, putting the past behind, making no reference to its ugliness.

Bill Dansky had no smile for Tanya and a hardness came over his eyes whenever he looked at her. Yet, of the three girls, she was the most sincere, seeking to know with every glance cast in his direction ... is he happy? ... is he well?

To Alisha, who couldn't understand her overt concern with a stepfather who had remained staunchly cruel to her over the years, she remained an enigma. And she often questioned her steadfast loyalty to him. Recently Alisha had been spiritually "born again" and now felt that she and Tanya could at least communicate on an equal plane. No longer did she think it odd whenever Tanya exclaimed, "Praise the Lord!" She understood.

74

THE CALENDAR INSIDE THE CUPBOARD DOOR read December 7, 1987. Outside it was quite mild and there was no snow on the ground. Tanya poured herself a cup of coffee and went to join Walter in the living room for the Monday night movie.

She was thinking of retirement. In November she'd turned 53 and Alisha and Anna were pressuring her to retire, as well as Walter. She feared it and yet desired it. At work she was still subject to stresses which undermined both her mental and physical health. Migraines plagued her nearly every day. Yet she was afraid that if she became housebound it might be boring. She'd miss her friends from the office. She'd gotten close to some of them. Without the daily contact, the ties were sure to be severed. On the other hand, there'd be more time to spend with Walter ... her stepfather. Maybe a trip somewhere with the three of them. At 82, he wasn't exactly in his prime anymore.

She nestled into a pale beige rocker, and turned to the television. Five minutes later she was fighting sleep and could no longer keep her eyes open. She forced herself to rise and shuffled off towards the bedroom. "Night, Walter."

His eyebrows arched in surprise. "Where are you going? It's not even nine o'clock!"

"I have to sleep. I'm exhausted. ... Good night!" Lately she couldn't seem to get enough rest.

The next morning they were both up at five-thirty. Tanya was usually at work by six-forty A.M., because Walter started his job at seven and insisted on driving her.

This morning she sipped the last of her coffee and sat down in a comfortable, padded office chair. The computer, as well as the chair, were a drastic change from the old mechanical typewriter and hard-edged oak chairs that she'd used when she'd first started working. Some years later it was discovered by a team of efficiency experts that comfort was indeed paramount among employees, since it increased their production.

She slipped the plastic cover off the computer and booted the machine into action. She'd barely started when Alisha phoned her.

"Tanya, now don't get upset."

She stiffened.

"Uh-h-h, I just had a call from a Mrs. Alldrit. You know her, she's the matron from Horizon Lodge where Dad's staying. Uh-h-h, she said that Dad was taken to the Grand Plains hospital by ambulance this morning."

Tanya felt a sickening crunch go through her. "What's wrong with him?"

"Well, she said that when he came down for breakfast, he was an orange colour, and he complained about feeling weak. She said she took one look at him and told him not to make a move until she'd called an ambulance. ... According to her, Dad wanted all of us to know about it."

Having recovered from the initial shock, Tanya now asked, "Did Mrs. Alldrit say if he'd been sick lately?"

"Actually, she said that he was feeling fine until today."

"Have you called Neil or Anna?" Neil was her stepfathers younger brother. A couple of years ago, they'd travelled together to Hawaii. "He might want to know."

"No, but I will. Look, I know you're busy. Why don't you call me after supper? And don't worry about Dad."

Tanya agreed and hung up. She felt the day was shattered. She had a sudden urge to call the hospital and find out whether he was all right. No doubt this early there would be tests. Later tonight, she'd phone. Matron had mentioned his orange color. Was it his liver, maybe jaundice? She sighed and resumed typing.

That evening she called the hospital and was surprised when Bill himself picked up the phone. His voice sounded weak. "So far those doctors they find nothing."

She decided at that very moment that she wanted to be with him. It was a relief when Walter agreed to go to Grand Plains without an argument. Thinking that Alisha might want to come, she called her as well.

"Uh-h-h ... no, I can't. Joseph is sick and Gloria needs help. ... I can't just take off. ... How long d'you think you'll be staying?"

"As long as it takes!" she snapped. Joseph was Alisha's four year old grandson. It irked her that both Alisha and Anna never had time for anyone other than their own immediate families.

"Could you call me as soon as you find out what's wrong with him?" Alisha asked.

She softened, knowing that Alisha's circumstances could not be helped and that Gloria did rely heavily on her. "Yes, I will. ... Uh-h-h, you know, last night I dreamed about Mother. I hate to say this but every time I dream of her, something awful happens."

"Really? ... What did you dream?"

"It was quite strange, actually. I remember sitting in a large room. It looked like a waiting room in a hospital, except that there weren't any people in it. I sat in a chair by myself. Suddenly mother appeared out of nowhere. She put her face very close to mine and smiled at me. But when I took a closer look at her she wasn't smiling. ... In fact, she looked as if she had a leer on her face. Then she turned and went outside and I followed her. There was a wagon with a team of horses hitched to it. Mother got into the driver's seat and took the reins. Funny thing about that wagon is that it had no sides to it. I got in with her and went to the back, and I sat down at the very back. Well, we started to go over something that looked like the High Level bridge. You know, the one with the trestle on top where the train rides? ... It was frightening, being way up there. Anyway, she whipped the horses until they started going at a gallop over that rickety trestle. Sitting up there, it felt dangerous."

"The wagon started to shake and I became really frightened. Once I looked down to see the river flowing directly beneath us. It looked black and ... and ... threatening. But she just kept going faster and faster. I sat there hanging on for dear life until we crossed it with the wagon almost ready to split apart. Once we crossed it she went so fast that the landscape became a blur. We went north. You know, I awoke with my heart pounding, it felt so real."

Alisha hesitated before answering. "Grand Plains is north. I wonder, seeing mother in the dream, would that represent death?"

Tanya flinched. Death had crossed her mind as well. "Yes, I know that Grand Plains is north. Uh-h-h, do you think that we should go there with speed? I wonder if that's what the speed in the dream meant? You know the blurred landscape?"

"Hm-m-m, it could be."

Tanya sighed. "We're leaving in the morning, Walter said. Quite early, too. I have to pack, now."

75

THE FOLLOWING SUNDAY, four days later, Tanya phoned Alisha to tell her that the doctor thought that Dad might have gall stones or cancer. "He's not sure which it is," she said speaking with a slight tremor.

"Oh Tanya, cancer!"

"Uh-h-h, actually, they're going to move him to Edmonton by air ambulance because they don't have the proper equipment to do the tests here. He'll be at the Royal Alex by nine o'clock tonight."

"And you and Walter, when are you coming home?"

"Tomorrow. Neil is here and so are Dad's two sisters, Martha and Sue."

"Can I speak to Walter?"

Surprised, Tanya handed Walter the phone, wondering what Alisha could possibly want to know from him that she couldn't tell her herself.

"Uh-h-h, Walter, how is Tanya taking all this? Is she okay?"

"No, she's not. Sorry, I can't say anymore." With Tanya beside him, he couldn't elaborate.

Alisha persisted. "Is she sleeping all right?"

"No. But this isn't a good time to talk, either. Ask me again when we get home."

"Yes, tomorrow." Alisha hung up.

76

FOR TANYA, THE WEEK SPENT IN GRAND PLAINS had been devastating, as each day she waited for the dreaded results of the tests. So far, the only good news from the doctor was the assurance that Bill did not have cancer.

Two days after they'd transferred him to Edmonton, neither Alisha nor Anna made any effort to see him. Tanya was surprised at their lack of concern. She reached Alisha by phone at Gloria's house the afternoon of the second day.

"Sorry, I'm babysitting," Alisha explained. "Uh-h-h, Dad, so how is he?"

Something within her snapped. "How do you think he is? You still haven't gone to see him or even phoned him ... and that goes for Anna, too."

"I can't just leave. Joseph is still sick. Very sick, in fact."

"Yes, I know about Joseph. ... Alisha, I did expect you to support me in this. Do you know what it's like to wait in a waiting room for all those awful tests? I'm at my wit's end. I can't be there day and night. I still have a job to go to. I need some help."

"I'm sorry, but Gloria needs me to help her with Joseph."

Now she all but shouted, "So when can you come?"

"I've got to stay until Gloria gets back from grocery shopping. He's only four, she can't leave him by himself. And the doctor told her that she can't take him out until his temperature goes down."

Tanya slammed the phone down. Was there no one that she could count on for help? Were they all deadened to a sick, old man's needs but her?

She fought back a stream of tears, and for the rest of the afternoon paced the hospital corridor while waiting for more test results. When it came time for her stepfather's x-rays, she pushed him in a wheelchair through drafty hallways then massaged his neck and back in the waiting room until his turn came. Alisha, who she thought would surely come after their talk, didn't show up.

As soon as the radiologist was through, she took Bill back to his room and watched a young, fresh-faced intern insert a feeding tube in through his nose into his stomach. It didn't take more than a minute before he was finished and gone. I'll leave him and go home now, she thought.

Suddenly, Dad's face began to turn red. The next minute, she was horrified to see him struggling for breath, his arms flailing in the air towards her.

"C ... c ... a-an't ... breathe! ... Help ... me!"

Tanya, panic stricken, watched helplessly as his face turned from red to purple. ... Something was not right! ... "What's wrong? Can't you tell me? It's the feeding tube? It must be the feeding tube!"

Her heart pounding, she ran towards the nurse's station. "Miss! ... Miss! Please, help me! My father, he's choking on his feeding tube! ... Come quick, please! ... Room 4ll!"

Unperturbed, the nurse answered with painstaking slowness. ... "Calm down, we'll get someone to look at it right away."

Tanya ran back to his side. She felt herself go limp. His breathing was coming in audible gasps. She'd have to do something to help him, or he'd die before her very eyes. Gently, she raised his head. "All right, Dad, do as I tell you. ... One, two, three ... now breathe in! ... One, two, three ... breathe out! Concentrate! ... Concentrate! Do as I say. You'll be all right. Breathe like I tell you to. The nurse said someone will come right away!"

Ten minutes later, Tanya, in an absolute frenzy, was still counting

and working with him and praying that a doctor would show up. Dad
had a heart condition. She couldn't keep this up much longer. "Dad,
please give me just a half a minute, I'll be right back! ... Keep breathing
... and don't stop!"

Once more she frantically confronted the same nurse. "Please!
Please, Miss! ... My father, his feeding tube, there's something wrong
with it! He'll die if someone doesn't help him! Quick! ... Please send a
doctor in to look at him!"

The nurse looked up, questioning her desperation. "Oh, yes, ...
I've sent out a call. The doctor will be there shortly, if you'll just be
patient."

She ran back to reassure her stepfather. ... "They're coming, Dad
they're coming! Hold on for just a little longer! ... Hold on!"

She began to tremble, realizing that his breathing had an anguished,
raspy gasp to it. Was he to die from a feeding tube? Tormented by this
fear, she lifted up his head and started counting with more intensity,
not altogether positive that it was doing him any good. But the effort
and concentration would keep him alive for at least a while longer.

Another agonizing five minutes went by before a doctor showed up
with a nurse. Beads of cold sweat drenched her stepfather's forehead.
Tanya felt that he was about to lose consciousness. "Thank God you're
here!" she cried out. "He's almost dead!"

The doctor turned to her, brusquely. "Could you wait outside,
please?" He pulled the curtain around the bed.

Tanya's tension lost its grip. She collapsed into a chair and burst into
a flood of tears. Through the curtain she could hear her stepfather's
agonizing moans as the pair worked on him. What if she hadn't been
there? He'd certainly have died.

Twenty minutes later the nurse drew back the curtain. Her stepfather
was propped up and breathing normally.

She dried her eyes and turned to the doctor. "Could you tell me what
was wrong?"

"The feeding tube was knotted in his throat. I'm afraid it caused
him a bit of pain. ... He'll be fine."

Tanya got up and walked to the side of the bed. Her stepfather looked
extremely worn out. The clock on the wall told her that she'd been there
for five hours. "Dad, I have to go home. I'm sure Walter's wondering

what's happened to me. And after what you've just gone through, you should rest."

He nodded assent, looking grateful.

The nurse at the front desk avoided Tanya's angry glare. It was six o'clock before she came home and told Walter the grim details of Dad's brush with death.

After they'd eaten she dialed Alisha's number again. Her nerves frayed, her energy level at its lowest, still she didn't think that Alisha should be ignoring him. Her stepfather had always liked her best and she should have the decency to at least spend a few minutes of her time to look in on him in spite of Joseph's illness.

However, after several rings, it was Allen who answered.

Tanya struck out without any preliminaries. "Alisha! Where is she? I want to know!"

"She's still at Gloria's, babysitting."

"Tell her tomorrow I want her to be at that hospital. She should be there; I thought I made it clear to her!"

There was a pause before Allen spoke in a cold, authoritative voice. "Well, she can't be there with you all the time. And the whole world doesn't revolve around your Dad. Some of us have other obligations. Now get off her back! Because whether she's there or not, it ain't gonna make any difference as to his recovery in the long run. ... Besides," his tone softened, "he's dying, you know that, and you can't stop it!"

The rebuke caught her off guard. Suddenly, she felt as if she'd been doused with cold water. "Oh Allen, I'm really sorry! I ... I didn't mean it that way. It's just that I need someone, uh-h-h, someone ... to help me. You understand, don't you? When she comes in, could you please have her call me?"

"All right, the minute she gets home, she will," he promised.

Alisha returned her call at nine P.M.. "Tanya? Did the x-rays show anything?"

"No. The doctor is doing more tests tomorrow." Her voice was dull with none of its previous anger. She sighed. "It's possible he may have passed a gall stone but they're not really sure. You know Alisha, I must tell you, Dad nearly died today. He was so scared." She told her about the feeding tube. "Uh-h-h, one of us should keep in touch with the doctor to see what's being done for him."

"He's lucky you were there. What about you, how are you feeling?"

She sensed the concern in Alisha's voice, but brushed it off. "I'm okay! I'm not sick."

"Now Tanya, be sensible, ... don't go getting so wrapped up that you do get sick."

"Yes, I know, but I want to be sure that everything is being done that can possibly be done for him. ... Alisha, I've got to go and lie down. I've had a long day. Good night."

"Okay, I'll go see him tomorrow. Tanya, you won't have to go. ... In fact, the three of us can take turns visiting him."

Tanya hung up thinking that she might as well save her breath, because regardless of what they agreed to, she'd see him whenever possible.

77

EARLY THE NEXT MORNING ALISHA FOUND her stepfather's bed crammed into a small room with two other patients. She hesitated, unsure of how to greet him, then came forward. "Dad, how are you?"

He turned and smiled at her. The jaundice had faded but his skin still retained a yellow tinge. There were dark smudges under his eyes, giving him a haggard look.

"Not so good," he said, weakly.

"Did the doctor say what was wrong?"

"No, they trying to find out. Right now, they just guessing. But I feel better than in Grand Plains. See the guy in the next bed?"

The patient in the next bed, a middle-aged man, let out a loud, painful sigh.

"What's wrong with him?" she asked.

"I don't know. But he make that noise all night. I can't sleep nothing. If you ask me, I think he's crazy. I tell you, I can't stand it here. I would rather be dead than be here."

His breakfast tray was untouched.

"Have you had breakfast?" she asked.

"No, I don't want nothing. It smells bad to me. I don't have no appetite. Nothing tastes good."

"But how do you expect to get better if you don't eat?"

"I don't care, I don't want it."

Alisha went home, promising to come again the following day.

The next morning when she walked in, she instantly noticed that the bed next to his was empty. "Where's your friend?" she asked. "Did they move him?"

Her stepfather threw her a disgusted look. "No, he died in the night!"

She recoiled at his lack of compassion. With death literally staring him in the face, how could he be so callous? The poor man who died was much younger than her stepfather. He must have suffered to have cried out as he did. Was Dad not afraid that the same fate might be awaiting him? Again she noticed that he hadn't touched his food. "Dad, don't you eat anything?"

"It doesn't taste good. There's no salt in it."

Alisha moved the tray closer. "Here, try some of this toast."

He turned his head toward the wall. "No, take it away."

78

As soon as Tanya found out that her stepfather ate almost nothing, she went to speak to the head nurse about it. "I think something should be done to improve his appetite. A bird couldn't stay alive on what he eats. He says the food is tasteless."

The nurse gave her a tolerant look. "Mrs. Kushinsky, Mr. Dansky has a menu and he can pick and choose whatever he likes."

"I see. ... Well, I don't think he really wants to do that. In fact, it would be better if you, or one of the other nurses, did the choosing for him. You see, my father believes that the doctors and nurses, have his best interests at heart, so he respects whatever they have to say. Now if

the doctor were to tell him to eat, he just might listen. It's worth a try."

The nurse nodded. "I'll speak to the doctor about it."

"Thank you. ... Now, about those tests you're putting him through ... are they really necessary? He can't get better if every day he has to starve until one or two o'clock, waiting to go through some test."

"I'm sorry, Mrs. Kushinsky, but we have to find out what's wrong with him, don't we?"

Tanya was unconvinced.

In order to coax her stepfather to eat more, Tanya and Walter began timing their visits to be with him at meal time. Usually they went to the hospital directly from work without eating anything themselves. The visit ended at nine P.M. when visiting hours were over. The rigid schedule exhausted Tanya, who found it impossible to unwind when she finally did come home.

One evening she walked in by herself to find his tray untouched as usual. Neil sat beside him. He looked up at her, smiling. Something within her snapped. "Dad, why didn't you eat anything? You're going to die if you keep this up. I can't be here to baby you every day! And don't complain to me about how weak you are! Eat all your meals! That's the only way you'll get your strength back. Don't give up so easy! If you give up, you won't live! And another thing, the next time I come in here, I want to see you moving around. Go for a walk! Nobody's tying you to the bed. Where's your will to live? If you need something, don't be afraid to ask someone for it. One of the nurses, they'll be glad to help you. Just open your mouth and speak out!"

Across from her, Neil's expression turned from smiling to disapproving.

Tanya sank into a chair. "Neil, I'm sorry you had to hear this. I didn't mean to carry on like I did. ... He won't eat, and it's frustrating." Her voice trailed off.

"Tanya, relax. You can't force him to eat. Don't take it so personally." He rose to his feet. "Gotta go. See you, Bill"

She didn't mean to be so rough on him. But the words had come rushing out before she could stop herself. Her hand touched a sore spot at the top of her head. The pain had returned. She felt fatigued, her energy depleted, alone in her struggle to encourage him to live. No one understood her or her reasons to do this but she knew that she would carry on to the end.

Last night, much to her dismay, she'd had another one of her dreams. This one had been so real that at this very moment she still carried a reminder of it. ... It had taken place on the block where they lived. In the dream, she was aware of a bright blue sky without a cloud in sight. She looked up to see what appeared to be a large black boxcar hurtling through the air. Suddenly it came crashing down to the ground and landed quite close to where she and Walter were standing. It shattered, exploding on impact and breaking up several houses around them. Even the sidewalk on which they stood was smashed. She remembered holding on to Walter's hand tightly, ... then falling with such force that she nearly dragged him down with her. Somehow he managed to stay on his feet. However the explosion caused a pain which seemed to explode in her head.

She awoke to find the pain was actually there.

Now she sat by her stepfather, trembling in fear, thinking that perhaps she'd suffered a mild stroke. ... The one positive thing was that whenever she rested, the pain left her ... only to return at the least bit of stress. Even now there was a constant, dull ache throbbing in her head.

She went home thinking that only God could help her. Tanya went directly to her bedside and knelt down, consoling herself that whenever she'd needed Him, Jesus had always been there for her.

More than ever, I need you now, Lord, she cried. ... "Oh my God, what am I to do? Oh, Lord, please help me!"

79

THAT EVENING NEIL PHONED ALISHA to complain about Tanya.

"Tell her to back off! She yelled so hard, she scared him half to death. We were laughing and talking and having a great time until she walked into the room. Then all hell broke loose. She starts screaming, she gets him all upset. She's not doing him any good. Especially when he needs cheering up, because that's what he really needs ... not someone yelling at him."

Alisha sighed, knowing that Tanya only meant it for his good. "I know what you mean. Neil, yes, I'll tell her."

"By the way, did you know that the hospital is going to discharge him for Christmas? ... Actually, he'll be spending three days with me."

"I didn't know that. But I'm glad to hear it. That sounds just fine! Maybe you can fatten him up. He looks awfully thin."

"Yes, really. ... Well, I'll try." Neil was divorced and lived alone and would have the time to cater to him.

80

ALISHA AND ALLEN WENT TO SEE BILL DANSKY on Boxing Day at Neil's house. He came to the door to let them in.

"How's he doing?" Alisha asked, after they'd shaken hands.

He looked sombre. "Uh-h-h, really, he eats so little I can't believe it. He was up most of Christmas Day ... played his fiddle for us. Some of my family were here." Neil shook his head, "He's awfully weak. I let him eat whatever he wanted."

"Would he be better off here than in the hospital?" Alisha asked.

"No. He needs twenty-four hour care. Actually, I can't give him that. I work. Last night he went to bed really early. Today he went to bed right after breakfast. He's been sleeping most of the morning. Come on, I'll take you to his room."

At first glance Bill Dansky seemed to be asleep, until Allen touched his arm. His eyes flicked open. He smiled at them. "Allen ... Alisha, you here?"

"How are you, Dad?"

"Well, maybe you can tell me. How do I look to you?" He closed his eyes while waiting to be examined. Snow white hair framed a face drained entirely of colour. There had been a dramatic weight loss, defining the bone structure more precisely.

"You look real good to me," Allen told him after a pause.

He looked surprised. "Do I? I don't feel too good. You know I'm weak like a kitten."

"You look fine," Allen insisted. "Do you have a shaver here?"

He pointed to the night stand. "Yes, in the drawer."

Allen combed his hair and began shaving him. "You want to look good for the nurses when you get back to the hospital, don't you?" he teased.

Bill broke into a laugh then quickly sobered. "Last night I dreamed that somebody was trying to get into my safe deposit box. So I said to myself, why you trying to get my money when I'm still alive? I'm not dead yet. It was a funny dream."

Was death so near that it was beginning to prey on his mind? Alisha wondered.

He shook his head. "No ... I tell you now, I'm not gonna get outa this. I'm going to die. I'm not getting better. I can feel it. I could have told you that from the first day I got sick."

Alisha thought it would be just as he said. It wasn't long before his strength gave out, and they left him to rest.

81

"BUT WALTER, WHAT IF WE DON'T COME BACK IN TIME? What if he dies when we're away?" Tanya looked forlornly at her husband, knowing that she could never forgive herself. The trip had been planned several months ago. All three couples were leaving for Hawaii on the fifteenth of January. Now she had misgivings, doubts, that she couldn't explain away.

Walter looked at her sharply. "Just pray that he doesn't. It won't be easy getting back. We're flying charter, you know."

"Walter, he's so sick, what'll I say to him?"

That evening Tanya forced herself to tell her stepfather about the vacation though everything in her being revolted against it. "Dad, would you mind very much if we went to Hawaii?" she began, knowing that it was for Walter's sake only that she was going.

He became still ... then slowly turned his head to look at the ceiling. Instantly she sensed that he didn't want her to go.

When he answered, his voice was barely audible. "Yes, go Tanya, don't worry about me."

She silently despaired, thinking that if only he was stronger, the guilt wouldn't lay as heavily. She came closer and took his hand. "Dad, are you going to be all right?"

He nodded. "I think so. I think I be all right."

"It's only for two weeks, you know."

Walter, hovering at Tanya's side, now spoke. "We've paid our deposit. We can't change it! ... Uh-h-h-h, we booked last October, so it makes it hard to cancel."

Bill Dansky nodded. "Yeah, I know how it is."

When they left, she kissed him good bye with the feeling that she was abandoning him when he needed her most.

Walter, seeing her downcast face, put a hand on her shoulder. "I know he's sick but we can't just hang around here waiting for him to die either. ... Tanya, I've worked hard for this vacation. And you need a break too. He's in good hands. ... We're going!"

"Walter, I know all that. But I still don't feel right about leaving him."

As with Tanya, Bill Dansky urged Alisha and Anna to go as well."

The two weeks slipped by without mishap. No urgent phone calls disrupted their holiday. When it was over they flew back, anxious to see how he'd fared.

82

ALISHA SAT IN ANNA'S KITCHEN TALKING TO LAURA. Laura was telling them about what had taken place while they were away. They listened intently; she had an expressive way of speaking.

"And you know, once when we went to see Dedee in the hospital he was running such a temperature that he began to hallucinate! It was shocking! At first I didn't know if he'd lost his mind or what, because nobody told us that he'd been operated on. Well he started talking about seeing bugs on the ceiling and saying words that didn't make sense. ... At this point I got upset, so I went to find a nurse. That's when they told us that he'd had an operation. Apparently, his doctor had found a cyst under his liver and he had to lance it."

Alisha spoke with annoyance. "I don't understand why they didn't operate on him before we left for Hawaii!"

Anna gave her a sharp look. "You know something, Dad could have died while we were away. ... I don't feel good about that. In fact, I wish that we'd stayed home."

Alisha nodded. "Yeah, all well and good, I wish it too. But you know very well that we could never have convinced Allen, Walter, or Anton, because they had their hearts set on the trip ... so really we didn't have a choice. Especially after paying for the trip in advance."

Anna looked up. "You heard, didn't you, that the hospital moved Dad?"

"No, where to?"

"It happened right after the nurses went on strike at the Royal Alex. Laura said that he was moved from there to the University by ambulance."

Alisha leaned forward. "Well thanks for telling me. The University is actually closer to our house. I think tomorrow I'll go see him. No point in going tonight, no doubt Tanya will be there."

83

THREE DAYS HAD ALREADY GONE by since they'd returned from Hawaii and Tanya still hadn't found a convenient time to visit her stepfather. Lurking in the back of her mind remained an ominous dread about his condition and what she'd find. After unpacking their suitcases she did the laundry and the housework, then stocked up on groceries for the week.

The following Monday, she sat down at her desk and opened her computer. Laura's account about the operation began to gnaw at her and her thoughts kept straying to her stepfather. She felt a small stab of anxiety mixed with guilt jab at the pit of her stomach.

Grimacing, she chastised herself for not making a move to see him sooner. But there hadn't been time.

At three-thirty five P.M., papers, letters, and unfinished work were quickly put out of sight. She wanted to be outside and waiting for Walter the minute he showed up. Hopefully he'd be early. She flung on a pink ski jacket and hurried downstairs to wait for him by the door.

Five minutes later his van pulled to a stop in a puddle of slush and snow. Tanya reached for the handle and got inside.

Walter threw her a sideways glance. "Hi. Have a good day?"

She hesitated before letting him in on what she was brooding about. ... "Actually, no; I worried about Dad all day. I'm glad we're going to see him. I mean, let's go now, Walter. I don't want to put it off another day."

"I'm sure he's okay. ... Tanya, I was wondering, can we go home and eat or, do we have to go see him this minute? I'm hungry."

It was the last thing she wanted to hear him say. "No, Walter, not tonight. We'll go to the hospital first and eat later ... if you don't mind!"

"But, can't we ..."

"No, Walter, please, I said later! Besides, it's been two weeks since we left. Aren't you at all concerned about how he's doing? ... It won't kill either one of us to wait."

He set his mouth into a firm line, turned the van southward, and headed for the hospital. Argument would be futile. The rest of the trip went by in silence.

As soon as she found out his room number, she ran towards the elevator doors with Walter striding behind her. They came to a stop. She walked swiftly to the geriatric wing. She paused long enough to see which bed he was in. Having caught sight of his silver hair, she turned to Walter, "That's him, by the window."

A few feet from the bed, she stopped short. Her mouth sagged at the sight of the medical paraphernalia surrounding him. There was an intravenous clamped to his wrist. A plastic bag with yellow fluid hung at the foot of the bed. A second plastic bag, half full, looked as if it might contain the bilious drainage from his operation.

The joy of seeing him was replaced with concern at the sight of his sunken eyes. It didn't seem possible that he could have changed that much in only two weeks! At the moment the darkening sky outside the window held his gaze. Tanya felt herself overcome with sadness. She forced herself to smile as she came closer. "Hi, Dad! How are you feeling?"

He turned to look at her, his eyes widening in disbelief. "You come back?"

"Of course we did. I said we'd be back in two weeks and here we are!"

His face crumpled as a tear quietly slid down his cheek. With a shuddering sigh, he broke into heart-wrenching sobs. "Oh Tanya, why did you leave me when I was so sick? Why did you go? Don't you care nothing about me? Doesn't nobody care about what happens to me?"

Tanya stood motionless, her feigned cheerfulness turning cold. She'd never seen him cry before! His sobbing tore at her heart. She reached out and touched his wasted hand. "Dad! ... Dad!.... We didn't leave you! We're here. We're back. Why do you say we left you?"

"Because all of yous ... you left me by myself ... to die ... that's what. I could have died and how would you know? And I was so sick. Oh, Tanya, do you know how I suffered? ... Do you know how bad it hurts? If I could die, it would be better." His voice sounded weak and thin as a child's.

Something inside Tanya withered. Her eyes began spilling tears. "Dad! ... Dad! Listen to me. I'm here, Dad. Don't cry! ... Please, don't cry. I'll never, never, leave you again! I promise, no matter what happens ... I won't leave you. Actually, I'm sorry we went. Forgive me, it was the wrong thing to do. You're right! I knew you were very sick, but still we went! We all did! We should have stayed home to be with you. I'm sorry!" She bent down and gathered his head in her arms. Holding him gently, she comforted him as a mother would a child, unheeding that her tears were falling on his face as she gave in to the pent up sorrow in her heart.

Walter looked away, moved by the old man's sobbing.

Suddenly she stopped, reminding herself that crying was a feeling that expended energy. "Dad, you mustn't cry. Here, let me get you a wash cloth. It's not good for you to cry," she consoled him, though still finding it difficult to stem her own grief.

Tanya wet a towel and came back to smooth it over his eyes and face. "It's okay ... it's all right, we're back now. Everything will be fine. You just relax and lie still. Remember, I pray everyday that God will heal you. You'll be all right, you'll see. I have great faith in God and you should too."

He calmed down, his china blue eyes following her movements. "Yes, I know, God has all the power."

"Well, you must pray to God too. If you have God in your heart everything will be fine. Does your incision hurt?" she asked.

"Everything hurts. I never had such a pain in alla my life."

"Then I'll speak to the nurse about giving you something to make it better. You shouldn't have to suffer like this."

Tanya reached down and opened her purse. Her face lit up. "Dad, I brought you these cookies all the way from Hawaii. How would you like some tea to go with them?"

He nodded.

"These cookies, they're "Mrs. Field's", and really delicious. I'll get the tea ... and I'll ask the nurse to give you something for pain."

"Maybe the tea will warm me up a little. You know, it's cold here. My feet are freezing alla time. The covers are way too light."

"Then you need another blanket." She thought a moment. "Tomorrow I'll bring you something warmer from home."

She came back a short time later carrying a pot of tea and a blanket. A nurse trailed behind her with his medication on a tray. After he'd swallowed the pills, Tanya leaned back in her chair, watching him eat the cookies and drink the tea.

"Dad, are you afraid of dying?" she asked. It was a subject that had to be faced with him as well as herself.

He looked at her evenly. "No! What's to be afraid of? The one thing I'd like is to have a heart attack. I go unconscious, and everything goes black." He raised his hands. "And it's all finished."

She sighed, remembering what Laura had said about the cyst that the doctor had lanced. As soon as she'd heard, she began praying that God would heal him. 'Then Lord You may take him, but first, heal him'.

His eyes began to grow heavy with sleep. Tanya rose to her feet, first tucking the covers around him. Then she laid her right hand on his forehead and said a prayer.

"Let's go, Walter." They left the room. Her eyes filled with hope. "Did you hear what Dad said about God?"

Walter sounded skeptical. "Yeah, so?"

"I think he's changing, I think he's starting to believe in God! Isn't that wonderful news, Walter?"

"I don't know if he is."

The next night Tanya brought him her very best wool quilt that Mama had given to her as a wedding gift when she married Lou. The material on one side was in a lively paisley print, the other side was a shiny, turquoise satin and completely impractical. It proved how impractical Tanya was when it came to her stepfather's care.

She flung the quilt over the bed. "Dad, I'm sure this will be softer and warmer."

That evening all three couples showed up at visiting hours. To the outward eye he appeared calm, listening to their talk, laughing at their jokes, with none of the sentiment of the previous night. Tanya having pacified his fears, he seemed content.

Later, in the hospital cafeteria over coffee, Tanya brought her sisters up to date on his medical treatment.

"You know, it just so happened that today I ran into his doctor outside his room. So I introduced myself. I must say that Dr. Lans is a very nice man. You know, I think he's a caring person. Dad had a Dr. Bellman at the Royal Alex, remember him?"

"Yeah. He sounded like a real mercenary to me from what you told us," Anna remarked, though she'd never met him.

"Well let me assure you that Dr. Lans isn't anything like Dr. Bellman was. I couldn't talk to Dr. Bellman because he always brushed me aside as if I was nothing. And he never did return any of my phone calls."

"So what about his operation? Alisha asked.

"The surgery? Dr. Bellman found the cyst when Dad was still at the Royal Alex, and he lanced it. There was a nurse's strike on and he had to be transferred by ambulance to the University. Dr. Lans said that Dad was so run down when they brought him in that they nearly lost him. It was touch and go, he said."

Tanya went on. "Uh-h-h, Dr. Lans said that he wasn't on any

antibiotics, intravenous, nothing! And he was swollen up like a balloon! Imagine that!"

Anna looked angry. "Maybe because of his age, Dr. Bellman expected him to die, so why bother with medication!"

"You're right. Anyway, Dr. Lans started giving him large doses of antibiotics. Right after that lo and behold, the swelling went down. A nurse at this hospital told me that it took all of ten days for the cyst to drain. ... It would be nice if you girls went to visit him besides me."

They both promised that they would.

84

TANYA WENT TO SEE HIM EVERY DAY until the infection under his liver actually healed. However, his zest for life remained flat.

Once Dr. Lans even mentioned discharging him and sending him back to the Grand Plains hospital for recuperation.

But Tanya disagreed. "He's not strong enough," she told him. The next day, she blurted out her concern to Alisha. "You know, the doctor wants to discharge Dad."

Alisha nodded. "Yes, so I heard."

"Do you know how Walter and I found him last night? He was curled up in a fetal position ... just like a baby!" She hung her head in despair. "I hate to say this, but I blew up again. I told him that he should at least make an effort to talk to someone, or to go for a ride in his wheelchair ... anything. ... Or even make some kind of a noise. It would be better than seeing him lying there, waiting for death to take him. I can't stand seeing him like that!"

As one day followed another, she became more vigilant of his well being. She tried to reform him in his very thoughts, hoping to rekindle the dying spark of life into a flame.

He came to depend on her, pouring out all his complaints into her sympathetic ear.

"Alisha, he needs another quilt. He's still cold. Do you have something at home? ... Then bring it please. He says he's cold."

Alisha brought the quilt to the hospital and they wrapped him up like a cocoon. As they were about to leave, Tanya motioned her aside. "Alisha, please tell your children to visit him. You know that he's always had such respect for Dan. Ask Dan to visit him. And tell Dan to impress on Dad that he must eat. He might listen to him."

"All right, I will. But I can't promise anything. Dan's busy, you know." Dan had graduated in medicine and was working as an intern at one of the hospitals.

However Dan's visit proved futile, and Bill Dansky's interest in food didn't change. Undaunted, Tanya remained adamant that there must be a solution. One day she called Alisha to check out yet another theory. "Do you think that he might be anorexic?"

Alisha exploded in anger! "I should say not! Loss of appetite is no indication that he's anorexic. He just can't eat, that's all."

Tanya carried on as if she hadn't heard her. "Alisha, what about a psychiatrist? Maybe he should see one."

"No! No psychiatrist! He's physically sick, not mentally. Why are you doing this?"

"Well, I'll only be satisfied when I know that all is being done for him that can possibly be done. That's all I want for him."

"I see. Well, I'd like that for him, too. ... But isn't he already getting the best of care? ... How come we don't talk about anything but Dad? What about you? How are you feeling? Are you getting any sleep at night? Or are you spending all your time worrying about him?"

"I'm fine. Don't worry about me!"

"I'm not so sure I shouldn't. You've lost quite a bit of weight. You don't look that great!"

85

THE NIGHTS SEEMED ETERNALLY LONG. Lying awake next to Walter, Tanya tried not to move, reminding herself that he was entitled to a good night's rest even if she couldn't sleep. At the same time, there'd be a ready lecture from him in the morning if he found her awake.

She turned on her side and silently began another prayer for a healing ... for a miracle. She was grateful that she could still function under the great emotional and physical strain that she suffered from daily. She thought that God Himself must be taking care of her. There were times when she felt it, and just when she thought that she could no longer carry on, some outside help became readily available. Now she stretched and closed her eyes, praying for sleep.

At the onset of morning she was first to get up. Tanya made her way to the bathroom and stepped on the scale. Another pound lighter! The weight loss worried her. The drop had been a gradual one ever since they'd returned from Hawaii. She wondered how much more she could afford to lose? Already, most of her clothes were a size too large. Her hand went to her head. And the pain, would she ever be free of it? She hurried to dress. Walter had promised to take her to the hospital for a morning visit before driving to work.

86

PERHAPS SHE OWED IT TO TANYA, but Alisha found that the increase in her daily visits to the hospital had actually brought her a little closer to her stepfather, even awakening a spark of pity for him, overshadowing the vengeful feelings she still carried from the past.

Each morning she rushed through her housework to be at his bedside just before noon. They lived close by; it took only minutes to get to the hospital.

As she walked into his room she was surprised to see him sitting in a chair by the window his feet covered with a plaid, wool blanket.

"How are you feeling?" she asked.

He turned, squinting at her through half closed lids. "I don't know. I can't see too good. To me, everything looks kinda fuzzy. I see grey."

She noticed his tray of food. "Have you eaten anything?"

"No, and don't tell me to eat, or I'll throw up. It makes me nervous just to look at it."

"I see."

He sighed. "You know, every minute seems like an hour in here. I don't know how I could stand it this long. You see this bed here? It just needs bars, because I feel like I'm in a jail. This is no life. ... I tell you, it's worse than dying." His face took on a hopeless expression.

Alisha sensed that a part of him had already left. Her thoughts strayed to Tanya and the appointed hour. How would she take it?

"I been sitting here for a long time, could you tell that nurse I want to lie down? I feel tired."

Alisha rose to her feet. She returned a short time later with an orderly and a nurse. They each took one of his arms and hoisted him to a standing position. He swayed on feet painfully puffed up with edema. Like a child taking its first steps, he brought each foot forward, his slippers sliding over the floor, his eyes dilated, his face stained red from exertion. Alisha looked away, agonizing for him.

She expelled her breath only when they lowered him to a sitting position on the side of the bed.

The orderly motioned to the nurse. "Okay, you get a hold of his feet ... I'll take his shoulders. At the count of three, we'll swing him over."

"One, two, three, over!"

"Ah-h-h-h," a sigh of intense pain filled the room.

Alisha shuddered, wondering if the very touch of a human hand had become unbearable to his deteriorating flesh. She walked to the bed and helped the nurse straighten the covers.

"Are you all right?" she asked him. "Do you want me to go so you can sleep?"

"No. Not yet. Alisha, could you wash my underwear and socks?
The closet, my clothes are in there."

She went to the closet and opened the door. She was happy to oblige him. It would be like doing penance for the years of hatred that she'd harboured against him. "Okay, I found them. Would you like me to go home now?"

"No, stay a while." He closed his eyes. "Why don't you tell me a joke?"

"A joke?" She smiled, marveling at the tenacity of the human spirit. He wanted to laugh ... to be cheered up. She wracked her brain, trying to think of something.

"I want to hear something funny."

She pulled up a chair and sat down. "Uh-h-h, okay. This one's about a dentist. He had a patient who came to see him. This patient, he was a logger from a camp. And the dentist was trying to convince him that painless dentistry was as simple as chopping down a tree. 'You just breathe in one whiff of laughing gas and poof, the tooth is out!' ... 'Any extra charge for that stuff?' the logger asked him. ... And the dentist said, 'Only fifty cents extra.' ..... The logger thought a minute, then said, 'I guess the old way is best. Go ahead, Doc, and never mind how much it hurts.'

Well the dentist was really surprised at his answer, so he said to him, 'You're a brave man. Open your mouth.' ... 'Wait a minute,' the logger told him. 'It isn't me that's got the toothache, it's my wife!'

Her reward was his laughter. She stayed on, talking about how she'd spent her day. It was a boring, mundane conversation, but perhaps the sound of a human voice was comforting and somehow helped to keep him connected to the fragile thread of life that he was about to let go.

After a time Neil showed up. Alisha looked relieved, thinking that at last she could leave without feeling guilty, for the afternoon was getting on and there was Allen's supper to prepare. Lord knows, I'd like to stay longer she thought, but ..."Hi Neil, how are you?"

"I'm fine, thanks." He turned to his brother. "Bill ... how're you? Feeling any better?"

Before leaving, she touched her stepfather's hand, clutching the edge of the blanket. The skin, paper thin, felt cold. She rushed off to the underground parking lot. No doubt Tanya or Anna would come by to see him later.

87

"ALISHA, I DON'T KNOW IF YOU KNOW THIS, but Dad's birthday is next Tuesday; it's the day after Valentine's." Tanya's voice sounded tight with emotion.

They had passed each other outside his room. Tanya was leaving, Alisha had just arrived.

"I'm sure he'll be all right." Alisha sounded reassuring.

"Uh-h-h, it's not that. But maybe next Tuesday we could all come at the same time and make it a kind of celebration. You know, with the family here, all of us talking, laughing. I think it would do him good to be in a normal, happy atmosphere." She looked beyond Alisha. "He said he only wants to live until his birthday."

"Tanya, eighty-three isn't all that bad. He'll have lived a decently long time, wouldn't you say?"

"Yes, but I still don't like to hear him talk about it."

"If you like, I could bring a cake, okay?"

"Oh, Alisha, would you? ... I'll phone Anna so her family can be here, too."

Tanya arrived carrying her gift in a paper bag. She'd bought it while on en route to the hospital.

Bill lay semi-propped up. Tanya, smiling, kissed him on the forehead and placed the bag in his hands. "Happy Birthday, Dad! Sorry there wasn't time to wrap it."

He gave her a wan smile. "Thank you." He pulled out a plum colored, knitted vest with buttons down the front. "Just what I needed!" he exclaimed.

"Dad, you know how you're always freezing! Well, I thought you might be able to wear it over your pyjamas. ... Here's Walter. Why don't you thank him," she said, remembering his patience with her while she debated about the colour.

Walter held out his hand. "Happy Birthday, Dad!"

Tanya pulled back the covers. ... "Come on, Dad, let's go for a walk. Walter, help me get Dad out of bed."

Walter put his hand under Bill Dansky's arm and heaved him to a standing position. The old man, too weak to protest, was balanced between them, with most of his weight on Walter. They walked out the door ever so slowly, limiting the walk to but a few steps from the doorway, with Tanya clucking encouragement to him.

She stopped when she noticed that he was perspiring. "Enough Walter, let's take him back. He shouldn't overdo it."

At that moment Alisha showed up carrying paper plates, napkins forks, a card, and an angel cake frosted high with whipped cream. Since Allen was out of town, she'd come alone.

Tanya knew that she'd tried to entice Dan, Gloria and Maria to come. However they'd made other plans and couldn't make it. The bonding that should have taken place long ago just wasn't there.

Seeing her stepfather on his feet, Alisha stopped short.

"We're taking Dad for a walk," Tanya explained, smiling. "Isn't he doing well? ... See, Dad, you can do it. You can walk. ... We're almost there. ... Just a few more steps."

Just then Anna, Anton, Laura, her husband, and their two small children came into the room. Tanya and Walter shuffled in with their charge. By now, he was in a considerable amount of pain.

"I think I lie down now," he said, panting.

Walter put him back into bed and adjusted the covers. Tanya motioned for silence. "While Alisha is getting the cake ready, let's all sing "Happy Birthday" to Dad."

Laura's two small youngsters jostled closer to the bed to help him blow out the candles. Tanya felt a gratified joy go through her at the sight. It was more than she had hoped for!

Alisha handed him a piece of cake. He graciously accepted it, but ate only a few scant forkfuls. A short time later, the nurses on the night shift surprised them by bringing in another cake complete with candles.

"Happy Birthday, Mr. Dansky. He's our very best patient. He never complains," a pretty, dark-haired nurse informed Tanya.

Tanya looked delighted. "This is such a surprise. Thank you. Look Dad, another cake for you! ... That'll make three already, because Neil brought him one earlier!"

At the first sign that he was tired, Tanya, ever watchful, made a motion that they leave. She lowered his bed and straightened the covers. They said "good night." Anna, before leaving, kissed him on the forehead. Tanya was the last to go, satisfied that the event had turned out exactly as she'd planned it.

88

THE NEXT AFTERNOON ALLEN AND ALISHA BROUGHT BILL HIS MAIL. Allen wished him a belated "Happy Birthday", then cranked up the bed to a semi-sitting position. "Uh-h-h, the matron from the lodge, Mrs. Alldrit, she sent all your mail to our house. ... Alisha, you can open it and read it to him. It dates back to the first week in December."

The old man nodded. "I never got even one letter since I got sick."

Alisha began tearing open the envelopes, which were mostly Christmas cards. Her stepfather motioned for her to stop when she was halfway through. "Alisha, you know, you're the executor of my will. ... The money is to be divided among you three girls. I promised your mother, so I keep my promise to her." He sighed.

"Last night, I had a very bad night. Very bad! I don't know what happened, but you know, I couldn't feel my arms. No feeling. They seemed like dead. The doctor came and two nurses. They work on me till I got some feeling back. I thought it was over for me. Allen, the key to my safe deposit box is in my suit jacket pocket. I want a cheap coffin. Nothing too expensive. I don't believe in that."

Allen nodded, sombrely. "Uh-h-h, what kind of a coffin would you like? Wood? Maybe oak?"

He pondered a moment. "Yes, oak."

"What about a service? Do you want a service?"

"Yes. United Church in Spirit Valley. Alisha, your mother was buried in United Church. I always did my business with them. ... I got some nice clothes. ... Allen, you pick me a nice suit."

Allen nodded. "Okay. Do you want a lunch to be served?"

"Yes. The ladies from United Church, they make a lunch."

They discussed the funeral arrangements, as if planning a wedding. Alisha wondered how Tanya would feel if she knew. She wondered whether he'd like to confess his sins to a priest?

Confession and Holy Communion would cleanse his soul of sin and prepare him for that final journey. The state of his soul was far more important then the kind of suit that would shroud him. His mother had been a devout Greek Orthodox and believed in confession.

Should she bring up the subject? The last time that she'd mentioned religion to him, he'd momentarily toyed with the idea, then put it aside. Watching him now, she felt that it was a door that had never been opened. However the right moment didn't present itself, and she left with the feeling that there was still some unfinished business that hadn't been attended to.

89

A WARM, SOUTH WIND TUGGED AT HIS WHITE HAIR. Behind him a brilliant sunset created a rainbow colored halo around the soft, white tresses. Tanya could see Dad from a distance, searching through piles of lumber which lay scattered about.

She noticed he was being very particular for it seemed that not just any board would do. He'd been that way from as far back as she could remember. He examined each piece, discarding the ones that were flawed. The good ones he put to one side, unconcerned and unaware of her presence as he worked.

She attempted to cry out to stop him! But her cries were as powerless as a feather carried away in the wind. She tried to move, but her feet felt rooted to the ground. Try as she might, she could not distract him, though she knew that he was putting the boards aside for his own coffin!

She awakened covered with perspiration. Slowly the dream returned making her wonder why, when finally she was able to sleep, she should be tortured by such a nightmare?

90

SHE OPENED THE DOOR TO HER STEPFATHER'S ROOM and stood stock still. The bed had been stripped bare; there was a pile of blue linen left on top of the mattress. Tanya panicked, wondering if he was? ... No! It can't end like this, she thought. Weakness coursed through her, as she rushed to the nurse's station to speak to a nurse. "I'm Bill Dansky's daughter, could you tell me where my Dad is? He's not in his room!"

The nurse reached for a list. "I'll check. ... Actually, he was having chest pains today, so-o-o, we've moved him to the sixth floor ... room 18."

"Thank you."

The sixth floor was the Cardiac Unit. Tanya, her heart pounding with anxiety, located her stepfather and went in. She was relieved to see that he was sitting up. As she bent down to kiss him, she noticed an unhealthy tinge to his skin.

"Dad, are you all right?"

"Today, not good."

She was about to say something soothing when Alisha walked in with Gloria, Maria, and Jonah, Gloria's six year old. "Dad, look who's come to visit you!" She was sure their presence would brighten his day. Especially Jonah, he was such an appealing child. She returned Alisha's smile, with approval.

"Dad, I brought someone to see you," Alisha announced.

His hand groped at the bedside table. "My glasses ... Alisha, would you?"

Alisha found the glasses and set them on his nose. He examined them separately, smiling in recognition. "Maria, how are you? And Gloria?" Gloria he'd loved from the time she was a baby. He held out his hand to her. Gloria leaned over and kissed his cheek. He noticed Jonah. "And this boy, which one is he?"

Jonah beamed at him, placing his small elbows on the edge of the bed.

Alisha put a hand on his shoulder with pride. "He's Gloria's boy. This is Jonah, your great-grandchild."

Their eyes met. He shook Jonah's hand. "Alisha, raise my bed up a little." As he spoke the oxygen tube slipped out of his nose.

Tanya reached up to adjust it, at the same time catching a faint sound that escaped him.

"Ah-h-h-h. ..."

It was barely audible, but it alarmed her. She bent down to examine him more closely. Was he in pain? His breathing sounded more laboured than usual. From under his pyjamas, she caught sight of a wire attached to his chest.

With eyes half lidded, he drank in the scene. His head moved from side to side, slack and uncontrolled, resembling a newborn.

Maria and Gloria sat talking by his bed.

Tanya thought it was just as well, since he was too ill to draw into a conversation.

"Gloria, your boy looks just like you when you were little," he remarked.

She looked pleased. "Oh, do you think so?"

Tanya rose quietly and slipped away to the nurse's station. "Excuse me, I'm Bill Dansky's daughter, could you tell me why he's been moved here? Is there something wrong with his heart?"

The nurse nodded. "Uh-h-h, there's some irregularity with his pulse. His doctor wants it monitored."

"I see. I'll leave you my telephone number. If there's a change in his condition, would you please call me?"

She went back to his room. "Dad, are you all right?" she asked, noticing that he was lying angled.

"You know, I think I have a nap."

Alisha stood up. "Jonah hasn't had dinner; it's already seven." She turned to him. "Jonah, say good bye to your great-granddad."

As soon as they left Tanya wondered whether she should go as well.

Walter, who was working overtime, did say that he'd be finished by eight. She felt that she should be there when he got home. It bothered her to think that she'd been neglecting him.

She touched the top of her head which was throbbing with pain. Exhaustion steeped every bone. She lingered over her stepfather for a few more minutes then trailed after the others to the elevator. Knowing that she needed rest, she wondered how long she could carry on without sleep?

As she entered the house she took a step back, frowning at the sight of unwashed pots topping the sink. The kitchen table hadn't been cleared from the night before. Walter had made a Kraft dinner casserole after they'd come home from the hospital, because she wasn't up to doing anything. He'd stacked the dishes in the sink and went to bed after the news.

Tanya examined the room, noticing that every chair had something draped over it. There were wet towels lying on the bathroom floor ... something that she ordinarily didn't tolerate.

She started walking away and nearly tripped over a pair of Walter's shoes blocking the doorway. However in her present state, cleaning was the farthest thing from her mind.

Tanya slipped off her coat, went past the mess and into the living room, then crumpled into a corner of the chesterfield. She acknowledged Walter, who was watching television, with a nod of her head. Though she knew that Dad was slipping away, she was beyond the point of being upset. She leaned over to pick up her testament from the coffee table. However her attempt to concentrate did little good. She gave in to the weariness and dozed off momentarily.

When she awoke, Walter had thrown a blanket over her, and the Bible was back on the coffee table. He was watching the news.

She stood up, intent on getting some sleep. "Walter, I'm going to bed." She changed into a nightgown and lay down on the unmade bed, thankful that sleep overtook her.

The shrill ring of the phone jerked her awake at twelve-thirty A.M.. Something told her that the time had come. Her heart leaped and began to pound madly, hearing Walter's hushed tone. "Yes, we'll be right there!"

"That was the hospital. Your Dad's very low."

"Oh, Walter!"

"I'll give Alisha a call. The nurse said they couldn't find her number. She can tell Anna. We'll all meet there," he said, already dialing.

As in a dream, Tanya rose from the bed. Quickly she doused her face with water and combed her hair. She dressed hurriedly, then stumbled outside to the van, shivering from more than the cold night air.

A policeman, sitting at a small desk at the entry of the hospital, momentarily blocked their rush. "And where do you think you're going?"

Walter pointed to Tanya. "We had a call that her father is dying."

He waved them on without comment.

Tanya burst out of the elevator as soon as it stopped. There was an intense, troubled look on her face as she ran past Alisha and Allen. Walter was behind her, protective and calming.

Alisha came to stand beside her, white-faced. Tanya went directly to the night nurse on duty. "I'm Bill Dansky's daughter, how is he?"

The young nurse answered her matter of factly. "Uh-h-h, we're working on him. The doctor should be out in just a minute. He'll be able to tell you more than I can. Why don't you wait here for the doctor? Your Dad's being moved into a different room." She pointed to a set of double doors in front of them.

"Is he still alive?" Tanya asked, fearfully.

"Oh yes, he's all right. ... Now if you'll excuse me ..." She hurried away in the direction of Bill Dansky's room.

Tanya walked a short distance from Alisha and, raising her arms over her head, began a silent prayer. She stopped when the door opened and three nurses came out wheeling a bed and an oxygen cannister. They moved slowly down the corridor. Tanya caught sight of her stepfather's forlorn face. His eyes were closed, his face ash grey against the blue sheets. He looks so helpless, so gaunt, she thought. ... Suddenly the double doors opened and the resident doctor emerged. He was slight, short, with a neatly trimmed black beard.

She went to meet him. "Please, I'm Bill Dansky's daughter. How is he?"

The doctor paused. "Uh-h-h, his heart has already stopped once. It was close, but we managed to restart it. I think it'll happen again very soon," he told her sombrely.

Alisha and Walter stood listening. Just then Neil arrived and joined them.

The doctor made a motion to leave. "I have to go and check on him. I'll be back in a few minutes. Then I'd like to talk to all of you." He disappeared through the double doors.

Neil went to the reception area and sat down beside Allen.

"How is he?" he asked him.

"We just saw him. He's still alive," Allen told him.

Alisha put a hand on Tanya's shoulder and examined her closely. "Are you all right?" she asked.

"Are you all right?" Walter echoed her words.

Tanya brushed off Alisha's arm and backed away from them. Though no tears were visible, her eyes looked bright. "Leave me alone ... both of you," she told them, angrily.

Alisha stiffened. "What do you mean, leave you alone? Don't you know that I'm worried about you?"

"Because I know that you're going to try to stop me, and I don't want you to stop me!" Tanya turned away from them and raised her arms over her head, a slight smile helped erase some of the tension from her face. "Jesus, dearest Jesus," she prayed aloud, "help my father. Lord Jesus, please save my father. ... Lord have mercy on him and heal my father!"

Alisha turned a shade whiter. "Tanya, are you all right? You worry me. You're my sister, I love you. I don't want anything to happen to you."

She dropped her arms and leaned momentarily against Walter. Suddenly it dawned on her that after all these years, Alisha was no longer excluding her.

Neil stood up and joined their circle as the doctor appeared again.

"He's dying," he said. ... "His heart is about to stop. You'll have to decide what you want me to do, because the next step is to put him on a ventilator."

"What's a ventilator?" Alisha asked.

"It's a breathing machine."

"A breathing machine? But what does it do?"

"It's life support," the doctor explained.

"Life support? For how long?"

"Oh, until he stops breathing ... or his heart stops. It'll prolong his life for a little while. Do you want me to put him on a ventilator?"

Alisha persisted. "But how long will he live?"

"Oh, perhaps a couple of weeks, or maybe months ... until his heart stops."

They looked at one another, wondering, searching each other's faces to see if they were all of the same mind. Tanya voiced what was uppermost in each of them. She sighed. "Oh Lord, help us to make the right choice."

The doctor glanced at his watch. "All right, you still have a little time left. I'll go check on him again. When I come back, you can let me know what you've decided."

It lay with them ... a life and death decision! In her heart, Tanya was thinking that she did not want to let him go. There was still the chance that the Lord would heal him and he would live. She knew that her wish would be different from Alisha's or Neil's. Now she turned towards Alisha, "Where's Anna?"

"I phoned her and told her to come, but she said she didn't want to wake Anton because he'd had such a hard day at work. She said she'd come later."

"What a pity that she never learned to drive. ... She should be here to help us decide. I'll have to phone her," Tanya said, making her way to the nurse's station.

A short time later, she came back. "Anna's going to take a cab. She said she wants to be here with us."

Alisha looked anxious. "But it might be too late by then! I hope she makes it in time! We have to decide ... I think soon." She turned towards Neil. "Neil? Tanya? What should we do?"

Neil, at first apprehensive, began slowly. "I know for sure he didn't want to live anymore, and I know that he wouldn't want to be hooked up to any machines. What quality would there be to his life that way?"

Alisha nodded. "Yes, once he told me that lying in that bed made every minute seem like an hour. He said it was like being in a prison without bars. ... And we all know that he was in a lot of pain."

Tanya looked from one to the other, the hope in her slowly fading. Yet she knew that what they said made sense. "Yes, you're right, he is in a lot of pain. ... He told me so himself many times. And many times he told me that he didn't want to live."

"Did you hear what the doctor said about the ventilator?" Alisha asked. "He said it could only prolong his life for a short time before his heart stopped beating for good. Actually, perhaps only a matter of days then he'd have to go through all this again."

Walter sat down by Allen and they started to talk in low tones, as the doors opened and the doctor came towards them. "Well?"

"Well," Tanya looked at the other two faces and dropped her eyes. One of them would have to say it. She couldn't.

"I know he didn't want to live anymore," Neil repeated his last statement to the doctor.

Alisha glanced at Tanya. "We won't use any machines on him. ... We're going to leave it in God's hands. If God wants him to live, he will live ... if he dies, then it will be God's Will."

Tanya nodded calmly. "Yes, let's leave it in God's hands."

"How long does he have?" Alisha asked.

"Not very long."

"Can we go in to be with him?"

"Yes of course, you may if you want to." The doctor pointed to the double doors. "He's in there."

"Tanya, shall we go?" Alisha asked.

Her face looked more relaxed. "Yes, I want to be there with him. He'll need me." She smiled at Walter. "Walter, come with us, ... we'll all go together."

At this moment, Anna came rushing up to them. "Sorry, I got here as fast as I could. That taxi, it took so long!"

"He's about to die," Tanya said to her, "do you want to come with us?"

She shook her head. "No I don't. I'll stay right here. I don't want to see him die."

"What about you, Neil?"

"Not me. I've always had a fear of death; I'd like to remember him as he was when he was alive."

Alisha turned to Allen. "Allen, will you come?"

"No, I'll wait right here for you. You go on in."

The doctor sat down next to Allen, and they heard him say, "They've made the right choice ......"

Tanya nodded. "Let's go." They went in through the double doors to where death waited.

A nurse stood over him, adjusting the oxygen mask over his nose and mouth. "Do you want the hospital chaplain?" she asked. "I can get him for you."

"Yes," Tanya said, "please get him." She moved closer to her stepfather. Her heart turned over at the sight of his intense agitation. He seemed more restless and anxious than ever before. She touched his hand. "Tata," she said using the ethnic word that years ago she'd called her real father. Tears glistened in her eyes. The nurse raised the bed, putting him into a more reclining position. They stood in a group at his right side.

Suddenly Bill Dansky gripped the iron railing surrounding his bed, and slowly began to raise himself, inching his way ever closer to the edge ... as if about to leave. Fear and panic were clearly written on his face; he was already half way up. Terror had injected a powerful will in him to live. Did he imagine that by getting up he could escape his destiny with death?

Tanya stood wondering what effort this must have cost him in his condition!

He began to swing his legs over the side, when the nurse gently, but firmly, pushed him back. "No, no, you mustn't do that. Lie still, please. You can't get up."

Tanya felt the back of her neck prickle as a cry of agony was rent from him. The sound imbedded itself into her mind. She started to pray: "Lord, please, please, Lord, have mercy on him. Forgive him for all his sins, Lord. Oh, Lord Jesus, we are all sinners. Please forgive him, Lord Jesus."

Once more he tried to rise and once more the nurse had to restrain him. Undaunted, frightened, he repeated the act a third and final time as though some demon had materialized to taunt him with the fear of hell for his past sins.

Alisha moved to the other side of the bed and Tanya moved closer to his head. Walter took his right hand in his own, and Alisha gripped his left hand.

The nurse began cranking down his bed, still unsure where to leave it.

Tanya gathered her strength together and focused her attention on her Dad. She was there to help him, to walk him as far as she could ... to that door where he would enter ... never to return. She thought of the light within her that God had instilled there so long ago. Gently, she put her arm over his head and smiled into his eyes. "Tata, I love you.

Don't be scared. You'll be all right, I'm here with you ... and Christ is here with you, too!"

He nodded.

"You know, I've always loved you. You were always my "Tata". ... Now look directly at me and don't take your eyes off me for a minute. It's going to be all right. I'll help you. Are you in pain?"

He shook his head. "No."

His voice was muffled by the oxygen mask. The nurse was still fussing close by. Tanya wished that she would leave. The oxygen mask! Why did he have it on? Oh Lord, what good was it now? ... The nurse finally left them.

Tanya knelt down. Walter and Alisha dropped to their knees as well. Tanya, her face radiant, extended her free arm over his head and looked upward. "Lord, Jesus Christ, send Your angels down to take my father's soul and carry him straight to heaven. Oh Lord Jesus, forgive my father for his sins. ... Lord, we are all sinners, and all of us fall short of the mark. ... But Lord, every knee shall bend at the name of Jesus, and every tongue confess that Jesus is Lord. ..." She touched his face. He gazed at her with implicit trust.

Alisha looked at Tanya in wonder. Her own presence, she felt, was only to witness this wondrous happening and to record it.

Tanya's perseverance to forgive and love her persecutor was astounding. To love him was to love her enemy, for surely in every sense of the word he'd been her enemy! Suddenly it became very clear that this was the love that Jesus spoke of in the Bible when he said to forgive our enemies ... to love our enemies. It was this kind of love that Christ wanted from us.

Oblivious to everything, Tanya went on: "Tata, now ask God to forgive you for your sins. Say, forgive me, Lord Jesus, I am a sinner."

His muffled voice repeated the words. Tanya went on. "Oh Lord Jesus, you are the redeemer of our souls, You shed Your blood for us. Forgive my father for his sins. Take away his pain, soothe his grief, bring him peace, calm his fears. ... Send down your holy angels to take his soul directly to heaven. Lord Jesus, let the angels carry him to heaven. ... Forgive him! Oh Lord, please, please, forgive him! Give him the peace that passes all understanding. Fill his heart with Your love, Your grace. ...

Dearest Jesus, blessed Jesus, wipe away his tears, end his

suffering."

As she prayed her face took on a special radiance; she was in the presence of the Almighty where nothing mattered but the prayer from her heart. Intent on saving him, her face glowed, her eyes shone with a soft light as she pleaded for a father who'd never had anything but contempt for her. "Jesus, oh Jesus, send down your holy angels to carry his soul to heaven."

Suddenly Bill Dansky seemed more relaxed. A look of peace settled upon him. The harsh lines of worry eased; his face took on a strange glow. He was no longer fearful or fighting death.

At that very moment, Tanya knew that God, being merciful, had heard and had answered her prayer. ... "Thank You, Lord Jesus! We praise You, Jesus! We thank You, we bless You!"

A long, unpleasant sound of a snore, the telltale death rattle, filled the room. Her stepfather expelled three long breaths before his china blue eyes glazed over to stare at them vacantly. He was gone!

Tanya lowered his head, removed her hand, and stood up. She sighed as Walter put his arm around her. The fight to save his soul had ended. "He's with Jesus," she said, her face illuminated by a smile. "Did you see how the angels carried him away? You know that they carried him away, don't you?" She looked from Alisha to Walter. "I saw them with my very own eyes!"

Alisha nodded and rose to her feet.

They walked out to break the news to the others, as the chaplain met them at the double doors.

Tanya went up to him, smiling. "My father's gone," she said. "and do you know that the angels carried him away to heaven? They just picked him up and carried him away. It was wonderful, it was really wonderful to see!"

THE END

About The Author:

Alisha Franklin was born and brought up in the Prairies of Alberta. She finished High School in a small town. As a young child, many evenings were spent telling stories to her two sisters, who listened captivated by her renditions.

Later, she moved to Edmonton where she met and married a lawyer. They raised three children. After the children married, Alisha underwent a spiritual transformation... an awakening of mind and spirit. This experience brought with it the gift of writing. where she could tell a story before, now she found that she could write it.

The Mourning Dove is a true story inspired by her sister. the novel spans an entire generation and will keep the reader's interest to the end.

ISBN 1-41205958-5

9 781412 059589